BLACK LIES

Other Lon LaFlamme iUniverse.com, Inc.
Writer's Showcase novels, presented by
Writer's Digest:

    Lords of Paradise
    Vanishing Breed

BLACK LIES

Lon LaFlamme

Ruth)
My best 2000
Lon [signature]

Writer's Showcase presented by *Writer's Digest*
San Jose New York Lincoln Shanghai

Black Lies

Published by Writer's Showcase presented by *Writer's Digest*
an imprint of iUniverse.com, Inc.

For information address:
iUniverse.com, Inc.
620 North 48th Street
Suite 201
Lincoln, NE 68504-3467
www.iuniverse.com

ISBN: 0-595-09636-0

Printed in the United States of America

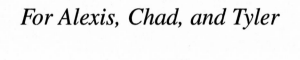

For Alexis, Chad, and Tyler

Acknowledgments

My wife had casually mentioned Red Lodge, Montana for years. Sunsets and fierce lightning storms stirred memories of the ten weeks each summer she had spent in the tiny western town from the age of two to fifteen.

I was convinced she was shielding me—or herself—from parental abandonment during her formative years. I seldom pursued the question why and how her parents could send her, and her two sisters, to Montana on a 1940s Northern Pacific passenger train every summer.

As years passed, I finally took the action to arrange a trip to Red Lodge with my wife and her parents to get to the bottom of the mystery. My suspicions proved to be totally unfounded. What I did discover about the infamous "river woman" Alice Becklen and her heroics in my mother-in-law's early years was incredible enough to inspire the birth of *Black Lies*.

While every character and circumstance in *Black Lies* is fictionalized, I hopefully captured the spirit, joys and struggles that permeate this little corner of Montana's Big Sky Country, still haunted by the state's worst mining disaster.

A special thanks to Jane Johnson; Red Lodge Carnegie Librarian Bob Moran; and Harry Owens and Shirley Zupan of the Carbon County Historical Society for their book *RED LODGE, Saga of a Western Area.*

I am also indebted to the tall and short storytellers up and down Red Lodge's main street who live with one foot in a thriving tourist town and the other in a colorful and dark past.

Other contributors who warrant thanks include Beartooth Mountain's Forest Ranger Patrick Pierson; attorney, brother-in-law and friend Chet Lackey; Captain Pearl Capanara, head surgery nurse, Madigan Military Medical Center, Fort Lewis, Washington; Michael Buckner, research director, United Mine Workers of America, Washington D.C.; and Michael Altman, iUniverse.com Publishing.

As always, I am indebted to my wife Karen, and agent Nancy Ellis-Bell for their support and guidance.

Cover design by Kat.

Chapter 1

A split second of silence followed the deaf-ening roar, suspending time for eternity. Brent Harrison held his breath, rooted to the spot, as hell exhaled an acrid wind with enormous velocity. From the bowels of the earth, the hot wind spewed, flinging timber like toothpicks as the ground beneath his feet began to tremble once again.

In the recesses of his mind, the immediate infiltration of the swirling black wind trans-mitted a message of impending doom. There was no time for thought or reason. Pure survival instinct prodded his feet toward the nearest tunnel exit. Robotically, Brent placed one foot in front of the other, laboring to inhale any semblance of breathable air in the midst of the tornadic vacuum.

Charred, twisted bodies lay sprawled across charcoal-crisp ceiling beams and wall timbers that littered the ground. Hell's flaming orange glow cast eerie shadows on the metal rail cars where they'd tumbled to a precarious resting place, their echoing clatter forever silenced.

Thoughts ricocheted through Brent's head, heard but unrecognized as he struggled toward the exit. He couldn't identify the cause of the disaster; he just knew it was bad. With each breath, his thinking grew more clouded and his path more difficult to navigate. The mine was collapsing. Men were down. There was no light visible. He had to get out. As he stepped over a fallen beam and rounded a corner, there was a sliver of light, beckoning him toward the entrance.

Another explosion, deep within the mine, caused the ground to shudder beneath his boots, casting him against the wall and freeing the thought that had been seeking a voice. "Damn! I told Bradford she was going to blow!"

Lungs straining eagerly for the miniscule amounts of fresh air lingering near the entrance, his brain transmitted with sudden clarity the events that had been unfolding at his feet. The gas, the danger, everything he'd feared was happening and he was powerless to stop it. With a reluctant glance at the two motionless bodies near his feet, Harrison swallowed fear that rose like bile in his throat. Nothing to do but continue his slow, steady move toward the entrance, one hand clamping his lamp-lit helmet to his head. A sliver of light revealed more bodies less than one hundred yards ahead. Dead. Like a heavy black curtain falling, Harrison's mind shut down, unable to consider the horrors that greeted him there.

Bolting out of the darkness, he gulped at smoke-tinged air that brought life to lungs drowning in the charcoal textured gases from inside the collapsed mine. Tears smeared the coal grime on the backs of his beefy forearms as he swiped at his blood-red eyes then stared, confused, at his empty hands.

"I forgot my lunch pail!"

Nothing made sense in the midst of the chaos. His brain refused to register the noise, the smoke, the hideous visages of coworkers and friends, both inside and out. Covered with charcoal, each breath causing agonizing pain in his throat and chest, Brent's mind zeroed in on the last pleasant memory he had, leaving the house after breakfast that morning. Then, as if knowing he should do something, he locked on the thought of the new lunch pail Delena had lovingly packed for him. All he could think of was the new pail he couldn't afford to replace. He worked too hard for that money in the mine. With a wife and child to care for, every dollar counted. Like a man on a mission, he turned back and vanished into the black hole.

Chapter 2

In her cabin beside Rock Creek, the familiar, dreaded rumbling launched Alice Beck from her chair in one fluid movement. As if sensing her master's distress, Autumn rolled over from her favorite spot by the fireplace to stand at rigid attention. The golden retriever responded as though she knew the reason for the blast that pierced the chill mountain silence.

Mobilize, stabilize, minimize, Alice reminded herself, adrenaline already coursing through her veins. Standard emergency procedure. She glanced down at her army fatigues and spit-polished combat boots and hurriedly forced her wool coat over a bulky sweater. Pulling a knit cap over her thick, short chestnut-colored hair and snatching her nurse's bag from its spot on the shelf by the cabin door, Alice bulleted out of the cabin. With singleness of focus, she hardly noticed the frigid wind in her face or the snow stacked three feet high on the path to her '39 Chevy.

Dropping her bag to the ground, she kicked the ice off her truck's snow removal blade attachment pins and yanked them out in swift movements. Wrenching open the truck door, she hoisted her bag and threw it onto the passenger seat, then climbed aboard the cold, threadbare driver's seat of the pickup. Autumn jumped in beside her, sniffing the air excitedly.

With practiced hands steady on the wheel, Alice navigated carefully as the truck lurched from its carved-out spot in the mountains of snow surrounding it and headed down the gravel road toward Red Lodge, three miles away. Just over the hill from Red Lodge lay Washoe and Bear Creek Mine, where over three hundred fathers, husbands, and sons clawed out a living as coal miners. Hardly a family in the valley wasn't related to the miners.

Alice had a reputation for driving speeds that teetered on madness. Today was no exception. The warning whistle had barely started blasting and she was already kicking up gravel and snow. Her truck careened through Red Lodge, past Washington Hall, beyond the General Store in Washoe, barreling toward the mine entrance.

Years of experience nursing front line casualties during the war were not easily forgotten and Alice was steady as a rock during crisis situations. She nodded with each anticipatory thought, mentally preparing for whatever was ahead. Red Lodge's Washington Hall could be set up as an auxiliary treatment center. Her mind raced, picturing Red Cross relief volunteers, beds and supplies filling the large meeting room.

Stomping hard to bring the truck to a screeching halt, Alice thrust the gearshift knob into park and catapulted from the cab. Her stern eyes, set off by high cheekbones and an outdoor honey-brown complexion, darted from one gaping face to another, assessing the situation. Her commanding inspector-general stride demanded attention.

"What happened? Who's in charge?" she barked, sensing panic in the air.

A man, tending to his injured comrade, looked up at her. In a tired, hollow voice, he said, "They're inside, all of them! There was an explosion in Tunnel Three. We've lost all contact. Give me a hand here, will you?"

Alice bent over the injured man. His head drooped forward onto his chest and a trickle of blood ran down from his mouth. Alice felt for a pulse, then lowered him gently to the ground.

"I'm sorry, he's gone."

Anger flickered on the despairing face. "Damn! Bradford's gonna pay for this." The miner stood wearily and wiped his hand across his coal dust and grime-streaked face. With jaded determination, he dashed back toward the entrance of the mine.

For a moment, Alice watched him go, then turned her attention toward those she might help. A small group of impromptu rescuers without gas masks were staggering out of the mine, choking and gasping. Alice shoved through the crowd and acted as a crutch, catching one of the men as he stumbled toward her and guiding his massive frame to the ground. Corded arm muscles pulled Alice close to his horror-wracked face. Blue and red pulsing veins bulged from his forehead, temples, and neck. His gaseous breath made her eyes water. She cradled his head and inclined her ear to hear his raspy voice.

"There's no air blowin' through. I saw three of 'em near the entrance before the rockslide. They're dead," he coughed, spitting blood and phlegm from his throat.

"Help is on the way," she assured him, attempting to make him comfortable in an impossible situation. "Try not to talk. You took in a lot of gas." Motioning to a woman in the small group of bystanders, she called, "Bring a blanket over here. I'm going up to the engine house to find Bradford."

A rancid odor assaulted anyone within a ten-foot range of the entrance to the mine, assuring not all visible tears were due to grief alone. The frustration of doing nothing until proper equipment arrived was more than some of the men could tolerate. Their friends and family members were inside that mine, but without equipment, they were helpless. Many disappeared into the killer's black mouth only to run out less than a minute later, gasping for air.

Alice strode purposefully up the hill to the engine house, yanked open the door and stormed into the room. Four men sat around a small table, listening to voices over the radio from the mine. The cold, calm atmosphere was a grim contrast to the panic-stricken urgency just a few feet away down the hill.

"Where the hell is Bradford? Those men outside aren't equipped to rescue anybody. We need help."

A smooth, oily voice spoke from behind her. "I'm Bradford. Who the hell are you? And what are you doing in my engine house?"

"She's that hermit army nurse that lives up Rock Creek," one of the men at the table offered.

"I was a lieutenant colonel in the U.S. Army. Been in front line combat action and dealing with blood and guts most of my life!" Alice spouted, her anger intensifying as she scanned the motionless group.

"Then why aren't you outside nursing, instead of in here bothering us?" Bradford asked.

Eyes narrowing, Alice stared up at Lawrence Bradford, owner of Bear Creek Mine. Neither his expression nor his voice showed even a trace of concern for the horrors that lay just a few feet outside the engine house door.

He smiled and blew cigar smoke in her face.

It was obvious there was no help to be found there. Without a word, she turned, grinding her heel on his foot, as she strode out of the room. The whistle continued to erupt like a pounding heart, obliterating any response Bradford might have made.

Men, women and children swarmed the area, arriving in vehicles and on foot. Some pitched in to help immediately, others just stood and stared with expressions of utter dismay. The snow around the mine was unusually deep and the near zero temperature made waiting even more intolerable.

Alice gathered those women who would accept her hands-on nudging up a hill to the engine house, a short distance from the mine entrance.

"Can't save anybody if we don't work together. I know what I'm doing," Alice said bluntly, her shortness of breath emphasizing the urgency of her movements.

She'd long been considered an oddity in the tight-knit community. Even the present crisis didn't totally obliterate that fact. Her announcement garnered only scorching glares and resentful glances; no doubt they wondered what right she had to tell them what to do. There was an uncomfortably long silence followed by grudging willingness to follow orders.

Alice expected resistance. After all, she was an outsider. But the situation left no time for differences. Alice went into action. "Please stay away from the mine entrance. Go up to the engine house and help set up medical support and food."

One by one, the women turned their attention to her. Alice knew it was important to maintain a sense of hopeful diligence, helping them block out their fear of loss and giving them something productive to do. Because of Bear Creek's location, ambulances from nearby communities took hours to arrive. From what she'd already seen, most of the damage was still contained inside the tunnels of the mine and the news, when they finally got some, wouldn't be good.

When the Red Cross arrived, more assignments were issued to help divert their fears. It wasn't like the community had rallied around a handful of victims. Virtually everyone on the mountain had some connection to the men that were trapped in the mine. The cavernous engine room, with its permanent coat of coal dust, echoed the bleakness of the grim scene. Busy teams went to work cleaning the metal lunch tables and filling them with food and medical supplies. As Alice had anticipated, Red

Lodge's Washington Hall was agreed upon as the best auxiliary medical treatment location for a catastrophe of this magnitude.

Within hours of the initial alert, mining experts and rescue teams came in from Red Lodge, Butte, and even as far away as Salt Lake City. The Billings Fire Department coordinated their efforts. Time seemed to be suspended as Alice worked tirelessly through the night, running on pure adrenaline.

By the time the sun rose over the mountains the following morning, enormous fans were set up in the poisonous catacombs to aerate the tunnels as gas-masked rescue crews began the first legitimate forays into the depths of the mines. Twenty-four hours had passed since the disaster, and the vicious monster had only released three miners alive in the first three hours of rescue attempts.

Settling yet another miner's family on a blanket in the overcrowded engine house, Alice paused before heading back out into the cold, gray dawn. Her heart broke in the face of their courage, knowing the rescuers were likely to recover far more dead than alive.

A radio announcer's voice caught her attention as it echoed through the engine house, "From the recovery center at Washington Hall in Red Lodge, Montana we bring you the first interview with a survivor of what rescuers fear could be the worst mining disaster in Montana history. His name is Alex Thompson. Mr. Thompson, what happened down there?"

"At about ten o'clock, me and Reid and Dewey felt a powerful pressure in our ears. It was followed by a God-awful hot wind that was full of garbage. When the mine timbers started to crack, I grabbed the phone and sent word to the engine house that something was wrong. Then we took off running."

An awkward silence was filled with the sound of ragged breathing as Thompson struggled for control. With a quavering voice, Alex Thompson whispered hauntingly into the microphone, "Reid, Dewey, Finny and me got the gas real bad. We knew we had to get out. We was knocked clear to the ground. I looked back. Reid was on his face on the tracks. That wind kept tearing at me, nearly ripping my clothes off my back. Reid was hurtin' real bad."

"He yelled for us to get out. Right after that, rocks came down between us and him. We should'a grabbed him when we had a chance. Just 'fore we got outta there we ran past another guy who didn't make it. He couldn'ta been more than fifty feet from makin' it out alive." Thompson coughed and choked.

Another airwave silence followed before the broadcast continued with a discernible tremor in the broadcaster's voice. "It's now confirmed that there was an explosion in Bear Creek Mine followed by the release of poisonous gases. No word yet on the number of dead."

Taking a deep breath, Alice squared her shoulders and headed back outside, determined to bring as many of the wives inside as she could. Good news, if there was any, would be welcomed anywhere. Bad news might be easier to hear in the warm, supportive environment a step removed from the cold devastation of the mine entrance.

Once she'd done all she could outside, Alice took advantage of the warmth in the engine house and waited anxiously for the first rescue teams to emerge. Wiping a clear spot in the coal dust covering the engine house window, she watched the first body bags surface from the mine.

Clad in asbestos suits and gas masks, the rescuers looked more like coldly detached aliens carrying mysterious inanimate objects. Mechanically, they trekked across the coal-stained snow and handed their cargo over to a receiving line of workers who precariously hauled the bodies across a narrow railroad trestle to waiting ambulances on the hillside road.

The hope of news after a long night emptied the engine house as everyone scrambled out the door. Previously silent relatives and friends watching the somber procession burst into tears at the sight of the bags and a crescendo of wailing rose to intermingle with the sounds of digging and the roar of the fans. Dropping the task at hand as the crowd pressing through the door dwindled, Alice exited the building and ran for the hillside edge of the trestle to prevent wives and children from seeing the remains.

"Who are they?" was the tormented cry from the crowd.

Shift foreman Sean McDonald raised his arms to quiet them. "I'm sorry. There will be no further announcements of the deceased until we have an accounting of every soul trapped in there."

Assured that Red Cross workers were offering comfort where needed, Alice surveyed the grim scene in the harsh light of day. The crowd ringed the immediate area as if waiting for a performance, some standing tall and defiant, others crumpling to the ground in devastated sobs. As the wailing subsided into a cacophony of whimpers and moans, Alice followed the men to one of the ambulances, pushing her way forward long enough to inspect one bag's contents. No one stopped her as she opened the bag and gritted her teeth as she glanced inside. The combination of unimaginable heat and carbon monoxide fumes had melted the man's features in a grotesque, unrecognizable death mask. Only their safety helmet lamp numbers would identify these men.

Closing the bag, she turned to the attendants standing nearby. "Under no condition are any of these bodies to be viewed by their families here, at Washington Hall, or even the funeral parlor. Leave it to the pros," Alice curtly instructed the ambulance crews. No more than an hour of sleep at a time for three days was wearing Alice down to raw nerves.

Chapter 3

At the urging of the Red Cross volunteers, Delena Harrison followed the group of wives and children back into the engine house. Instead of the subdued murmuring and forced hopefulness prevalent there earlier, the atmosphere was dark. Smothering. Despite the frigid temperatures, she had to get back outside where she could breathe while she awaited word of her husband's condition. Instinctively, she followed a path in the worn, dirty snow that led back to the entrance of the mine, skirting a group of exhausted miners taking a break from their rescue efforts.

Delena paced nervously along a stretch outside the mine, hoping and praying for good news. Brent was a hard worker. He knew his way around the mine, for sure. He knew the dangers and he knew how to protect himself. He was probably still in there trying to help someone else. With her mind focused on positive thoughts, she tuned out most of the chatter in the area, but the resting miners' conversation intruded on her thoughts.

"Can't believe it," Harry Clarkston mumbled to his crew buddy. "That dumbbell went back to get his new lunch pail. Harrison was outta the mine, and he went back in. Poor son-of-a-bitch, he was one of the best foremen we had."

Delena stopped, mid-stride, as though she'd been slapped. Suddenly, her blood ran colder than the freezing air that took her breath. Her tightly clenched throat halted rising nausea and she struggled to breathe. Closing her eyes, she forced the words out, "Excuse me. Are you talking about Brent Harrison? My Brent?"

The quiet, childlike voice behind Clarkston caused him to wheel around on one pivoting foot to face her. Delena stood tall, bolstered by the wild-eyed ten-year-old miniature of herself holding on to her waist like a body brace.

"No, Ma'am," he stuttered. "We was…We was just jawing 'bout some of our buddies trapped down there."

Delena knew better. It was written all over Clarkston's face. "You said there was a man with a new lunch pail. I just bought Brent a new one along with a new thermos. You said Harrison."

"Don't know, Ma'am." Clarkston avoided her eyes, looking to his companions for help.

"Was he one of the three they just carried out? Do you know that? How would you know?" Delena insisted. She had to know.

The men's awkward silence told Delena more than she wanted to hear. She bent down and clutched her daughter Clara so tightly the girl started struggling. Then, as if understanding the cryptic exchange, she fell limp in her mother's arms. There were no howls or tears. Shock and numbness wrapped around them like a thick winter blanket.

The men gradually got to their feet and slipped away, leaving the woman and child alone with their grief. Much like the rumble that shook the mountain twenty-four hours before, anguish rose from the depths of Delena's soul, building in intensity until it erupted from her throat in great whooping sobs that filled the air.

Alice looked on, numb, her eyes raking over the growing number of gawking onlookers. Nothing she could say or do would ease the pain of that woman, or any other. That fact only served to intensify the anger building inside her over the callousness of Lawrence Bradford. The injustice of irrevocable loss. Unfortunately, her response seemed equally callous. Just stuff the compassion and deal with it.

"What the hell are you all looking at?" Alice snapped at the onlookers. "There will be no announcements of who is who until this rescue mission is complete."

One of the miner's wives curled her lips in disgust and shot a pointed glance in Alice's direction. "Who do you think you are? Running around here like you're family?"

"Get the hell outta here," Lawrence Bradford's voice barked from behind Alice, "This ain't your damned army. I'm in charge here."

Alice wheeled around to face him. The intensity of his dislike for her mirrored what she felt toward him. She opened her mouth, ready to lash out, then clamped it shut again. Suddenly, the exhaustion and realization of how little help anyone could provide drove any remaining strength she had from her body. The crowd closed in behind her and a hard shove against Alice's back underscored the point. There was nothing more she could do there. If she'd learned anything from years of experience, it was knowing when to accept her own limitations. Pushing her way through a tightly forming circle, without a word Alice signaled to Autumn that they were leaving.

~

A stone's throw off the Beartooth Highway, hidden among the cottonwoods and aspens lining Rock Creek, Alice lived three miles from Red Lodge, Montana's most infamous mining town with a population of thirty-five hundred doggedly self-proclaiming spirits. "Nature with an attitude" was how she referred to her cherished hideaway. The limber pines best captured the defining vision of her natural hideaway. Most pines couldn't endure the weather extremes. The limber gave up its symmetrical beauty to survive. Twisted and bent limbs reached out in celebration of living another day. She might describe herself the same way.

Alice anxiously longed to return to the security and protection of her wooded private fortress. Life in the army was anything but private. A sense of purpose and mission had engulfed her upon her return, conveniently leaving little time for social camaraderie. What did her hometown understand of a hostile world governed by military madmen who never had to touch civilian life?

Determined to put the last thirty-six hours out of her mind as she navigated the roads that led toward home, Alice forced her thoughts toward the issue that was most pressing before the warning whistle sounded. Robert Ren. She exhaled a deep, shuddering sigh. Just thinking his name again gave her a strange, sensual rush.

An unopened letter from Ren was propped up against the lamp base on her bedside nightstand. She'd received it mid-week and planned to wait until Sunday to slowly devour the words from the only man she'd ever loved.

Chapter 4

Easing the truck into its designated spot between the snow banks by the main cabin, Alice got out, taking a fresh look at the life she'd crafted since leaving the service. She'd purchased the dwellings and two acres of land along Rock Creek from a family in Billings who had owned it for summer outings since the turn of the century. The cabins were badly in need of repair, and while Alice had cultivated many skills, carpentry wasn't one that came easily. She'd re-shingled the roof of both cabins and resealed the rustic log exterior and interior walls. Her proudest achievement was the construction of a spacious covered porch overlooking Rock Creek.

The main cabin had a floor-to-ceiling Rock Creek stone fireplace. She'd studied a five-mile stretch of the river, carefully selecting each rock and carrying it to her nearby truck to haul to the cabin. Its majestic presence created a binding link between the river and the cabin.

A high-back, dark green fabric-covered chair, a Beck family heirloom, was next to the hearth, perfect for evening reading and meditation. A secretary desk and chair nestled against a nearby wall, only a few feet from the dining room table. The small kitchen area had a simple white fold-out table with seating for two, enhanced by a green and white-checkered plastic table cloth and fresh wildflowers five months a year. A new icebox, white porcelain sink, water pump and simple white curtains completed the kitchen furnishings.

The full-size antique bed was covered with a green and white Amish quilt, purchased at her last U.S. post in the Northeast. A nightstand and matching antique mirrored armoire that held her unfashionable, but highly functional, wardrobe finished off the cabin's motif.

Unfortunately, she was too far up the Beartooth Canyon to access a septic tank for indoor plumbing, a major issue six months of the year when she had to dig snow tunnels to the outhouse. The smaller cabin served as a yet-unused summer guesthouse. All things considered, it was a place that Alice was proud to call home. After the exertion of the last thirty-six hours, surrounded by the comforting cabin presence, Alice fell almost immediately into a long, dreamless sleep.

Following ten hours of uninterrupted slumber, Alice awoke. The clock by her bed read ten o'clock. She turned on the nightstand light, hesitated once again, and then snatched the letter like a child reaching for the last cookie. Like a talisman, the mere touch of the envelope hurled her mind back to three months in 1919 that created a stormy blueprint for a life unfulfilled.

~

Savenay, France was so small it was even missing from some road maps, yet it still held the magic of Europe for a nineteen-year-old Montana girl. Women with bad teeth and hairy legs were hardly the Moulin Rouge beauties that danced through Alice Beck's head when she got her first Red Cross nursing assignment overseas. The village's charm and lush green floral countryside were intoxicating.

On the heels of the Armistice, Alice cared for the wounded at a makeshift hospital located on a quaint college campus. Operating tables replaced rows of desks where doctors performed life-saving procedures. Alice's shy and caring demeanor along with her petite beauty and long, wavy chestnut hair made her a popular bedside companion to disfigured victims of German mustard gas and amputees whom others nervously dismissed from direct eye contact.

She couldn't believe her good fortune when Robert Ren, one of the richest and most popular boys from her hometown high school in Red Lodge, Montana was under her care. He'd sustained severe burns while saving a fellow soldier from a warfront inferno.

The relationship started out with coy teasing—conversations skipping along the surface—occasionally accented by small admissions of insecurities and worries. While she was a humble coal miner's daughter and he the son of the president of Red Lodge's only bank, they soon served as each other's touchstones to the sanity of growing up in the infamous western town at the foot of the rugged Beartooth Mountains.

The ravages of war displaced a lot of childish notions, including Alice's perception of Robert's childhood as idyllic. As their conversations grew more intimate, her wistful envy was readily replaced with compassion for Robert's brutal childhood, enduring an abusive father. Before long, the relationship erupted into a shared, unquenchable passion and deep lifetime commitments. Their lovemaking was as raw and wild as their love, culminating in a luscious peak of rapture on a rain-soaked wood floor of a French countryside windmill. At the time, Alice was naïve enough to believe it would last forever.

Even when Robert was called back home to the bedside of his mother in the final throes of a life-threatening illness, she'd dreamed of the time they'd be together again. Long letters, mostly about the severity of his mother's cancer, came to Alice twice a week at first. She carried them with her to work, tucked deeply in the pocket of her uniform nearest her heart. Although it troubled her that he didn't write much beyond the bare facts of his mother's health, she consoled herself that he was a man of few words. The time between letters gradually increased until they came randomly, and finally stopped coming altogether. The hope that Alice had for her future dwindled like a worn candle, slowly extinguishing its own flame.

Alice never told her lover that she got pregnant that night at the windmill. She wondered, later, if the little part of her that died had any effect on the child conceived from their rapturous union. In any case, it was no surprise to her that she miscarried right after receiving a telegram from her own mother stating that Robert vanished after his mother's death. It was final confirmation to her that Robert, and all the joy he'd brought into her sparse existence, was no longer a part of her life.

Alice never heard from or about him again.

The innocence of youth caught up in the rapture of her first love was lost. From that point, Alice Beck exchanged the promise of a lasting relationship for a manic, career-driven life, avoiding even the mention of the name Robert Ren.

With a sigh that transported her back from memories of the past, Alice weighed the envelope in her hand and wondered if its heaviness represented years of words left unsaid. What could Robert have to say to her after twenty-five years? Taking a deep breath, she settled back onto the pillow, holding the expensive watermark stationary up to eye level.

"My Dearest Alice,

You have never left my thoughts since the moment we parted in France. You were so right about how the world changes things. I saw Red Lodge as a small western outpost in the middle of rugged, lonely country.

Nothing changed at home and yet everything changed. After my mother's death, my father and I turned on each other like caged beasts. Not a day went by that he didn't try to drive a stake through our lives and marriage plans.

You should know my mother was highly supportive of us through the night she died. She left me a beautiful letter praying for our happiness together.

My father nearly went mad. He blamed me for leaving home, as if that had anything to do with her cancer. I became so full of rage I couldn't stay in Red Lodge another day. I ran until my wallet was empty.

I don't know if you heard the army helped pay for me to go to college and get a law degree. I've been a corporate attorney for many years with my own small practice.

I married and had a child. I won't bore you with the details, but my wife left me. I have a wonderful and talented daughter— she's a writer—who's gone through hell over the breakup.

And yes, the reason for this letter… My father is dying, so I'm coming to Red Lodge. Please keep this a secret. He doesn't know. We haven't said or written a word to each other since I left. I heard you moved back. I'd love to see you.

I've never again felt passion and ecstasy like the time we made love at the windmill.

While you were timid and delicate, I always felt you were the stronger of the two of us. When my mother died, I didn't know what I needed. Somehow I just needed to get control of my life. Control. Sounds like my father, doesn't it?

I've followed every step of your career. Congratulations on becoming the army's first woman lieutenant colonel and doing our country proud in both wars and eight U.S. posts.

I've been concerned that the folks in Red Lodge say you not only live alone, but also stay alone all the time. Did something happen over the course of your life that made you want to live without social contact?

I'm sure this letter shocks you after all these years. There will
be no expectations, except, I hope, your willingness to see me.
      Always,
      Robert Ren"

Alice carefully folded the letter and sat motionless, staring unseeing
at the words on the paper. Surprisingly, no tears appeared. Gradually,
the self-protective walls she'd erected around her heart began to
crumble, replaced by a swirl of unrecognizable emotion. She leapt
from the bed and ran to the bathroom mirror, pulling off her pinstripe
flannel nightgown along the way. A full examination of a forty-eight-
year-old body started with the eyes. Clear, electric light-blue eyes were
now accented by fine crow's feet, revealing a hard life of focus and
little pampering.

Once long, thick chocolate brown hair was now cropped short. At
least there was still a lot of natural luster and few signs of gray. A
lifetime of self-neglect hadn't substantially changed her strong but
attractive facial features or her lean, toned and still-shapely figure.
Would the woman she'd become withstand the scrutiny of a man who
hadn't seen her in so many years? Would she even care?

What if the years had taken the towering muscular young man she
remembered and changed him into a middle-aged pear-shaped bag of
pains and psychosomatic illnesses? Hard as she tried, she couldn't
picture Robert any other way than the way she remembered him that
rainy windmill morning they embraced with commitments to a life
spent together regardless of the obstacles.

Sinking slowly back into the safety of her bed, Alice considered her
situation. After twenty-five years, Robert Ren was coming back to Red
Lodge. In a few minutes time, that simple fact had unleashed a whole
range of conflicting emotions she'd been stuffing for years. Closing her
eyes, she waited for the confusion to subside. The thought of seeing him
again excited her, she had to admit. But the excitement was followed
almost immediately by fear. Fear that he'd find her undesirable after so

long. Fear that they'd never be able to bridge the gap of the years. Fear that maybe he wasn't the man she'd thought him to be. And even if he was, would she be able to forget the hurt? The sense of abandonment she'd felt? She'd been devastated and the subsequent loss of the child they'd created had been almost more than she could bear. And there, beneath all the questions and uncertainty, was an anger that had smoldered for a long, long time. A sense of betrayal. The one man she'd loved more than her own life had left her alone, without a word or a concern for her feelings or her safety. What kind of man would promise undying love and commitment then just vanish, never even knowing about their baby? Never caring about her hopes and dreams?

One thing was sure. She wasn't as gullible and naïve as she'd been at nineteen. At least he'd given her fair warning this time. She'd meet Robert Ren again, but this time she'd be prepared. Her anger flashed, then gave way to meditation and sound sleep like she hadn't experienced since she was still a nurse catching a few hours of shut-eye between shifts.

Chapter 5

Over the next few days, Alice concentrated on living life as usual, minimizing the undercurrent of anticipation that caused her to wonder frequently when Robert would make his appearance. Each day, she opened the *Carbon Courier* to tragic reports of the mining disaster. Clean up crews reported messages found in chalk on walls and the sides of coal cars. "Walter J Jounny. Goodbye wife and daughter. We died an eary death. Love forever. Be good." Another scribbling read, "It's five minutes past eleven o'clock. Dear Agnes and children, sorry I had to go this way. God bless you all. Your Emil, with lots of love."

The news of Montana's worst mining disaster was picked up by the media from coast to coast as the last words from loving husbands, fathers and sons captured the kind of human drama radio and newspaper reporters knew made provocative human interest stories. Anxious reporters swarmed Red Lodge looking for additional scoops about rumored premonitions and other juicy angles.

Alice felt a surge of antagonism when she spied a story by Red Lodge mayor, "Captain" Frank Blethum, inside the front page. Blethum had capitalized on the descending media like a one-man chamber of commerce. It seemed like every time she went to town anymore she saw the Captain walking along Main Street, trailed by reporters with notepads in hand. Never mind that it was a self-titled military distinction no one bothered to challenge. His long, well-groomed black beard was accented by hair as white as new fallen snow. His heavy plaid wool Pendleton shirt and black suspenders holding up a pair of baggy beige pants and flailing arms perfectly finished off his near-comical rugged appearance. While his girth made it nearly impossible to guess his waistline size, it was easy to surmise why no clothing stores in Montana carried a belt with that much leather.

The story was obviously written for national release. The Captain was quoted dramatizing a rich Western history that made it sound like Red Lodge rivaled Dodge or Virginia City. He announced that, at one time, Red Lodge had over twenty saloons and twelve whorehouses on the single main street. Western lore characters like Billy the Kid, Calamity Jane and Buffalo Bill Cody peppered the story, more bent on tourism than the mine disaster.

"Since the early 1900s, it was often the case that coal mines had been marginally safe. The mine owners and miners knew it. Most of the families chose not to speak or think about possible consequences," the newspaper article concluded. With a snort, Alice slammed the paper down on the table. It would be nice to think someone as important as the mayor would be more concerned about the families of the miners killed in the incident than in declaring themselves blameless.

~

As time went on, Alice settled back into a familiar isolated routine, but couldn't go an hour without thinking about the widow and child she'd seen at the mine that day. The daily headlines of post-disaster events and related stories were gradually replaced by World War II updates and typical small town coverage. There was one exception: an article no more than two column inches long reporting that Delena Harrison, on behalf of the fifty-eight widows, was threatening to sue Bear Creek Mine owner Lawrence Bradford for safety negligence. The story stated that damages were rumored to be as high as nearly one million dollars.

A smile crept over Alice's face. Now she knew why she was getting restless since leaving behind a life dedicated to helping others. She needed a cause. Maybe she'd found one. Delena Harrison.

Chapter 6

On an average day before the disaster, Delena Harrison rose with the sun to feed the pigs and chickens, collect eggs and start a fire in the stove before waking Clara for school. The Harrison family garden was one of the most ambitious of the thirty families randomly scattered on Bear Creek's many gullies and valleys, providing ample fresh vegetables nearly half of the year. Produce stored in the root cellar provided food for the winter.

Her husband had worked consecutive time-and-a-half shifts at the mine, including grave-yard, scheduled from ten p.m. until six a.m. After hours, Brent worked as a union foreman, organizing and leading evening meetings on every issue, ranging from fair wages to safety concerns. Usually, Delena sat quietly in the back, knitting sweaters she sold to mining families every fall.

The explosion that rocked the mine destroyed her world, as well. There was no such thing as an average day anymore. Delena's contagiously optimistic personality reverted to that of a lost, tortured soul. After spending days shut away in their one bedroom house lying listlessly on the bed, or just staring at and fondling clothing and other articles that belonged to Brent, she found a black, pocket-sized diary containing Brent's daily mine foreman notations. She leafed through it.

> "February 4, Spoke to Alex Thompson today. He agrees with me. Must get an inspector into Tunnel Three."

Delena sat up straight on the edge of the bed, feeling a jolt of excitement laced with dread. She turned the pages, finding more similar entries.

> "February 10, Met with Howard Wellington. He's the mine inspector.
>
> February 18, Met with Wellington and Lawrence Bradford, the mine owner. Bradford refuses to shut down Tunnel 3, even for a few days to allow for repairs.
>
> February 22, Men are getting kinda jumpy. Harvey Williams passed out today. Seems to be okay. They still want to work.
>
> February 24, More overtime, Bill Henry left early complaining of headaches and feeling sick."

Delena turned another page.

> "February 25, Carbon monoxide levels getting too high. Not enough venting. Stop mining operation long enough to fix gas leaks. Meet with Bradford Feb. 27."

Delena perked up, remembering back to February 26th, the day before Brent died.

"I'll be home late in the morning, Delena," he'd said. "I've got another meeting with Mr. Bradford and the mine inspector. Bradford's just got to listen to us this time. That damn mine's gonna blow sky high one of these days! And we're gonna be inside!"

Closing her eyes, Delena felt a shiver run up her spine. She was right. Brent knew. Bradford knew. Those men should never have died.

Summoning the last reserves of her determination, Delena flipped through the pages again. Every entry in the journal showed gas level readings. She turned back to the beginning, dated June 10, 1942. The last entry was February 25, 1943.

With a deep sigh, Delena closed the book and hugged it to her chest. Inside its pages were the answers she needed. Carefully, she tucked the book inside her drawer, under her panties and nightgowns. Her first thought was to contact mining officials and demand a better explanation of why her husband had died when there was black and white evidence of safety hazards.

Since Brent had been a union man most of his life, Delena decided to enlist the cooperation of mine steward Clint Franich, one of her husband's best friends. Being home in bed with the stomach flu had saved the miner's life the day of the disaster. Marching determinedly through the snow over a slight gully rise, Delena was surprised to see the front door fly open before she could scrape the mud off her feet and lift a hand to knock.

"Howdy, Delena."

Delena cleared her throat and put a hand to her chest to calm herself. The miner's face drew to a sharp pointed nose shading a mouth full of crooked and missing teeth. "Please, come in a spell." He leaned a little too close as he beckoned her inside, causing Delena to shrink back from him instinctively. The man's odor followed him like a loyal dog.

Taking small steps, Delena crossed the small room, carefully avoiding piles of clutter. She sat nervously on the edge of the worn couch, while Clint pulled up a chair near her.

"What can I do ya for?"

"I, I need to share this with somebody," she said, carefully extracting her husband's work log from her bag and placing it in the man's long, thin hand.

"Won't be needin' to see that," he hardly even glanced at the book, still closed in his palm.

"You know what it is?"

"'Course. It's Brent's bitch book," he looked at her steadily.

"Those men could have lived."

The miner's dark eyes sparked when his brow shot up. "I got some possible mighty good news for ya."

Delena slipped the book out of his hand and scanned it for indicting entries, thinking he surely just didn't understand. Maybe if she just read him some of them, he'd see what she meant.

His eyes narrowed and he leaned forward to get her attention. "What are you going to get out of blowing up at everybody? Tell me that?" The sour smell of tobacco and liquor on his breath made it hard for Delena to concentrate. "Here's the thing," he continued. "The company's talking about up and givin' every widow a big hunk of money to shut up and get on with their lives."

"I can believe that," Delena whispered, looking up.

"Yup," he nodded in emphasis, "upwards of one thousand dollars. Pretty hunk a change."

The dark, stale atmosphere was closing in on her and she felt confused. "That's not what I'm here about. This diary could be useful."

Clint's expression shifted as he leaned even closer. "I'll help getcha that money for a little favor."

"Favor?"

He nodded and moved over to the couch. "You help me a little and I help you."

Her eyes narrowed as she tried to interpret the change in him. Suddenly, she felt a hand on her leg and it started to make sense. "What? What in the world?" Delena leapt to her feet. "I can't believe you. Brent's best friend." Her stomach churned and disgust left a bad taste in her mouth.

"True enough," he got up slowly. "Always had a sweet tooth for you, but until Brent was in the ground I didn't do nothin' about it."

"I made a mistake coming here." Delena stormed to the door and headed back home before her neighbor could apologize. She was running low on people to trust and new ideas.

~

At first light, Delena scratched out notes to each of the other fifty-seven surviving widows, announcing a meeting at the local work hall in three days. A night's sleep helped her focus and keep things in perspective. Methodically, she wrote and discarded one speech draft after another until she was comfortable. Finally, she had a reasonable—although potentially debatable—recommendation to make to the widows, suing mine owner, Lawrence Bradford. Even though the newspaper announcement had been premature, Delena had probed many of the women on their receptivity to the bold move. Unanimous encouragement had prompted the meeting. Now she had the ammunition they needed to proceed.

~

After anticipating the meeting for so long, it was hard to believe it was time to begin. Delena stood and straightened her dress, stylish by Red Lodge standards. Nauseating spurts of adrenaline coursed through her veins until she looked into the faces of longtime friends. For such a good crowd, the room was still. Pasting what she hoped was a pleasant smile on her face, she cleared her raw throat and held up a one-page speech in her trembling right hand.

"Speak up," a man growled from the back of the room.

"As most of you know," Delena cleared her throat again, "my husband was one of the union foremen in the mine. He was very careful about keeping records."

Delena's voice was interrupted by another loud outburst from the back of the hall. "This meeting is being held without the coordination or input of Bear Creek Mining officials." A tall, boxy man lumbered

from the shadowed back wall of the meeting hall to the front of the
room as though he'd been awaiting an introduction. "I'm Jed Patterson,
Bear Creek Mining Company legal counsel. I have to tell you ladies
that we are providing each of you with a generous sum of money. It
isn't required by any insurance claims or legal action, but we are doing
it because we feel deeply over your loss."

Ill-equipped for a confrontation with a lawyer, or anybody else
representing the mine owners' interest, Delena dropped to her seat,
trying to decide her next action.

The attorney offered a plastic smile. "I'm sorry you didn't come to
me for the facts before troubling all these people." The look he shot at
Delena was laced with daggers that belied the smile. "Ladies, if you
have concerns on any subject, please give me your name before you
leave. A company representative will come to your home and resolve
your concerns. Lawrence Bradford is committed to helping each of you
through this difficult time."

A frail, liver-spotted widow near the front of the assembly was the
first to respond. "I, for one, am grateful for all the mine has done for
my family. I figured we came here to share personal grief and get ideas
on how to provide for our families."

Heads nodded agreement. Delena rose, eyes turned downward. In a
whispered, shaky voice she spoke again, determined to finish what she
started even though her heart was failing her. "As I was saying, my
husband kept records of issues that were of concern to mine workers. I
never heard him speak poorly of anyone in particular, recognizing he
and the others were helping the war effort and all." Delena lifted her
husband's safety booklet for all to see. "But, he did write down serious
safety concerns in this book. Carbon monoxide levels were getting
dangerously high. Many of you aren't strangers to these safety
concerns." Delena's voice built more resolve with each statement. "You
know how often the men spoke of them. It just isn't right." She abruptly
sat down, awaiting a response.

Not a word was spoken as the women got up and left, one or two at a time at first, then in mass, abandoning Delena on center stage.

Waiting until the room was emptied, with a smug expression, the attorney clambered over to Delena. "That was pretty dumb."

She felt pretty dumb; she didn't need him to point it out. Without a word, she looked up at him and examined his face. What kind of man knew the miners were in danger and still did nothing?

"When we read in the newspaper article about this 'black book' and meeting to rally a lawsuit, I have to tell you the first thing we did was eliminate you from the list of those who get money. You blew it, sister. This move just cost you one thousand bucks!"

"My husband and I have never been trouble makers. He was the best roper you had in that awful mine. He was only doing his job."

He made a guttural sound and lurched for her purse. "I'll take that book. It's company property."

Delena was too fast, snatching it away before he could touch it. "It is not. It's a diary my husband paid for with his own money so he could keep track of what the union assigned him to do. If this goes to anyone, it goes to the union."

Patterson made a sharp about-face and rushed out the door into the night.

Feeling the weight of the world on her frail shoulders, Delena gathered her things and walked silently out into the night. Her sense of purpose had taken a beating and she wasn't sure what to do next. Upon reaching the outskirts of her yard, she was surprised by two rangy miner widows in worn dresses and warm smiles waiting on her front steps.

The corn-kernel toothed older of the two warned in a frightened tone, "We're all with ya, Delena. With that company guy there it was best no more be said in front of him. Got it all in that book there, huh? Better hold onto it."

Delena collapsed into the arms of her friends in tearful relief. Her two champions sauntered into her house and plopped into chairs by Delena's wood-burning stove.

"Didn't believe a damn thing that slick-ass attorney said, did we, Flora?"

Gladys leaned over and tapped her neighbor's knee.

"Nope. Don't let 'em git ya, Delena. We're all with you. God knows we need the money that rich son-of-a-bitch Bradford owes us all. Now read us that diary."

~

The next morning, Delena resolved to go to the home of every widow to solidify support. She asked each one to sign the handwritten document that stated personal loss claims due to careless and fore-warned safety problems, requiring Bradford to pay one million dollars collectively for the future well being of the widows. Once all the signatures were gathered, Delena mailed a copy of the document to the publisher of the *Carbon Courier*.

Chapter 7

Alice drove into Red Lodge for breakfast at the Bear Creek Cafe. "Morning, Sally. Your pancakes sure smell good. Got any hot coffee?" she slid onto a seat at the counter.

"Alice, what brings you into town for breakfast?"

"Just picking up supplies. Besides, I don't see much of my friends these days. What's this?" Alice picked up the newspaper from the countertop. A long, front-page story heralded the compassion of Lawrence Bradford in giving generous sums to widows whose husbands died in the mine explosion. Halfway down the page, another headline caught her eye: "Bear Creek Mine Owners Frown On Delena Harrison Lawsuit." Alice's eyes raced down the article. "I'll be damned," Alice thought, "She did it!" Settling in to sip her coffee, Alice read Bradford's scathing response.

"We're deeply saddened by Mrs. Harrison's attack on those who care the most about Red

Lodge and Bear Creek Mine. While we have no animosity towards Mrs. Harrison, we know the town will stand behind us."

Alice threw the paper down without finishing the story. "Hot damn! Sally, did you see this?"

Sally looked nervously around before answering. "Shh, Alice. There's some that come in here who are scared they won't get their money if Delena keeps this lawsuit going. People are getting real steamed."

"Well, that's just fine, because now I'm getting mad, too. I knew Delena Harrison when she was just a little baby, before I went off to war in 1918. Her folks were my friends in high school. I think I'll just go on over to the library and see what I can find out about this mine business." Alice tossed some coins on the counter, then walked out the door and across the street. Something deep inside churned and rebelled at the way this thing was panning out. She took the steps two at a time and burst through the library door.

The pale-faced librarian turned from directing a finger-tapping woman to the romantic fiction section. "Alice! Shush! I'm helping someone." The elderly woman pushed her silver wire-rimmed glasses back up her nose and peered at Alice like she'd walked in wearing a pair of manure-caked boots. "Alice, you were always the noisy one, even as a little girl. Now, what do you need?"

"I'm sorry, Miss Jones," Alice demurred, more out of respect than genuine repentance. "This article about Delena Harrison. What's the scoop?"

"You mean the article this morning about her husband?" Miss Jones adjusted her glasses and rested an elbow on the counter.

Alice approached the counter and leaned in close to the librarian, lowering her voice. "No, the lawsuit."

"Well, I don't really know much about that." The elderly librarian cupped her hand around her mouth and spoke in a whisper. "The real news is about her husband, Brent. You know, the one who died in the mine explosion?" Pursing her lips daintily, she leaned toward Alice and adopted a conspiratorial tone. "The paper says Brent Harrison had a drinking problem." Her eyes darted around the room. "But there's more. They're saying he slept around a lot, a regular at Bella's. You know, the whorehouse." She took a long, deep breath. "Now here's another thing. I heard this morning Delena's been doing some sleeping around herself, for extra money since Brent died." The old gossip's eyebrows went up and she nodded knowingly.

"Holy shit," Alice yelled, then looked around and lowered her voice. "And you believe that?"

"Don't believe or disbelieve. You know this younger generation; it's just what people are saying."

Chapter 8

At first, Delena was fortunate enough to avoid hearing the vicious gossip. Her daughter, Clara, bore the brunt of it, hearing huddled whispers and giggles while braving school halls and entering classrooms with a downcast head. Girls who'd been her playmates, suddenly avoided her, but exclusion didn't satisfy some of her former friends.

"How many fathers did you have?" a freckle-covered, crimson-haired girl politely asked Clara, loud enough for friends to enjoy.

Clara looked at her in defiance. "I had one dad, just like you."

"Your mother didn't make you call her other boyfriends 'Daddy'?" the girl taunted.

Gritting her teeth, Clara slammed a fist into her tormentor's face until blood started running down the girl's chin. A trip to the principal's office and after school chores are worth it, Clara thought, just to see that smug expression erased.

~

Store manager Ole Winther had long been close to the Harrisons. He knew that they were God-fearing Christians, like most miner families. While the mine was still in operation, as far as he was concerned, Lawrence Bradford called the shots. After all, Bradford owned the store. He didn't much care for his latest instructions, though. Just yesterday, Bradford demanded that Delena Harrison get no more credit and that she pay off the balance she owed in full. Winther put off the confrontation as long as he dared, but once he locked up, the aging store manager trudged reluctantly to the Harrison home to explain his dilemma.

Approaching the front door, he stopped when he heard Clara's sobbing followed by Delena's soft voice as she tried to comfort her daughter. Already feeling regretful, he waited awkwardly on the front porch until he heard silence before knocking. He shifted his feet nervously as Delena opened the door.

"Mrs. Harrison, I'm sorry to interrupt you at your home, but I need to let you know that I've been required to extend you no more credit at our…" His voice failed him before he could finish, seeing the startled expression on her weary face.

"But everybody who works, ah, worked for Bear Creek Mines, gets some credit. Please Mr. Winther, I've sold all I can. Even my house is for sale, but nobody wants it. There are rumors that the mine is going to close. Don't do this to us right now. I'm out of staples. My daughter…" Delena's face wore a stricken expression as she, too, seemed to run out of words.

Even before she finished speaking, Winther realized he'd made a mistake in coming to her home. Bradford or no, he couldn't inflict even more hardship on this woman and her fatherless child. "Miz Harrison," he held up his hands, "forget I said anything. Don't worry anymore. You owe the store nothing." As he watched tears of gratitude fill her eyes, Winther felt inspired. "In fact, I recall you not only don't owe me any money, you have a credit I wish you'd hurry in and use. I'm trying to balance the books," he said, his eyes glistening.

"I'm not looking for charity, but I'll help you in straightening out your records just this one time," said Delena gratefully. Without warning, she startled the brittle old man, giving him the kind of all-arms hug that she'd been known for since childhood.

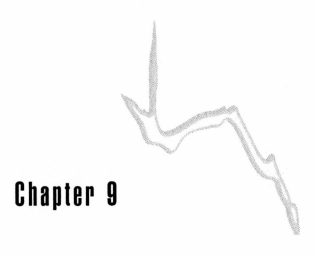

Chapter 9

Days turned into weeks, and while the widows persevered in their support of the lawsuit, Delena was painfully aware that the mining company's wrath was singularly focused on her. Knowing the contorted way public opinion could be used as a brutal weapon of destruction, even Delena's closest friends kept their distance.

Having spent her life surrounded by loved ones and a wide circle of caring and attentive friends, her exile was nearly intolerable. She hadn't been a reader or one who took much solace in meditation. In her unwanted and uninterrupted solitude, she started questioning the wisdom of her intention to sue Bradford. Maybe she shouldn't have struck out so boldly at the main provider of employment in the area.

Through the grapevine, Delena learned that the other widows were receiving small gifts and free employment counseling from Bradford. Widows in both mining towns were having their modest homes lifted from the foundations and moved to the Red Lodge's ethnic neighborhoods like Little Italy and Finntown in hopes of finding employment within walking distance. At least they had each other and some help to start living again. Delena had neighbors who avoided her for fear of incurring Bradford's wrath and having nowhere else to turn. Worse, while Delena's house served as refuge from gossiping neighbors, little Clara had nowhere to hide.

~

Wandering back to the house from the mailbox, Delena heaved a long sigh. The legal process was suspiciously slow. Delena's appeal to the National Mine Workers' Union for legal representation and support got nothing more than uncommitted condolences and promises of support of the widows' case "if our independent investigation into the safety violations reveals that established standards weren't being practiced."

Without the financial means for strong legal representation, each of the widows donated no less than one hundred dollars from their payment from the mine. Delena used the cash from selling her pigs and chickens to contribute her share since she received no payment. She kept the fifty-eight hundred dollars in a fruit-canning jar, wrapped in newspaper and placed in an old cardboard shoebox, stored in her open closet next to her four pairs of high heels and well-worn slippers. With the money tucked safely away, she hadn't anticipated difficulty in finding a qualified attorney in Red Lodge. The search she'd begun with high hopes had failed miserably and she soon realized her attorney would be subject to the inevitable ridicule of representing such malicious women. With local resources exhausted, Delena had to seek representation in a neighboring town.

With a Montana regional telephone book in hand, Delena had Clara pack a modest lunch and placed it in their 1936 Ford sedan for the two-hour drive to Billings. Missing a day of ridicule at school meant a lot more to Clara than Delena first realized. She had to help her daughter find some answers before her next inevitable classmate battle.

"Did you see other men while Daddy was alive?" Clara asked in a timid voice, intentionally looking out the car window at yet another spectacular mountain-and-stream view.

Delena's heart lurched at the bitter insult and unfair indictment, delivered by the solemn voice of her own child. She chose her words carefully, "Clara, before your father was killed in the mine, he used to talk at the dinner table about dangers he and his men were being subjected to. Do you remember what he would say?"

Clara turned toward her, chin quivering, "Never mind, Mom. It doesn't matter."

Delena swallowed hard, determined to be strong for her baby, "I assume you've been hearing horrible things about me at school. You haven't told me much, but I can tell every day you come home that things haven't been easy. Of course I never saw any man except your father. The men your father worked for at the mine didn't take the time or spend the money to make it safe for your dad. He didn't have to die. I have proof in this little book." She wiped tears away with her sleeve and pointed to her purse. "We're trying to get money from the owners of the mine for taking your father away from us. They're trying to stop me by destroying my reputation, even making up stories that even my daughter might believe."

"I don't want to go back to school, Mom. Can we go somewhere else to live?" Clara asked.

"I'm glad you feel that way. You know that I've already decided to sell our home in Bear Creek and move to Red Lodge. I think we can get enough, because of our large garden and over an acre of land. I can find new ways to earn money, too. I've got some ideas."

"But Mom, everybody I know is moving to Red Lodge. Can't we move somewhere else?"

"Honey, I've never lived anywhere else. After the trial everybody will forget all this and it will all be fine," Delena murmured unconvincingly.

~

After a long day of waiting in lobbies and only getting in to see two attorneys, the Harrisons approached the dirt road leading to their home near dusk. Delena was surprised to find the living room light on, knowing the lights were out when they left that morning. Upon entering the house, they found what little furniture they had ripped apart and the kitchen drawer pulled out with its contents strewn across the floor.

Standing in the doorway, Delena gasped and placed a firm hand on Clara's shoulder. "Stay right here," she told her, venturing inside. When she reached the bedroom, she uttered a shrill cry and fled to the closet in search of the cash-filled shoebox. It was gone.

A dense cloud of confusion and despair settled around her head as she walked dejectedly back to the front room where she'd left Clara. While the thieves failed to find the black book she had taken with her to show potential attorneys, she suddenly realized it was of little consequence without the money. She went through the motions of cleaning the mess and preparing Clara for bed, feeling nothing so much as a chilling sense of numbness.

There was no sleep for Delena Harrison that night, only torturous staring at the clock as each hour passed. When dawn approached, Delena could tolerate the isolation no longer and dragged her emotionally torn body from the bed. Soundlessly, she pulled down the covers that concealed her most precious possession and delicately slipped in the bed beside Clara, snugly wrapping one arm around her last reason for living.

Chapter 10

Alice silently took note of the week's hot topic. The word around town was that Delena Harrison had stolen the money the widows donated for a defense fund. Gathering bits and pieces of information, Alice deduced that the gossip consisted largely of strategically planted rumors maliciously spread through the mining town within an hour after Delena reported a burglary to the single law officer who oversaw the residents of Bear Creek and Washoe.

Alice's lip curled in disgust at the thought of the local law enforcement. A company man if she'd ever seen one. Seldom having to address more than public intoxication and disturbing the peace, the sheriff had determined that the alleged house break-in and theft was best handled by Red Lodge authorities. The now infamous Delena Harrison was driven in the sheriff's car down Red Lodge's Main Street to the small stone police headquarters behind the Pollard Hotel. News of her arrival didn't escape the *Carbon Courier* reporter or the growing throng of locals who hurried from their businesses and appointments to get a glimpse of the miner's wife.

Alice Beck completed her miscellaneous purchases at the Main Street Coast-to-Coast hardware store, simultaneously listening to and ignoring conversation about the town's new arrival at the police station. Reluctantly, she lingered by the front door of the store to hear all the details on the latest indictments—theft of money, duping helpless widows—growing angrier by the minute. They had the poor woman convicted without a trial.

Aside from the incident at the mine's engine house the day of the tragedy, Alice hadn't seen Delena in years, yet she felt drawn to her.

When she'd heard enough, Alice stepped out of the store and headed directly for the police station. She had no concept of what came next, but trusted her instincts that she was needed immediately and wove her way through the small gathering of curious onlookers, opening the police station door with a strong shove that got the attention of its occupants. Delena was seated directly in front of Red Lodge Sheriff Willy Hays and flanked on both sides by deputies hovering over her. All eyes turned toward the door.

"Can I help you, Ma'am?" Hays inquired, peering over Delena's shoulder at Alice and squinting at the intrusion of the blinding midday white light in the open doorway.

"Alice Beck, Sheriff. Like to sit in on the discussion you are having with Mrs. Harrison. I'm… I'm a friend of the family."

Alice Beck had few, if any friends in Red Lodge, and the sheriff and everybody else in the room knew it.

She couldn't read his expression but apparently he wasn't impressed. "Let's get back to your theory," he redirected his attention to Delena. "You claim the thieves were looking for this black book you keep talkin' about."

Alice didn't hesitate. "Sheriff, there isn't a person in this town who doesn't know about that black book and a lot of other books where union men recorded problems in the Bear Creek Mine." She put a beaded eye on each officer's face. "All of a sudden everybody's got their head up their ass playing like conditions were perfect. Enough play actin'! Why is it so difficult to believe that somebody wants that book when I read about a one million dollar lawsuit, and that book has got 'em nailed?" All her frustration at the morning's critical gossip spilled out.

The sheriff pounced to his feet. "That's it. I will ask you to leave, Miss Beck. This case has nothing to do with you," he flailed at her like he was shooing away a dog. "Now go on, leave my office. And by the way, don't you dare use that kind of tone with me." He glanced at his men with a devilish smile. "You're not back in the service giving orders. Now get the hell out of here and go on back to your cave."

Alice felt a flash of anger, but managed to contain it. She smiled calmly and looked over at Delena. "Mrs. Harrison, if you'd like to talk further I can be reached at my 'cave.' Just ask one of the three muske-teers here and they'll point the way." With a last pointed look at the sheriff, she turned and marched out the door.

~

That evening, Alice settled in with a good book to forget the troubling events of the day. In the quiet glow of a flickering fire, her head whirled up to keen attention when she heard a knock at the door. *Robert Ren.*

Despite the forewarning, Alice had persistently put thoughts of Robert's return out of her head. The thought that it might be him on the other side of the door had her on her feet in seconds, frantically speeding from her high-backed chair by the fireplace to a mirror, any mirror. "Be there in a minute!" she yelled, smoothing her hair with trembling hands. *Damn him. Doesn't contact me in nearly twenty-five years and I am running around like a teenager.*

Suddenly, she stopped all movement, deciding that she wasn't going to change a thing: not even comb her thick short hair. She took a deep breath, trying unsuccessfully to calm her hammering heart and the torrent of surging emotions.

Looking more like a sergeant than a lady in her drab green military fatigues, she slowly approached the front door, her teeth nearly drawing blood from her lower lip. All she could do to deal with her adrenaline was throw open the door. She must have looked frantic. Delena and Clara Harrison looked startled as Alice gave a loud gasp and covered her mouth with her hand.

Wide-eyed, Delena grabbed Clara by the arm and headed back toward the Ford. "I'm sorry. We shouldn't have come here," she said over her shoulder.

It took a moment for Alice to grasp the situation. As Delena backed away from the porch, she struggled to regain the use of her voice. "No, don't leave. We need to meet," Alice yelled, finally. Delena turned, paused and suddenly started to laugh. Clara was slow to recognize what was so funny, but Alice, realizing the absurdity of the situation, burst out in a deep belly laugh that even ignited the young girl in giggles.

"I'm sorry. I thought you were somebody else. Someone I haven't seen in over twenty years," Alice said through the relief of laughter. "Please come in. Isn't much, but I can set us up a comfortable place to talk."

The women entered the house together, with Alice nimbly moving to place two of the four wood dining room chairs by hers near the fireplace and tossing some kindling in to restore the blaze. Lacking in the social graces of entertaining that are a high priority in the military, Alice darted around the kitchen area trying to think of what to serve. Hurriedly, she prepared hot cider for Clara and reheated the last of her government-rationed coffee for Mrs. Harrison and herself.

When Alice returned to her guests, Delena looked away, wearing an expression of humiliation. "I'm afraid I don't know where to begin. I did appreciate you coming to my defense with the police. There have been a lot of ridiculous rumors about me, so I don't know what anybody really thinks anymore." Delena took a deep breath, sighed and placed a hand on her heart as if to stop the pain.

Alice quickly poured and handed Delena a cup of coffee then waited for her to continue.

"Thank you," she offered Alice a weary smile as she accepted the coffee. "I've lost my friends by losing their money and their hopes to get what we deserve. I'm sorry for going on like this. I just don't know what to do. Nobody wants to buy my house. I was going to use the money to pay back the widows. I would have had enough left over for Clara and me to move into town and rent a little place. I have to sell it anyway." She took a jagged breath and looked from Alice to Clara who was seated on a rug next to Alice's dog, rubbing Autumn's belly. "We have no way to live. No one in Red Lodge will hire me. Besides, I'm not skilled at anything." Delena finally allowed herself a sip of the hot coffee.

"Did you bring the black book with you?" Alice asked.

Delena nodded, reaching for the bag that had settled at her feet. "Keep it with me at all times since they tried to steal it," she said. "You can't tell me the mine owner wasn't trying to get his hands on it. Brent had carefully recorded the high gas levels for over a month in his diary. I don't know what the readings mean, but his comments tell it all. They were too high. Dangerously high." Delena extracted the book from her purse and handed it to Alice for her review.

Alice skimmed the first pages, then, as she started reading continual notations regarding gas level and air circulation problems, she became totally absorbed. When she reached the abrupt and painful end, she looked up, remembering that Delena was still there with her. Delena's delicate vulnerability and compassionate eyes began to seep into Alice's starving soul. After staring into the fireplace's dancing flames with only the sound of Delena's uneven breathing, she decided she needed the mother and child as much as they needed her.

"You don't know me any more than I do you." Alice turned from the fire and scooted her chair opposite Delena. "Look, I'm not crazy, or a hermit like some people say. I've just needed to be alone, except for my dog.

"Have no husband or children. My parents died while I was away. I wonder sometimes why I ever returned to Red Lodge," Alice spoke as though she was talking to herself, although Delena's eyes were fixed on her face. "After I got malaria so bad they had to ship me home, my first thought was this place. I never had the time to enjoy nature or a place of my own, so I came to Rock Creek. When I first drove into town, I stopped at the snack shop by the river. Beautiful July day. Took my lunch to one of the picnic tables by the river." She sighed and offered Delena a tiny smile. "Its sound was hypnotizing. Looked for a place in town, but one day when I was hiking at the base of the Beartooth Mountains I decided the second chapter of my life was going to be totally different. No more orders doing what was required." She stood and looked around, suddenly feeling awkward at so much self-disclosure. "Bought this cabin and the one next to it. Only had a few weeks for the exterior work before the first snow. Went to Carnegie Library in town. Checked out every 'how to' book I could find." Alice turned her eyes to her attentive listener.

"Towns like this, everything from religion to cowboy boots have to be the same." She paused and walked over to gaze out the cabin window. "Funny, I thought the military was regimented. Found in just a few conversations that I had nothing in common with these people. Keep in contact with friends still serving in the Philippines in the War right now. Keep in close touch with a family I lived with during one of my two tours to the Panama Canal."

After a hesitant pause, Delena spoke. "I've never lived anywhere or even traveled much outside of Montana. With my family and all my history here I've never felt like I missed much. Didn't it get lonely moving from one place to another?"

Alice shrugged a shoulder. "Got a lot of friends I care about. Just turns out none of them are here, unless Autumn counts." She smiled over at her faithful canine companion.

Clara had long since stopped paying much attention to the grownups' chatter, but she looked up as Alice glanced her way. "Does your dog know any tricks?" asked Clara.

Alice felt the tug of compassion, considering the child's questioning gaze. "Tell you what. If you and your mother will stay for dinner, I can show you how talented she is. Can't say I'd be able to make good food like I'll bet your mom does, but it'll do."

"We really appreciate the offer," Delena interjected, "but I'd like to get back to Bear Creek. After the sheriff took me home, I went straight to the school to pick Clara up before classes were over. We came right here. I don't know what you can do to help. Frankly, I don't have a lot of others that want to do anything other than run me out of town." Delena guided out the words between clenched teeth. "This is my home. Damnit, Clara and I aren't going anywhere."

Clara's head jerked up like a pointer when she heard her mother swear. Profanity was as rare as ice cream at their house.

"Once our house sells—"

Alice bluntly interjected, "Yes, you said that will finance the legal battle and move to town. A couple of questions, though. What if Bradford and the bank make sure word gets 'round and nobody buys it? Hardly a mortgage in these parts that doesn't go through the Red Lodge Bank. They'll probably have to approve the loan. Only a local would buy your place now, I would think, since people are moving out faster than the original miners moved in." Alice lifted one foot onto the fireplace hearth and rested a fisted hand on her hip like a country lawyer.

"My second question has to do with the court case. Attorneys for the defense will be aware of the exact amount of money you had in your war chest, especially since Bradford had someone steal it." Alice stood, back to the fire, with both arms folded. "In a million dollar case you can be sure that money would be gone before the second day the trial was held." She turned back to the woman, erectly perched on the edge of her chair. "Delena, litigation on a case like this could take months. There's no way that I can see you and the widows would have made a valuable use of the money, anyway, even with your black book evidence."

"If we could have been taken care of that easily, why did somebody go through my house like a cyclone and steal the money? They must be scared," Delena argued.

"Doesn't hurt to be overly cautious. They don't have any idea what's in that black book. There could be a lot more incriminating evidence of illegal activities than just what we know is there on gas levels and air quality.

"Don't mean to upset or discourage you," Alice said. "Please do stay for dinner. We can figure something out. Already have some ideas that might help." Alice glanced over at Clara and half-smiled. "Won't tell you what they are if you and the young one don't stay for supper."

Delena stood and paced the cabin, rubbing her brow. "It's all so complicated. I've got Clara and me into a real mess." She turned to Alice and spoke softly, "I guess we'll stay if it's all right." With that decision, Delena, towering nearly a foot above Alice, wrapped both of her thin arms around her, burying Alice's head between the cleavage of her perfumed breasts.

Not knowing how to tactfully pry herself free, the normally distant former colonel stood stiffly erect, waiting for the dramatic show of emotion to pass. The problem was nobody gave a longer, tenderer hug than Delena Harrison. Clara was so used to her mother's affectionate behavior that she looked up from Autumn at the embrace and sighed, shaking her head back and forth grinning.

Alice flashed on a strategy to release the hug. "Clara, maybe after dinner you and I could go on an evening nature walk." Delena relaxed her arms, then wiped tears away with the back of her wrist. "That's a good idea, honey. I bet Alice knows the Beartooths better than a mountain goat."

Alice served up a dinner of fresh-caught cutthroat trout and rice, followed European-style with a garden salad, and cheese and bread for dessert. The simple meal was a feast to the Harrisons. A relaxing atmosphere settled over the honeycomb beeswax candlelit table as the desperate group of Red Lodge outcasts began to meld. Their shared exclusion alone was a solid foundation for a growing relationship.

As the two women lingered over cups of coffee, it grew dark, prompting Alice to convince her guests to stay in her nearby cabin for the weekend. Alice suspected the idea of returning to the holocaust and emptiness of their Bear Creek home made the decision an easy one. Brent had died months ago, but no doubt his presence was felt in their little house. Delena told Alice she hadn't been to his gravesite at Red Lodge Cemetery since the funeral, making his death even more of an abstraction.

Alice put down her coffee cup and signaled to Clara that it was time for a moonlight walk. Clara put on her coat and nervously followed her to the front door.

While early June can mean snow in Beartooth Canyon, a recent burst of heat had melted most of it making Alice and Clara's walk even more magical. Alice loved the "blue" time of day best, when everything turns to a twilight shade bathed in the color of deep tranquility.

At first Clara did all the talking. She was an outspoken child, mature for her age, but in the impending darkness, with pine trees looming like monsters and winter wildlife stirring nearby, it wasn't long before she slid her hand into Alice's hand, trudging toward the partially ice-covered creek only yards from Alice's front door.

Alice was a bit uncomfortable with physical contact at first, but the gesture helped her with her own clumsy shyness. Alice's mind reeled back to the first few hours of the mining disaster where she'd watched Clara assume the role of nurturer, patting her mother's long dark wavy hair and whispering the words, "It'll be okay, Mom."

"Mom said you know a lot about nature. Can you tell me something about where we're walking?" Clara asked.

Alice glanced around and wondered what would most interest an inquisitive child. As her eyes fell on a familiar, flattened area, she pointed. "That's what's called the Beartooth Plateau. As the granite was uplifted or compressed, or basically heated, the pressure becomes metamorphosed." She paused a moment, suspecting she'd be more successful trying to teach Clara a new language than a bombasting of geologic terminology.

Glancing down at her captive student, she tried again. "Look up at those rocks. If you look closely, you see clear striations." Alice looked into emerald eyes pretty as Delena's. She kneeled down to Clara's level and used her finger to point the child's eyes to the night skyline. "If you could climb to the top you could talk to your ancestors." Alice rose and stood erect, pointing to the river's edge. "See that bent-looking tree? It's a limber pine, my favorite. Guess I'm a little crazy to pick the ugliest as my favorite."

"If my mother brought me here again, could we go on a camping trip together and you could teach me more about the woods?"

"It's too cold at night right now to go camping. Later this summer we'll hike to the 'big boot'," she said, pointing to a distant mountainside where natural spring runoff drainage had cut away one side of an enormous grouping of ponderosas into a distinct outline.

Clara seemed riveted by the mountain woman's voice. "That's enough for tonight," Alice said. "We'd best get back to the cabin and see if your mother is hugging the life out of Autumn." Alice stopped and stood motionless. The sound of a nearby tree branch cracking from the weight of the recent snow pierced the silence. "What really matters are mountains, trees, and rivers like this."

While Clara couldn't grasp most of what Alice had told her that evening, she seemed calmed by their walk with nature.

As the two explorers entered the cabin, they found Delena huddled with Autumn on the floor, both of them staring into the popping pine log fire. Delena looked up as they entered and offered a smile.

"Alice, can we get Clara settled into the guest cabin?" she asked. "We have a lot to talk about before the night's over. I think we're starting to figure this mess out."

Alice nodded and called Autumn to her side, then stood by the door, waiting, as Delena got slowly to her feet and shrugged into her coat.

The second cabin was closer to Rock Creek, and the eternal sound of the river, just a few steps away from Alice's main cabin. There was no separate kitchen area or fireplace like in the master cabin. An ornately carved canopy antique bed, nightstand, and dresser, with a yellow down comforter and complementing lace window curtains stood opposite a pot-bellied stove in one corner.

Alice stepped back out onto the front porch, listening to the night while Delena helped Clara change into an oversized nightgown she had provided. Alice had been taught since childhood that the ritual of making a child feel at ease in a strange surrounding was sitting near or on the bed telling a story until their eyelids closed. Once the child was dressed and ready to snuggle up in bed, Alice offered, "Would you like a bedtime story to help you sleep?"

Wide-eyed, Clara eagerly nodded her acceptance as she climbed beneath the comforter.

Alice perched on the corner of the bed, cleared her throat and began. "It was probably some time in the 1700s when the Absarokee, or Crow tribe as it was later to be called, migrated to the area later to be known as Montana. They were forced out by their hated enemy, the Sioux, first from the area of Minnesota, later the Black Hills and parts of Montana.

"There were the River Crow and the Mountain Crow. If you took the time, you could probably go anywhere in Red Lodge and dig through the surface of the soil to find arrowheads and stone tools. These were their hunting and fishing grounds. This was Crow country. Snowy mountains and sunny plains. All kinds of good things to enjoy every season. The air was sweet and cool, the grass fresh, and the streams full of cutthroat trout."

Already, Clara's eyelids were starting to droop.

"In the fall when their horses were fat and strong from the mountain pastures, they'd go down into the plains and hunt buffalo or trap beaver in the river."

Clara was in a deep sleep with her right hand still clutching Alice's. She lightly placed the girl's arm under the cover and patted Autumn on the head. Alice sat staring at the child, losing all concept of time, refilling her soul with a sense of purpose.

Chapter 11

With Clara tucked safely in bed, the two women returned to Alice's cabin, talking like old friends. Alice paced back and forth in front of the fire, too agitated to sit down.

"When my father died of black lung in his fifties I did some investigation into safety standards. Knew my mother couldn't make it on her own having never worked outside the house. Figured there had to be some union protection," she said, ferreting through her desk for the paperwork she'd gathered during her investigation.

"Turns out that at the turn of the century there were so many people dying in the mines there were federal laws enacted to supposedly protect human life and run the mines more efficiently. Things like enough exits in case of explosions or fire. Stuff like that. Problem was, there were different safety codes for different mines. Some states, including Montana, adopted their own regulations. Ever hear your husband talk of the Montana state coal mine inspector?"

"He came to some of the night meetings Brent and I went to. Why?"

Alice's eyes lit up with excitement. "Good. Did you contact him after the accident to see if he would confirm your husband's reports?"

"I remember he said once that Lawrence Bradford had to enforce safety standards to stop the chance of accidents. It was something like that. His name is Howard Wellington. Do you think he could make a big difference in our case?"

Alice's eyebrows shot up. "Enormous! What else?"

"As foreman, Brent was assigned each day to check out the ceilings of timber to see if they were safe. He would examine the way explosives were handled and stored and, of course, check the air quality and proper ventilation. He was supposed to keep it in a book he signed each day. That was a different one than the one he carried with him to remember what to write down daily."

"Wait a minute. What happened to the daily foreman's log then?"

"I think I heard it was never recovered."

Alice's attention returned to her yellowing paperwork. "Here it is. Dating all the way back to the early 1900s there's been a coal miners' Workmen's Compensation Act. Not much but it helped." She continued reading, then glanced up with a beaming smile. "It was set up at the federal level to not only help widows and orphans of workers killed on the job, but it also protects the employer from excessive awards and damage suits." Alice dropped the pile of papers and kneeled down to Delena's seated eye level. "Delena, the money for the widows is federal, it doesn't come from Bradford's pockets. Did Bradford pay you the money owed after the accident?"

"He took the money away from me after I got the widows to sign a petition to sue. You mean he had to give me money? And he took what is legally mine?"

Alice stood and laughed. "You bet that bastard did. Until this giant disaster, these things were worked out with individual families, quietly I imagine. I can't tell you what your settlement is, but I bet it isn't a dime more than the amount Bradford claims he is giving. Probably not costing him a thing."

Delena's expression reflected the thoughts that flitted through her mind. "Miner families have always taken care of their own. When someone died, about two or three a year, it would get reported at the union meetings. Each miner, and I mean every one of them, donated whatever they could, knowing it might be them one day. The donations got pretty high before the War, near a thousand dollars once, if it happened near payday."

Alice nodded, content that they'd found something useful at last. "We'll get the money owed you. Let's contact this Wellington to get the money for you. No need to deal with those asshole attorneys. While we're at it let's see if Mr. Wellington is man enough to admit what every idiot in a twenty-mile radius knows about the lack of safety of the mine," Alice barked, a gleam now in her eyes.

Chapter 12

Delena felt a renewed sense of purpose that night when she crawled into the cabin bed with Clara. The sound of Rock Creek's water tumbling over the nearby boulders settled her into sleep.

They awoke the next morning to a chorus of birds and inviting breakfast aromas from the neighboring cabin. Delena's compact mirror had to serve all grooming purposes. Putting the finishing touches on their appearance, Delena was delighted to note that Clara rose that Friday morning as momentarily happy as when she was part of a whole family, at a time when everything was dependable. Back then, the child's most monumental problem had seldom been more troubling than homework assignments or getting permission to sleep at a friend's house. Delena longed to give her that kind of security again.

Delena and Clara joined Alice in her cabin for breakfast, but the serenity of the meal was interrupted by the sound of a car pulling into the dirt drive. Alice got up and went to the dining room window to find a car in the parking spot adjacent to her's and Delena's vehicles.

Emerging from the driver's side was Red Lodge Sheriff Willy Hays, with a look of consternation that just possibly meant something more than the fact that he was passing gas.

With a quick look at Delena, Alice braced herself for trouble and headed for the door.

"Are Delena and Clara Harrison here, Ma'am?" the sheriff called from where he stood when Alice opened the front door. He made a point of glancing at the Harrison family Ford parked next to him. "I'm here on official business and I need to talk to her about a serious matter."

Without inviting him in, Alice acquiesced to the order and motioned to the Harrisons to join her on the porch to hear whatever the sheriff had to say.

"We've been looking for you since three o'clock this morning, Ma'am. The Red Lodge Volunteer Fire Department wasn't able to get to your home in time. I'm afraid sometime during the night something happened to start the blaze. Your house has burned to the ground. I assume with everything you own in it. Sorry to bring you this kind of news. Guess you should've been home watching things." The tone of his voice offered more rebuke than condolence.

"Guess you and that highly alert police officer at Bear Creek should have been doing your job," Alice seethed, shocked at his news. "This family just had their home ransacked and all their money stolen. Just might have given you the idea that she was in some kind of danger."

"Look, Beck, I told you to stay out of police business. If you give me any more lip, you're going with me for verbally assaulting a police officer."

Alice bit back a retort and turned to Delena who stood motionless, trying to absorb the latest horror. Clara held her mother's hand so tightly her little knuckles were white.

"Come on, Clara," Delena's voice shook. "Let's gather our things and go home."

"I'm afraid you don't understand, Mrs. Harrison," he said with a stern expression. "I said your home is gone. Burned to the ground. You're in no condition to drive. I'll take you to the site if you want to see it. We planned on going back to see if we could find what caused the blaze. Did you leave anything on the stove that could have started the fire?" the sheriff asked.

"I'll drive her, Sheriff," Alice said. "If you'd leave us alone now."

Without waiting until the sheriff got back into his car, Alice turned to Delena. The poor woman looked as though she'd been jolted with a high voltage electrical current. She started shaking uncontrollably, pulling free of her daughter's hand. "Oh my God! Oh my God! This isn't happening. There's a mistake. It's not my house," she choked out. Her body danced to the adrenaline racing through her veins and her breath grew so short she started gasping for air.

Alice forcefully grabbed her, hoping somehow her presence would lend a calm. "Come on inside," she guided Delena back through the door. "I'm going to give you a sedative. You're with friends. We'll find an answer in all of this. Try and lay still for a minute," Alice said, motioning Clara to help keep her in place while she went to her medical bag on the floor of the armoire. She produced a sedative from the bag, moving at a speed that was second nature for a front-line nurse.

"I don't think you should be doing that," the sheriff said, following them inside. "She needs to get to a hospital."

"Just leave us alone now! We'll see your sorry ass at her home or in your office later," Alice snapped without looking up.

The officer thundered away, cussing the crazy river woman who would soon get hers.

Alice had no time or patience for his problems. She went to the kitchen and pumped some water into a glass so Delena could wash down the pill.

Once she had Delena settled, she turned to the frightened child. "Clara, we're going to need you to be strong. Stay right here with your mother. I'm going to your house to see if there's anything left that hasn't been damaged. I'll go through everything, Delena. Try not to worry. You're going to live here for now until we get everything worked out. Okay?" The child stood motionless.

"I know it is a considerable distance from home. But summer is almost here and I'll drive you for your last week of school," Alice continued, clearing breakfast away as she talked.

"But I don't have any clothes. I'm going to get in trouble at school because I have their books at home, and they're burned up. I don't have anything." She stopped and returned to her mother's bedside.

There was no more Alice could say. The loss the Harrisons had faced was mounting up to the point at which even Alice's "can-do" attitude was beginning to wane. No wonder the child couldn't respond to her hollow assurances that she had things under control.

Chapter 13

The charred remains of Delena's house reminded Alice of the devastated city blocks she'd seen in France after World War I. A gathering of neighbors from Washoe and Bear Creek created a swarm of cars and a crowd of people filled the dirt road leading up to the house.

Alice parked as near as she was able, then got out and pushed her way through the crowd to examine the ruined home. Only charcoal debris from the roof and its collapsed supporting joist structure remained. Alice forged ahead, joining a handful of volunteers that were making a methodical search of the remains. Within minutes Alice was covered with soot as they pried up beams to sift through burned housing material with their hands in a futile effort to find even the smallest surviving household or personal item. There was nothing left to find. Delena Harrison lost every possession she owned.

As Alice backed away from the rubble hours after she'd arrived, she overheard the snide remarks of a woman, as wide as she was tall, garbed in a worn pale blue chenille robe with hair curlers rounding out her fashion statement.

"Probably burned the place down herself so she could get out of town with the money she stole from us."

Alice turned on the woman, firmly planting herself less than six inches from her face. "Did I hear you right?" Alice's voice began to rise. "Of course, none of this would have to do with the Bear Creek Mine lawsuit, would it?"

One of the woman's front metal curlers tumbled out, releasing a long string of hair over her right eye. Alice's small, but imposing body forced the woman back to where she finally lost her balance and fell on her rear, causing a puff of dust to rise from the sooty ground.

A police officer swooped over to the commotion and circling crowd. With one fluid motion he had Alice slammed, face against the car, legs apart, and handcuffed. "You're coming to the station with me for disturbing the peace."

"I had Sheriff Hays' approval to look for any of Mrs. Harrison's belongings, damnit!" she snapped over her shoulder.

"Hey lady, I don't buy your story but I'll check it out. You wait here." The officer stomped off toward a neighboring house. Alice waited impatiently until he returned, at which time he shoved her into the back seat and headed for the police station.

Alice promised herself no outbursts this time. Regardless of what the sheriff rationalized, she prepared to appreciate his reasoning and offer a calm explanation. She was never an effective listener when idiots tried to make a point, but Delena and Clara needed her right now. She would be a model prisoner.

~

As the police car roared to a stop outside the stone police station, Alice took deep breaths, trying to maintain control of her well-worn natural instincts.

Sheriff Hays looked up from his desk as the deputy escorted her in the back door.

"I told you to stay out of Delena Harrison's business. Now you've really done it, Beck." He looked at his deputy and pointed to one of two temporary holding cells. "She goes in the right one for the night." Alice glared at him, but held her tongue.

Once she was behind bars, Hays rose and came around his desk, sighing deeply. He placed both hands on his slightly bulging waist holster and walked over to Alice, staring at her with a malicious smile curling the corners of his mouth.

"Snooping around in everybody's business is going to end. You assaulted a woman at the scene of the fire and forcibly pushed her to the ground. Sounds pretty serious." Hays narrowed his eyes with a predatory expression. "I won't have any of that bullshit in my jurisdiction. Think about that all night."

Alice threw her hands up in disgusted resignation. "Is the woman pressing charges? Have you even talked to this supposed victim?" she muttered. "I'm sure you haven't even moved your fat ass to investigate the facts. Considering there were at least twenty witnesses, you would have found out the woman fell down on her own with no help from me." So much for good intentions.

Whether he heard her or not, Hays walked away without a backward glance. When he released her the following morning, Alice found her pickup parked in front of the station with no impounding fee notice.

~

More determined than ever to see justice done, Alice headed for Lawrence Bradford's High Bug house to get Delena's money. High Bug was local jargon for the rich and ritzy neighborhood. She checked her purse for the copy of the Workmen's Compensation Act she'd obtained and filed on her father's behalf. Unfortunately, black lung disease, contributing to nearly a quarter of the premature deaths by miners, wasn't covered under the Act. While she assumed it had changed to some extent in thirty-eight years, it still had basic provisions for severe injury and death. She pulled the aged copy out and read the applicable sections.

Burial expenses weren't to exceed seventy-five percent of wages received at the time of death. As she read the provisions, her bitterness grew. Her mother received nothing for hospital expenses or funeral costs: a personal injustice that contributed to her conviction to make Bradford pay for all those cheated by greedy mine owners and an oblivious government.

Alice hadn't been to High Bug since high school. After Robert Ren vanished from her life it was too painful to see his parents' grand home and all the wealth she so bitterly envied in her youth. She turned off Red Lodge's Main Street at the south end of town. There it sat, Robert Ren's home. Weeds spread like a terminal disease with occasional outcroppings of yellow dandelion petals replacing the immaculately sculpted bushes, colorful flowerbeds, and lawn of the past.

Alice stopped in front of the house, impulsively considering a visit with Robert's father. When she'd returned to Red Lodge, she'd inquired about the old man. A shut-in, she was told, a recluse since retirement from the bank. All of his groceries and personal items were delivered. Alice shook her head. No, that visit would come later.

One street up, on Broadway, stood Lawrence Bradford's home. The architecture of the ten thousand square foot mansion, complete with spacious guest quarters above the garage, was as ostentatious as a tuxedo in Red Lodge. Towering columns and far-spanning curved bay windows, all in a crisp white, made the edifice look more like a miniature White House than the residence of an executive. The professionally groomed lawn and the flagpole set in the center of an island accenting the circular driveway added to the pretension. Alice pulled her mud-splattered truck up to the entrance, climbed out and marched over to the towering double front doors.

While Red Lodge society would never approve of the pretense of a butler or maid, Lawrence Bradford got around this potential social faux pas by having a needy distant relative stay permanently in the guest quarters. Only his lack of uniform separated him from the role of house servant.

A somewhat distinguished looking gray-haired man slowly opened one door in response to her knock. "Yes?"

"I have urgent news for Mr. Bradford regarding the mining disaster," Alice said, "May I come in?"

While the greeter considered her peculiar request, Alice noticed with a sideward glance that one of the bay window curtains moved, revealing the shadow of a woman. The old man shook his head and closed the door. After waiting for nearly ten minutes, he returned, waving Alice to enter.

He left her standing in a spacious foyer. While she waited, Alice realized her appearance wasn't making much of a positive impression. Her black cinder-covered clothes, hands and face made her feel more like a chimney sweep than an authority on the Workmen's Compensation Act. Mrs. Bradford's appearance at the top of the curved staircase interrupted Alice's feeble attempt to clean up in the powder room beneath the dual spiral staircases.

"Please come in," Mrs. Bradford said with all the grace and polish of a first lady. "My husband is detained momentarily, but he is most anxious to hear any news you have relating to that tragic accident." The woman's curvaceous figure, inappropriately revealing cream satin dress, and clear spike high heels told a different story. "You know since those men died we've kept a candle lit in their memory. Would you like to see it?" Mrs. Bradford asked.

"If you don't mind, I'd like to meet with your husband as soon as possible. I think he'll consider the news of great importance."

At that moment Lawrence Bradford entered the foyer, emerging from the main floor study. "This way, Miss Beck," he said, holding onto the curved brass handle of one of the room's double doors.

Alice was surprised by the unpretentious way the man was dressed and carried himself. In spite of his luxurious surroundings, he had the demeanor of one of his miners. Alice followed him into the oak-lined study and seated herself in a high-back dark maroon leather chair opposite the mine owner who took a seat by the fireplace.

Bradford scanned his guest with a prosecutor's disdain. "Where the hell have you been?"

"What I'm covered with is what's left of everything Delena Harrison owned. Were you aware her house mysteriously burned to the ground last night?"

"Of course," he certainly didn't look surprised. "This is a small town. It wouldn't be hard to find out how many fish you caught recently from Rock Creek by your cabin," Bradford said without blinking while staring into Alice's blue eyes. "As a matter of fact, Miss Beck, I'm all too aware of how you're tangled up in all this." Bradford stood up and walked over to the fireplace then turned like an animal on its prey. "When somebody is trying to sue me for a million bucks, doesn't it make sense that I'd be trackin' them?"

"Your attorneys have acted like they're doing the widows a favor by 'giving' them money that you know damn well comes directly from survivor provisions in the Workmen's Compensation Act passed in 1915. The union people and the state mining inspector haven't said a word about anything, including the widow entitlements."

"Do you have any idea what it's cost me and our nation's war effort since the mine closed down? That mine produced over a million tons of coal, lady. Coal. Every poor son-of-a-bitch in that mine was saving lives."

"I appreciate your patriotism," Alice interjected with not a little sarcasm. "Delena Harrison will appreciate the money you're required by law to pay her. Were you aware your patriotic attorney told her she'd get nothing because of the lawsuit?" Alice rose and stood chest-high to Bradford, not backing down. "That's illegal, and unless you write a check out to her right now, I'm going to the *Carbon Courier* and see if they think this makes a good story."

With a smirk on his face, Bradford went to his desk and pulled out a checkbook. "Of course Mrs. Harrison is entitled to one thousand dollars like all the other widows. I wasn't aware of any such oversight. It will be corrected immediately. By the way, good luck with the paper. They'd never print your bullshit no matter how you slant it. Dying's part of what mining is all about." Bradford withdrew a cigar, bit off its tip and lit it. "The government has us working around the clock, seven days a week. Bitch to Uncle Sam."

"So glad you brought that up. My father worked in the Red Lodge Mine and died of black lung disease before he was fifty-five years old. While I was trying to get financial aid for my mother, I looked into the history of mining disasters in Montana. Six men died in a 1906 accident and two more lost their lives trying to save them. The state and local coal mine inspector happened to be in Red Lodge at the time and jumped into the rescue attempts. Just three months before the fire, the inspector found deficiencies in the ventilation, just like this time. Nothing came of it. I assume it was because, for some reason, the inspector changed his story later and the earlier records just disappeared. No war effort going on that time, just a mining company more interested in profit than human lives."

Bradford lowered himself slowly into the chair behind his desk and sat, puffing his cigar. "It's impressive that an army nurse has such a memory for the history of mining in Montana. I'll remember this conversation and try to be more prepared for our next meeting, if we ever have one. Now, if you don't mind, I'm going to write a check." He sent her an icy glare. "You're going to get the hell out of my house and go home to your shack in the woods. I hear they have no showers or indoor plumbing up where you live." Bradford's eyes twinkled at the imagery. "It must be hard living like an animal, but I guess you probably got used to that in all those wars."

Alice snatched the check and left for the cabin.

Chapter 14

Alice knew the sedative she'd given Delena had long since worn off, leaving only Clara to contend with the consequences. With the summer ahead, there were months before Clara would need to return to school, which gave them time to find a place to live. The second cabin wouldn't be suitable when the snow fell. Alice had only remodeled it to accommodate summer visits from friends around the world.

These thoughts crowded Alice's mind. The twenty-five thousand dollars she had left of her retirement fund should at least, in part, be used to help Delena and Clara get by through a court trial. She decided not to share all of her ideas with the widow, knowing Delena's pride would prevent her from accepting what was needed.

As Alice turned onto the private unpaved road to her cabins and parked the truck, she saw the Harrisons sitting on the granite boulder surrounded by grass in her yard and hesitatingly approached the two.

Clara was looking down and suddenly found a four-leaf clover. "Look, Mom. I think it means something. I like it here at Miss Beck's cabin. I like Autumn, too."

Alice ambled up to the child. "Clara's right, I do have some good news."

"Where were you last night?" Delena asked.

"Cooling my heels in Sheriff Hays' jail for some trumped up charge of disturbing the peace. I'll explain later." Alice joined them on the rock. "While nothing survived the fire, I have here a check made out to Delena Harrison for one thousand dollars. You were federally entitled to it, so I went and got it from Lawrence Bradford, nasty bastard that he is. Sorry, Clara."

The money was obviously an enormous relief to Delena. She leaped from the rock, and before Alice could get away, pulled her into a hug that caused her to break out in a wheezy chuckle.

"Hold on here. You're going to get your only dress black with soot," Alice said. Slipping away from Delena's grip, she stood and stretched. Jail cots were less than comfortable. "How about no more discussion of any worries until the weekend is over? It's near dinnertime and I could use some help making biscuits to go with the cold cuts and cheese I bought. Told you I'm not much of a cook. Never had to learn in the service."

~

The next morning Alice was gone before the Harrisons had left their cabin. Anticipating Delena's resistance to her plan, she left a note about needing to tend to bank business. It was Alice's first stop, with the singular purpose of withdrawal. She'd spent her life putting away a small sum each month since her early twenties. The security it represented ranked low compared to the need for fifty-seven hundred dollars to repay the widows and another three hundred dollars to buy replacement clothes and basic necessities for Delena and Clara.

All eyes were on Alice when she entered the bank. One of the three tellers scurried to a closed door to alert the president of her arrival.

Before Alice finished writing out a withdrawal slip, a tall, long English-faced man, immaculately dressed in a midnight blue pinstripe suit and starched white shirt, joined her at the customer service counter.

"Miss Beck, we rarely see you at the bank. Is there a problem?" he asked in a low, hollow voice.

"Just here to withdraw a bit of money. Got some more improvements to make on those cabins. Cost me a bloody fortune, but I'm getting there. Why do you ask? Doubt everybody who walks in here is greeted with questions from a busy president." She eyed him curiously and watched his discomfort increase.

The bank president's eye twitched while his outstretched fingers toyed with a fountain pen. "I assumed you'd finished the place last fall after you stopped coming in. None of my business. Just curious since the town folk see you so seldom. Nasty business with Mrs. Harrison, isn't it? It was so tragic to have her house burn down at a time like this." He pinched his eyebrows together in an unsuccessful attempt to halt the twitching. "Wonder why she kept all that money in her house when it could have been safe right here? The days of hiding your money under the mattress are gone in today's world. She could have been earning interest instead of the predicament she's in now."

Alice smiled. "Maybe she thought you were tied just a little too closely to Lawrence Bradford. Of course I can't imagine where she'd get that idea. Your concern would be for her as a customer, wouldn't it? I can't see an important man like you watching the comings and goings of some miner's wife."

The banker slowly nodded his head in agreement and returned to his office. Alice knew his next call would be to Bradford, telling him the exact amount of her withdrawal. "I've decided to withdraw my entire balance," Alice announced to the teller loud enough to be heard behind the president's slightly open door.

~

Soon, Alice was on the road again. The trip to Billings would allow a greater selection for the Harrison's needs as well as a little privacy from prying eyes. Never having given more than a magazine glance at women's fashions, Alice relied on a well-dressed saleswoman at Hart-Albin to help in her undergarment, dress, and accessory selections for Delena. A longtime bachelor would have fared as well when it came to women's makeup, night creams and other feminine basics. Assuming the purchases were for her, the cosmetic saleswoman bubbled with enthusiasm. Alice couldn't interrupt as she kept pushing away well-intentioned hands from her face.

"I hope you don't mind my telling you, honey, but that classic-looking face of yours shouldn't be so taken for granted. It doesn't appear you use any makeup. I could highlight those magnificent blue eyes, high cheekbones, and full luscious lips."

"Save it. I'm here to buy makeup for a real beauty. She's got dark-brown hair with naturally black eyebrows and eyelashes. I think she has green eyes. Her skin is nearly flawless. She doesn't need foundation, at least it doesn't look like it, but she does wear powder," Alice said, clueless to the nuances of makeup.

Selecting clothing for Clara at Cole's was much easier. Youth fashions were basic: pedal pushers, cotton pants, and dresses. Alice found a liberating excitement in purchasing the gifts as she anticipated that Clara would have a wardrobe far superior to the one lost in the fire. One dress led to another. She dashed from one rack to the next, moving from the initial concept of necessities to the unabated joy of giving.

Six shopping hours later she loaded the back of the pickup truck with everything from a Zenith radio, washboard and kitchen replacements to piles of clothing. She still felt guilty that the mother and child would need furniture once they moved to Red Lodge in late August.

As she drove home, Alice hummed along with the radio's big band sounds of Tommy Dorsey, tapping the steering wheel and laughing out loud in the unbridled happiness of what kind of response awaited her.

Clara was whiling away a warm cloudless Saturday with her nose to the grass seeking the magical four-leaf clover when the truck pulled in. Her mother sat vulnerably on the porch of the large cabin with her arms tightly hugging her knees. She had resigned herself to an uncertain future. Her loss of possessions was of far less consequence than the rejection of her wide circle of friends. Everything from the grief of death, the dramatics of divorce, the early stages of romance and marriage as well as plans for a better tomorrow had all been welcome at Delena's home. The indictment on her character and the social isolation was the worst punishment.

"Got just a few things to help out here," Alice said, trying to contain her enthusiasm over the surprise she was about to reveal beneath the old canvas tarp. "'Course I know when things get better, and they will soon, I'll be looking for you to knit me some warm sweaters for myself and presents for overseas friends. There'll be some chores like chopping wood and helping out around here in the meantime."

She was successful in underplaying her generosity. Both of the females didn't more than glance in Alice's direction while she untied the tarp ropes.

"Clara, would you help me?" Alice called with a smile.

Clara slowly arose, brushed off a little clinging debris from her bare knees and went to the back of the truck. As the tarp was pulled away, she yelled to her mother to come over and see the bulging bags and boxes. Delena rose and lethargically marched to the truck.

"Delena, sorry if I got you the wrong size and style of clothes. I can see you've always made sharp looking dresses," Alice said, loading the woman's arms hairline high with dress, hat, and shoe boxes.

Delena was too shocked to speak.

"Now, how about taking these things inside and let's see just how many need to go back."

"Alice, I can't, I can't." Delena's shoulders started shaking before the tears fell.

"I saved all the receipts knowing I probably made a lot of bad choices," Alice laughed.

The women carried the purchases into the cabin. It was like magic on Christmas morning.

"I love you, Alice Beck," Delena kept repeating as Alice's flushed face turned away in embarrassment.

The mother and child tried on everything Alice bought. "Look at the craftsmanship on this dress, Alice. These are the finest clothes I've ever owned."

"Now Delena Harrison, don't you dare come over here and hug me," Alice said, wielding a large carving knife she had snatched from the kitchen drain board. She didn't need to concern herself. Delena was lost in the fantasy of the opened boxes that surrounded her. She sat giggling in the center of the room. Clara ran to Alice despite the knife and locked her arms around her waist, repeatedly saying "I love you."

"Delena, when you two get this all cleared away I want to talk to you about an idea that just might help us out in this lawsuit. I'll tell you this, Lawrence Bradford is running scared. If we plan this right, I think we've got a chance to win."

Delena's eyes were moist with joy. "How are we going to go on with anything now? I don't want to sue anybody anymore. I just want everything to go back the way it was. Clara doesn't need to be picked on at school either. I've been thinking, if we apologize to Mr. Bradford and drop all of this, the rumors will stop and we can try to rebuild our lives."

Noticing how attentive Clara was to the conversation and Delena's delicate emotional state, Alice said no more, giving the impression she agreed. The gifts had accomplished more, at least momentarily, than intended.

Chapter 15

Alice arose at daybreak to catch her beloved cutthroat trout for breakfast. Without including her friend in the next step of her plan, she slipped away.

The desolate summer weed and tumbleweed-covered gullies had so little to offer. Even wild animals were scarce. She trudged through a blinding dust storm to the front door of a Washoe widow's humble, patched roof home. Judith Sarvonen was not only the spark plug for the many Finnish women who lost their husbands in the disaster, but also had been the most vocal, accusing Delena of stealing their money and was the very same woman that Alice had allegedly accosted. Convincing her to shift her energy to fighting Bradford instead of Delena would make the other door-to-door visits more successful.

Alice checked her carry bag, making sure she had her dated copy of the coal miners' Workmen's Compensation Act along with

Brent Harrison's journal Delena had left with her for safekeeping. Certain she was armed, Alice raised a hand and knocked sharply.

The Finnish widow peeked through the tattered curtains, then opened the door just enough to see through the crack. "Whatcha want? Don't want no trouble. I'll holler for help if I need to."

"Not looking for trouble. Here to give you your money back," Alice said in haste to prevent the door from closing.

"I knew she stole our money. Don't she have the courage to give it back herself?"

"If you'll let me in for just a minute, I'll give you your hundred dollars and be on my way," Alice added, pushing past the woman into the living room area of the one room house. She quickly pulled out a one hundred dollar bill and flashed it in front of her opponent's eyes to tease her into a conversation. Judith grabbed for the money, but Alice jerked her arm back with a mischievous smile.

"First, we're going to get a couple of items straight. This money is a loan from me to Delena Harrison. She doesn't know I'm wiping out her debts. Doubt she'd even approve. I'm doing it because I know she's innocent. The woman has nothing after she lost her home, especially fifty-seven hundred dollars. Oh, and by the way, she has no intention of leaving the area. This fall she'll be moving to Red Lodge. This is her home and until all this happened I believed people like you were her friends."

Judith Sarvonen didn't bother to completely close her well-worn robe. She planted both heavy arms between her legs and plopped onto the worn floral couch like a hippo in a shallow wading pond.

"Now you're gonna tell me about the evil Lawrence Bradford and how he caused my husband's death, I suppose."

"I'm going to show you something that will change your mind."

She gave a dark, smoldering look. "You don't mean her husband's little black book, do ya? I already seen that with a bunch of scribbling and numbers that Delena told me herself she don't understand."

Alice turned her back to the woman and shook her head. "Okay. If you feel that way, I won't bother you by telling you how a wrongful death suit could win you over thirty thousand dollars." She paused and turned in time to see the woman's jaw drop. "No, won't bother with that." Alice reached into her purse and pulled out the folded stack of papers. "Just wanted to show you a little federal legislation that'll prove Bradford didn't give you anything. That one thousand dollars you got was rightfully and legally required to go to you and all the other survivors based on the coal miners' Workmen's Compensation Act and Montana state law. Wonder why there hasn't been a word from the union since the accident? Bradford was only doing what was legally required and it should have been handled by the union." Alice leaned down to the woman with a wry grin. "He arranged things so widows like you would think he actually cared about something other than profit, which he doesn't."

The woman took a careful look at the document and said nothing. Alice handed her the money and went to the front door. She turned before leaving for one parting attempt to sway the woman to her point of view.

"Delena Harrison's been one of the best damn friends the miners' wives and families have had. All she got in return is everybody swallowing Bradford's lies hook line and sinker. What you haven't figured out, Mrs. Sarvonen, is that her enemies are yours, too."

The home visits that followed over a three-day period went from explosive displaced aggression over an impoverished future to gleeful celebration of the money and Delena's vindication. Years of being a nurturing neighbor were paying dividends. Through countless stories of the active role Delena had played in helping families through challenging emotional times, Alice gained an appreciation for the woman far beyond her early feelings of protecting the innocent.

~

While Alice was talking with one of the widows, an Italian woman with four small children, they were interrupted by a knock at the door. Judith Sarvonen, hardly discernible out of curlers and in a dress, shifted her heavy torso from one side to the other, ready to spring into action.

"Hope I ain't interruptin' nothin'. I seen Miss Beck was here and I got something I want the two of you to see."

One more element of confusion was nothing new to the mother. She rose and put her arm around Mrs. Sarvonen's large rounded shoulders, guiding her to a seat on the couch adjacent to Alice.

A purse that could have carried a picnic for a family of eight was hoisted off the woman's fat, jiggling arm. She rummaged through it while mumbling to herself, "Here it is. Maria, sign right here. We need to let Delena know we're with her on goin' after them bastards." She grabbed the pen and handed it to her neighbor. "Hell, we all knew it wasn't safe months ago." Mrs. Sarvonen turned to Alice, pausing long enough to take a needed breath. "I didn't press no charges on ya even though ya scared the bejebees out of me."

"Yes, they only kept me overnight," Alice said. "Mrs. Toreno is the second-to-last widow I need to see."

"How soon are we gonna git this show on the road so we can git what's coming to us?" Mrs. Sarvonen asked.

"The next step is to get the state mining inspector and the union involved. We're hoping Mr. Harrison's evidence in his daily journal will correlate with the official mine log that's supposed to be checked on a thirty-day basis by the state mining inspector. Even if those records were lost in the explosion like they say they were, the inspector's testimony along with the diary should give us a case. I know it would be unaffordable for any of you to contribute any more money to the cause. I don't see why the union shouldn't shoulder the expense to pursue this. Seems to me, that's what they're there for."

Mrs. Sarvonen's chin vanished into layers of neck blubber when she nodded. "Yeah, that sounds good. How soon do ya think we'll get the million dollars?"

"First things first. There is something you can do to help the effort right now," Alice said, leaning up close to the smell of Vick's Mentholatum the woman must have rubbed all over her chest like body lotion. Alice patted her surprising crusader on the back. "I'm glad to see you used carbons so we'd have extra copies. Get the original back to me. Gather three or four of Delena's closest friends. I have some names if you need them. Have each of them write down on a sheet of paper the nice things Delena Harrison has done for them and why she deserves community respect and support. If the judge and jury hear all the outrageous stories going around about Brent and Delena Harrison without it being convincingly denied you'll never see a cent. She's got to look lily white if you're going to get any money."

Mrs. Sarvonen paused to consider the wisdom of the request. Knowing no one had been more accusing than she had, she quietly acquiesced and excused herself, leaving with a quick peck on her neighbor's cheek.

~

Alice's mysterious disappearance all week had Delena wondering what she was up to. Querying her on the subject of the lawsuit and her determination not to take it one step further should have caused heated discussions, but there was no rebuttal. The fact that nothing was said for or against her position made her wonder. Alice, leaving to take Clara to school some mornings without even returning to fly fish or visit, was even more peculiar.

Delena was surprised one morning when Alice had a visitor. No one besides the sheriff had set foot on the property since Delena and Clara came to stay. Cautiously, Delena opened the door and looked up into a surprised face. The man, who stood about six-foot tall, trim, around fifty, dressed in a dark olive suit and brightly-colored tie, had the presence of a well-accomplished businessman. He cleared his throat and said, "Alice Beck here?"

"No, sir, she's not," Delena answered, not sure what to say. Oddly, he looked a little relieved.

"Just tell Miss Beck that the caller had a particular liking of windmills," he said and hurried to his car.

With a shrug, Delena closed the door and returned to her worries, particularly focusing on how withdrawn Clara had become. In fact, she didn't even think to mention the caller to Alice when she arrived home at dinnertime.

Alice noticed Delena's contemplative mood and was pretty caught up in her own thoughts. Between bites of venison stew, Alice kept looking over at Clara until she caught her eye. The child loved their outings and Alice could always think better outside. "Clara, let's go for a nature walk at dusk. This evening's lesson will be a rock hunt for all the types of stones that comprise the Beartooth Mountain range." Clara immediately perked up at the suggestion. "We could make it into a collection you could use for a school project." Clara's eyes began to sparkle.

As usual, they chatted about inconsequential things, then Clara did a little exploring while Alice sorted her thoughts. Once they returned and Alice settled Clara into bed with more tales about the Crow Indians, Alice prepared some coffee and urged Delena to join her near the fire for what promised to be a highly enlightening discussion.

Allowing a relaxing moment to pass before she shared the news, her plan was interrupted.

"Oh, Alice, I forgot to tell you," Delena said suddenly. "A man stopped by when you were gone today. I can't imagine what he wanted. He wouldn't even leave his name."

Alice dropped the steaming cup of coffee she was lifting to her lips and the hot liquid splashed onto her lap. She yelped and leapt up from her chair, brushing the spill from her faded olive army fatigues. "Just what exactly did the man look like?"

"Are you okay?" Delena jumped up and retrieved a towel from the kitchen, handing it to Alice.

"I'm fine," Alice assured her, mopping at her lap. "What did he look like?" she asked again.

Delena sat back down, still wearing a surprised expression. "He was tall and his hair was going just a little gray. He wore a dark business suit. I've never seen him before. I'm sure he isn't from around here. Oh, and he had a long thin scar on his forehead."

Alice's heart was all aflutter. "What did he say? Is he coming back here tonight?"

"He said something really strange. Something about a windmill of all things."

Robert Ren, Alice thought. Just like he'd promised, he was back. There was nothing more personal to Alice Beck. It would have been easier to talk about the horrors of the war. Knowing there was no way to hide their love story and his abandonment that seemed centuries ago, she decided to open a door of her heart to the one woman she knew would understand.

Alice took a deep, jagged breath. "I was just getting ready to give you some news that might have made you spill your cup when you beat me to it," she chuckled nervously, wishing the pounding in her chest would subside. "Yes, I know the man. When I was in my early twenties I fell in love so deeply it almost killed me. I can't even think about it now." Tears formed in Alice's eyes and she stopped for a moment.

Delena didn't need to hear anymore. She reached for Alice's hand, pulling her up from the chair into her arms. "We don't need to talk about this. I think I understand. When he comes tomorrow, do you want to see him or should I turn him away?"

"I don't know what to think. If I'm gone when you get up, I'll be fishing."

"From the little time I've known you, I've learned to trust what your heart tells you. You'll make the right decision, Colonel. That's what you do, isn't it?" Delena succeeded in making Alice smile through her tears.

"I have some news for you that might be just as shocking in its own way," Alice said, changing the subject. "I know you told me to stop anything having to do with suing Bradford, but I just couldn't let it end like that."

Delena stiffened. "Alice, I told you that for Clara's sake more than my own there would be no more said or done on the issue. It's already cost me my reputation and just about everything else. I plan to pay you back for every cent of it you know."

"I can't let it end like this. And you don't owe me a thing." Alice lowered her voice. "I did do something that you can pay me back for if you want, but only if you can someday."

Delena got up and turned her back to Alice. "Please, no more."

"Did you know that there isn't a widow who hasn't apologized for what she said or believed about you? I'll also tell you that not one of them still believe you stole their money."

Delena whirled around, returning to the chair. "How did all this happen in less than a week? It's not possible. Besides, how would you know how all the widows feel about me?"

"'Cause I talked to every one of them when I gave them their money back."

Delena froze in amazement.

"That's right, Delena, I went to the bank and withdrew enough to give the one hundred dollars back to every one of them. I knew it had to be done if they were to listen, and listen they did. Didn't take much nudging on my part to get them thinking straight. You can't believe how much those dummies think of you when they take five minutes to consider what kind of a friend you've always been."

Delena stared into the burning ponderosa pine logs. The enormity of what Alice had accomplished in three days was just starting to settle in.

"There's no way I can make enough money for Clara and me to find a place to live in the fall. I won't be able to pay you back anytime in the near future," Delena said.

"No more talk of money," Alice insisted. "The widows have all signed a new document supporting our wrongful death lawsuit idea. There's even a good possibility that some of the women are going to see the *Carbon Courier* publisher with letters in hand denying all the rumors about you and your husband. I'll bet he'll print a story about those signatures. The contents of the letters will get around town faster than a stallion in heat."

Delena gave a tearful laugh and kept nodding while Alice unfolded her plan.

"Okay," Alice shifted her chair to face Delena, anxious to get on with the details, "the next steps are the most important. We need to get collaboration from the state mining inspector that his record keeping and Brent's matched. His name is Howard Wellington and he lives in Billings. Let's go to his home unannounced and wait for him if we have to. I think we need to look him right in the eye to get to the bottom of this. Keep in mind he's said nothing since the accident."

"I bet Bradford got to him," Delena said.

"Maybe. If he doesn't play ball, we could fry his ass in court."

Alice went to bed that night wrestling with the sheets and blankets as vigorously as her mind wrestled with the memories and hopes of things to come. Should Robert Ren be confined to memories? She wondered until her stomach ached.

Chapter 16

By religious interpretation, Howard Wellington considered himself a good man. It had long been an acceptable reality that the work of a hard rock and coal miner was hazardous. Previous state mining inspectors had been instrumental in shaping laws regulating the health and safety of miners.

Howard proudly placed himself among his predecessors, assuming they, too, exercised situational ethics when it came to negotiating with mine owners like Lawrence Bradford. The fact that a number of mine owners provided automobiles and miscellaneous items for his home and family was simply proof that he was an effective partner to all mining interests in the state of Montana. That was his reasoning.

At times his responsibilities overwhelmed him, requiring a time-out for meditation and fishing at his lake cabin near West Yellowstone. The Madison River raged through the back two acres. In the spring, high water created a soothing sound his family could hear from open bedroom windows.

Alice and Delena were disappointed when their unannounced visit to Howard Wellington's large two-story home in Billings only yielded a note taped to the front door for his gardener, leaving the telephone number of his West Yellowstone residence.

The two proceeded to a Billings truck stop cafe to phone Mr. Wellington. None of the widows had heard from him since the mining accident weeks earlier. Even if he didn't answer the phone the first time, they decided not to stop their quest until they met the man in person and tested his mettle.

"This is Howard Wellington," an evenly measured voice answered.

"Yes, my name is Alice Beck. I just came from your home here in Billings and got the number off the note to your gardener on your front door. I hope you don't mind me calling."

"I'm on a little vacation with my wife and kids. You caught me at a good time. My son and I just returned from fishing. What can I help you with, Miss Beck? Couldn't have anything to do with the Bear Creek Mining disaster, could it?"

"There are just a few questions that the widows need a smidgen more information on. No great issue as it relates to you, Mr. Wellington. The widows haven't seen much of you since the disaster, and Delena Harrison and I would appreciate a moment of your time. It would be no problem for us to come to West Yellowstone and see you at your cabin if you like," Alice said.

"Oh no. No need for that. We're leaving tomorrow morning to come back to Billings. Sounds like it's pretty urgent. I hate to have you make a six-to-seven-hour drive to get here just to answer some minor questions. Tell you what, I'll meet you at Natali's Restaurant tomorrow at three o'clock for coffee. How does that sound to you, Miss Beck?"

"Much appreciated, Mr. Wellington. We'll be there."

~

The two women arrived a half-hour early to be sure they got a table at the popular Red Lodge dining spot. Unfortunately, there were no private corners. Anything that was said of any consequence over a whisper moved out the front door faster than a Kansas tornado.

"Good afternoon, ladies. Am I late?" Howard Wellington asked as he joined them. Alice's eyes icily scrutinized the mining inspector's dark blue suit and large leather briefcase with an imprinted H.M. near the brass latch. She shrugged and gestured for him to sit opposite them.

"How about ordering our coffee first? I'm extremely tired after the long drive," Wellington said.

Delena leveled her gaze at him. "That sounds like a good idea to me. This doesn't have to be so formal, does it, Mr. Wellington? My husband never had anything but good things to say about you. In a way, you were partners with him as he recorded what was inspected every day in the log for your review."

Wellington's brows knit together. "I have no words to express my feelings over what happened." Wellington sighed deeply and signaled for a nearby waitress. "Yes, I knew your husband and many other foremen who took a chance every time they set foot in a mine." He steepled his fingers together like a choirboy. "Ladies, there have always been tragic deaths associated with mining."

"Whatcha havin'," the waitress interrupted his monologue.

"It's on me, ladies. Want to look at the menu first?" She glanced at the waitress circling around Wellington with pad and pencil in hand.

"Coffee, and give us a minute okay?" he told her.

The hefty woman nodded and moved on to the next table.

Wellington pulled a notepad from his briefcase, the first page meticulously outlined with the heading of 'Montana Mining Deaths'.

"The first recorded mine disaster in Montana where there were deaths occurred June 7, 1906 with eight fatalities," Wellington said.

Wellington paused when the waitress brought over a pot of coffee and poured some into each cup.

Alice's face reddened. "We didn't meet with you to talk about how dangerous mining is, for God's sake. My father died from black lung and everyday he went to work, he knew it was dangerous."

Alice's outburst provoked an awkward silence and the three sipped with no further discussion.

At last Howard Wellington broke the silence. "Just what is this meeting about, then? I have an appointment in town in thirty minutes so if either of you would get to the point, I'd appreciate it." It sounded as though his patience was wearing thin.

"I think we could discuss this in a more private place," Delena said, glancing around the cafe. "These deaths are still open wounds."

"All right. That bench outside the restaurant should work," Wellington said, rising from his seat.

Alice glanced over at the two men whose table abutted the restaurant's front window. "Better than here."

Once seated outside, Alice narrowed her gaze on Wellington. "At the coroner's inquest held April 12th through the 14th, less than two months after the disaster, you failed to introduce the official logs that verified a flagrancy in Bradford working men around the clock in unsafe conditions. Where's that log? Why didn't you speak up? The integrity of the ceilings and timber, levels of deadly gas, inadequate air ventilation. Mr. Wellington, cut the bullshit. What is your job, if it isn't to protect those men?"

"Before you started this unfounded tirade, Miss Beck, I was pointing out that regardless of what efforts I make to protect miners, there's an inherent danger that no regulations can totally control."

Delena motioned that she wanted to talk. "My husband knew the dangers and the safety laws. He provided you all the information needed to stop mining coal until it was safe. You know that, Mr. Wellington. You had to have recorded it. Not only did I lose my husband, but—in case you haven't heard—rumor says I'm a whore who cheated on my alcoholic husband and stole the widows' money. The people you represent not only stole the money, but they burned my house to the ground, and I wouldn't put it past them to try to kill Alice or me for wanting the truth to be told!" Delena's voice was loud enough for the two men on the other side of the restaurant window to hear with ease.

"To my knowledge, there is no proof tying Lawrence Bradford to any of these reckless allegations. As to these rumors about you and your husband, I find them as crude and unfair as you do. I did know Brent Harrison. The man gave no evidence of being under the influence of alcohol at any time during our monthly meetings."

"You'd say that in court?" Alice said.

"Of course, but I only saw him once a month. I also resent you suggesting that I've played any role in hiding evidence that the mine should have been closed. Those records were destroyed along with those poor men."

Alice's features hardened. "And what about your own records? They missing, too?"

Wellington's nostrils flared. "This ends our innocent conversation to get a few things straight. I will tell you, Miss Beck, that your reputation precedes you as an irrational hothead who's managed to insult the sheriff, bank president and now the state mining inspector, all in a matter of a few days." That said, he turned to Delena, "I am sincerely sorry, Mrs. Harrison, for what you and the other widows are going through. There needs to be more effective safety practices for all coal mining in the U.S., and I for one am going to do my part to keep fighting for higher standards." Wellington looked at his watch, then straight into Delena's eyes. "You should keep better company."

"There are seventy-four dead men whose voices can't be heard right now!" said Alice.

Delena's head dropped to her friend's shoulder and Alice stroked her hair like a child with a cut knee.

"You've made it clear how your bread is buttered, Mr. Wellington," Alice said as the inspector got up to walk away. "See you on the witness stand."

Chapter 17

A spasm of irritation crossed Lawrence Bradford's stony face. "Somebody close those bay window blinds. Stop fidgeting and tell me what that bitch is up to."

The inspector let the intensity of the moment pass. His eyes raked Bradford's library and his hand shook as he took a deep sip of scotch before responding. Attorney Jed Patterson stood with one arm propped up against the fireplace mantel. He and his Billings-based partner were hovering over every word like focused vultures.

Patterson sounded earnest. "Mr. Bradford appreciates you working so closely with us to minimize any trouble the Beck woman and her widow friend could cause us and the community. We're all trying to get this tragedy behind us, Mr. Wellington. Given a sympathetic jury that doesn't begin to understand the dangers of mining, the outcome could close the Bear Creek Mine permanently, putting over one hundred and fifty families who desperately need these jobs on the street. I don't need to tell you how hard it is to find work right now." Patterson's warning didn't escape its intense listener.

Wellington cleared his throat, twice. "I anticipated the outcome of the meeting as soon as Miss Beck called me at my West Yellowstone home."

Bradford's tone became matter-of-fact. "By the way, Wellington, I meant to talk to you about that property the mining company leased to you. It seems you'll need to pay a single dollar to keep all the papers in order. Isn't it something like that, Jed?"

The attorney nodded.

"I researched all mining fatalities in Montana since the turn of the century," Wellington said. "There's a clear path here that provides irrefutable proof that it's impossible to prevent tragedies like this one, even under the most responsible management." Wellington paused. "I do have a bit of a concern, however."

All bustling in the room fell to dead silence and heads unanimously turned for the next statement.

Wellington continued, "For the past six months I spoke with you regularly, Lawrence, about legitimate safety concerns requiring the mine be temporarily closed to make needed air ventilation passages. The combustion potential was a lot higher than I ever recorded in my monthly reports."

The room remained as quiet as a monk's bedroom.

Bradford went to his desk and drew out Wellington's property papers for West Yellowstone he'd referred to earlier, and handed them to the inspector.

"If you could give me the dollar now and sign here, I think that's all we need from you. Howard, I really don't recall any such conversations. I do remember you assuring me that everything looked safe and sound, especially in light of the twenty-four hour shifts needed by our country at a time when the future of the whole fucking country is at risk."

The inspector said nothing, withdrew a dollar from his wallet and handed it to Bradford.

"I fully appreciate your point, Mr. Bradford. You've always had a great concern for your employees and our country. The contributions you've made to the war effort with personal money and time are well-known and respected from Red Lodge to Washington, D.C."

Wellington's eyes darted to the closed door. He crouched forward and lowered his voice. "It's important that the role of the state mining inspector isn't undermined by those who don't understand the big picture. What we don't want is the leadership of the United Mine Workers of America involved here."

Bradford clenched his fists. "What the hell are you talking about?"

"My safety concern discussions with your shift foremen, including Brent Harrison, were heard by a lot of the men, not all of whom died in the blast. I told you about them, remember? And how we should shut—"

Bradford was on his feet. "I want every one of my miners to rest assured that you and the Bear Creek Mine owners have always addressed safety concerns with the operation. You never said a damn word about shutting down. You wouldn't want to make a false statement like that again, or people might think you didn't end up doing your job. In fact, if you felt so strongly about that, you could have forced action to close the mine." Bradford moved from around his desk to putting an arm around Wellington. "What I'm saying, Howard, is the death of seventy-four men could be placed at your doorstep."

Chapter 18

Robert Ren breathed deeply of the crisp, mountain air, hoping to fortify himself against whatever was still to come. When he'd first arrived, his thoughts were of Alice but he'd felt so distinctly separate, foreign. A few days to acclimatize in the achingly familiar surroundings might be best. He'd walked the back streets of his childhood and revisited the soul-soothing beauty of Rock Creek and the Beartooth Mountain Range. Gradually, his restless spirit was calmed and refreshed as he felt the tug of the years. Again and again, his mind wandered back to the time he'd spent with Alice years ago. Would she be glad to see him after all these years?

Oddly enough, by now it felt as though he'd never left Red Lodge, but it hadn't erased the years. Whatever happened to the wisdom that came with age? He'd stopped and parked by the creek to work up his courage to approach Alice, but it occurred to him that passing years didn't so much provide answers to unanswered questions, but rather helped pinpoint those questions that most needed answering. Fat lot of help that was, he chuckled to himself, putting the car in gear and heading out on the road.

After weeks of indecision, he was determined to at least see Alice. Talk to her. See if just maybe she'd consider starting over with him. She'd never married, that much he knew. That could be good or bad. But the time for speculation was over. He'd already done that. Pointing the car down the last road, within minutes he was firmly entrenched on a rickety bench on Alice's front porch, knees together, face taut, with a bouquet of wild flowers in his hand. The afternoon sun baked the deck with an intensity that made each minute seem like an hour.

"What you doin' here, Mister?" a childlike voice startled him out of his reverie and he squinted into the sun, searching for the source. There, behind a clump of weeds, seated on a nearby rock, was a waif of a girl eyeing him intently.

Robert got nervously to his feet. "I'm hoping to see Miss Alice Beck. Might you know when she'll be back?"

The girl shook her head without comment, then proceeded to watch him from her station on the rock. If anything, her surveillance made time creep even more slowly. Who was the child? Was it possible she belonged to Alice? He couldn't have missed something like that, could he?

Suddenly reality seized him, with stomach cramps and sweaty palms and brow. Maybe too many years had passed. He felt like he was going to throw up. Unable to contain his anxiety any longer, he got up and started a short hike along the cabin side of Rock Creek.

~

As difficult as it had been, Alice had done all she could to avoid thinking about Robert that morning. A sleepless night had done little to untangle her feelings. He'd been to the cabin and he was bound to be back, but it was just easier not to think about it than to try to sort through all the conflicting emotions that sprang up at the mere mention of his name. As if on cue with the thought, Alice steered the truck around the last bend in the road and spied the tall stranger holding flowers in his hands, standing in the center of the grassy area in front of the large cabin.

In those few short seconds, her mind was bombarded with all of those thoughts and questions she'd worked so diligently to avoid. Was she angry with him for abandoning her? Angry with herself for letting him go? Or maybe angry that he'd waited so long to write. It wasn't entirely rational. She knew that. Unfortunately, she had little control over it. Clenching her teeth, she accelerated the pickup, creating a dust cloud as it screeched to a halt. She waited for Delena to approach the man with an outstretched hand of greeting before stepping out of the cab.

The hazy fog of memories followed Alice as she exited the truck and approached him slowly, inspecting a middle-aged male who had some resemblance to the phantom still haunting her dreams. Delena had greeted him kindly, then stepped aside, waiting for Alice's reaction with a look of obvious anticipation on her face.

Alice, on the other hand, felt nothing aside from a vague sense of dread and unease. Rational thought escaped her. The only thing that seemed even remotely familiar was the way her heart leapt at the sight of his handsome form, a response that was followed almost immediately by serious, self-protective measures. This man that stood before her had the power to break her heart all over again. Alice didn't think she'd survive that.

"Delena, will you tell this man that I will see him at his father's house only after he restores it to the condition it was in when he vanished a lifetime ago?"

Alice had no idea where such an inane comment came from. It was almost as if she'd gone on autopilot. She knew his father deserved every misery he got but it was so far removed from anything she'd anticipated discussing at their first meeting. It was too late to retract it.

Robert's face reflected his surprise, followed instantly by a flash of irritation, but he didn't miss a beat, picking up the strange woman's name from Alice. "Delena, would you tell Miss Beck that I made a mistake coming here and will not attempt to contact her again. Tell her I didn't travel over two thousand miles to be insulted with a comment like that."

"Delena, would you tell...?" Before Alice could continue, Delena looked at them like they were crazy and signaled Clara to join her in the cabin, leaving them standing in the yard.

Without the shield they stood and gazed at one another as if staring at an alien entity. When Alice made no further move to speak, Robert shook his head and walked over to his car.

Alice stared at the dust cloud in the road long after his car was gone. Her words reverberated through her mind, and she grabbed hold of the porch's log rail with the last of her strength. What was wrong with her?

When Alice entered the cabin alone, Delena didn't broach the subject of the stranger, letting it take whatever course Alice's heart would steer.

That evening Delena prepared dinner, usually Alice's domain. Immediately following the silent meal, Alice disappeared into the curtain of green to one of her cherished trails winding away from and back to the river. In her mind, she repeatedly envisioned Robert's appearance and demeanor as adrenaline rushed through her in anticipation. Anger melted into meditation and later a giddy happiness that added even more vibrant hues to the impending sunset. She would see Robert again, even if only at a distance as she awaited the completion of his first of many trials before he could enter her heart and bed.

Chapter 19

Howard Wellington had no trouble finding the Beck cabins. He cursed to himself that the primitive woman didn't have a telephone, which would be far more covert for the discussion he had in mind. After careful consideration of his personal vulnerability in a court of law, he surmised that he needed to create a silent alliance or at least sympathy with the women's concerns.

Without knocking on the front door of the main cabin, Wellington left his carefully worded, unsigned note, fully aware of Alice Beck peering out the window. His nervous, quick actions and departure made it clear he wasn't there for another confrontation.

Shooing Clara away, Delena and Alice threw open the door once the sound of the car had faded away and rushed to the clean white envelope with both of their names typed in the center.

"Getting interesting," Alice said, then ripped the envelope open and began reading out loud.

"'Meet me at the Bear Creek Campground three miles up the highway in one hour' is all it says," Alice said. "Didn't even sign his name. He's Bradford's boy, all right."

~

Alice's truck roared to a stop ten minutes early. She'd already spotted Wellington's car parked a few yards from the wooden park bench and rock-piled fire pit carved out of a thick grove of Ponderosa pines. He paced nervously in a circle, not far from his car. Alice and Delena got out of the truck and walked toward him, watching as Wellington's face grew hot and pinched. He gritted his teeth, turned, and then pasted on a plastic smile as he saw the women approaching and got up from the picnic bench with an outstretched hand to greet them.

"Sorry for the short notice, but in light of how strongly each of you feel I assumed my spontaneity would be appreciated," Wellington said.

"You know our position. What's changed with yours?" Alice replied, in no mood for small talk.

"I want to apologize for the flippant way I acted over coffee. I thought you needed a better opportunity to tell me exactly what role you feel the state mining director should play in your case."

Alice stifled a snort at his smooth pronouncement. Wellington was a tricky one; they'd have to watch him.

"I think I'm best suited to answer that," Delena said, motioning everybody to sit down at the picnic table. "First, tell us why all the records were destroyed in the explosion when this safety issue had been a subject with you and my husband for months. It would be naïve to assume that you don't file any reports over a long period of time outside of the mine. Did you destroy your entire paper trail?"

Wellington rubbed his clean-shaven chin and focused all his attention on Delena. "That's a fair question. The reports I file with the state lack the specifics often discussed and recorded in the mine logs. That kind of detail is inappropriate in the summary reports. You know my responsibilities go far beyond the Bear Creek Mine. They include oversight of every mining operation in the state."

"I don't understand your role clearly, Inspector. Exactly what does go into your summaries?" Alice asked.

"First, I have to acknowledge the necessity of coal as the lifeblood for heat and energy at a time when Uncle Sam is depending on us more than ever before. Secondly, Montana's coal mines are in continual need of improvement. It's the nature of underground digging that the job is never done, especially as it relates to the integrity of the roof and wall supports. After a shaft reaches a depth of one hundred feet, it has to have two or more exits. The second exit is there to provide an escape in case of fire or gas. In the Bear Creek Mine, they've been mining over a million tons annually. The mine goes miles underground." He turned to Alice. "Ladies, that's a lot of shafts, and the potential for an accident goes up accordingly, especially when I inspect once a month and production is going on day and night."

"Let's get to it," Alice said. "When this gets to trial, will you repeat the safety concerns you discussed with Brent Harrison? It would be corroborating evidence of what he recorded in his daily work diary."

"Without knowing exactly what he wrote, I can't answer that. Would you loan me the diary? I'll get it right back to you."

"A little early in our wonderful new relationship to trust you that much, Inspector," said Alice. "What we could do is read you some key statements that you can confirm or deny right now."

He didn't look convinced, but there was no room for argument. Alice nodded at Delena.

Delena proceeded to read the daily logs with no real indictments until she got to the middle of the book recorded three months before the disaster. Wellington sat expressionless while the declarations of dangerous gas levels and inadequate safety measures for storing explosives with dwindling air ventilation were repeatedly inserted after readings of carbon monoxide levels.

After an uncomfortable pause, Wellington cleared his throat. "Ladies, there's a checklist of thirty-six health and safety concerns the foremen and I review regularly. At any given time, there can be problems in different areas. I don't disagree that those problems were correctly noted, but at what level they constitute real danger is the question here. I don't mean to be condescending, but you can't jump to conclusions based on issues the foremen and I wrestle with every day. I feel for you and your loss but you don't really have a case here," Wellington said flatly.

"We'll trust that those gas readings will tell a different story," Alice said. "It has to reach a point when precaution isn't optional, Inspector. Bear Creek Mine had already reached that point and you know it."

"In no way did I act deceptively at the coroner's inquest. I told them just what I'm telling both of you. Please understand that I take my responsibility seriously. Today's laws and regs for health and safety exist because of people like me."

"People like you?" Alice said.

"The law establishing the eight-hour work day and the one prohibiting children under the age of sixteen from underground work, my predecessors all had a role in those critical changes." Wellington absently raked his fingers through thinning hair. "Ladies, you're not here with the enemy today, but someone who shares your concern for laws protecting miners."

Delena's eyes narrowed. "One of your jobs was to insure there were escape routes and enough air. If you didn't point these concerns out to Bradford, you weren't doing—"

"But, I did!"

Alice's eyes widened into saucers. "You what? You're admitting that you did tell Bradford of these dangers and he did nothing?"

Realization of his mistake was evident on Wellington's stricken face. "I didn't say that."

"When you're called to the stand, Mr. Wellington," Alice said, "I trust you won't perjure yourself. You can be sent to prison if you're caught lying."

"You're putting words into my mouth, Miss Beck, and I sure as hell don't appreciate it. I never said I instructed Lawrence Bradford to do anything. You're twisting my words. I've tried to explain."

Alice stood up and clapped her hands together. "Thank you, Inspector. You were right, this conversation has been extremely comforting. We look forward to your testimony."

Howard Wellington left the women with polite good-byes though he felt anything but polite. He'd deny he ever met with them and wait for the trial for the potentially incriminating admission to be revealed. The typed invitation to the meeting would cause no lead to him. He'd prepared it on the typewriter in his fishing partner's vacated office. Of course, Lawrence Bradford would never be told of any such meeting.

~

"Howard, this is Lawrence Bradford," Wellington cringed at the sound of Bradford's voice. "How long has it been since you've been to the mine?"

"Oh, I guess about three weeks, shortly after you resumed limited operations. Why?"

"There are some safety issues I want to go over. Every possible precaution must be taken to insure absolute safety after what happened. I'm still having a hard time sleeping after the explosion, all those lives and families without a father or son. We did all we could, but mining is a nasty business. Just want to be overly protective in the future, that's all."

The telephone line was silent except for the breathing of the other listener on his party line. Wellington weighed his response in puzzlement. Bradford knew the party line drill. What was he trying to accomplish? His best bet was to play along.

"I wish every mine owner was as proactive as you are concerning your men's safety, Mr. Bradford. Of course I'll meet you at the mine at whatever time or day you recommend."

"How about when the afternoon shift gets over at about ten thirty, so we have access to the mine for our own inspection?"

"No problem. Since the disaster, it would be prudent to keep detailed reports of every step we take to insure the men's safety. If you have the time, I'd like to read the foremen's daily logs with you and then conduct our own safety check," Wellington said.

Approaching his car by the light of the moon as it neared the appointed time, Wellington tried hard to swallow the lump in his throat and shake off the skin-crawling fear that had grabbed him with Bradford's phone call. He imagined scenarios explaining why such a delicately worded conversation took place, and even more importantly why Bradford himself would commit to spend the over three hours past midnight that it would take to go through the mine. Maybe Bradford was trying to build a history of the concerned owner in case there was a trial after all. Maybe one of his lawyers had become overly cautious in suggesting the approach that should be made to all telephone conversations. These wise moves contrasted dramatically with the stupid stunt of trying to reason with those irrational and dangerous women, Wellington thought.

Still, the closer he got to the mine, the harder it was to keep his foot on the accelerator. He steered his Buick up to the crest of the steep, winding road separating Red Lodge from the Bear Creek plateau and mine. His eyes darted maniacally, picking out phantoms just beyond the perimeter of the headlights.

An old, drab green, unlicensed Chevrolet sedan lunged out from the shadows, ferociously ramming Wellington's passenger side front door. The thunderous crash split the calm summer night. Before Wellington could right the steering wheel, his car soared off the road, flew through an ocean of darkness for over one hundred fifty feet and exploded into a fireball on the road below.

Chapter 20

"Oh!" Delena gasped sharply as her eyes fell on the *Carbon Courier* headline.

"What is it?" Alice looked up at the deep intake of breath. She and Delena had just finished clearing away the breakfast dishes when Delena collected the morning edition from the front porch.

Wordlessly, Delena crossed the room to her side and sank down into a chair beside the table, positioning the newspaper so they both could read at once.

The car was discovered just before midnight by a convoy of three cars overflowing with miners from the afternoon shift. While the flames were gone, the first approaching car's headlights illuminated streams of white smoke rising like ascending angels from the mound of twisted metal and rubber.

The body, found with the head and shoulders protruding through the shattered windshield, was mutilated beyond recognition.

License plate identification confirmed the car belonged to Montana State Coal Mining Inspector Howard Wellington. The dirt road between the mine and Red Lodge was notoriously dangerous in winter months, claiming eight lives over a ten-year period. While only two intoxicated teenagers had gone over the side on a summer night three years before, the cause of Wellington's death—if indeed the driver was Wellington—was considered an accident by all concerned, except Alice Beck and Delena Harrison.

"You don't suppose someone else was driving his car, do you?" Delena looked up at Alice, wide-eyed.

Alice shook her head, "I don't suppose any such thing."

Previous coverage of the mining disaster had clearly proven to Alice that the Red Lodge bi-weekly newspaper publisher was an assumed member of the elite fraternity of men who reported to Lawrence Bradford. She was nevertheless convinced the former *Associated Press* bureau chief's journalistic integrity would outweigh community power dynamics.

Already, Alice's mind was reeling, preparing for battle. She grabbed a notepad and sat back down at the kitchen table to outline the subjects to be addressed with the publisher. Delena leaned over her shoulder to inspect the topics.

She finally pulled her chair close to Alice and sat down with a glare of determination. "It's one thing to rightfully fight for the other widows and myself. After my reputation got trashed, it was pretty obvious Bradford would do anything to protect his secrets. Wellington wasn't an accident."

Alice waited, suspecting there was more where that came from.

"Murder doesn't scare you, but Alice," she reached for the woman's hand. "Please stop and think about Clara."

Alice nodded, deep in thought. The same thing had occurred to her.

"It isn't crazy to consider they would arrange another 'accident'."

Alice slowly pulled her hand away. "We're either going to proceed with the suit or not. If you ever had any reservation about the guilt in your husband's death, this murder should give you even stronger resolve. By going to the publisher and telling him what we know, I think we make ourselves more safe, not less. I really don't believe Bradford's attorneys would be party to murder. This was conceived by him alone, I bet, and followed through by some out-of-towner. We get real visible and our deaths would be too obviously connected to Wellington."

"I hadn't thought of it like that," Delena said slowly. "Talking to the publisher is a bit of an insurance plan if we say Bradford must be behind it. I'm glad you aren't against me," Delena sighed. "You're right. Let's do it."

~

With some reservation Tom Lloyd, publisher of the *Carbon Courier*, had agreed to meet the women in his office for no more than thirty minutes. He was on deadline.

While the bi-weekly was widely distributed in the area, as far away as Cody to the south and Billings to the north, the tiny ink and galley-proof-covered floor resembled a startup publishing business more than the location that produced the local news everyone relied upon as gospel. The prematurely gray-haired, aristocratic-looking newsman glanced up from his front page proofing at the sound of the two women entering his world. Without invitation Alice cleared still-wet, discarded galley proofs off the chairs occupied by reporters before press time.

"I don't have much time, so I hope you don't mind holding on for a moment as I finish and run the page back to my pressman. This is the worst time of the week, but the urgency of your call made it sound like the news you have couldn't wait."

"We appreciate you fitting us in, Mr. Lloyd," Delena politely interjected before Alice could respond. "We're in no hurry. We'll wait outside for a few minutes to let you concentrate."

Upon their return, the newsman seemed appreciative of the courtesy extended by Mrs. Harrison, not to mention her beauty. He paused, took off his glasses and pinched the bridge of his nose.

"Now ladies, what big news do you bring me?"

Alice spoke. "For the sake of your time, best get down to it. Before Howard Wellington's death we contacted him to confirm that he had told Mrs. Harrison's husband and others about the dangers in the mine that needed fixing.

"At first he had reservations about saying or admitting anything. You could tell he was scared of how he might get caught up in the lawsuit that Mrs. Harrison and the other widows still planned to proceed with."

The publisher raised an open palm. "Would you mind if Mrs. Harrison spoke? This matter really concerns her most."

Delena nodded and began. "As Alice was saying, we couldn't get any cooperation out of Mr. Wellington until a day later, when he must have thought over what I have in my husband's daily diary that he recorded as shift foreman. He left us this note." Delena passed the folded paper square to the publisher.

He read the typed message, then looked up at Delena with a frown creasing his brow. "This isn't even signed."

"He left it at Alice's front door. We both saw him. It's pretty hard to drive to that cabin without everybody hearing and seeing who it is. We met with him shortly afterward at his designated location. He tried to be cautious. While he was explaining his job as mining inspector, he accidentally let it slip that he told Lawrence Bradford to close the mines because they were too dangerous to keep running until things were fixed."

Still wearing a skeptical expression, Lloyd looked from Delena to Alice and back again. "Are you suggesting Howard Wellington's death wasn't accidental?"

"We told Mr. Wellington that we would make him repeat it on the witness stand. Of course, we have no proof, but it's strange he died right after we met, late at night on his way to the Bear Creek Mine. It just seems suspicious and we thought you ought to know. We're a little concerned for our own safety." Delena paused and took a deep breath, "If we have some 'accident' before or after the trial, please tell me you'll look into it."

The publisher's eyes widened in alarm. "I know this million dollar lawsuit has made things pretty nasty on both sides. It's wise not to accuse someone of murder when you have no evidence. There's no solid lead other than speculation for me to follow on this. I'm afraid unless there's some way you or the police can provide new incriminating evidence associating Mr. Bradford with the death, you really have no news at all. You should be meeting with the sheriff, not me. I do understand there's a small communication problem with you, Miss Beck, and the local law enforcement."

Alice laughed. "Not really, Mr. Lloyd. Sheriff Hays is an asshole, but of course you already knew that."

~

After the women left, the publisher tried to return to his press proofs with his usual focused intensity. His thoughts kept returning to the strikingly beautiful Delena Harrison and the remote possibility that the hypothesis of Lawrence Bradford orchestrating murder wasn't absurd.

The benefactor to many local charities and national defense causes had never shown anything but the face of a patriot and humanitarian. On one recent occasion the publisher made an unannounced visit to get further details for a front-page story regarding Bradford's presidential recognition for contributing to the war chest. Bradford had failed to conceal the cruel way he treated his wife. While at the door, Lloyd overheard Bradford abusing his wife. When settled in the house, Mrs. Bradford appeared fifteen minutes later, with face foundation thick as house paint. It unsuccessfully disguised a sizable bruise around her right eye.

The story did run on page two, with a picture of Bradford standing by the flagpole. He was quoted as stating he personally raised the flag each morning before offering a silent prayer for God to protect American soldiers engaged in the greatest battle of good and evil in the history of the civilized world.

Without the women knowing it, their visit had confirmed uneasy feelings the publisher had always had toward Lawrence Bradford. With Red Lodge so dependent on its largest employer, the former investigative reporter had been more focused on relations than finding hidden truths. Only Bradford's future actions would determine which direction the town newspaper was now going to go.

~

"Mind if we head up to High Bug to see something?" Alice asked Delena after they got in the truck. The question was really a nicety, since she'd already started to drive the pickup to the south end of the town's exclusive neighborhood.

Delena nodded.

"There's a house up there that needs some serious attention. Just wanted to see if there's been any progress. There are advantages to being a former military officer. You know," she said, trying to lighten her real reason for driving in that direction, "my 'C' ration sticker allows me twelve gallons of gasoline a week, compared to the four gallons with your 'A' sticker. It's important to start consolidating trips."

"Alice, you don't need to defend anything with me," Delena smiled. "It would be interesting to see if that mysterious caller has been helping out that poor old man."

"He's no 'poor old man'," Alice assured her. "Don't want to stop, anyway. Even if he's in the front yard. Just check it out," Alice said before turning the mud-covered vehicle off Main Street to the neighborhood. Her chest tightened and she got a little dizzy in anticipation of seeing Robert again.

To her relief, he wasn't in the yard that had been transformed into the early stages of its previously groomed beauty. A mountain of weeds, and shrub and tree trimmings made the house easy to find. There was still much to be done in grass reseeding and flower plantings, but considering how recently she had given her stipulations for their first meeting, she smiled at the possibility that it could soon be renewed.

"Look at that house. It looks pathetic. When I think of how this was once one of the most elegant and well cared for homes in High Bug, it really makes me sad," Alice said.

"You don't look too sad to me," Delena said. She giggled and playfully poked a finger into Alice's ribs, provoking laughter that nearly put the two in tears.

"I've got a great idea," Delena said. "Why don't you leave a note at the front door letting your friend know you're impressed with his progress and look forward to seeing him?"

The suggestion abruptly ended Alice's spontaneous joy. Her lips curled with disgust.

"That man, Delena, abandoned… Oh, never mind. If he thinks he can do a little yard work and house painting to make up for a lifetime of inconsiderate behavior, well, that's bullshit."

"My mistake." Delena put her hand on Alice's knee. "I said I would stay out of this and I know you don't like to talk about yourself, Alice, but for once, trust someone and admit it when it hurts."

Alice pulled the truck to the side of the road; her shriveled heart only made a dull gnawing on her soul. Delena was right, she knew, but it was much easier said than done. The occupants of the truck were quiet all the way back to Alice's cabin.

Chapter 21

Alice and Delena had agreed to avoid conversations about the lawsuit when Clara was close by since they seemed to bother the child. She'd already suffered so much. Watching her, though, Alice wondered if they'd made the best choice. Delena and Alice's frequent absences were taking a toll on the isolated girl. She slowly withdrew, saying less and seldom smiling. While not acknowledging it, Alice suspected she was acutely aware of her mother's renewed commitment to battle with the mine owners. If she was feeling betrayed by her mother after the redundant pain of her father's death and the surprisingly vicious rejection and persecution by her former friends, she was being crushed like a dandelion in a young boy's hand.

Alice was ever more aware of her depression in recent days. Even their rock hunting and search for bird feathers failed to stir any enthusiasm. While she was still a little young and awkward at fly-fishing, their ritual of creating their own nymphs and dry fly hooks on Saturday afternoons was the only thing that squeezed out even a forced smile. This time, like so much of their time lately, was spent mostly in silence.

"My mother lied to me. I hate her," Clara's comment was so soft-spoken it didn't register with Alice at first.

"Clara, now watch again, you float the fly above and into there. See, I've got a bite. It's a big—"

"I hate her!" Clara hurled her pole into the low water stream, then got to her feet and stomped toward the cabin.

With a sigh, Alice hooked the trout, reeled it in, picked up Clara's pole and got to the front door in time to have it slammed in her face. Alice set the gear down and slowly opened the door. The weeping child was crumpled in a heap with her arms around Autumn.

Alice glanced quickly around the room, grateful that Delena must be busy elsewhere. She slowly approached and sat in a high-back chair near the child and dog. "If you feel lost, you picked the right companion. A dog's ancestors are the wolves."

Alice held back a smile when Clara stuck a quivering bottom lip out further. "A wolf has a roaming territory of up to five hundred miles without getting lost."

"What about Autumn?" Clara asked in a shrill falsetto voice.

"One night I decided to follow her with only the moonlight to guide me." Alice glanced over at Autumn, her flopping ears all attention. "She knew I was behind her. I gave up after too many miles to count. I bet she has a one-hundred mile territory before the remote possibility of getting lost."

Clara's defiant expression gave way to interest as she grudgingly looked over at Alice.

"You, Autumn and I are going camping right now. We'll leave in less than an hour. Make it before dark. Okay, get on your feet and help me get things together."

"Where will we sleep?" Clara whispered.

"I think the stars make the best ceiling. Never use a tent unless I have to." Alice nudged Clara and Autumn up from the floor.

Alice found Delena in the kitchen and hastily explained things to her. Soon, she, Clara and Autumn were on their way. Their destination was a challenging five-mile hike from the Custer National Park trailhead. It was late in the afternoon when they emerged from the woods and established camp in an open wildflower-blanketed meadow. A fawn snuggled up to the side of a doe, settling in the shade of cottonwood trees at the perimeter of the open area.

As the coals of a mesmerizing campfire started to lose their glow, Clara moved close to Alice, putting her delicate hand on her shoulder.

"I've watched you listening to your mother and me talk. You know why it's important to go to court, don't you?" Alice asked.

A frown clouded the child's expression. "My mother promised we would make everything like it used to be. She went to the newspaper people today about a man getting killed."

"Do you also know that the money stolen from your burned home has been given back to each of the widows? I went to every one of your friends' homes and got them to support your mom's court fight. There'll be no more bad stories about her now. When we get back I want you to have your mother take you to one of your friend's houses. They'll be your friends again. You'll see."

Alice reached Clara's hand and squeezed it. The two watched the last of the firewood melt into streams of smoke.

Chapter 22

Robert had shared Alice's shock at first sight of his father's home. No urging from Alice Beck was required to inspire him to restore it, regardless of who lived inside. It was as hideous as his childhood memories. Somehow, beautifying it seemed the best way to fix his ugly past, if that was even possible.

Its outside appearance wasn't nearly as shocking as the first sight of his father. A withered six-foot frame, stooped over with gnarled arthritic fingers replaced by sharp claws. Grizzly bear eyes that had turned to a distant dusty road gray, inset from white furry eyebrows and long, ungroomed salt and pepper hair. All made even more bizarre by the immaculately clean plush interior of the home.

No calls, no letters, no father, no son for a quarter of a century. Only a call from his father's doctor notifying Robert of the man's rapidly deteriorating condition.

Robert couldn't ever imagine what his father's first words would be when his disinherited son came unannounced to care for him in his last days. His eyes haunted with playback memories, his stomach tighter than a brawler's fist, Robert had bolted from his car to his childhood home foyer without even knocking.

"Dad, it's me. Robert."

The music of Vaughn Monroe belted out when the upstairs bedroom door opened. The old man came to the top of the stairs, squinted and took five steps down, then stopped.

"Robert who?"

The words sounded as hollow, echoing down the stairs as they had in Robert's heart. Beads of perspiration on Robert's brow formed streaming lines that were stinging his eyes. "Your son."

No questions, no response. The old man turned and went back to the golden voice of Vaughn Monroe.

Taking the train from Pennsylvania, Robert had envisioned and rehearsed either a tear-filled embrace for all the years lost or a fierce argument between lifetime warriors. Nothing. His father said nothing. They ate in silence. No hellos, good-byes, goodnights. Robert concluded his father was already dead. All of his thoughts had then turned to Alice Beck.

~

Restoration on the exterior was extensive, and proceeded at a manic pace. His only interruptions were to go to the Coast-to-Coast Hardware Store on Main Street for supplies. With the war going on, it was easy to find workers. Robert hired four recent High Bug high school graduates on a high hourly rate to re-roof, repair and paint the exterior of the house. He also hired two capable mine disaster widows to wash windows, assist with the garden, and tackle the tasks that had been building up since his mother had died over twenty years ago.

The cost of a new home was, on average, three thousand to thirty-five hundred dollars. When through, Robert figured the Ren home would return to the grandeur of days gone by, and would some day sell for ten times the average. It had once been distinguished as the most impressive home in the area, according to Red Lodge standards, until Lawrence Bradford built his mansion nearly two blocks away.

Robert's father took no interest in the exterior restoration. He shut himself in his upstairs bedroom listening to the radio, his only dependable companion.

Since the mine disaster, Red Lodge had been the focus of national media, making it easy for Robert to stay abreast of developments, including Delena Harrison and the crazy woman at the river. The recent death of the state mining inspector and rumors of the widows' lawsuit whirled through conversations in every part of town.

Bob Wise, the chief librarian at the Carnegie Public Library had been a friend of Robert and his mother since childhood. As time allowed between directing work crews, Robert journeyed less than two miles to the library for the latest on the women's crusade. While scanning back issues of the *Carbon Courier*, Robert noticed a large story recounting Lawrence Bradford's visit to Washington, D.C. President Roosevelt had commended Bradford and other industrialists on the critical contribution they had made to the war effort. The story also highlighted a meeting Bradford had with Tony Pozereli, president of the United Mine Workers Union of America. No details of the purpose or outcome of the meeting were revealed in the story.

Having heard the news, he was curious why local and national union representation was conspicuously absent from the disaster inquiry process.

"Number please," the telephone operator said in a highly mechanical voice.

"Yes, Washington, D.C., please. The number is 344K," Robert Ren said, studying the phone number for the United Mine Workers Union of America from one of the library's directories.

"UMWA, may I help you?" the receptionist asked.

"I want to speak to Tony. He's a friend of mine," Robert said nonchalantly. A moment later, the call was transferred.

"Pozereli here. What was the name again? My secretary told me something, but I didn't get it."

"Well, we don't actually know each other, but I do have a question that should be of great interest to you."

"I'm listening."

"You recently met with Bear Creek, Montana mine owner Lawrence Bradford."

"Yes, I recall. Is this about the mining disaster? I'm not the one to talk to about that."

"Did you know that two days ago the Montana state mining inspector died in an automobile accident? And the home of a union foreman who died in the mine mysteriously burned to the ground? His widow had all of her money stolen right before that, all because she led the charge to sue Lawrence Bradford for running an unsafe operation. Did you know that?"

"Hold on there. You're going too fast. Who is this?"

"I'm a citizen of Red Lodge who seems to be the only one concerned about the fair treatment of fifty-eight widows whose husbands and sons may have died needlessly. My name is Robert Ren. I'm an attorney from Pennsylvania, born and raised in Red Lodge."

"Mr. Ren, I have no comment on this new information. I can't make it out to Montana with all we have going on here right now. There are strikes everywhere."

"I think there's been a murder and maybe more to come," Robert said. A crackling transmission noise filled the silence.

"I'd be willing to keep an open mind if somebody came to Washington to give me the details in person."

"I might be able to arrange that. Sure you couldn't come to Montana?"

"Have the widows hired an attorney and filed a complaint to go to trial?"

"I don't know. I understand they're having a hard time finding appropriate legal representation. In fact, that's exactly where I was hoping the union would come in. Do you do that kind of thing?"

"You're moving a little too fast here. The union does have a legal arm, but it's unprecedented to provide legal counsel."

"I'll be getting right back to you with who'll be at the meeting in your office. I assume this doesn't include representatives from the mine owners at this stage."

There was a moment of silence on the line. "No, I haven't heard from Lawrence Bradford at this point. I do want to observe that this meeting in no way means I agree or disagree with any of the indictments you've made in this conversation. I've read the coroner's inquest and at this stage it appears there's no hard evidence of wrongful doing. Mr. Bradford was just recognized by the President for doing the mining industry proud, based on the role his mine and personal contributions have played in helping out in the war effort. I will, however, hear what the widows have to say. It was a real tragedy."

"We'll be there."

Robert impulsively rushed to his car and headed for Alice's cabin. Alice and Delena's vehicles were parked near the cabin when he arrived. It wasn't until he was marching across the yard that he felt the first tremors of misgiving. What if she didn't appreciate his interference? He hesitantly went to the porch and struggled with whether to knock. The door soon opened in front of him.

"Mom, it's that man who came here before," Clara said as she closed the door in the stranger's face. Alice reopened the door garbed in her usual drab army fatigues.

"Mr. Ren," Alice swallowed hard. "What brings you out here?"

"Would you go for a ride with me? I have something to show you." Robert's voice sounded stilted, even to him, but he couldn't deny a warm glow in the pit of his stomach at the sight of her lovely face.

"Not exactly what we talked about before," she said.

"I know," he held up both hands in mock surrender. "I heard you before. But I think you'll be surprised with what I have to show you."

"Would you mind waiting here a moment while I change?"

Robert smiled and agreed. Alice reappeared minutes later in a blue, red, and white floral summer dress and white low heels. Robert turned from the spot on the porch he'd staked out, staring off into the pines and a smile tugged the corners of his mouth as his eyes fell on her. Uncertainty lined her face as she squinted up at him. He wished he dared reassure her that she was a sight for sore eyes. The dress skimmed her slight figure, accentuating curves he'd dreamed about for years. Nylons weren't available, and bruises on her legs from daily life in the woods were obvious. While the length of the dress helped, she couldn't conceal her unstable gait in unfamiliar high heels. Her first haughty glance into Robert's eyes gave him warning that it wasn't a time to find humor in her predicament.

"Lovely dress, Miss Beck. I'm afraid now I'm underdressed," he said, grinning broadly.

"I don't have long. Need to do some shopping for the crew for the weekend," she said, avoiding his glance and turning toward the car. Robert followed behind her, trying to not laugh out loud at her wobbly ankles and the crooked path she took to his car. He couldn't remember anyone looking so delightfully amusing, with the proud tilt of her head and the set of her jaw. Rushing to the passenger side, he opened the door without ceremony.

Robert took care to keep conversation light and to help them both through the discomfort of being alone. He jumbled into trivial conversation about the beauty of Beartooth Highway and how it had recently been selected as America's most scenic summer drive. He rambled on about the weather and how little Red Lodge had changed since his youth. Although she appeared to be listening intently, Alice's face gave no indication of what she was feeling. She gave no response at all until he mentioned his father's house. "We're heading for your father's? You have it all done already?" The look she gave him was one of genuine surprise, followed by a darkening expression. "I had no right to say what I did."

"I don't know how he let the exterior get away from him that far," he chose to ignore that last remark. "I know money wasn't the issue. You should see how beautiful it is inside."

"No, Robert, I doubt money was the issue. Losing his wife, then son gave him nothing to care about. Frankly, I'm surprised he's still with us."

"Okay, goddamnit, I got your point the first time I saw you. He's dying. Okay?" Robert kept his eyes glued to the windshield as the tension crept up his neck started drumming out a rhythm in his temples. "Even though he hasn't acknowledged my existence since my mother died, I came back to be with him to the end. I'm not the bastard you seem to think I am."

Alice looked down at her feet, launching no protest. She remained silent until they arrived at the Ren home. The yard had been completely replanted, with freshly turned flowerbeds and new shrubbery. A stark white gazebo had reappeared in the back yard from the earlier jungle of overgrowth, adding a festive quality to the grounds. Painters were still busy putting the last coat of pale yellow on the wood siding, having already painted the ornate gingerbread trim in white that matched the picket fence and gazebo. Two large white wicker chairs and a love seat graced the spacious front porch.

"Robert, it looks beautiful," she said softly.

He nodded, arm propped on the steering wheel and eyes still straight ahead. "It's not done for another week, but I have something to talk to you about that couldn't wait." He paused, willing his defensive posture away, then turned to her and reached for her hand.

Alice scooted back against the car door, obviously not ready for any sign of intimacy. "I don't think I want to hear this. We haven't been together for more than twenty minutes. I don't even know you anymore, and you sure as hell don't know me. A lifetime has happened since you met that sweet innocent girl in France. She's gone, Robert."

He burst out laughing, although the sound had a bitter edge. "Really? You've been so shy since I first saw you at your cabin that your observation really surprises me."

"I'm seri..."

He interrupted with a wave of his hand. "There's always time to be serious. I'm not trying to whisper sweet poetry in your ear, Alice. I've been following what's been going on since the mine accident. There's been a hell of a lot happening, and from what I can gather you've been in the middle of it. I just want to help." That much, at least, had a ring of truth because it was true. But deep inside, he had to admit he wanted much, much more.

"Everything is under control. Don't need any help. Thanks." Alice's hands fluttered nervously, brushing a strand of hair back from her face as her eyes flitted around.

"That's not exactly how I see it. When the state mining inspector died you lost your key expert witness, if you are, in fact, continuing with the suit. Has your attorney filed a complaint, or do you even have an attorney yet?" Legal posturing had been his refuge for many years now. He could only hope a sound business-like approach would appeal to her, draw her out so she'd let him help.

"No, we don't," she admitted reluctantly. "We plan on picking one in Billings next week, and yes we are going to file. The inspector's death could be to the widows' advantage." Alice eased her blazing glare. "Look Robert, I do appreciate that you want to help out, but I don't know how."

"I do." Robert gingerly placed a hand on her twitching leg, then removed it. "Now Alice, don't get that temper flaring again. I have an idea that could make a lot of sense. I contacted the president of the UMWA and—"

"You did what? You had no right doing that. Who do you—?"

"Damnit, would you just listen to reason for a minute? We have an opportunity to meet with him in Washington, D.C. to get the investigation reopened, and possibly have the union provide legal representation. They aren't the enemy, and neither am I." He watched her steadily as she avoided meeting his gaze. "I think Delena, you, and I should take a train to D.C. and see this man before you get other legal representation."

Silence. No fireworks.

"Why would you want to get in the middle of this?" Alice asked after a long pause.

"It's obvious that this has become very personal to you. I appreciate the fact that you've taken the lead in this and I wouldn't try to change that. I wouldn't want to. Just let me help. Hell, I'm an attorney. I could be of some use in this mess."

"Those bastards killed Wellington."

"All I know is that the sheriff and everybody else considered it an accident. The focus, it seems, needs to be getting the money for Mrs. Harrison and the other poor widows... Don't ya think?"

Alice huffed. "Can we go back to the cabin? I have a lot to do today. I'll give it some thought."

"Of course. I'm glad you like the house. What day should I tell Pozereli?"

"You're as bull-headed as..."

"As you are?" he laughed.

"I'll get back to you," she groused, but Robert thought he saw the edges of a small smile before she ducked her head.

~

The next day Robert returned to the Beck cabins, but this time his arrival wasn't unwelcome.

"What grand scheme have you got cooked up this time?" Alice said, daring to look into his glistening eyes. He stood still, his expression unreadable.

"Would you ask Mrs. Harrison to come out onto the porch, Miss Beck?"

"If you insist, Mr. Ren," she said, then paused to take in his attire. He was wearing navy blue trousers, stylishly pleated—a luxury during the war—and a V-neck sweater of pale blue lamb's wool. Beneath was an open collar white cotton dress shirt that set off his dark features. Alice watched his still-handsome face. She was taking close notice of every line that middle age had created, and examining the pale scar on his forehead that had just about vanished. But his eyes looked exhausted. She sensed he was either a little ill, or maybe he'd pushed himself to a point of excessive fatigue repairing his father's home. She decided to treat him a little more civilly as she went in search of Delena.

Clara followed the two women out onto the porch. Robert greeted them each in turn, then launched immediately into a discourse of his planned trip to Washington as though it was already a done deal.

"Let's assume Clara can stay with friends or family for just a short period," he said, crouching down to her eye level and then slowly rising. "I've made all the arrangements and taken care of the expenses for the three of us to take the Southern Pacific out of Billings, connecting into Washington, D.C. to meet with the union president, Tony Pozereli. The train leaves in forty-eight hours for the four-day trip across this beautiful country. Sorry for the last minute notice." Robert glanced at Alice and smiled. "It couldn't be helped, based on Pozereli's travel schedule."

Delena clutched and hugged Robert Ren tightly. "I can't believe it. This is fantastic."

"Pretty confident in our decision, Mr. Ren," said Alice, feeling a little off balance both from Robert's initiative and Delena's apparent acceptance.

"It's the right thing to do and you know it, Alice. My only requirement is that I tag along to make sure you two stay out of trouble. Alice might slug some poor stewardess/nurse or porter, you know," he said while still being held in Delena's grip.

Reluctantly, Alice had to chuckle. Her peripheral vision caught Clara with head down leaving and walking toward the river. She followed the child to the edge of Rock Creek. "You know, Clara, I'll bet you that there will be kids fighting to have you stay at their house when we go back East."

"Really?" Clara said, averting her head, tears welling.

Alice turned the girl around and squatted down to her level. "Clara, I will never lie to you. That's a fact. I know. I met with those women, and your mother has a lot of people who care about her. They don't believe those ridiculous stories anymore."

Alice stood up and braced closed fists on her hips.

"Delena, we're going to go to Bear Creek today to make arrangements for Clara to stay with one of her friends, if that's all right with you." Clara's now wide-open eyes couldn't be missed. "Wouldn't hurt you any to see those women again and make your peace." From the determined expression on Delena's face, Alice figured she'd think it over.

Alice made a quick, nervous glance from the cabin porch's river view to the man beside her. "How about a ride up the highway?" The soft answering light in Robert's eyes gave her a shiver.

There was a surrealistic sensation about walking out before him to the car. Sensing his stare behind her, she fought to submerge feelings of familiarity already cropping up. The way he leaned sideways from the hip when he opened her car door, the sound of his footsteps coming around the car, his own peculiar movements as he settled into the vinyl seat of the large passenger sedan, the smell of his shaving lotion in the confined space. All the motions of a man in the car. Already she knew in which order he would do them, wrist over wheel as he started the engine, the unnecessary touch of the rearview mirror, the single shrug and forward jut of his head as he made himself comfortable. He automatically turned on the radio after starting the ignition. The big band sound of Tommy Dorsey filled in gaps of awkward silence.

"Look, I know I jumped the gun," Robert said as he pointed the car towards town. "I was afraid not to lock the appointment with the Union while the guy was still agreeable, and..."

"Robert, I'm not going to yell at you. I thought about what you said and you're right."

While Alice was speaking, he pulled the car to the side of the road. He started moving over to her. Her startled eyes widened. She laid a hand against his chest in an overt gesture to hold him off, but he captured it, along with her other hand, and carried them around his neck.

"I can't believe we're finally together again," he whispered. Then he lowered his lips to hers, caught them opened in surprise. Alice was completely aware that he wasn't playing fair, but she melted beneath his kiss. Their tongues touched wetly, unleashing just a hint of the passion she'd stifled for so long. Then a single fingertip found the skin of her neck and gently he tightened the arm about her waist, running a hand possessively up and down her back.

Gradually pulling herself away from his intoxicating touch, she righted her blouse and grabbed the passenger door handle, stepping out in a daze that almost caused her to trip and fall. "I'm not ready for this, Robert," she gasped. "I may never be."

"Alice, we've been away from each other for over twenty years. You'd think I could be patient, but I can't. I want to make..."

"Don't say that!"

"Don't be afraid of me," the soft timbre of his voice compelled her to turn and examine his face. "The next time we kiss you'll be the one who does it," he assured her, moving back beneath the steering wheel. "And you will do it."

His earnest expression reassured her somewhat, but she wasn't so sure she could trust herself. "Doubt that." She got back into the car.

Chapter 23

While Robert, Delena and Alice were making final preparations for a four-day trip to Washington, Clara's classmate greeted her with enthusiasm. The visit to each widow increased Clara's circle of friends; upon arriving at the modest Bear Creek home, she found three girls anxiously awaiting her. Her fear and shy hesitation after being so harshly treated soon gave way to feelings of acceptance and comfort. Ironically, the crisis had elevated her popularity, as mothers shared their unencumbered confidence of a successful trial settlement, often within earshot of their children. Delena had been elevated from the town tramp to the role of heroic crusader.

~

Robert had a wealth of choices for accommodations and luxuries as he opted to pay a little more and purchase rail tickets on Southern Pacific. There were literally thousands of possible route combinations, including innumerable scenic side trips, most of them possible at no additional cost. Glass-topped dome view cars glowed softly above the roofs of coaches and lounge cars as the trains were routed to wind through breathtaking wheat-field plains and mountain ledges, capturing America's vast and diverse terrain.

At a steep round-trip cost of one hundred forty-five dollars apiece, Robert made connections from Billings through Denver, Denver to Chicago and then on to Washington. Delena and Alice would share a Daylight Express bunk car. He reserved a premier two-berth unit for himself, convertible for day use with its own bathroom and shower in anticipation of opportune moments or nights with Alice.

"I've never been on a passenger train before," Delena admitted during the ten-minute ride to Red Lodge's turn of the century train station. "What kind of people ride the train?" she asked Robert.

"Just about everybody these days," Robert said. "A year ago I took the Southern Pacific from Chicago to Los Angeles. You wouldn't believe the number of families traveling with everything they owned, going to California because the land is so cheap and they heard there's still a lot of plane factory work. 'Course there are a lot of GIs and businessmen, just about anybody you can think of."

"Do you need a lot of clothes? I mean I only have a couple of pretty dresses," Delena said, focusing on Alice in appreciation.

"You'll be fine, Delena," Alice noted. Her stomach fluttered when she pictured her own wardrobe, not exactly Paris's latest fashions. Not even Montana's.

"Since the government has restricted the kind of fabric you can buy, my sewing's lost all its flair," Delena said.

Robert nodded his head attentively.

"Delena's a gifted dressmaker," Alice said, never having seen any of Delena's wardrobe.

"Before the war, the French were the final word on style," Delena said, quoting a dated fashion magazine. "I'd have an advantage over the manufacturers right now if I could make and sell clothes. The restrictions are ridiculous. A skirt can have no more than a two-inch hem, and one patch pocket on each blouse. You can't even buy a top with an attached hood or shawl."

"Sounds pretty serious," Robert said. "So I guess everybody will be at a disadvantage. I think you'll pass inspection." He veered into an open parking place at the train station.

During her many journeys across the country by train, Alice had always been in uniform. The thought of mixing with civilians and also being accompanied by her beautiful, fashion-oriented companion made her palms sweat and stomach hurt.

"Delena, this is a business trip, not a fashion parade," Alice said. "Never did get into all the frilly stuff. Only got a couple of old dresses, but they'll do fine," Alice quickly glanced at Robert, then brushed against him while the porter attempted unsuccessfully to offer her a hand with her luggage.

"Now why doesn't that surprise me?" Robert said, laughing.

The two women settled into their first-class cabin accommodations. Delena pounced around the small space, giddy like her daughter exploring every feature of the berth. Her spontaneous joy was interrupted by a knock on the cabin door.

"I'm to deliver these packages to a Miss Alice Beck," the smiling black porter announced to Delena. He loaded five boxes of all sizes into her arms.

"Alice!" Delena yelled toward the closed bathroom door. "I know what you just got," she chided.

The cabin bathroom door flew open. Alice forgot her usual cold reserve and rushed to the brightly wrapped packages.

"There's a mistake. These aren't mine," she told the porter, who was patiently awaiting a tip.

"If you are Alice Beck, Ma'am, they are for you from the gentleman in the next car."

Alice scrambled to find some change to tip the man.

"If you're not going to open them, I will," Delena said.

"What's all the commotion?" Robert asked, peering over the porter's shoulder. The porter turned with a smile never leaving his face and made his exit. Robert entered the women's cabin, taking Alice by the arm and pulling her to the lower bed. Delena hurriedly loaded the boxes next to both of them.

"Now look, Miss Beck. If I choose to buy you a few appropriate clothes for our important upcoming meetings, that's my choice. Too late to return them now. I just hope they fit. My information was a little dated on your size, but I think I have a pretty good idea of your proportions," he winked.

"That's enough of that kind of talk, Robert Ren," Alice's eyes affectionately betrayed her tone.

Robert stood and went to the berth door. "I'll leave you two women alone until dinner. I've made reservations in the main dining car for each evening at seven p.m. No need for reservations for lunch and breakfast. We'll just take those meals as we feel like it."

Alice didn't even glance at the packages until the cabin door closed. She quickly brushed away a tear lining her cheek and turned from Delena, who had already started opening the first package. A slinky black evening slip dress, spike high heels, black silk stockings, French cut panties and a lacy garter belt were the first treasures beneath carefully folded tissue, sealed with a gold leaf stamp.

"Silk stockings. A single pair cost over ten dollars if you can get 'em. These are from Paris. So is the dress. The high heels. Gal, you just hit the jackpot!"

Alice fought off tears as she opened the rest of the presents. Robert had selected two three-piece ensembles in emerald green and red. The "convertible suits" were designed to be appropriate business attire with a no-nonsense jacket by day and a soft blouse and calf-length skirt to be worn alone at night for dining and dancing.

"Alice, you have to admit, this guy is really trying. I wouldn't be surprised if Frank Sinatra has been hired to sing to you during dinner."

"I don't wear these kind of clothes. I would look ridiculous. I can't even walk in a low heel anymore, let alone these things. Ridiculous."

"Come on. You know he must have bought these some time ago. He sure didn't buy them in Billings." Delena detected a hint of a smile on Alice's stony face. "Now don't get mad, but I could apply just a hint of makeup to your face this evening to go with that black outfit. You know, you have classic features and gorgeous eyes that wouldn't take much to make you look like a million bucks."

"The only million I care about comes from Lawrence Bradford. Okay, but I'm not about to make an ass out of myself in those heels."

~

Robert took extra time preparing for dinner, deciding that though it might seem a little inappropriate he would wear his tuxedo, a perfect complement to the black dress, assuming Alice was willing to get out of Army fatigues. He was seated facing the dining car entrance as his two dinner guests entered the diner. Delena appeared in front with her five-foot-ten-inch sleek frame in high heels, making it difficult to see the woman behind her. Delena approached the table and stepped aside, giving a small bow.

"Mr. Robert Ren, I would like to introduce you to..." Her words fell away.

"Alice, you look stunning!" Robert said, bumping the table when he rose from his seat.

"Didn't look so good when I tripped into a passenger on my way into the car. I told you I can't walk in high heels. Especially these French jobs," she said without a smile.

"I don't know how you did it, but you are better looking today than the first day I spotted that beautiful hair tied in a chignon in the hospital. I mean it. You look stunning."

Alice blushed and seated herself opposite Robert, quickly picking up and hiding behind a menu so she wouldn't have to respond to his boyish grin. Robert was relieved she hadn't taken a close look at him. His recent weight loss made the tux drape loosely on his shoulders and arms like it was two sizes too large. The cummerbund had comfortably cinched up his sagging pants. He had already scanned the menu completely before their arrival to ensure he could find food he could digest. He found thoughts of something worse than stress creeping into the back of his mind.

"Delena, it wouldn't be fair not to acknowledge that, outside of Alice, you are clearly the most beautiful woman in the dining car," Robert said, realizing his rudeness in solely complimenting Alice.

Delena started to respond when she saw Bradford's attorney, Jed Patterson two tables away. "I know that man behind you, Robert. He's Bradford's attorney. Don't turn around in a hurry. He's staring right at us," Delena said.

"I see him, Delena," Alice said. "Somehow they must know we're going back to see the union. Couldn't be a coincidence he's on the train. Robert, what are you…?"

~

Robert got up from his seat and went to the nearby table where the solitary man was now focusing all attention on a quickly grabbed menu.

"Let me introduce myself, Mr. Patterson. My name is Robert Ren. I assume you know it's rude to stare at people while they're eating."

"What are you talking about, buddy?" the bull-necked attorney looked up from the menu in feigned surprise.

Robert seated himself opposite the man. "You know exactly what I'm talking about. Now see if you can convince me that it's a coincidence that you're on the train headed for Denver for any other reason than to follow Delena Harrison."

Patterson's eyes narrowed slightly. "Not that it's any of your business, but I regularly go to Washington, D.C. to represent the interests of the coal mining industry. My being here is normal." He rested both wrestler's arms on the dining table and leaned into Robert, "The question is, what are you people doing here?"

"Enjoying ourselves, not that it's any of your business. And if you keep watching us we're going to have a hard time doing that, so I'll keep it simple. Wherever we're at, you won't be. We'll be dining at 7 p.m. every evening. You won't be." Robert pushed the rounded handle of a dinner knife into the top of Patterson's hand, pinning it with nearly all his strength.

The man's fingers desperately tried to grasp the tablecloth; with his free hand Patterson grabbed Robert's clenched fist. "Let go of my hand, you son-of-a-bitch, and meet me in the luggage car."

Robert released the pressure and straightened up in his chair as though he'd only reached out his hand in friendship. I'm not about to spoil my dinner. Besides, this is a friendly conversation among a couple of Montana boys who were surprised to see each other. We'll meet, just as you say, but only if you don't do what I ask. This trip means a lot to me, and you're not going to ruin it by getting my lady companions upset. It wouldn't be good for your health."

The attorney glared, but Robert offered him a devilish grin before turning to walk away.

Robert returned to his table, signaling a waiter to avoid a continued focus on the attorney. The man behind them abruptly left without ordering.

"Take it you encouraged our friend to leave," Alice said.

Robert shrugged. "Didn't take much. You won't be seeing him at dinner. If you catch him watching you any other time let me know and he and I will have another visit. Let's eat," he smiled broadly at the ladies. "I'm starving."

~

The next day passed uneventfully, but as the hours slipped by, Alice grew increasingly uncomfortable. Thrown together night and day in close quarters had its up side, but she couldn't help but feel there were too many loose ends. Delena knew the two of them had a history and managed to make herself scarce despite Alice's efforts to the contrary. Still, she enjoyed the private time with Robert except for the nagging feeling that they were doing something wrong.

Alice and Robert wrestled with where to begin to get reacquainted as middle-aged people. Maybe they were trying too hard to begin a new relationship when they'd never gained closure on the old one.

On the third evening of the journey, Robert broached the subject of their relationship, something he was ordinarily inclined to avoid.

"Damn you, Robert, damn you!" Alice exclaimed aloud.

"What?" he looked surprised. "I thought you wanted to talk about it."

"Oh, Robert," she moaned. All night last night she'd wrestled with the realization that they'd wasted half of their lives apart. Her forehead fell to her arm and tears lined her cheeks. His face, his voice, his body, all the things she had learned to trust once before were tempting her again, but this time with a wisdom that gave her a torrent of warning signals.

Abruptly her head jerked up and she stared into his eyes. She dragged the back of one wrist across her nose in a masculine gesture, sniffed, dashed the errant tears from her eyes and swallowed a lump of memories in her throat.

"I got over you, Robert Ren. Now you traipse back into my life with gifts and loving smiles like nothing ever happened. It's not that easy. I've built up a lot of bitterness over the years. I compared every man I met to you. You got married and had a child. I, well, I only had the service."

Robert looked away out the window. "Nothing is impossible if you want it badly enough. I'm not asking for any commitments, Alice. Just let me enjoy being with you, showing you every day how important you are to me. I don't want anything more than that."

"I can't be the woman you imagine, frilly and shy. We're totally different people. Things happened to me you'll never understand. I've been alone too many years."

"Is it so normal to live every day with one woman when you love another? That's probably why she finally left me for another man."

"Robert, you have to end this fantasy. You don't even know me. We were kids who spent a few months together a lifetime ago."

There was a pause in the conversation, and Alice suddenly felt reluctant to end it. Robert Ren was turning out to be one of the most congenial and warm men she had ever known.

"You know, I think my daughter, Karen, knew something was wrong in our marriage since she was very young. Her mother buried herself in church and community work. She always found a reason to never be with her family." Robert raised and scratched his slightly stubbled chin. "Poor Karen. Guess it would be a shock to anyone if your mother runs off with your best friend's father."

For a long time Alice looked out the expansive curved dome window at a pale full moon glimmering on the tumbling Colorado River. The outline of the rugged Rocky Mountains was bathed in eerie rose-tinted shadows as the diesel snaked its way through the formidable terrain.

"This Vista-Dome is really something, isn't it?" Alice said finally, trying to lighten the mood. They might never agree on some things, but she wasn't ready to have Robert Ren vacate her life again.

The train nearly bumped against warm red canyon walls, soaring until they seemed almost to meet half a mile straight up from a sage- and scrub oak-covered floor. East of the gorge they could begin to catch distant outline glimpses of Pike's Peak, the most famous of the Rocky Mountains.

Robert chuckled softly as he squeezed Alice's hand. "There's one thing a person can't accuse you of, and that's trying to finagle your way into a man's heart."

At this comment, Alice's heart began to beat furiously. A tight restricting feeling settled across her chest. Robert avoided her eyes, allowing her to intermittently study his downcast mouth and the forlorn droop of his shoulders. Her eyes moved to his left hand. No ring.

"Stop me if I'm being too forward, but my name is Retired Lieutenant Colonel Alice Beck, and I would like to get to know you. Committed to anyone at the moment?" Alice said in a rare moment of humor.

"I'm afraid I am," he responded with an intense look in his eyes. "I hurt you and I'm going to make sure nobody does that again."

Her lips parted slightly, and for a moment she feared she might cry. Then she slipped her hand from Robert's, her throat working convulsively. "It wasn't your fault. Your home life was a nightmare. I should have been with you after your mother died."

His sober eyes rested on her questioningly. "My name is Robert Ren. No, I am not spoken for, and would be delighted to get to know you, Miss Beck."

The two drifted into a blissful sleep, Alice's head snuggled against his shoulder. They were the only remaining occupants of the Vista-Dome compartment for the rest of the night as the train stopped in Denver and an hour later pulled away for the second leg of their journey.

Chapter 24

Delena didn't mind eating breakfast alone, knowing that Alice and Robert were making spectacular progress in their relationship and inaccurately assuming they'd spent the night together in his berth. How such a slim woman could eat like a miner and never gain an ounce was always a topic of humorous discussion with her husband Brent, she thought, momentarily picturing him at home with Clara awaiting her return from her greatest, and first, travel adventure.

"Two eggs scrambled with potatoes and the old-fashioned railroad French toast with coffee and orange juice," she told the black waiter dressed in a crisply pressed white serving jacket.

"May I join you?" Jed Patterson said from behind her.

Delena was too startled to answer, but he apparently mistook her silence for consent and sat down across the table from her. "Waiter, just hot cereal and coffee." He raised one eyebrow and made a lofty expression. "I understand you have an appointment with old Tony. I don't know what he can do to help your cause. The union already stated its position at the coroner's inquest."

Delena cleared her throat. A trap door opened in the floor of her stomach. "I don't have anything to say to you, Mr. Patterson. It does seem a little strange that you would be on this train when we are, unless you're worried about our meeting with Mr. Pozereli or your Mr. Wellington."

"What do you mean 'my Mr. Wellington'? I hope you're not inferring that the Montana state mining inspector had anything but the health and safety of the miners as his sole concern. Lady, that's what he was paid for." He took a deep breath and lowered his raspy voice. "If you carry an indictment like that back to Washington, D.C., all you're going to do is embarrass the union. Look, this Beck woman has got you all confused from the get-go. Bradford thought long and hard about the crisis you and your daughter Clara…"

The sound of her daughter's name on this vile man's lips shot through Delena like a spear. "You leave Clara out of this! How did you know her name? If anything happens to her or us, there are people in Red Lodge watching every move you scoundrels make. Important people who know what's really going on," Delena screeched.

Patterson raised and lowered an outstretched palm. "Settle down, for God's sake. You're acting paranoid. You see, this is exactly the kind of twisted thinking I was talking about. I've said nothing to threaten you or your family," he said with a warning stare, then softened his voice. "As a matter of fact, I was saying that Bradford wants to help all the widows through this tough time, and no one more than you, with the loss of your house and everything. The bank is prepared to make you an interest-free loan for three years on a wonderful little place near downtown Red Lodge."

"I don't have any money," Delena said flatly, numbness creeping over her. "I don't have a thing and you know why."

"No, no, you don't understand. Lawrence Bradford will give you enough money to not only make a sizable down payment, but enough for you and your daughter to live on without a day's work for at least three years," the attorney said, his consoling tone suspect. "This gift is in no way a settlement because there's no wrongdoing here. Bradford just thinks it's the right thing to do considering all the hardship you've been through."

Robert and Alice fast-stepped to the table.

Patterson looked up at them, his eyes hard.

"Mrs. Harrison and I were having a friendly conversation that has nothing to do with either of you. In fact, I'm still trying to figure out what you two have to do with any of this, except to stir up trouble and create illusions and paranoia in the poor widows' minds."

"If you don't mind, Mr. Patterson, I'd like to have breakfast with my friends," Delena said haltingly.

"Not at all," Patterson offered her a gracious smile and got up from his seat. "I hope you'll consider the genuine sincerity of the offer made in our conversation. Not everything is as it may seem to some people," the attorney added while pointedly glaring at Alice and Robert before leaving.

Delena concealed her sweaty shaking hands in her lap, but her furiously tapping leg did little to conceal her anxiety. She waited as Alice and Robert took their seats and ordered breakfast before launching into an explanation. "I think he just offered me money and threatened me about Clara. We have to go home right now."

"What?" Alice shrieked. "He said what?"

"Calm down a minute," Robert spoke in soothing tones. "Tell us from the beginning, Delena."

With a quivering chin, Delena spoke slowly and deliberately, re-enacting the confrontation for them with a little prompting from Robert.

"Okay," Alice breathed an audible sigh of relief. "You're overreacting, Delena," Alice whispered. "His reference to your daughter's name was only a way of trying to seem like a caring friend, wanting to warm you up for the buy off. If there was no concern for the outcome of your meeting with Tony Pozereli, he wouldn't be chasing you down with generous offers." She turned to Robert. "This is encouraging. I'm looking forward to this meeting more than ever, thanks to that dummy."

"Alice is right, Delena," Robert said patting her hand. "Enjoy the train ride. It's starting to look like we're the ones holding the aces."

"I think I'll send a telegram to Tom Lloyd when we reach Chicago," Alice interjected. "The *Carbon Courier* ought to know about our trip to Washington and the offer just made by Bradford's man."

"Good idea, but I'll do it." Delena laughed nervously, feeling relieved but not entirely convinced.

~

Following dinner, Robert and Alice again excused themselves from Delena's company to spend their last night together on the train alone with at least thirty other sightseers in the Vista-Dome. Enough had been said. Threats and indictments were gone from all of their conversations. Alice was beginning to connect with her feminine side, enjoying her sensuous tight-fitting new wardrobe. Robert was awakening, or maybe even creating, a new woman.

"Miss Beck, because I like you, and I've enjoyed being, working, with you, I think kissing is a helluva nifty way of telling a person things like that."

There was little she could do, and in another moment, little she wanted to do to combat his advances. She quickly pulled away from the clutch of his arm. "Mr. Ren, I thought you were going to wait for me to make the first advancement in this relationship," she teased half-seriously, looking around the near-empty view deck to see just what privacy they might be afforded.

He didn't bother to reply and pulled her closer, lowering his lips the remaining fraction of an inch, touching her mouth lightly with warm, moist lips. Her eyelids slid closed, and her guard grew shaky while the gentle pressure of his mouth lingered, growing more welcome as the seconds passed. Without removing his lips from hers, he pulled her hot, rapidly breathing chest close to his, guiding her resisting arms around his sides, then clamping them securely with his elbows. When he felt the last of her resistance melt, he slowly, cautiously, moved his hands to her back, nudging, now harder, now softer, back and forth while she felt the warm proddings of his tongue. The warning voices, reminding Alice of an abandoned past, faded into silence. Only the pounding of her heart filled her ears as her hands rested on the back of his tuxedo jacket, holding him lightly. He guided her to an empty seating area.

Her lips parted, and his tongue came seeking. She met the warm, wet tip with her own and felt the heart-ripping thrill of wet flesh meeting wet flesh. Behind her she felt his hands moving brusquely and wondered what he was doing as the motion jerked his mouth sideways on hers momentarily. At that moment he was reaching down the low back of her black dress.

"No, Robert."

Her heart throbbed as she peered at him, desperately searching for probing eyes. The tall-backed seat they shared provided at least the illusion of privacy with no one watching. She drifted back beneath his warm, wet tongue while it slid along the soft, velvet skin of her inner lips, making a complete circle before widening again, the kiss now wholly demanding.

He removed his hand from her back. Then he moved both his hands down to her hips, pulling her so close that she could feel his hardness as if they were one. Before she knew what she was doing she was moving in after-beats, making circles with her hips that chased those he made with his.

Without realizing it, he'd taken the kiss further than he'd intended in such a public place. Robert closed his fist around Alice's short, cropped hair, tugging gently as he dropped his head back and swallowed convulsively.

Their breaths came strident and rushed, falling in blended clouds of dreams. She leaned her sweating forehead against his chin to calm her wild breathing.

"Geronimo," he got out in a guttural half gulp.

She chuckled, a high, tight sound of unexpectedness before two strained, little words squeezed from her throat, "Yeah, wow."

Her hips rested lightly against him. She waited for her body to cool down and be sensible, but against him she could feel the difficulty he, too, was having talking sense into his body.

"One kiss," she managed in a whispered voice. "That's what you said I had to do first. And you were right. If you wouldn't have, I would have grabbed you by the neck and pulled you to me."

"Now that's what I like about you, Miss Beck. Your shy manner that requires a man to be assertive."

Seeking to control emotions that seemed to have run away like wild horses with bits between their teeth, she teased, "Would you believe I did that so convincingly so you'd stop pursuing me and let me focus on the real reason for this trip?"

"Absolutely. Who am I to question the discipline of the Army Nurse's Corps' first lieutenant colonel?"

The two returned to their respective berths hand-in-hand, not wanting to spoil the evening with a physical commitment that could lead to complications.

When Alice walked into her sleeping compartment, Delena had just finished the *Saturday Evening Post* Robert had bought her aboard the train.

"Isn't it about time we had a little 'girl talk' about this guy that you're wearing high heels and learning to wear make-up for?"

Alice's cheeks felt a blush and she shot Delena a wry smile but deftly changed the subject. "We have to prepare for our meeting tomorrow. I assume you aren't interested in what Bradford's attorney has to offer,"

Alice said without bothering to wait for a reply, while shedding herself of her uncharacteristic feminine attire. She rummaged through her suitcase for a notebook to begin outlining their presentation.

"Before we go further with any of this I want to check in with Clara when we reach Washington. If I feel everything is okay, I'll meet with the union, but not before I know there hasn't been some stranger around watching her or the house she is staying at. I better check with Mrs. Brewcowski, too. I won't say anything to alarm her, but she needs to watch out. I can't wait to get back home."

"Delena, we don't even know yet if we have a case that will stand up in a jury trial."

"That didn't stop something from happening to Howard Wellington, did it?"

Alice sighed. She had a point there. Conversation petered out and the two women got ready for bed, each lost in their own thoughts.

As the lights went out, Robert's touch lingered. The imaginary scent of his cologne caused a sexual desire that Alice celebrated as she drifted into sleep. An hour later she awoke, unable to resist him even in her sleep. She silently arose and reached for the cocktail dress nearby, gathered her undergarments, and heels and dressed in the sliver of light seeping under the cabin door.

Chapter 25

It was another sleepless, pain-filled night for Robert. Something was starting to encroach like a flesh-eating parasite. The last few days with Alice had been the first in weeks where he had moments, hours, when he physically felt like his old self. He had, soon after the departure from Red Lodge, dismissed the possibility of making love to her. While he tried to convince himself that his desires for her could be realized through their kisses and close embraces, he burned with a man's desire to devour every inch of her firm curvaceous body.

A light tap on his berth door suggested someone other than the porter. He panicked. Fumbling in the dark, he found a nightshirt to cover his withering frame. Without fully opening the narrow wood door he asked, "Who is it?"

"Hurry, Robert. It's embarrassing standing out here in the middle of the night."

Without allowing himself to consider options, Robert slowly opened the door to allow Alice in.

"Can't see a damn thing in here," Alice whispered.

Robert quickly moved to control her movements by pulling her close to his chest. He manipulated her at will, kissing her all the way to the bed while she unsuccessfully flailed at him, trying to break out of his embrace to turn on the lights.

"Don't," she mumbled weakly with her lips pressed against his. "Don't. I just came to see you."

He danced her backwards with slow, deliberate pushes of his naked thighs against hers, kissing her open mouth as he pushed her down on the tangled covers. Her arms were now firmly looped around his neck, and her words were nearly unrecognizable, her tongue pressed flatly against his. "Please. Don't waste so much time."

He smiled in the darkness, devouring her mouth while his hands slid down her shoulders, releasing the thin straps of her dress. She arched back to aid in removing the weightless garment.

"Make love to me, Robert."

He leaned his head low in the dark, feeling with his mouth. When she was free of her dress, lacy black garter belt and stockings, his lips pressed warmly against the skin above the bra. She hesitated, lost as the touch of his tongue delighted her flesh. He breathed outward gently, warming her skin and sending shivers of desire to the peaks of her breasts.

Her hands sought his waist in the dark, and her fingers spread wide on his ribs. She paused momentarily as she discovered harshly protruding bones and a concave stomach. He immediately tensed up and began pulling away from her touch.

"Robert," she murmured, "don't be tense. There's no need to be."

He released the breath he'd held captive for too long and forced his weakened muscles to relax one by one, as he nuzzled the warm hollow behind her ear until her head dropped to his shoulder.

He circled her with both arms, just below her breasts, renewing a sense of freedom. His arms tightened more firmly around her, and he rocked her soothingly a time or two. "Oh, Alice, we've got to enjoy every minute together."

She relaxed against him as he wet the soft skin of her neck with the tip of his tongue and slipped a hand over her breast. Shudders of pleasure prickled her skin. Doubts of their future together fled magically. She no longer hesitated in touching the body that wasn't sturdy and hard as it once had been. She only reveled in how good it felt to be caressed by him.

"Mmm, Alice, you feel so good." He dropped his head to her chest like a child.

She covered his hands and pressed them firmly against her supple breasts. His warm palms moved beneath her hands, gently arousing at once, appeasing the need for more exploration. His hands began to stroke away any lingering misgivings. His right hand slid over her flat, taut stomach, where his thin fingers spread wide for a moment, then closed again before pressing the hollow beside her well-defined hip. His touch became feather light, and with a single fingertip he was outlining every contour of her body as though trying to scribe it to memory.

Alice became powerfully aware of her own sensuality from a touch that was part loving caress; part desperately hungry and all aroused. She sensed him gauging her reactions, listening to the accelerated beat of her heart, and feeling it beneath the palm that still pleasured her breast. At last he slipped his hand over the moist curve of her femininity, bringing her to know the wild rapture they had briefly shared only once before on a cold, stone, windmill floor.

He whispered her name over and over as though trying to convince himself that it was really her as he tenderly kissed her ear, her jaw, her shoulder, and her stomach.

She smiled in the dark, thinking back to their lovemaking in the windmill, realizing she had been fighting a losing battle ever since.

"I've tried not to think of you for so many years, but it was impossible," she whispered.

His touch drove the breath from her lungs and set her pulse thumping; she was now the one starting to get tense as her mind raced from girlish uncertainty to womanly yearning. It had been so long, but during these moments of sweet expectation she realized their intimacy had been almost predestined. A shivering thrill rushed through her.

She pulled his hips firmly against hers. Her fingertips found his bare chest and she moved up to settle her breasts securely against it. He ran his palms over her back.

He asked only a single word. "Now?"

She groaned, a strangled sound of abandon as he grasped her firm backside, filling her with a wild sensuality she'd lost somewhere along the years. She pushed herself up from her shoulders and guided him into her. She chose to follow the wild tempo of force she savored as she unleashed a raw wantonness that shook him into an ecstatic stupor. When it was over, she fell heavily into his arms.

"Colonel," was all he could find the breath to say, but the single word was an accolade. "You're gorgeous."

"Not bad yourself," she responded in a breathy voice as she soothed the damp hair on his temples. Though it was still dark, her eyes had adjusted to the dimness, allowing her to discern the outline of his contentedly smiling face.

He ran an index finger along the rim of her nose. "Tough as nails, huh? Looks like you're as good at being a lover as a spitfire nurse."

Alice abruptly arose and turned on the light to dress.

"Keep that light off!" Robert leaped to the switch. "I'm sorry, Alice, that light is blinding me. Could you get dressed in the bathroom?"

She gathered her clothes in confusion. "Got what you were after, huh?" she whispered, surprised at her own blunt rudeness.

Robert put on his pajamas and robe. As Alice emerged from the small bathroom compartment, he turned on the berth light.

"I'd have more room dressing in a foxhole."

"Alice, I can't tell you what it means to me for you to have the courage to come here tonight." His sparkling eyes pleaded for forgiveness. His glare shifted to her stockings. As she turned to bend down to find her shoes, he admired her legs. He arched an eyebrow. "I bet if you keep wearing heels you would soon be walking without my assistance. In about a year or so!"

"Don't go banking on me wearing this kind of get-up when we get back to Red Lodge. Doesn't work too well at the cabin and those high brow social establishments in downtown Red Lodge," she said, laughing. "I don't know why you've gone to all this bother. I'm not even a very good…" Abruptly she gulped in embarrassment.

"Lover? Is that what you were going to say, Miss Beck? Because if it is, you might be interested in knowing that I only have a remote idea of what kind of nurse you made, but you're a hell of a lover." He continued to wipe the sweat from his forehead.

"Don't you start thinking that just because of this bump in the night I'm going to be your little girl. We're here to—"

"I know, crusade for all the injustice in the world," he said as he tried to pull her to him for a last kiss.

"Okay, Robert Ren," she said giggling, resisting his advances. "Let's see if we can show a little more self-discipline and dedicate our attentions to winning those widows a fair settlement."

"Yes, Ma'am!" he said, standing at attention.

Chapter 26

Jed Patterson paced in Tony Pozereli's outer office while the union president's secretary nervously reassured him that he would be with him shortly. Introductory topic scenarios raced through his mind. The secretary's intercom buzzer rang moments later, and he entered. The modest government office was decorated with the mandatory picture of Franklin D. Roosevelt. A large American flag occupied a stand opposite a large leafy plant.

Pozereli pulled a pocket watch from the vest of his expensive, dark, pinstriped, three-piece suit. Charcoal gray, bushy eyebrows accented his full gray hair, parted down the middle. A drooping mustache gave him the appearance of a white owl.

"Mr. Patterson," he said, rising from his chair with an outstretched hand. "I met your client Lawrence Bradford during his last visit to the Capitol. Most impressive what he's done for the war effort."

"He spoke highly of you, as well. May I call you Tony?" the attorney asked without awaiting an answer. "Mr. Bradford would like to extend an offer to assist in the war effort any way the government deems appropriate."

Pozereli waved the attorney to the seat opposite his desk. "Well, tell him I appreciate his offer and will consider what role his operation can play in representing the interests of our miners." The union president rose, stepped around his desk and sat knee to knee with his guest. "For starters, how about filling me in on the details of the Bear Creek Mine disaster. I heard the state mining inspector had a timely accident."

"Surprising death is more like it," Patterson offered. "Howard Wellington did his position proud, serving as a watchdog over issues that were of equal concern to the union and the company. Before he died he gave a full report at the coroner's inquest, vindicating the Bear Creek Mining Company of any safety violations."

Pozereli began petting one of his eyebrows.

Patterson sensed more than an attempt at effective listening and unknowingly started accelerating his speech. "Shame to lose such a fine man. That road has taken a lot of lives. It's incredibly steep going over from Red Lodge to the mine. He shouldn't have been out there at night."

Patterson fidgeted nervously while Pozereli spoke his piece. After a long pause that had Patterson holding his breath, Pozereli took a deep breath, slapped his open palms on his knees and sprang to his feet. "I read the summary of the inquest and it does leave a few questions. Why were there no records of the daily logs or monthly written reports? Mr. Wellington wasn't filing on a timely basis with the state, it appears. Why wasn't there any testimony from the union foremen on the two shifts that weren't caught in the explosion, either confirming or denying what Mr. Wellington only gave in verbal testimony with no supporting documentation?"

"Now… I can explain," Patterson became visibly agitated.

"Why was the rightful compensation paid the widows based on legal responsibility of the mine owner made to look like a discretionary gift? I have a few more questions but those will do for openers, Mr. Patterson."

"There seems to be some confusion of the facts. I—"

"Please just answer the questions one by one before giving me a summation of guilt or innocence."

Patterson addressed each question with similar ambiguities, doing his best to effectively evade the facts, but judging by the way Pozereli's furry eyebrows pumped up and down, he wasn't buying it. Pozereli never interrupted but he did aggressively take notes, making Patterson's anxious stream-of-conscious defense seem lame, even to him.

Finally, he said, "Thank you, Mr. Patterson. Before you walked in here I had a casual curiosity about allegations of wrongful death at the Bear Creek Mines. I felt Wellington's explanation was probably accurate. You've given me a different interpretation. I can see now that regardless of our patriotic duty, my first obligation, as well as Lawrence Bradford's, is to the safety of those miners. I'm not so sure this accident couldn't have been prevented now. I thank you for that, Mr. Patterson."

"But—"

"It will make upcoming meetings far more intriguing than I might have imagined."

"What did I say to give you that impression?"

"It's what you didn't say, counselor. It's what you didn't say." Pozereli reached over his desk to press his secretary's intercom button. "Miss Miller, will you show Mr. Patterson out so I can make my next appointment? Oh, and send a telegram to Lawrence Bradford in Red Lodge, Montana thanking him for his national and union support."

Patterson left the office with his hat in his hand, already dreading Bradford's response to this disaster.

~

Tom Lloyd had been in such a hurry to be on time for the Red Lodge Kiwanis luncheon that he snatched the telegram to reread when he got a chance. Every meeting eventually evolved into an address on the progress in the war and usually a lot of grousing about how America should be more merciless.

Lloyd settled into his usual seat at the speaker's table just as Lawrence Bradford was finishing the invocation. Following his prayer, singularly dedicated to fighting men overseas, Bradford took the opportunity to read a telegram he had just received from Tony Pozereli, president of the United Mine Workers Union of America. It gave commendation for all Bradford had done to advance the war effort through personal contributions of time and money by providing coal for the war machine.

Bradford stood at the podium deeply inhaling the applause from the gathering. He made a point of sitting next to Tom Lloyd as he returned to the half-empty head table.

"Here's the telegram, Tom, for a story. That Pozereli is a helluva guy. I think I told you about my meeting with him in D.C. I never saw the big follow-up story. Did I miss it?"

"I didn't write one, Lawrence."

Bradford's cheeks turned red. "The President of the United States is a pretty non-newsworthy event in Red Lodge. Yeah, I can see that. We have a school meeting or something that bumped it from the front page?" He squeezed his water glass so hard it should have exploded in his hand. "And now getting these glowing remarks about all I'm doing for the GIs isn't much either? Shit Tom, what does it take?"

"Everybody is committed to winning the war. There's a reminder in it every time you try and buy something, if you're lucky enough to have a job in this town." Tom felt distinctly uncomfortable, being on the receiving end of Bradford's wrath. But what he'd been learning in the last few days made it impossible for him to continue ignoring the man's dark side and still be able to live with himself.

"What do you mean by that, Tom? I provide all the employment and good wages, too, for just about everybody in Washoe and Bear Creek, let alone Red Lodge. What's going on here, Tom?" Bradford's words took on a cold, measured tone. "Have you got something against me all of a sudden?"

"I'll write a little something and include your telegram from the union president. You've got a good point there, Lawrence, I'll admit. It's not front-page material, but it does warrant a story. It'll be in the next edition." Tom felt in his pocket for the telegram.

Bradford nodded his head in less than enthusiastic agreement, then turned to talk to the bank president sitting to his left.

The publisher unfolded and slowly reread the message he'd received earlier:

"Mr. Lloyd,

Bradford's attorney made big offer to buy me off and stop filing lawsuit. No way. He's on train to get to the union president first and bribe me. Worried about my daughter's safety. Please watch her for me until return.

Delena Harrison"

He quickly folded and returned the message to his coat jacket. After a moment's pause he tapped Bradford on the arm. Might as well get a first person comment before he goes to print.

"Lawrence, I had a brief visit from Mrs. Harrison. She seemed to have some concern for the safety for herself and her child following the mysterious burning of her home and the death of Howard Wellington. What do you make of all that?"

The glare shooting out of Bradford's eyes as he turned on him was enough to make Tom shrink back. "It's all the fault of that crazy bitch that lives in the canyon. She got these widows full of ideas. Crazy ideas." Bradford spoke harshly, then again turned his back on the publisher to continue his conversation with the bank president.

Lloyd tapped his arm again.

"What is it, Tom?" Bradford snapped. "We were just talking about a piece of real estate I'm about to buy."

"Do you feel Mrs. Harrison should get some special consideration from your company for all she has gone through?" Lloyd tried to keep his tone casual.

"They haven't done it yet. But as everybody in this town knows, Mrs. Harrison is filing a civil action for wrongful death for as high as a million bucks. What am I supposed to do, donate to the cause? Come on, Tom. The mining business is dangerous. Every miner that enters that hole knows it because his father, uncle, or a friend has already died from living underground. We have a hard time even getting them to wear a helmet. They put little value on their lives." Bradford shifted in his chair, gaining steam. "We do all we can to protect them from themselves. Tell you what, I'll take you on a tour of the mine and show you all the precautions we take, from protecting the explosives to blowing air through the shafts. Damnit to hell," Bradford boomed, "You've gotta see it to understand what a shitty business it is, and always has been."

Tom Lloyd nodded but at the same time, he had to wonder why the mine owner was driving every point home with a sledgehammer.

Chapter 27

Tony Pozereli cleared his schedule to allow ample time for the next appointment after his distasteful encounter with Bradford's attorney. As the two attractive women and attorney, Robert Ren, entered his office, he leapt from his chair and rushed over to arrange the group in a circle of chairs in his surprisingly small office.

"We're not much for fancy space. That's not our job around here." Pozereli scanned the expressions on his visitors' faces and their fidgeting demeanor. "Please, have a seat. Get comfortable. When you're ready, begin your story. Take your time." The entire group looked anxious and he didn't want to miss a word of whatever they had to say.

"I'm the one who called from Red Lodge," Robert said, comfortably settling back into a wing chair across from the desk.

Pozereli lifted a hand and interrupted. "It might interest you to know, before you begin, that I've had a visit from Bradford's attorney.

He was here just yesterday," Pozereli's glance flitted from one face to the next, resting on Delena. "While the gentleman never really told me why he insisted on the meeting, I suspect it had something to do with our visit today."

"We saw him on the train," Delena said softly. "He tried to buy me off so I wouldn't go ahead and file for a fair settlement for me and the other fifty-seven widows I represent here today."

"Did it work?" Pozereli asked, fighting a wry smile. From the fire in her eyes, he'd bet not.

"Of course not," Delena sounded indignant. "I don't know where to begin. Sorry if I ramble. I…"

Alice had been fidgeting in her chair from the moment she sat down. Unable to resist any longer, she burst out, "My name is Alice Beck, retired lieutenant colonel, U.S. Army. I assisted in the rescue effort at Bear Creek Mine and have been actively involved in assisting in this legal effort ever since. I've prepared a written chronology of all of the key things that have happened since the explosion and the resulting death of seventy-four miners. I hand wrote it on the train. If you'd have one of your secretaries type it up, it'll help us get down to the reason for our visit, and how we feel your continuing investigation into the mining disaster is more than warranted."

Pozereli's eyebrows shot up in surprise. He expected the truth, but he hadn't anticipated this much forethought. "An excellent suggestion, Miss Beck. You can breathe now," he teased, rising from his chair. "If it's acceptable to each of you, I'll do just as the lieutenant colonel has recommended and have a copy for each of us to refer to over dinner on the Potomac this evening. There's a small Italian restaurant with a back room providing privacy and a notable view. We can end this meeting now to allow time for the preparation of the document and my review so we don't waste any time in getting down to brass tacks," Pozereli chuckled in an English-style reserve.

Looking surprised, but more than a little relieved, the trio got up, nodding and shaking hands in turn before exiting the office.

~

Robert had already booked rooms at the Washington Hotel on Pennsylvania Avenue, only a four-block walk from the White House. He delighted in Mr. Pozereli's suggestion, leaving them time for the White House tour and maybe even a quick peek at the Lincoln Memorial. Robert whisked Alice and Delena through the Capitol high-lights, including a stop at the Congressional Longfellow Building to meet the administrative assistant for a Montana Congressman. Afterward, they returned to the Lincoln Memorial to more fully absorb the overpowering monument. Although they all enjoyed the time exploring the nation's capital, it was a relief to head for the restaurant in hopes of a positive outcome to the meeting with Pozereli.

~

Alice's head was spinning after the train ride, her impetuous reunion with Robert and their letdown to finally arrive at the destination of Pozereli's office only to have a decision postponed yet again. It was wonderful to tour the sights with Robert and Delena, and to feel hopeful, at least, that Pozereli would listen to reason. As they entered the restaurant, the dim lighting and festive ambiance was a welcome contrast to the hectic traffic and bright sun of the late afternoon.

Alice and Delena stood close together, waiting, as Robert sought out the maître d' and confirmed Pozereli's location. The two women followed close behind as he led the trio to Pozereli's table. A moment later, a more relaxed looking Pozereli greeted them and watched as they were seated.

"You have to try the linguini," Tony Pozereli assured them once they were settled and basking in the warm yellow glow of the candlelit table.

The spacious private room, as promised, overlooked the Potomac River, and bright distant lights that Alice knew to be Arlington, Virginia.

"Ah, here's my associate," Pozereli said, turning his eyes to a thin-as-a-broom stick man hurrying toward the table. "Tim Poulson, these folks are from Red Lodge, Montana, representing the rights of the many widows whose husbands were killed about six months ago in the Bear Creek Mine disaster. Tim has long been our legal counsel. I felt he might be able to assist in this evening's conversation."

Alice sized the man up, hoping the surprise visitor wasn't a bad sign. He appeared pleasant enough, but she'd learned through the years to be suspicious.

Poulson smiled and nodded at each of them in turn, then took a seat next to Pozereli. Once their dinner orders had been taken, he turned to Robert and said, "I've read the notes one of you prepared giving a chronology of events leading you up to this moment, and Mr. Pozereli and I have concluded—"

Pozereli stopped him with an uplifted palm. "Before we conclude anything, I'd like to see your husband's mine diary, Mrs. Harrison. Did you bring it?"

Delena nodded. "Yes, sir. It's always with me since the fire." Hesitantly, she pulled it from her purse and handed it to Pozereli.

The union president leaned into the flickering glow of the candle-light to focus on the hard-to-read scribbling and took a moment to scan through some of the entries. Looking up with a serious expression, he asked, "And you said these written concerns were expressed and collaborated with other foremen and the state mining inspector?"

"Mr. Wellington accidentally admitted as much shortly before he was, well, before he died," Delena volunteered.

"As Mr. Poulson was about to say, your appeal has fully captured my fascination," he glanced around the group. "I've taken the liberty of totally rearranging my schedule to take the train out to Montana early next week. I think I need to see the mine for myself and look into your allegations."

"Then you'll provide legal counsel so we can take this to trial?" Alice asked.

Pozereli began stroking an upturned eyebrow and gave an uncertain expression. "That's not exactly what I said, Miss Beck. So far, there's absolutely nothing proving negligence on the part of Lawrence Bradford or the deceased state mining inspector. This is purely a personal investigation to determine if there's any validity to these indictments."

Conversation was suspended as the waiter began setting their cocktail orders on the table.

"Now let's turn our attentions, if only for a moment, to this spectacular menu," Pozereli said with a smile.

"That's not what—" Alice couldn't switch gears quite that fast. She wasn't about to give up that quickly.

Robert interrupted her, smiling at Pozereli. "Miss Beck has a tendency to get a little dramatic, Mr. Pozereli," Robert said, lightly kicking Alice's shin under the table. "But I will tell you that she's been in there every step of the way fighting for these widows in a town where Lawrence Bradford runs the stores, bank, and public opinion. We wouldn't be here if it wasn't for Alice."

She knew he was right in stopping her from speaking too hastily and tried to contain her frustrations.

After the group had feasted on the chef's original creations, Pozereli asked the union attorney to give an overview of the legal steps if Mrs. Harrison was to proceed.

"Unless Mr. Bradford is arrested for the alleged murder of Mr. Wellington, what we're talking about is strictly a non-criminal, non-contractual wrongful death civil action you'd file with the superior court at your county seat. It's called per se negligence based on the alleged violations of federal mining safety act standards. As the plaintiff, you have to prove there has been a breach in established regulations."

"Is it like a criminal trial with a jury and everything?" Delena asked.

"When you file a complaint, those accused will file a response," Robert interrupted, turning to the shocked Mr. Poulson. "Sorry, I'm an attorney, a corporate attorney. It's then up to the presiding judge to determine if a trial is warranted. And yes, there would be a jury. I should note that the statutes for a civil action are considerably different than criminal trials. You don't have to prove the elements of negligence, just the violation of the statutes. Then you have a wrongful death cause of action."

Poulson gave a disapproving look. "It's easier for you to win. The primary burden is on them, not you."

"Do we have to file a specific amount of money we want at the beginning?" Delena asked.

Mr. Poulson shoved his glasses up the narrow bridge of his nose. His eyes darted over to Robert to ensure no further interruptions. "There was a reference to one million dollars. Mrs. Harrison, I don't know where that figure came from, but all survivors of the mining accident, not just the widows, are automatically included in the amount you file for. I've taken the liberty to rough out the unrealized salary of the seventy-four men, using an average of five dollars a day for twenty-five years with a twenty percent overtime factor for the hard damages, and for pain and suffering as well. A better figure would be three million dollars."

In hearing the amount—three times what they'd discussed—Delena caught her breath.

"That, of course," Poulson continued, "is if you are going to actually follow through with this. I read the coroner's inquest and it appears you have a real uphill battle."

"Doesn't that diary mean anything?" Alice asked. "We could get an expert witness to verify the gauge reading recorded in there."

"You'll need corroborating evidence beyond the diary in light of conflicting testimony from the state mining inspector," Pozereli said, beating his attorney to the same conclusion. "I'm particularly curious about the absence of solicited testimony at the inquest from the foremen from the other two shifts. They were living in the same supposedly dangerous conditions."

Alice sat quietly for a change, watching the expression on Pozereli's face. It was clear that nothing was going to get past Tony Pozereli without being properly scrutinized. She said little more as the evening wound down, listening to a serenading violinist perform some favorite Italian classics.

~

The three walked up Pennsylvania Avenue one last time at Delena's insistence before checking out of the hotel. As a memento of Delena's first travel adventure, Robert and Alice presented her with a fashionable new dress to enjoy on their return train trip, along with matching heels.

"I think we ought to change cabins," Alice whispered to Robert before they boarded the train.

"I need to talk to you," Robert said. "The Vista-Dome."

Once seated in the Dome in a private spot he turned from her, staring out the window while the train started pulling out.

"What's the topic, soldier?" Alice said, snuggling up under his arm. Anticipating a private moment, she wasn't sure why he seemed so aloof.

"I'll be getting off in Chicago, and..."

Alice swallowed hard, wondering if she heard him right. "Getting off? Everything's still up in the air. We don't even know if we have an attorney."

"I've got to make a quick stop in Chicago. There are some urgent things I have to get back to at home."

His voice sounded calm but he was still avoiding her eyes. "What are you saying, Robert? Got to take off again just when we get back together?"

"I have to."

Alice jerked away from his draping arm. Her face darkened faster than a Kansas summer storm. Only knowing him for snippets of time

before and now, she instinctively knew he wasn't the type to move
slowly or be overcautious, particularly when it came to the obsessive
behavior he had shown her until this moment. "I think I understand.
You aren't sure how you feel about us now that I'm a real woman and
not that fantasy you've been carrying around for twenty years. Bad
idea. I'll bunk with Delena!" She half rose from the seat.

Robert pulled her back. "There you go jumping before you look
again. Damnit Alice, what did I say to give you the impression that I
don't love you?"

Alice froze at the words. In her confusion, anger overwhelmed her
and she feared another abandonment. "Nothing about you is consistent,
Robert Ren. Since the first day I met you, you say one thing and then
do another. You're right. Why should we make love ever again? Who
knows how you'll feel a month or a day from now?" She ripped her arm
away from his grip and stormed out of the view compartment.

Chapter 28

The first night of the four-night journey home, Alice ate in her berth to avoid any contact with Robert. Delena eagerly joined him for dinner. She'd bought Clara a little gift for each day she was gone, feeling a pinch of guilt for leaving her behind. She feared the postcards she'd sent wouldn't beat her home, creating the longest period of non-communication the two had ever known.

During dinner with Robert, Delena steered away from any probing into his emotionally charged relationship, pointing out jagged mountains and rivers exploding with white water between bites. She began feeling as protective about his feelings as Alice's and couldn't avoid seeing the suffering in his eyes as he moved food around his plate, eating less than a child. He offered her no clues about his upcoming plans.

~

Jed Patterson folded his arms and planted his feet the moment Robert saw him block the narrow corridor outside the sleeping berths. They were alone. A face-off.

Robert slowed but didn't stop. "I've been wondering when you and I would meet…"

Patterson didn't give him time to finish the sentence. He rammed his fist into Robert's stomach, doubling him over. A well-placed knee rocketing into his forehead was the last thing Robert remembered before he saw the porter's eyes peering down at him.

"You all right, sir? I don't know how long you've been laying here. What happened?"

"Just must have passed out, I guess." Robert staggered to his feet and dragged himself as far as Delena and Alice's cabin.

"What in the world?" Delena gasped when she saw him in the doorway.

Robert stumbled into the room and slumped over on one of their berth beds. "Everything okay with you two?" Robert asked, coughing up drops of blood in his hand. "Bit my tongue."

"Good God, Robert! What in the world happened to you?"

"Patterson, that son-of-a…" It was all coming back to him now.

"We better get to Alice," Delena looked panic-stricken. "I think she went to the Vista-Dome, but she's been gone too long. Are you all right to go?"

The instant Robert realized what she was saying, he was on his feet, dashing out the door with Delena in hot pursuit. Taking the stairs two at a time, he raced up into the Dome, scanning the mostly empty seats for her familiar form.

He breathed a sigh of relief as he spied Alice, asleep against one of the enormous curved windows. He'd just started to sink into the chair in front of her when a familiar voice sliced into his consciousness.

"Expecting a problem?" Jed Patterson asked, his head barely popping up from the seat directly behind Alice's.

Robert knew, in his degenerated condition, he'd be no match for the muscular attorney. He paused before responding.

"I told you once that this mining case doesn't have a thing to do with you and the little lady here, unless of course you want it that way," Patterson whispered looking down at Alice.

Adrenaline alone propelled Robert to Patterson's throat. In a burst of fury, he lunged, his fingernails digging in. Patterson's contorted mouth slobbered out a desperate breath. Even his strong grip couldn't release the vice lock on his neck.

"You're killing him!" Delena screamed, running up behind Robert and clutching at his shoulders, trying to break him from his murderous spell.

Robert's hands popped open and Patterson collapsed, fighting for breath. Robert fled as train personnel responded to the scream and the gathering crowd.

The scream awakened Alice in time to see the lingering insanity in Robert's eyes.

"What? What's going on?"

"Shh," Delena hushed her, helping her to her feet. As the two made their way shakily down the stairs, Delena overheard Patterson mumbling something about choking on a piece of food.

"We've got to get home as soon as possible," Delena whispered as they neared their room. "Anything could happen to Clara. These people only know how to get their way through violence."

~

When their train pulled up to the Chicago station, Delena rushed to a telephone for reassurances that Clara was safe. Alone, Alice paced their cabin berth, reaching for the doorknob countless times to run to Robert, and then stopping herself. Everything seemed surreal. She wasn't sure anymore what had really happened and what she'd dreamed.

"Why aren't you with Robert saying good-bye?" Delena asked when she returned from making her phone call.

Alice rushed to the window. "Oh damn, are we pulling out?" How could she have forgotten he was leaving the train in Chicago?

"Go, go and see him before he leaves. Right now!" Delena urged.

Alice pushed by Delena in their confined space and scrambled out the door, down the sleeping car aisle, weaving and bumping through people and luggage. The whistle blew before she made it to Robert's berth in the adjoining car.

Oh God, please not again. Robert, where are you? Damnit, did you really get off? The train started to pull away from the station. Robert Ren faded back into her haunted dreams.

Chapter 29

Lillian Hutton had no intention of listening in on Lawrence Bradford's conversation with Howard Wellington, but party lines present tempting opportunities. Delena Harrison had gone to Billings and officially filed with the superior court for millions of dollars. Her knowledge of the telephone exchange between the two men could be worthless. Or, it could be worth a small fortune.

"Bradford residence," an older man's voice responded as Lillian's quaking hand held the receiver to her ear.

"Yes, I have an important message for Mr. Bradford regarding his business."

"Your name, please."

"He doesn't know me, but I know he'll want to talk."

"I'm sorry, Ma'am, it's ten o'clock at night. He doesn't take any calls after nine unless it's an emergency."

"This is an emergency!" she insisted. After a long silence Lillian started to hang up considering the foolishness of her idea.

"Yeah, this is Lawrence Bradford, who's this? It better be good."

"It doesn't matter who I am. What does matter, is that… I know what you said to Howard Wellington the night he died."

"What in the hell are you talking about?"

"Isn't it curious that the same night Mr. Wellington died, he was on his way to the mine based on your instructions?"

"I don't know what you're insinuating lady, but talking to the state mining inspector when you're a mine owner is as natural as a bookie talking to a gambler. What in Christ's name are you trying to say? You've got thirty seconds before I hang up."

"You were probably the last person he spoke to. Why in the world would anybody want to meet at a mine at that hour of the night? If you can give me a good answer, I'll hang up right—"

Lawrence Bradford slammed down the phone and less than a minute later placed a call to Los Angeles, careful to make sure Lillian Hutton wasn't listening in.

"She was just testing you," the deep velvet voice said on the other end of Bradford's line.

"Civil suit is one thing. Murder rap is another. I don't like it. Maybe she knows a lot more than just what she heard on my line. It'll take me ten minutes in the morning to track down who's on my party line. And when I find out, I'll make sure that bitch doesn't start talking around town. If she did, it could open up questions and start people going after me. I just don't like it."

"Consider it yesterday's problem."

~

Premature as it was, Tony Pozereli was convinced without even talking to Bradford that his miners in Bear Creek, Montana could have been saved. His battle to convince mine owners all over the country that there was an opportunity to place a small royalty on each ton of mine coal to better protect their employees and families in the event of an accident had fallen on deaf ears. Pozereli knew Roosevelt was singularly focused on not interrupting the production of energy. He couldn't afford to ignite the mine owners. He sighed heavily at the thought of having to tell the widows the best he could do was be an expert witness. He couldn't chance taking sides so openly.

~

The train pulled alongside the well-worn, wooden platform at the rail station. Everything looked like classic Red Lodge, with coal-covered miners or wives waiting for a loved one, and a handful of Crows sitting on the weather-stripped benches. There was one exception.

Pozereli was dressed in an incongruous gray flannel, double-breasted suit, starched white shirt accented by a paisley tie, and a pocket-handkerchief. The outfit wasn't only dreadfully hot on a blistering late July day, but prompted condolences for what must be a man waiting for a casket.

Alice was the first to spot the distinguished figure. "Mr. Pozereli, what are you doing in Red Lodge?" she yelled while pulling Delena by the arm.

Pozereli uncrossed his legs and rose slowly, waving the group over to him. His reserved smile signaled their meeting was by design rather than coincidence.

"You've decided to support us. This is fantastic," Alice grabbed and starting pumping Pozereli's hand. The surge of excitement at seeing him there outweighed her customary trepidation. While Alice's nostrils were still flaring she calmed her voice. "I've been thinking about your itinerary, Mr. Pozereli, and—"

Pozereli gulped spastically and absently straightened his tie. "No, ladies." He looked over at Delena. "I'm here to investigate for myself."

Alice dropped his hand. "No attorney?"

"You have to understand, that isn't our role. I can serve as a…"

Alice reeled back in astonishment. "If defending the unnecessary deaths of union members isn't your role, what the hell is?"

Pozereli paused with a distinct look of embarrassment on his face. He reached out and gently took Delena's hand. "I'm sure the truth will prevail. Let's take this a step at a time."

Already kicking herself for believing he'd really come to help, Alice ignored that last comment. "Town publisher is Tom Lloyd," she snapped. "Make sure you let him know why you're in town."

~

Protocol dictated that Pozereli's first contact in his investigation would be Lawrence Bradford. It took him no time at all to realize that the dusty road he was driving on was the site of the accident. It wasn't treacherous. Without talking to anyone outside of getting directions, he found Lawrence Bradford at the engine house's administrative office.

The mine owner was huddled in a quiet conversation with a coal-covered miner whose helmeted head was bobbing up and down in agreement. Bradford left Pozereli waiting in a chair behind the glass wall while he completed his instructions to the employee.

"Mr. Pozereli, it's a surprise to see you way out here in Montana," his smile big as the Montana sky. "I wish you would have given me some notice. We're working around the clock."

Pozereli's eyes darted around the near-empty building. "Would you be too busy to show me around? I'd like to go in the mine and see the area where the accident occurred." Tired from the trip and a little on edge after the altercation with Alice and Delena, Pozereli just wanted to get his facts and be done.

Bradford's smile diminished just a touch and his expression became guarded. "That part of the mine is demolished, closed off after the explosion. We were digging over a million tons a year, doin' our part for the war effort. Doin' half that now. If we could go down tomorrow, I'll show you the rest of the mine and have you meet whoever you want."

Pozereli weighed his options, then decided it was the best he could do. He nodded. "I'd like to talk to each of the other shift foremen who had that job before and during the blast."

Bradford swallowed hard. "No problem, except if you want the same guys that'll be tough since they both quit after the disaster. I lost a lot of men after that tragic accident for a thousand different reasons. The real issue, though, was their wives were afraid to send them back down. Mining's always been a dangerous business. I don't need to tell you that."

"Do you know how I can contact those men?" Pozereli queried in a non-threatening voice.

Bradford shrugged. "I think they both moved away, since this mine is what keeps the town alive. Without Bear Creek Mine all you'd find in these parts are ghost towns. This community needs these mines to stay alive. Not much work, otherwise."

"You must have records or something."

"Sure. Everybody in a town this small knows what everybody else is doing. We'll be able to track them down. Would you do me the honor of having dinner at my house tonight?"

"I'd be delighted. You should know, however, the union's looking into the entire issue, including the widows who are pursuing a sizable settlement from you. I don't think I'd make very enjoyable company."

"I heard about that. I'm convinced you haven't been given the full and real picture. 'Course, that's up to you to decide. Is seven o'clock a good time?"

Pozereli was reluctant but there was no way around it without offending Bradford further. "That'll be fine. And yes, I'd like a tour of the mine tomorrow and to have a short meeting with your stewards and foremen."

~

Tom Lloyd leaped like an electrical current just traveled through his typewriter keys to his fingertips when Alice threw open the front door of his newspaper strewn office. "I'm on deadline. Not now!"

She moved piles and took a seat, ignoring his outburst. "Here's the news. United Mine Workers of America believes us, even if you don't. Fact is Union President Tony Pozereli is here at the Pollard Hotel right now to talk to everybody and find out for himself how Bradford's been getting away with all the bullshit for so long."

The publisher's pecking fingers froze mid-air. He sat back and locked both hands behind his head, looking at her intently. "You got me. And how are you, Miss Beck? It's been so quiet since you left. By the way, did Mrs. Harrison file a complaint yet? I don't have a thing until she does."

"Over three million dollars on behalf of all the survivors, not just the widows. All we need is an attorney to get it going."

"That could be expensive," he said with raised eyebrows.

"If it takes every last dime of my savings, we're going to win this thing."

A small, tight smile flitted across Lloyd's face. Maybe this time, Bradford would finally get what he deserved. "The minute you get an attorney and officially file, let me know. Now that is a story I'll run on the front page."

"Don't know how long Pozereli will be here. You'd better hustle over to the hotel." Having made her point, Alice disappeared as abruptly as she arrived.

Turning his attention back to the front-page story about the upcoming annual rodeo, Lloyd's mind kept wandering to the possibility of the first legitimate story he'd written since his days as an investigative reporter. If those women were right, there was no telling how big this story could be. As soon as he was able to wrap up the rodeo piece, Lloyd took off to find Pozereli. He didn't get as much information as he'd hoped, though. Pozereli volunteered little to answer

Lloyd's questions, except to confirm that the union was adequately concerned with the plight of the mine disaster survivors that it warranted further investigation. He remained cautious not to indict Lawrence Bradford, singularly focusing his comments on the role of the union to continually improve health and safety standards for its members. The union president did capitalize on the opportunity to espouse the critical need for improved safety regulations regardless of the demands of the war effort.

While the man's reserve frustrated Lloyd, he came away from the interview confident that a man of his position wouldn't have followed Mrs. Harrison back to Red Lodge if he wasn't suspicious about major violations leading to the death of seventy-four men.

At that moment Lloyd realized the tragedy of the Bear Creek Mine disaster would be his ticket back to legitimate journalism and national recognition.

Chapter 30

"Vinnie, it's got to look like she had an accident," Bradford told him. "You'll be well-paid only after her death raises no suspicions."

It was an insult. He just nodded at Bradford, holding his tongue even though he could feel the anger rising in him like an Italian volcano. That was the kind of comment you made to an amateur you picked up from the streets. Of course, he could more than manage that. She could slip in the bathroom, inadvertently fatally hitting her head like a client's cheating wife. Or, she could have an accident outdoors. He'd done it before. He could even break her neck falling down the stairs, just like his mother when he was sixteen. She could be given an intravenous amount of insulin creating a massive coronary, just like the bank president in Chicago, rubbed out by a too-anxious executive vice president.

But the killer said none of these things, enjoying his own imagination working on another perfect crime in a home he was amazed existed in Red Lodge. He was a little afraid of the man sitting opposite him, even though they'd done business once before. He'd heard too many chilling stories about him, and had reason to believe them.

The Italian said nothing, studying his client. He always studied his clients. Finally he spoke. "If you leave the method up to me, I think you'll be impressed with the results. Who's the target?"

"A nobody who had the misfortune of overhearing a conversation I had with the late Mr. Wellington. She might have nothing, but we've got a vicious bitch after us who could turn a civil case into a criminal one in a hurry. No reason to take any chances. First I have to make sure she hasn't spoken about the call before I give you the okay."

"I don't wait around places like this," he gave a sidelong glance at Bradford's log-burning fireplace bordered by floor-to-ceiling book-cases. "Not where I could be noticed. You've got one day to get an answer or I'm gone."

Bradford's nostrils flared, but he didn't argue. "Where are you staying?"

"Does it matter? One day and I'll find you. Get me her address so I can see her, the neighborhood, and the house."

~

Since making the reckless call to Lawrence Bradford, Lillian Hutton had reconsidered attempting to contact him again. The decision wasn't hard. Disturbed dreams and sweat-pooled sheets, night after night. Always the same nightmare: she was in her kitchen mixing up an apple pie while humming, "You're nobody 'til somebody loves you," when there was a faint knock at the door.

"I'll be right there," she would yell as she untied her bright floral cooking apron and quieted her yapping poodle. She shuffled to the front door. An enormous shadow with no face pushed past her, grabbing her from behind into the bathroom where a full tub of icy water was soon nearly overflowing. He forced her head to the tub floor. She awakened each time gasping for breath, soaked in sweat.

She'd told no one of the call she overheard. Somehow today she was going to lay Lawrence Bradford's mind to rest. His polite conversation with Howard Wellington had nothing to do with the poor man's accident.

~

Except for the cruel glares and vicious innuendoes the man's wife endured during the meal, dinner at Bradford's house had gone without incident. Afterward, Bradford and Pozereli retired to the library for nightcaps and cigars.

Bradford directed Pozereli to a sitting area away from the formality of his desk. "I don't get it, Tony. Why would you want to jump into a mess like this? I've got a pretty good reputation ya know, in Washington."

"Mr. Bradford, I'm not the careless type." He gave Bradford a slow appraising look. "I thoroughly read the coroner's inquest. I talked at length to your legal counsel and made sure I had the needed background from the survivors to draw an opinion," Pozereli sat up rigidly in the firm, high-backed fabric chair and helped himself to a glass of whiskey from the crystal decanter on the coffee table.

"You and I never talked about your concerns!"

Pozereli's eyes widened incredulously. "My concerns, Mr. Bradford, are singular: the health and safety of every member of the union. You aren't the only owner with questionable safety standards during this war. Working conditions for coal miners are deplorable. If these men choose to live this way, that's one thing. But it's your duty and mine to fight for far stiffer safety standards, where a mine is closed down immediately when a problem arises and stays closed until it's fixed." He took a finishing gulp and put the whiskey glass down. "It's that simple."

Bradford leaped to his feet, eyes blazing. "Wait a damn minute! The President has squeezed the hell out of you and me to get that coal. Shit, Tony, I hope you're not confused who the enemy really is.

I provide jobs for nearly everybody in this town. Deliver over one million tons of coal a year to our country and pay the best wages a miner can make in Montana!"

Pozereli shifted uncomfortably in his seat. "I'll certainly take what you've said this evening into consideration," he offered, his tone calm. "News of my investigation hasn't yet hit the national press. Your concerns on what kind of a national mine owners' uproar this could create are legitimate, and frankly deserve my further consideration. I'd like to meet with union representatives and anyone else you deem appropriate at the mine tomorrow."

Bradford raked his fingers through his hair. "Sorry, Tony. I guess I got a little carried away. But damnit, I'm proud of what we do for the miners and our great country. I feel terrible about what happened to those men and their families. It haunts the hell out of me. It's the business I'm in, and every miner that enters that mine knows that one day it could be him."

~

Whatever reservations remained after Bradford's impassioned appeal would have to be set aside, Pozereli concluded. Right now he was savoring a surprisingly elaborate breakfast, served to him in the crystal chandeliered dining room of the Pollard Hotel.

The *Carbon Courier*'s front page headline, "Union President Investigates Mine Disaster," was supported by a comprehensive story recreating the drama of the tragedy and how Delena Harrison had survived the loss of her home and endured vicious, unsubstantiated rumors while crusading for the survivors' rights.

The article quoted Mrs. Harrison and the union president extensively in their common goal to better protect America's coal miners and provide for their survivors. It cited two previous deaths where the families only made ends meet through the generous donations of the mining community.

"Pass the plate and bury the hate," was being replaced by "Fight for the right," the article stated, forecasting that the outcome of the legal battle could change the industry.

As he read further, breakfast lost its appeal for Tony Pozereli. He swallowed hard on the possibility that taking a position could mean a national uproar and his job, regardless of the outcome of the case. He had no reason to pause at the *Courier*'s obituary that reported fifty-seven-year-old Lillian Hutton had died of a massive coronary.

~

Over thirty men gathered around the lunch tables between shifts for a look at the union boss. Two formally dressed attorneys flanked Lawrence Bradford. They were brought along to insure there were no inappropriate comments that could lead to a strike or create further legal problems.

"Men, as you know from today's paper, the union has taken no position, but is further investigating the circumstances leading to the unfortunate incident some seven months ago. I've met with Mr. Pozereli, going over our strict safety standards and the fair hearing at the coroner's inquest where any questions of misconduct were fully addressed. Nothing was wrong. We returned to full speed so you'd have no paycheck interruption and we could get back to what we're doing to help win this war. I, ah, I'm proud of every man here. If you find anything that threatens your safety, my door is always open. We'll fix it, even if it means shutting down operations temporarily. Mr. Pozereli," he concluded, waving him up to join him standing on the bench seat.

Pozereli slowly hoisted his rounded frame up onto the bench and looked out over the faces for an uncomfortably long time before beginning his remarks. "Men, I don't need to caution you of the dangers you live with each day." He turned and reached an open palm out in the mine owner's direction. "I've heard Mr. Bradford's appreciation for the important role each of you is playing in the war effort. I don't disagree, and, like him, I think you should be proud of what you're doing for our country.

He raised his voice to an oratory level for impact. "Without a union, you would have no voice in what precautions are taken in handling and storing explosives, the integrity of the ceilings and walls that shield you from being buried alive, the air passages and escape routes you need. Fire needs oxygen to burn. You need the union to survive the daily threat of poisonous gases. I challenge anyone to find an industry that needs to be protected by a union more than yours."

The crowd broke into applause.

"The mission of your union is to protect your welfare and your loved ones. I can tell you without reservation that we aren't doing a good enough job. Whose fault is it? The mine owners? The union? Are you afraid of losing your job if you speak up? Is our great country placing unrealistic demands on the amount of coal we produce daily, weekly, annually? I put forth that we all have a role in creating the conditions that killed seventy-four men and boys here just a few months ago."

Pozereli scrutinized facial features for clues. "Be honest with me and yourself as I take a few moments to explore what happened and what is happening today. Mr. Bradford is right in much of what he says. After further discussions with him, I feel I, ah, we, may have been premature in taking any position until there is a further exploration into the possibility of misdoing."

Bradford hurried to pat fellow speaker Tony Pozereli on the back but the union leader jerked away. Lawrence Bradford's earlier one-way discussions with union stewards and foremen had left a lingering dark shadow.

Bradford's hovering attorneys blocked any potential private conversations with the union president after the mine tour. Bad strategy. Pozereli was beginning to feel manipulated. By the end of the visit, the union president suspected from the too-similar responses to his probing questions that every meeting was scripted. The less he was told, the more he learned. Shifting eyes, a tripped word. All clues sought after and found.

He'd made the right decision to come to Red Lodge regardless of the outcome, he thought, before settling into a restless sleep that night.

Chapter 31

The all white and silver examining room, two miles from his law office, was the perfect sterile setting for Robert's doctor's pathetic bedside manner. Robert Ren tried to prepare himself for the sleepy-eyed physician's preliminary diagnosis of his x-rays.

"Cancer. Cancer. I'll be dead in a month, just like mom," Robert said under his breath. The doctor's voice grew more and more distant. The horrors were rolling in like near-black rain clouds.

"And pancreatic cancer is a highly malignant disease, the greatest killer of all forms of cancer," Robert's doctor said without even raising an eyebrow. "Nasty. It often sentences its victims to death, usually even before it's diagnosed. The organ is hidden behind the stomach, the small intestine, bile ducts, gall bladder, liver, and the spleen. The signs of pancreatic cancer resemble those of many other illnesses, with virtually no evidence of the killer in the early stages," he droned on.

Robert felt like he wandered into someone else's nightmare. A wave of terror welled up in his belly.

"Robert, are you comprehending what I'm saying? What stage you're in?" his doctor blandly asked.

"A stage of firing a doctor with the sensitivity of a longshoreman. It's my life we're talking about here, not some case!" Robert stormed out of the still-passive physician's office with such speed that a pile of paperwork on the edge of the receptionist's desk went flying as he whisked by.

Robert Ren was still in the early stages from what little the medical world could tell. He resolved to live every day he had left, healing his heart and soul.

Abdominal pains came and went for short intervals day and night during the cross-country drive in his new white Plymouth Special DeLuxe convertible to Red Lodge. Soon they became prolonged, creating a severe stabbing pain that radiated to his back.

He'd read that before hospitalization the blockage of the bile duct would create jaundice, a yellowing of the skin. His mother's rapid decline caused by lung cancer took her in less than two months, and the similarities were beginning to look too familiar.

"I'll leave after the trial so Alice doesn't have to endure any more pain," he said out loud to himself as he crossed the Montana state line.

When Robert returned to his father's home it was as though he'd never left. Of course, that meant it was still like he'd never arrived. He only took time to unpack his bags before tearing up the Beartooth Highway to Alice's cabins.

Her mud-dressed truck made him smile. Autumn leaped from a stretched-out position on the main cabin porch to an upright barking attack position. Robert waited in his car for signs of life. No one came out so he ambled up to the steps with friendly locked-eye contact and an open palm to Autumn, who finally stopped yapping and licked his hand.

Robert knocked, and knocked again.

"There's no one here you want to see," the familiar voice yelled through the closed door. Robert could hear Clara being hushed inside.

"Delena, it's about your court case. Open up."

Robert shrugged his shoulders. Of course, he'd hoped for a better reception, but the idea that Alice was still angry that he left the train so abruptly wasn't really a surprise. Too discouraged to fight, he returned to his car without looking back at faces he could sense were in the windows. A moment later, he gunned the car back to his father's house.

Feeling a little better after a night's rest, Robert sat down to examine his situation. There was no question in his mind that if he let it go on, Alice was stubborn enough to exile him for days, even months, he didn't have. He made arrangements for flowers to be delivered to Alice every afternoon by a young man who worked at Red Lodge's library. Sometimes Robert would pick August wildflowers for a change, anticipating that Alice wasn't much for the domestic floral varieties most women would ogle over.

On the seventh uninterrupted day of delivery he decided to deliver the flowers himself. He knew he'd have to prepare himself for a battle that would make fighting the Nazis child's play. He pulled into the dirt drive and turned his car into the center of a dust explosion when his foot leaped to the brakes. Along the cabin's dirt road he found six dead flower bunches, each propped up in a can with no water, lined in a row.

He stopped himself from getting worked up, burst out laughing, and then proceeded into enemy territory. That Alice was one tough woman! Delena, Clara, and Autumn were not around from what he could see on his approach. Alice's pickup was there.

There was no sound of movement inside in response to his repeated knocks. On a hunch, he took off down the well worn path toward the creek. There she was, just as he'd suspected. A small smile lit his face.

"Just what do you think you're doing?" Alice yelled from the center of the stream, reeling in her fly-fishing line.

Robert turned to the small figure in full fly fishing regalia. With the rolled up sleeves of her drab green men's military fatigue shirt and her short-cropped uncombed hair, she looked more like a seasoned Montana fishing guide than the elusive woman of his pursuit. "Now don't go nuts on me, Miss Beck," he yelled back without smiling. "I had to fill in for the delivery guy today. Have you got an empty metal can somewhere I can put these in?"

Ignoring his jest, she pulled out some line and dropped the rabbit-hair nymph strategically above one of the low river's many rock pool hideaways for rainbow and cutthroat trout. Seconds later she jerked the pole straight up, insuring she'd set the hook into tomorrow's breakfast. The fish was quickly tucked into the plastic-lined fish bag on her shoulder and the line was dropped to float past the same spot for her third catch in the six-foot long hole.

"Hey, remember me? I'm the guy on the train that worships your body. Ring a bell yet, Colonel?"

His persistence and unyielding positive attitude finally pulled her attention from the river, only after she was convinced she had temporarily drained the hole. She stomped out of the water, splashing what she could on his dry clothes.

"You can't shake me off that easily, Miss Beck. I'm here to convince you, by heroic deeds if necessary, that I'm a knight who can be trusted now and forevermore." He laughed while standing at military attention.

His antics failed to get her to turn around before entering the main cabin. Unwilling to relinquish the game, he knocked once, then again. "An important message for Colonel Beck. Urgent! Answer the door immediately!"

He waited but there was no sound. Robert took a step back, like he was leaving and the door flew open. With arms folded the fisherman waited.

He fought back a smile. "I've got it here somewhere. Don't panic. I'll tell you what. Just in case of such predicaments I've memorized the message. It was too important to chance losing. Are you ready, Colonel?"

The door closed in his face.

Damn, she was stubborn! "Okay, if I'm forced to yell it through the door, I will!"

Alice opened the door again as soon as the yelling momentarily stopped. "What is it you have to say? Say it and get the hell out of here, Ren."

"Even your sweet enchanting comments won't stop critical war messages, Colonel. I've been instructed to tell you that Sergeant Robert Ren is madly in love with you and will do anything you say, including going to hell if that's where you prefer, Ma'am."

"Took the words right out of my mouth, Sergeant!" she snapped and again slammed the door an inch from his nose. Her one mistake was the smile that unknowingly began to sneak up on the corners of her lips and in her eyes before she could make her final exit. That glimpse of a smile warmed his heart.

"I'll just leave these flowers for the can right here on the porch. If you want to reach me, I'll be in hell until I can kiss you again, Colonel."

The next morning, Robert drove past the cabin to find six, not seven, cans with dead flowers.

Chapter 32

Delena was nearly out of time. School for Clara would be starting soon. She still had most of the money left from the settlement, enough to make a small down payment on a modest home in Red Lodge. Besides, she grew more uncomfortable every day with Alice's unqualified generosity, and a little uncomfortable about the way Alice's relationship with Clara had quietly blossomed into a second mother kind of dependence. There was no way the little bit of mending Alice allowed her to do for her could repay the cost of supporting a household of three, even if Alice insisted it was the most satisfying experience she'd known since leaving nursing.

Knowing the subject of her leaving would be as hard on her daughter as their benefactor, Delena slipped away for a few hours to explore Red Lodge's housing market. Her dreams of an elegantly simple home in High Bug were doused quicker than a brush fire in the front yard of the fire station. Even the one-room houses recently moved by flatbed truck from the rapidly abandoned Washoe and Bear Creek mining communities came at too high a price.

With guarded optimism about the outcome of the trial at some undetermined future date, she and Clara would need to get settled before school resumed. Delena sipped a cup of coffee alone at the Red Lodge Cafe as she re-examined the few sale and rental listings in the *Carbon Courier*.

"Ya look to be a bit lost, lass." A deep familiar voice rang out from the table behind Delena. Her husband's longtime Scottish friend, Sean Campbell, sat down at Delena's table. He patted her head like one of his hounds. "A man goes through a lot, but nothin' hurts like watchin' a woman in pain. You gunna tell me what ya up to now?"

"I've got to find a place for me and Clara to live. We can't even afford a shack," she said with a sigh. Tears formed in her bright hazel eyes.

"Don't let it bother ye, lassie. Still got a sewing machine?"

"No. I don't even have a way to make a living. I lost that in the fire, too. I've been afraid to use what little money I have on one."

"Enough of this. Aye, lass, ya never had a meal from my Bertha. You'll never live on tatties and porridge as long as the Campbells are around. We'll 'ave a grand meal with howtowdie, hairst bree, cabbieclaw and skirlie. You and the wee one will be our guests of honor this Saturday."

"I, I don't know."

"See ya at seven, lass," the Scot said as he returned to his hearty breakfast.

Delena knew she could build a business if she had a sewing machine. She could work right out of her home, making skirts, blouses, and even dresses in the latest European fashions for the High Bugs, maybe even sell some of the clothes in neighboring towns. But the idea could only work with a sewing machine.

After eliminating Little Italy, Finntown, Slavtown, and Little Norway from consideration due to their reputation as generous but closed societies, Delena was forced to consider the Dirty Thirty she had abhorred since her youth. The four-street neighborhood had always been home to transients and the unemployed. Before widows started moving their houses from Washoe and Bear Creek, there were thirty houses all in need of a firehouse hosing down and more than one coat of paint.

None of Delena's longtime friends or her daughter's classmates knew any of the unfortunates forced to live in squalor before the mining disaster. After obtaining a key and walking through one of the filthy hovels, she rushed to her car, crying all the way back to the cabin. As hard as it must have been for the widow families moving in to the Dirty Thirty, at least Clara would be able to find friends facing the same humiliation.

Delena allowed herself two more weeks before she and Clara would leave Alice's house. On learning of Tony Pozereli coming to dinner, Delena wisely decided to delay the news until she had the courage to put a deposit down on a home. The cost of rentals had skyrocketed when the army of widows simultaneously began to search for less-expensive accommodations. Most of the houses being moved to the Dirty Thirty were being bought by a handful of well-to-do people in town for an unrealistically inflated resale price.

~

In appreciation of the publisher's well-balanced story, Alice stopped by Tom Lloyd's office to invite him to join Tony Pozereli for dinner at her cabin. While it sounded more like an order than an invitation, he hesitatingly agreed. A healthy share of the criticism was being laid at the union's doorstep for being ineffective in gaining government support to pressure the mine company owners into imposing a royalty on coal to better provide for miner safety and family benefits. The dinner would be a perfect setting to probe the union president.

With one of Bradford's men following every movement Alice and Delena made, Alice's visit to the publisher was the impetus Bradford needed for an overdue discussion with Tom Lloyd. Within an hour of her departure he was in Lloyd's office.

"Tom, have you got a minute?" Bradford uncharacteristically inquired.

"Lawrence, perfect timing. I've been meaning to reach you."

"Some crazy rumor is going around town that you're having dinner at Alice Beck's cabin with Tony Pozereli. I knew it couldn't be true, or people could get the wrong impression that the paper is taking a sympathetic position whether there's a trial or not."

"Oh, I think there'll be a trial. Didn't you hear? Robert Ren, the banker's son, is back in town. Guess he's going to be the widows' attorney. He filed a three million dollar suit in Billings yesterday."

Bradford's jaw dropped.

Lloyd shot him a sharp glance. "Fact is, Lawrence, I'm going to have dinner there tonight. I don't see any impropriety in such a thing. I've had dinner at your house, I don't know how many times. What's your point?"

Bradford quickly overcame his surprise. "That front-page story for one thing. I see the President of the United States gets pushed to the back pages, and this bullshit makes front-page headlines. It's your job to at least give this fair coverage. Forget the fact that you and I have been friends for years, doing everything we can to help this community." Although he was struggling to maintain control, there was a slight edge creeping into Bradford's voice.

"Lawrence, you're overreacting." The publisher's face lit up. "Every time somebody has a story about them it's never big enough. I'm not in the public relations business. I'm a reporter. This multi-million dollar civil suit against the main employer in the area is big news that went national when the president of the union decided to take the unprecedented action of providing legal counsel for the plaintiffs. It's a hell of a big story, biggest since the disaster itself, Lawrence. If I don't cover it, the *Billings Gazette* will just take my place." The veins in Bradford's neck stood out in livid ridges. He was using every ounce of energy to contain himself. "It doesn't mean you should be sending signals to everybody that you've taken a position on this. Guilt or innocence is up to a jury, not the media."

"Lawrence, I hear and respect what you're saying. I'll be cautious to write no story that doesn't fairly represent the facts coming out of the trial. That's all I can and should do. Now, if you don't mind, I've got a paper to get out."

"Look, Tom," Bradford finally deflated, "I didn't mean to jump all over you. I've got a lot riding on this and I thought that after all we've done together… I just wanted to know if there was something I've done to upset you."

"Tell you what, Lawrence. Why don't you and I have lunch at the Red Lodge Cafe tomorrow for the whole town to see I never play favorites? We'll discuss what I covered at dinner as I determine what is appropriate."

"That sounds great to me. I knew we could work something—"

"We're not working anything out. I'm just being sure there's no misinterpretation of what I hope to accomplish at this dinner, that's all. It's a rare opportunity to talk to Pozereli about the big picture besides the upcoming trial."

Bradford nodded his head in agreement and left to learn a little more about Lillian Hutton's sudden heart attack. He couldn't help but smile at the fact that her name hadn't and wouldn't come up with the publisher or anyone else he knew.

~

"I barely have enough plates that match for us, let alone having enough for presidents and publishers," Alice said to Delena, as if the dinner was her idea.

"Alice, I know you don't like me to use his name, but Robert—"

"Don't use that name around this house."

"Wait a minute," Delena said. "Stop a second and sit down." She pulled Alice to the small kitchen chair. "I have an idea that will save the day, if you'll just stop being bullheaded long enough to listen." Delena took the unprecedented liberty of putting her finger on Alice's lips to hush up her interruptions. "You can be so impossible. I don't know why I love you so much. Now please shut up for just a minute. I don't know what Ro—that man—has done to deserve your wrath for everything that's gone wrong in your life, but I'll tell you this, I think he's one of the kindest and certainly most patient men I've ever known. He's offered to be our attorney and I've gratefully accepted."

Alice finally relaxed, delighted in her companion's uncharacteristic assertive behavior. "What's your idea?"

"I've got to believe that Mrs. Ren had some of the finest china and silverware in Red Lodge just sitting there covered in layers of dust. If you'd allow it, I'd like to go to Robert and ask to borrow what we need. We don't have much time."

Alice absently ran an open palm over her mouth and off her chin. "Have to admit, Delena, that's a good idea, the attorney thing, I mean. Why don't you take Clara with you? She's starting to go crazy with only Autumn to play with."

Delena did just as Alice suggested and loaded the car, humming happily along the way to Robert's house. Once she pulled up, the house looked so different she took a moment to recheck the address. She hadn't been there since she and Alice took a sneak peek some time ago. With a new light yellow color accented by bright white on all the gingerbread trim and porch, it looked like a new home, complete with landscaping that competed with the well-tended houses in the neighborhood.

"Good for you, Robert," she yelled as she approached the front door.

"Delena!" Robert appeared from behind an enormous hedge with gardening tools in each hand.

"Robert," she smiled warmly as he approached, "you're invited to dinner tonight at Alice's cabin."

"Really? Are you sure about that?"

She nodded, still grinning.

"All right," he returned the smile, "I'm not going to question anything. You bet I'll be there. Is there anything I can bring?"

"As a matter of fact, there is."

~

It wasn't quite two hours before the guests were due to arrive. Alice's temper had grown explosive and she stormed around the cabin, waiting for the dinnerware to arrive from Robert's house. Delena had only changed her story slightly, leaving out the part about Robert being the fifth guest, since Clara would be eating before they arrived so she could retire early with Autumn to the guest cabin.

The roar of a familiar engine sent Alice flying to the window. She pulled up the window sash and leaned out.

"Delena, you told me someone was delivering everything, not Robert." She caught herself before Robert got out of the car.

"Oh, I forgot to tell you he's having dinner with us too," Delena smiled broadly. "It looked like you were preparing enough to feed a barracks full of soldiers."

"We don't even have enough chairs!"

"I've thought of that. We'll get a couple from the other cabin. I know…"

The knock at the door was followed by Robert letting himself in, his arms full of the first of many loads of formal serving settings, tablecloth, silver candelabras and even a small serving table that would allow more room at the dining table.

Robert was dressed in a re-tailored dark pinstriped suit that no longer draped over his thin frame, but now stylishly accented his lean build. "My lady, would you consider wearing that simple black dress you look so gorgeous in?" Robert said with a smiling persistence that pried Alice's lips upward.

"Robert Ren, you are impossible. Considering my options, I guess I'll have to dress as inappropriately as you," Delena said.

Alice followed close behind, her arms full of boxes. "For God sakes," Alice snapped. "Come on, people, we're in a cabin. This isn't the Waldorf. We aren't kids playing dress up. This is just a measly cabin." She looked around in embarrassment over her foolishness in having the dinner at her modest retreat from the outside world.

"It'll be just the kind of novel experience Tony Pozereli will take back to his friends at home as he describes the Wild West and a crazy beautiful woman who lives by a river in the mountains," Robert beamed. "He'll love it."

The three worked madly, closely following Alice's direction on how to set a formal table. They finally finished everything with plenty of time for Alice to somewhat calmly get herself ready. Robert shuttled two glasses of wine into her bedroom just as Alice was stepping into her slip.

"Robert Ren! Get the hell outta here."

Robert set the glass down on her nightstand. "Just a little something to tame the tiger."

Chapter 33

The three greeted their guests like the dinner was a common occurrence. Robert couldn't have been more insightful as the dinner party grew to a high pitch of laughter and storytelling. A magic atmosphere enveloped the evening. Flickering light from the candelabras and fireplace danced across their pleasured faces.

Tony Pozereli snatched Alice's hand and kissed it. "The dinner was superb," he assured her, taking the last bite of his second helping of roast pork with applesauce.

"As a former lieutenant colonel in the Army, I have to admit I get privileged classification for everything, from the amount of gas I can purchase to the meat I can buy," Alice said, relieved the subtle lighting hid her blushing.

"You're a woman of many surprises," Tom Lloyd added. "One minute you're a paratrooper and the next a beautiful hostess and gourmet cook."

Knowing how difficult it was for Alice to be the center of attention, Robert diverted the conversation to the intended topic of the evening.

"Mr. Pozereli, I have to admit I was surprised by how fast you came to Red Lodge to validate what we told you."

"Please pardon me when I tell you that the union's concerns are far larger than the tragedy that occurred here. I've been trying to get an appointment with President Roosevelt for some time to demand the government take steps, if necessary, to better protect our coal and mineral miners. It hasn't gotten me anywhere. I guess, understandably, he has other priorities. He needs that coal and that's all that seems to matter." Pozereli shook his head in frustration.

"So, do you think that the successful outcome of this civil suit could change the focus long enough to get what you're after?" Tom Lloyd asked.

"The thought crossed my mind, particularly after Miss Beck got through filling me in on all that's happened since the disaster. It's the worst one we've had in three years."

"What could Roosevelt do?" Robert asked Pozereli, not moving his eyes from Alice's still-flaming face.

"It might sound ridiculous, but I believe there's about to be a national strike that will stop the production of all coal right when Uncle Sam needs it most. If that happens, Roosevelt could put in force the Smith Connelly Act, allowing the federal government to intervene into private business if it threatens the security of the country. I think we're going to win this war, and, please don't misinterpret," Pozereli said as he glanced at the publisher, "but we have to get national attention now while coal serves such a vital role. I assume, Mr. Lloyd, that insight was off the record?"

"I appreciate what you're saying. I'm not here to write a story tonight and I assure you no one will be given any information that suggests you have anything other than miners' welfare at stake."

"That's what I'm talking about."

"I, too, see this as a story larger than Bear Creek Mines. I plan to submit all stories relating to the trial to the national press. Is there anything more you want to say officially relating to your support?"

"I intend to return for opening testimony and spend a lot of time in Red Lodge throughout the trial until we insure that justice has been done," the union president said with a tone that ended further discussion of the matter.

The two men moved their conversation to the high-backed chairs by the fireplace as Delena insisted on washing the dishes and serving coffee. She not-too-subtly nudged Alice and Robert to the outside porch. The night sounds of birds, crickets and Rock Creek filled the air.

"Your father mind you clearing out his kitchen?" Alice asked.

"Alice, we have to quit fighting like this. Life is so short. With all the time we lost, every day counts. I don't care what you say or do, I love you."

Alice tensed at his words. "Don't say that."

"Bullshit. Every day I live I'm going to do something to prove it to you."

Alice turned away, then back. She took a chest-deep breath. "I compared one man after another to you. Can you begin to understand what I'm saying? Robert, I finally found peace with myself, by myself. You can see how I've changed."

"Yes, I can see. I still see a woman helping people in need, just like you did for me. I see a woman who's lived alone long enough to think she not only doesn't need men, but almost everybody else as well. Words like 'I'm sorry' don't help either of us. I lived in a dark world without you."

"You had a family!"

"Yeah, a daughter I love very much, Alice." He reached for her hand. "Please let the past go. It's our destiny to be together. Stop fighting it."

"I'm not the one who is passionate one minute, then only wants to be friends the next."

He put his arm around her slim waist. Electric pleasures raced through him from even the slightest touch. Alice immediately moved her hand to his upper outer leg, responding in full to his gestures. Robert quickly arose, pointing to shimmering moonlight on Rock Creek.

"Seems like Rock Creek has always been a part of my life," he said, looking away from her lost expression.

"When you were in the hospital in France, you told me about what the river meant to you when your parents were fighting. I guess moving here was a way of getting close to you, even though I thought we'd never see each other again." Alice snuggled both arms around his waist, noticing how thin he had become. This time, she didn't let him pull away.

"It's getting late. I'd better go," Tom Lloyd said quietly to the entwined couple from behind.

"Me, too," Tony Pozereli added as the two said their good-byes and headed toward the parked cars. The publisher lingered long enough to steal another glance at Delena Harrison.

As their guests drove away, Robert joined Delena in the last of the cleanup, leaving Alice on the porch to enjoy the soft summer night.

"Robert, Clara and I will be leaving soon," Delena admitted. "I don't know when the right time is to tell Alice. For the last two days I've tried, but with you out of the picture, I've been afraid to leave her alone again. She could go right back into that shell. She deserves more."

"Delena, I have something I need to tell you, too. But under no condition can you tell Alice."

Chapter 34

The next morning Delena found Alice at her favorite fishing hole, fifty yards up-river, well into catching their breakfast trout. Delena carefully sidestepped mud, balanced on rocks and swerved around branches until she reached the river's edge.

"Alice, would you help me look for a house today? School starts soon, and we need to get everything settled in for Clara."

Alice winced. "Is it that time already? I've been thinking. I could take her to and from school every day. It's not far. Besides, there isn't much that has to be done to the other cabin to winterize it."

Delena's toes felt the water's edge. "You've already done more for me than anybody ever has. If my parents were still alive, they couldn't have done more. I don't know how long it will take to pay you back."

Suddenly, Alice lost her interest in fishing. The thought of the Harrisons leaving panicked her to the point of nausea. "There's no need to pay me back. Told you that already. Clara is going to need school clothes. Let's go to Billings, shopping."

"Alice, I have to start taking care of myself." Delena put her wrist to her cheek to catch a tear. "This is really scary for me. I need your support."

Alice didn't look over. It hurt too much to see Delena so vulnerable. "Suppose you've already been out looking."

"There isn't a lot to choose from in Red Lodge. I did see a place in the Dirty Thirty I—"

"Dirty Thirty! Okay, let's find something together. Don't go rushing into anything." Alice shook her head and mumbled something about Dirty Thirty all the way back to the cabin.

~

After only a half-day of searching, Alice shared Delena's reality of where she'd be forced to live if she insisted on being self-sufficient. Rather than persist in offering the cabin, Alice silently decided to once again draw off of her dwindling savings before the first snow fell to winterize the second cabin in case Delena found the experience too degrading for her and Clara.

A week later Delena found a place for the two of them. Alice's reservations were minor compared to Clara's, who was too young to be sensitive to Delena's vulnerable state as she declared her new home a "dump" that only "hobos" would live in.

Delena's only reprieve from what felt like an engulfing nightmare came the Saturday night before she was to move. The day of her move was also when she was to begin her daily journey to Billings for jury selection in the long-awaited civil suit.

~

While indistinguishable from the road, each ethnic neighborhood in Bear Creek buzzed with native language, music. The aroma of garlic, sauerkraut, or something else wafted in the air.

As Delena parked and walked through the area alone where thirteen Scottish homes were huddled, she heard the boisterous singing of "The Bonnie Banks O'Loch Lomond" by, what sounded like a slightly inebriated chorus of male voices.

The majority of the Scots who settled near Bear Creek and Washoe had migrated from Pennsylvania, Ohio, and Wyoming. The most solid Scottish settlement "Over the Hill", as the Washoe and Bear Creek areas were called, was Caledonia. Near the Bear Creek Mine itself was another settlement mostly made up of Scots. In addition to migrating from other states, a handful of the Scottish miners came directly from the hills and glens of Scotland. As was the case with most of the area's immigrants, the father would come first, accumulate enough money for ship's passage for the family and then send his precious earnings home. In some cases, quite a few years elapsed before enough could be saved to reunite the family.

The Scots were the mining towns' most infamous Europeans. With rugged independent spirits, they were openhearted and open-handed to a fault, great lovers and even better drinkers. With a national disposition to wandering and adventure, only a fraction of Scots stayed on home soil in the late 1800s and early 1900s as they sought out more agreeable climates and dependable work. Scots could be found exploring and leading on nearly every continent in the world.

Sean Campbell had come with his family directly from the Inverness Highlands near Loch Ness. He was a classic-looking Scot from head to toe, with long unruly blond hair and mischievous aquamarine blue eyes always in search of a little fun.

"The House of Campbell produced cowards and turncoats. They lay down for the English like grovelling dogs. Betrayin' their own kind."

"You don't know wha' you're talking about, as usual, Roy. 'Twas the Campbells that stood up to the English. 'Twas the House of Stuart that turned coat."

"Campbell, you're an idiot, and your clan is spit upon in Scotland."

The last insult had gone too far. Delena's host planted his fist in his neighbor's face with such gusto his friend was lifted off his feet and over the railing of Campbell's porch, landing in the freshly turned chrysanthemum bed. He lay there still as his opponent folded his burly arms, relishing his perfect contact and waiting to see how long Stuart would lay unconscious. He finally looked up from his gaze at his dinner guest.

"Don't let it bother ye, lass. I've given him much worse," Campbell grunted. Stuart slowly arose and headed home to the house next door.

Delena couldn't believe how the men were fighting over things that had happened hundreds of years before. Reading her surprised expression, the Scot assured her that when you got any two Scots together they would fight over an empty glass.

Tales of Campbell bravery, accented by pictures of the Highlands and a wall-mounted family coat-of-arms, was no disappointment.

"There's nothing like the pure guts our Scots are showing those Germans. The lairds are proving what courage is. More medals for bravery than any regiment in Uncle Sam's Army. There's one thing no one can take away from the Highlanders, their courage in battle."

Delena could visualize what immigrants like the Campbells had given up to chase the American dream. It seemed as though Stuart wasn't the only idiot for leaving a dearly loved homeland rich in family and heritage for a two-room shack steeped in sagebrush and unfulfilled dreams. Their stories and gestures grew louder and more animated with each drained mug of ale.

After the "black bun" dessert, a spicy mixture enclosed in a pastry jacket made from a pound of butter, Delena was about to leave when Mrs. Campbell carried an object from the kitchen drain board covered with a tattered towel, placing it directly in front of her guest.

"My man thought of it, Missy, but all our neighbors put some money in."

Delena pulled off the towel, revealing a new Singer sewing machine far superior to the one she'd lost. Upon seeing her salvation to self-sufficiency, Delena leapt to her feet in tears, hugging the Campbells one by one, including the two young men whose arms were awkwardly dangling by their sides, their faces bright red. Fighting was one thing. Getting uninhibited hugs from an attractive woman was quite another.

~

Alice focused on the practical issues of Clara's school wardrobe and essentials to start a new household.

"Let's only buy a few clothes. I can make Clara beautiful dresses the likes of which you couldn't even find in Billings," Delena announced, dismissing all the practical necessities on Alice's list like a teenager dreaming of setting up house. It had become obvious too soon after the Harrisons had moved in that Delena's husband had always been the one to struggle with the bills to make his wife's high-fashion fantasy occa-sionally touch reality.

~

Robert rapidly gathered background information and a potential list of witnesses to provide expert testimony supporting Brent Harrison's documented concerns over lax safety standards. While he wasn't able to find any witnesses to corroborate conversations Harrison had with the deceased state mining inspector, he did get professional verification that the gas readings were at unacceptable levels. He worked feverishly to prepare jury instructions in concert with Delena and other widow plaintiffs. Character indictments of Brent and Delena Harrison crept up like uncontrollable weeds, indictments that had to be addressed directly to avert any surprises in the courtroom.

Robert sat nervously on the solitary chair in Delena's rented two-room house, anticipating an emotional torrent. "Delena, I'm nearing the end of my jury instructions. The defense will be doing the same thing for the judge to review before the jury's selected. If he agrees, away we go. There are a few personal items. You know, the rumors. I don't know exactly where to begin."

"Clara, would you leave Robert and me alone for a moment? We've got to talk about some boring legal things."

Robert sighed. "Thanks, Delena."

Delena smiled and smoothed her skirt on her lap. "Shoot!"

Robert winced in stomach pain when he uncrossed his legs, cancer's hourly reminder. "Did your husband drink to excess?"

"He drank like every miner in Bear Creek. Sometimes to excess, but only on the weekends when he was off the job." Delena made a pained expression. "Is something wrong Robert? You're white as a sheet."

He shook his head. "Not a thing. Your husband—"

"He wasn't a drunk, if that's what you mean."

"Did he ever go to work after he had a drink?"

Delena paused and rubbed her chin. "The men worked on rotating shifts. When he was on day shift he never had a drop of course, or afternoon shift from three p.m. to midnight. Sometimes when he was on graveyard he had a couple of drinks early in the evening. Nothing that would affect his judgment."

"If he went to work with alcohol on his breath, the defense can make a case that he did have a drinking problem."

"No way, Robert. I just won't say that. He never drank in excess on a workday. He had a lot of friends who would've testified to that, but most of them died when he did. Oh, there's a Scot named Campbell who was best friends with Brent. He'd tell ya."

"I prefer to suggest that your husband didn't drink on the job and leave it at that. I'll talk to Campbell as a back-up only if there are amendments by the judge to jury instructions." Robert leaned over and patted Delena's knee. "Here's the ugly one. It's been rumored that you had relationships with—"

Delena rushed her hand over her mouth in embarrassment. "Please don't even say that. I met Brent when I was sixteen-years-old. He's the only man I've ever been with." She took a deep, quivering breath. "Nothing pisses me off more than that one. Excuse me."

Robert nodded, trying to keep a rein on his own anger. "You deserve to be pissed off."

Delena looked around to reassure herself that Clara couldn't hear anything, then lowered her voice to a near-whisper. "Even my own daughter was told lies about me at school." The pain in the back of Delena's throat, damming the tears, cut her short.

Robert was ready to change the subject and move on. "Who do you think stole the widows' money and burned your house? Could you have inadvertently left the stove on or done something else to start the blaze?"

"When I left the house there were no lights on. I returned and noticed the living room light was on soon as I pulled up. Did the police reports tell you how I found my house? Everything turned upside down. The money was stolen. As if that wasn't enough, then they burned it down."

"The police reports were sketchy about the break-in, with statements like 'maybe' and 'you were the only witness.' As far as the fire was concerned, it's recorded as an accident, possibly unintentionally started by the home owner."

"Those buggers. Excuse me, Robert, but that chief of police is in Bradford's back pocket like everybody else in this town."

"When you're called to the witness stand, please don't refer to the defendant as anything other than Mr. Bradford," he warned. "You and the widows will inherently have the sympathy of the jury over your loss. This case needs to focus on the liability and damages. Their best bet is to make this a personal vendetta between you and Lawrence Bradford. Let's not let them trap us into that."

In Delena's confusion she'd lost touch with who the plaintiffs really were. The thought that she was only going to be one of fifty-eight widows making their case caused an enormous relieved sigh. She listened closely to Robert's explanation of the courtroom nuances that would likely determine the outcome of the jury's judgment. It didn't take long for Robert to become noticeably weary and he soon took his leave.

Once he was gone, Delena's eyes darted around a dingy room desperately in need of new surfaces from floor to ceiling. Torn, dirty beige burlap served as drapes over windows that hadn't been washed in years. The used ice box and stove Alice had bought from one of the widows leaving town were the only items of value she owned. The old maroon worn cotton sofa and mismatched chair each had more than one leg broken. The double bed Delena and Clara shared would have to do until there was enough money from sewing jobs to get two new singles. She tried to allow Clara privacy to cry over the shock of her surroundings. She couldn't afford tears.

Alice's arrival was well timed; she seemed to have regular premonitions of when Clara needed to be whisked away from frequent depressed moods to the mountains for hikes and meals over a campfire. As Alice looked around the neighboring houses, she concluded that housing on an Indian reservation was better built and kept up than where the Harrison's were forced to live.

After getting through Delena's bear hug, Alice didn't need to ask for her friend; Clara's sobs filled the small house with an emptiness she wouldn't soon forget.

"She hasn't stopped crying for long since we moved in," Delena said in a whisper. "None of her friends from Washoe or Bear Creek have moved over here. The few that are here aren't her age. If I could, I'd find a way to get her over the mountain, but I need all the rationed gas I've got to look for sewing jobs."

"I could use a new winter coat," Alice responded, "and one or two more for Christmas gifts for my friends overseas."

Delena strained to smile. "Great! What style and color?"

Alice looked around the room and slowly responded, "Maroon and brown."

Hearing Alice's voice, Clara stopped her whimpering, and moments later Clara ran to her, throwing both arms around her waist. "It's horrible here, Alice. I hate it."

Alice silently nodded in agreement and led the child out to her truck. "You don't live in a house, or even in this town," she assured the child. "You live at the base of the Beartooth Mountains and the Rock Creek River. That house is only where you sleep. Your friends are close by, and I can get you to them any time you want, starting today," said Alice. With her long dark hair flopped in front of her face, the slender child reminded Alice of Delena. Alice gingerly placed her delicate porcelain hand over her sun-dark wrist. "Let's go to our mountains today."

~

Delena set out for Red Lodge's Little Italy first. The largest of the ethnic communities in Red Lodge, it was known for open hospitality. There was a seat open at any dinner table in Little Italy. Delena turned down invitations at nearly every door. Clinging women hung on every word about the lawsuit and their share of the settlement, but Delena knew it made bad dinner conversation.

"No, no, no dear. I could never afford to have custom clothes made. If there is any sewing to be done I do it myself. I only have one good dress, but why do I need more? Mario wouldn't know what to do with a tailored shirt. If we could afford it, where would he wear it? He wouldn't. It would be too valuable. It would just sit there and turn yellow."

"I understand, Mrs. Dominico. If you ever need…"

"No dear, but if you and your daughter ever want a homemade cannelloni like you've never tasted, there will always be a place at the table waiting for you. I don't care when."

"Please let your neighbors know that I can make clothes faster and for not much more than the cost of fabric."

"Can you make a stitched buttonhole?"

"Yes, I have the attachment with my new machine."

"Now that's something that's got some people needin' it. I'll pass the word."

"Not a lot of money in buttonholes, but thanks." Delena lowered her head and trudged a mile back home.

After a week of Delena's door-to-door solicitation, she was shocked to come away with only a small amount of dress, blouse, and shirt work. However, word of her being the "buttonhole woman" spread quickly among the many family dressmakers in town.

~

Alice sat at her dinner table over a bowl of homemade lentil soup, observing the dark lines under her friend's usually sparkling eyes. Delena's exhaustion and discouragement couldn't be concealed any more than her good moods.

"Really Alice, everything is going great. My sewing business, and Clara."

Alice dropped her spoon on the kitchen table. "Bullshit, Delena Harrison. What we have to do right now is concentrate on winning this trial. The jury's been selected and Robert tells me the trial begins—"

"Next Monday at nine a.m.," Delena seemed to perk up at the thought. "Hope I don't have to get up on the witness stand. Robert has been rehearsing with me, but we both agree the jury has to think about all survivors, not just me. Do you think we have a chance, Alice?"

"From what Tony Pozereli told me before he left, it's going to be a race to see who can track down the foremen that left town. At least the ones who were working with Wellington, like your husband. For some obvious reason, nobody seems to know where they moved. You can be damn sure Lawrence Bradford does."

"You sound like we're going to lose. We can't," Delena gasped breathlessly.

Alice refused to think about it and changed the subject. "'Buttonhole woman' is what I'm hearing around town. It really peeves me. You could be a fashion designer in New York with your talents, and the only business you get in this hell hole is stitching buttonholes."

"I have other work."

"Not enough for you and Clara to live on, especially if you don't win the court case. Plan for the worst."

"You really think so?"

"My money's on the widows. Just being cautious."

"I've been to nearly every home. I didn't really think about how tough everybody has it. People in Red Lodge can't afford the luxury of having their clothes made. Oh, an occasional dress, but Clara and I never had to live on that before. I've tried to find other work."

Alice tried to shake off her pessimistic outlook and be encouraging. "Just one day at a time. You're not alone in this. We're not going to let a drop of rain fall on Clara's head."

Chapter 35

The *Carbon Courier* whetted a national appetite for the mining trial of the century: Desperate widows going head-to-head for millions of dollars against a wealthy prominent mine owner recognized by the President of the United States as a great patriot.

The red brick courthouse building in downtown Billings spanned across half a block at Yellowstone and Broadway. Of the twelve courtrooms in the building, only two were reserved for criminal trials. Land, cattle, and water issues continued to dominate the always backed-up Superior Court caseload.

Because of the enormous interest in the Bear Creek mining disaster, the trial was being held in the largest courtroom, forty feet wide and nearly three hundred feet long. Seats were divided into three blocks, six feet apart, with nine wooden benches to each row. At the front of the courtroom, a raised dais stood behind a six-foot mahogany partition with a high-backed, worn leather chair for the presiding judge.

In front of the dais was a witness stand, a small raised platform, upon which was fixed a reading lectern, and, against the far wall, the jury box, now filled with twelve jurors. In front of the defendant's box were the lawyers' tables.

Montana's most dramatic mining trial was spectacular enough, but the piece de resistance was the defense counsel, Paris Diamond, one of the preeminent criminal and nationally famous civil suit lawyers in the country. In recent years, Diamond had tried only multi-million dollar, celebrity civil cases and he had a remarkable record of success. The Los Angeles attorney's fee was rumored never to be less than five hundred thousand dollars.

Paris Diamond was a thin, emaciated-looking man who seldom smiled or showed any facial expression. His uncompromising hunger could only be seen in his eyes, the antithesis of all other aspects of his demeanor. They were so intense, rapidly scanning everything within range for information, that they hinted madness or genius, or both. He dressed blandly, bringing no attention to himself until he spoke. Where other famous attorneys showcased grand gestures and theatrical intonations and pauses, Paris Diamond was known for his whispering voice, causing a deathly quiet in the courtroom as he wove intricate magic, based on studious attention to every detail contributing to the vindication of infamous clients.

The press speculated furiously about why Paris Diamond agreed to represent the Bradford Mining Company in a remote place like Montana. But behind Diamond's bland manner was a brilliant strategist who'd built his wealth from cases like this one.

While the unassuming attorney had no apparent sexual appetite, he did have an insatiable need for possessions. His mansion in a compound just off Big Sur and Highway 1, several hours by car from his downtown Los Angeles office, was where he spent most of his time.

He also had a plush apartment in Manhattan and another in Zurich, Switzerland. He had over a million dollars, earned by masterfully defending high-profile businessmen with low-profile friends. He trusted few people and had no friends as he dedicated every waking hour of his life to quietly building his lavish lifestyle.

The 1942 Chevrolet Fleetline and a tattered, mostly gray wardrobe were effective diversions from one of the most cunning criminal attorneys on the West Coast. Not bad for a dispossessed Jewish boy brought up by distant relatives in a rough Manhattan neighborhood. With alcoholic guardians who abused him sexually until he ran away at the age of sixteen, Levi Goldstein lived out of garbage cans and street corner handouts until he found work as a delivery boy for the Swartz, Bridge, and Hammerstein Law Firm near Times Square.

The three partners were notoriously cagey, representing many of the underworld's East Coast Mafia leaders in everything from tax evasion charges and drug dealing to murder. As fate would have it, Howard Swartz was bisexual with a penchant for young boys. His selection of the rag-and-filth-covered young man was based mostly on his plans for the lad outside the office.

He worked patiently for two years as a delivery boy, gaining precious inside understanding of criminal law and legal strategies. Swartz often gave in to his wishes of sitting in on a lot of "war room" discussions, which in most cases could have had every attorney in the room disbarred and prosecuted. Levi had, over time, convinced the partners that he was serious in his interest in becoming a lawyer. He finished high school through home study, with high hopes of attending law school in upstate New York in the fall. He had become a trusted companion for all of the firm's attorneys, learning their favorite foods, casual reading material, and other little niceties. He then provided each with those favorites from the generous allowance his lover had provided.

Levi was the hardest working student at the university's college of law, often correlating relevant cases to class assignments and coming up with legal arguments that frequently outmaneuvered his professors. Group discussions on case assignments with his extended family at the law firm gave him a decided advantage over his classmates.

Everything had gone as planned since his graduation. He legally changed his name to Paris Diamond. With Howard Swartz's patronage, he was given cases only successful and experienced lawyers could hope for.

His first highly publicized case, a paternity suit by a secretary who claimed her wealthy boss got her pregnant, was just the big break Paris needed. With only five hundred dollars, he had bribed a heroin-dependent teller at the bank to confess that he was the father. Revealing the young man's nasty little habit was just the incentive needed for the closing testimony clincher Paris had timed to maximize the courtroom drama. The press was sure to eat it up with front-page headlines, and they did.

Paris' partners weren't informed of how he won the case, and they preferred not to know, considering the victory landed them another high-profile client only a few days after the trial.

"I want to open up a West Coast office in Los Angeles as one of the firm's partners," Paris told Howard.

"I think that's an excellent suggestion," said Howard. "I'll do my best to pull it off. I'll make it happen."

Within less than six months, Paris had moved to Los Angeles, opened an office, and started making calls to the leading underworld figures made available to him by Howard.

When Lawrence Bradford contacted Paris to handle the mining disaster civil suit, it took little time for him to surmise that Bradford had arranged the state mining inspector's "accident". It didn't hurt to have a little leverage on your client, particularly when the case was such a high profile one involving women and children. He agreed to take the case for his standard minimum fee.

The only thing missing for drama was a murder. Too bad no one had the investigative sense to link Howard Wellington to the case. He would have returned to criminal law for that one, he thought as he once again straightened the files at his courtroom desk.

Robert Ren, prosecuting attorney, was completely unaware of Diamond's impressive record at first. He had some trepidation when he found out that the highly successful Paris Diamond was defending Lawrence Bradford. Yet, with testimony from two brave miners supporting Harrison's safety concerns, Robert felt even Diamond couldn't stop his victory.

Delena Harrison was seated at the prosecutor's table in a simple summer floral dress Alice had bought her only two blocks away from the courthouse. Even with no jewelry and little makeup she was stunningly beautiful.

In contrast, Lawrence Bradford was dressed more like an attorney than his attorney. He wore an expensive dark blue double-breasted suit and white starched shirt and tie. Lawrence's dress shirts were all personally tailored for him in New York, complete with French cuffs and his initials stitched in small letters on his shirt pocket.

As Delena gave a nervous glance over at the defendant's table, she was momentarily confused by who was the attorney and who were the defendants. Diamond caught her in his peripheral vision, and turning to her, he shot back a stare that burned right into her soul. She jerked back with a spontaneous deep breath.

"That little man scares me," she whispered to Robert.

"Me, too," Robert said with a smile.

Chapter 36

Tom Lloyd surveyed the overflowing courtroom as competitors from the wire service and
other national and regional media hungrily
awaited the inevitable fireworks. The widows,
their families, and other surviving relatives
settled into their bench seats, leaving others
standing in the back to get a glimpse of the
drama's main characters.

Tony Pozereli sat directly behind Alice,
deciding that morning the trial had become
such a national event he would arrange his
schedule to not miss a day of the proceedings.
He'd concluded there were going to be major
repercussions to his career, and more importantly, the entire coal mining industry, regardless of the outcome of the trial. Other coal mine
owners had telegraphed him en masse,
expressing their concern over the union's on-
sight involvement. Whatever support they'd
previously committed to his proposed national

miner health and safety coal royalty tax was being held back until the trial ended.

Clad in the emerald green dress suit Robert had given her, along with her silky French stockings and heels, Alice looked more like a big city spectator than the infamous river woman who'd ignited the legal battle. The only thing that gave away her roots was the crooked eyeliner she'd applied without the benefit of Delena's steady hand.

Robert jotted down a note, folded it into a tiny square and passed it to Alice as the judge was giving introductory instructions to the jury, reminding them of their role and obligations.

Alice glanced at Robert in annoyance when the folded note was passed back to her.

"I want to make love to you tonight," it read. "You look so beautiful, you're driving me crazy."

"What are you doing?" Alice mouthed back with just a hint of a smile.

Robert turned, straightened his tie and rose at Judge Ron Snider's call to address the jury. He slowly approached the jury box and rested both hands on the rail. His unblinking eyes trolled across the rows of faces. "We will prove beyond a reasonable doubt that under the guise of providing our country vitally needed fuel at a time of war, the defendant, Lawrence Bradford, worked his employees around the clock, flagrantly disregarding federally established safety standards to maximize production and personal profits. This action resulted in the death of seventy-four—"

"I object, Your Honor, " Diamond said. "The plaintiff's attorney is inferring criminal intent. This is a civil, not a criminal trial."

"Over-ruled, Mr. Diamond," the bald and heavy-jowled judge interjected. "The plaintiff is appropriately establishing his position. There are grounds for these proceedings. Continue, Mr. Ren."

"Thank you, Your Honor," Robert nodded to the judge. "Ladies and gentlemen, sometimes in a multi-million dollar civil case, a trial takes up to three or four months. But I don't think any of you are going to have to worry about staying here for that length of time. When you hear the facts in this case, I have absolutely no reservation in saying that you will agree there is only one verdict, wrongful death that requires retribution. I will prove that the defendants willfully disregarded the pleas of the shift foreman and others who had to enter the death trap referred to as Bear Creek Mine. There were pleas to open more escape paths in case of a gas explosion or cave-in; pleas to close the mine until dangerous gas levels were lowered to federally acceptable levels before continuing around-the-clock work. Pleas that are now nearly all silenced as seventy-four grandfathers, fathers, and sons lie in the Red Lodge Cemetery. No, this isn't a case of cold-blooded murder, but greed and profit."

"I object to these slanderous suppositions," Diamond said calmly, barely above the mounting murmur coming from the spectator section.

"You'll strike that last remark from the record," the judge said. "Be careful, Mr. Ren."

Robert kept his eyes locked on the jury while pointing to Bradford. "We'll prove that the defendant had a motive beyond helping our country with coal for the war. A motive of record-breaking profits that could have been seriously interrupted if the mine had closed down to address violations in federally established health and safety standards. With no current laws allowing the state mining inspector or the union to require a shutdown when violations occur, we will prove the defendant chose to risk men's lives solely for the purpose of profit. Thank you."

The judge turned to Paris Diamond. "Is the counsel for the defense prepared to make his opening statement?"

Diamond rose slowly to his feet, his eyes intentionally dull. "Yes, Your Honor," his muted response completely quieted the courtroom. He moved toward the jury in an uncertain shuffling manner. He stood quietly for a moment, as though he couldn't think of what to say. "Husbands, grandfathers, fathers, sons buried alive in a vicious explosion and air-sucking fire that melted men's skin to the bone."

Diamond's horrid description caused members of the jury to gasp. He paused, allowing the full visualization of the tragedy. "Horrible, tragic. Families without their main provider. Mothers losing their nineteen-year-old sons. A slow, torturous death for those who had to wait for the gas and heat to finally overtake them, some as long as two days after the initial blast. Ghastly."

Judge Snider rubbed his chin, his eyes locked on Diamond.

"Nothing can be done for those men, and probably a lot more men to come, until there are stronger and better enforced laws governing the health and safety of the men who choose to make a living doing one of the most dangerous jobs in the world today." He leaned up close to one of the middle-aged female jurors and whispered loud enough for everybody to hear, "Is this a case about Bear Creek Mine or is it about mineral and coal mining everywhere in the United States? Thank you." He returned to his seat.

~

Newspapers heralded, "Flag-Waving Mine Owner Raises Questions," "Miners Could Have Lived," and "Mine Owner Accused of Needless Deaths." Radio interviews with crying mine disaster widows created a national fervor of sympathetic support for the survivors in less than twenty-four hours after opening statements.

~

"Just what in the hell do you think you're doing, Diamond?" Lawrence Bradford growled at Paris Diamond when he got him behind his home library's closed door. "You're costing me hundreds of thousands of dollars to scare the shit out of the jury with images of men screaming from melting flesh. This keeps up and I'm going to find myself a new attorney."

The attorney waited for the millionaire to finish his explosive indictment.

"How do you feel about the death of those seventy-four men?"

"What the hell do you mean, how do I feel? It happened and there was nothing I could do about it. Every miner knows the danger they face."

"I understand, but I asked you a specific question. How do you feel about it?"

"Like shit, of course."

"Good. It's a beginning. I assume you feel the same way about Howard Wellington's untimely death."

Bradford hesitated in his response, wondering what his enigmatic attorney knew about Wellington. "Of course."

"Of course," Diamond whispered.

Chapter 37

Robert was scared. Once again, he'd led the dance, but feared he was too sick to hide his illness from Alice any longer. Unlike previous intimate moments with her, his pancreatic cancer wasn't giving him the respite he needed to romance her back into his short life.

He was getting a more sallow look every day, but at least his weight loss had stabilized, putting him about twenty-five percent lower than his normal healthy frame. He tried to get sun for short intervals in the privacy of his father's backyard, but the heat nauseated him after only a short time.

As evening approached, he grew more and more regretful of his uncontrollable urge to make love to Alice every time he saw her. His mind was more than willing, but his body wasn't, something of which he was painfully aware as he dressed for his overnight stay at the cabin.

~

"To hell with it. I'm not going to be his puppet," Alice said out loud to the empty room. She walked into her bedroom and took another look at the stranger in the mirror. "Acting like some French whore," she said while undoing then reconnecting the stockings to her French garter for a third time. She couldn't deny the pleasureful surges. She giggled as the form-fitting dress settled into place. The knock at the door had to be Robert. Alice absently ran her hands down her hips, but couldn't smile at the stranger in the mirror. "I'm coming," she yelled from behind closed doors. It was Robert, standing on the porch with gifts in hand.

"We have so many formal entertaining plates, platters and silverware that have been, and will continue, collecting dust and tarnish. This is a little present from the Ren household," Robert said. He followed her inside and stacked the boxes near Alice's kitchen sink.

"I've made us a tuna noodle casserole," she smiled. "A little less formal, if you don't mind."

Robert lifted his chin and scratched his head. "A black evening dress and a casserole. Mmm. Sounds like a perfect combination. You should have told me you were dressing up, I would have put on a suit."

"There are so few chances to wear it, I just thought it would be nice. I don't want you to feel uncomfortable, though. I'll change."

"Oh, no you won't," he pulled her into his arms.

As she looked into eyes shadowed with pain, she couldn't avoid it any longer. "There's something you need to tell me isn't there, Robert?"

He released her and turned away as if she'd slapped him.

"I've felt it since we were on the train," she continued softly. "One minute you're pleading to make love, the next, your skin crawls from my touch."

"What have you heard? I'm feeling fine," his denial sounded weak, even to him.

"You're still in love with your wife, aren't you?"

Robert stopped, assimilated, and finally let his breath out. "Have I seemed like that? There's never a minute I don't desire you. I'm just not the muscular man you first met. You've gotten even more beautiful with age." A dagger-piercing pain attacked his stomach, causing him to fall to his knees.

"What's wrong! What in the hell is going on?" Alice had prepared herself for admissions of undying love for his former wife but this took her completely off guard.

"I've got to go," he gasped, trying to lift his tortured body from the floor.

"You're in no condition to go anywhere." Alice helped him up and into her bedroom, easing him down onto her bed. As he continued to spasm in a fetal position, Alice again noticed the yellow pallor of his skin and felt like kicking herself for being so dense. Of all things, a nurse should have recognized the signs of serious illness. "Robert, when did you start losing weight?"

"I've been this thin…" He couldn't finish a sentence without acute pain.

"I've wondered about your health since that night we made love on the train. You felt too fragile. What's wrong? How can you expect me to trust you if you keep hiding things from me?"

"It must be the stomach flu." His jaw locked to clenched teeth. "I've gotta go."

"Robert," her voice took on a softer tone, "You're not talking to some stranger on the street. I've been trained most of my life to detect symptoms of serious illness. You've got—"

"I've got to go," he interrupted and struggled to his feet, taking determined short steps to escape her probing questions. "Alice, I'm really sorry about tonight. I really have to go."

"Yes, you do, to a hospital. Weight loss, sallow skin color, acute abdominal pains. Do you think I haven't watched you move the food around your plate? You never have an appetite. Come on, damnit."

He hobbled to the front door, desperately trying to get to the car without falling. "There you go again with all the answers."

"If you leave, don't ever come back!" she warned.

"I won't be back." It spewed from him, using the anger to drive strength to leave.

Alice shrugged as though his answer was fully acceptable. Once the dust cloud was gone, she allowed herself to feel dizzy and nauseated, unwilling to accept his possible diagnosis. He was, indeed, going to leave her again and close himself away at his father's house without the medical attention critical to any chance of recovery. Her nervousness became manic as she madly unpacked the boxes of magnificent place settings. Finally, she couldn't resist any longer and rushed to the truck, oblivious to the mud splattering on her dress.

Chapter 38

Delena was busy washing her few mismatched dishes when Alice's truck roared up in front of her house. Without knocking, Alice stormed into the house and dropped to the couch in silence. Before Delena could even get out a question, Alice's pain couldn't be retained any longer. She burst into a wailing cry that jolted Clara from her bedroom.

Delena rocked her in her arms, knowing she had finally found out about Robert's secret. "He told you."

Alice pulled back, stammering. "He told you and not me?"

"He was afraid you wouldn't be able to see him through his illness. Alice, he loves you more than I've ever seen a man love a woman. He didn't know he had cancer when he came back to care for his father and see you. But when he kept feeling worse, he knew he had to take the train back to his doctor."

"Cancer? With the right treatment..." Alice's voice trailed off and she was wracked with silent sobs.

Delena threw her arms around Alice and tightly held her. "Alice," she whispered, "He needs you right now. He's dying. There's nothing anybody can do."

"Oh, my God. Oh, my God." It ripped through her as if broken glass.

~

Robert sat in the darkness of his childhood room, still as his childhood furniture and void of all emotion. The muted, hypnotic sound of his father's seventy-eight RPM record of Frank Sinatra crooning "I'll Never Smile Again" was driving him into an even darker listlessness.

At that point, he felt he should have never come back. He felt guilty leaving Karen behind without even letting her know if she'd see him again. He felt like an empty shell. He was too late for Alice. Too late for everything, except to win the trial. The drive to win for Alice, Delena, Clara, and himself was all he dared to hold.

"There's someone at the door, Robert," his father yelled over the music. "Would you get it? I'm staying in my room today." Mr. Ren had seldom left his bedroom since Robert's return.

As he leaned on the handrail to slowly descend the stairs, he thought that he didn't even do his father any good in coming back. He looked through the side window before responding to the uninterrupted pounding on the brass doorknocker.

"We're not here!" he yelled through the closed door.

"Then I'll wait until you are, if I have to sit on this damn hard porch for days," the voice said.

Robert reluctantly opened the door just enough to see a line of her body. "I told you—"

"Question. Did your wife divorce you officially?"

"Yes. What's this all about?"

"How could we get married if you already had another wife? Answer me that, will you, Robert Ren?"

The door flew open wider than his gaping mouth. "I can't marry you or anybody else."

"You have cancer. I know." Alice had cried all she intended. Now she was back to her old, practical self. "We let over twenty years stand in our way. I'm not about to let cancer stop us now. Robert Ren, will you marry me?"

"Even in the proposal of marriage you have to get in the last word," he smiled weakly, still not believing what was happening.

"Why don't you get to work on it? You've got a court case and a wedding to plan. Hurry and invite that daughter of yours to one of the most romantic weddings to ever take place in the Beartooth Mountains."

"Now wait a minute, Colonel, just why couldn't we have a wedding right here at one of the most elegant houses in town?" he managed a laugh.

"Now you're finally starting to think straight, soldier."

Chapter 39

Not knowing where to channel his anger, Lawrence Bradford confronted Tom Lloyd in the courthouse corridor with papers in hand from the *New York Times* and the *San Francisco Chronicle*.

"Lloyd, you had a part in this, didn't you?" Bradford said waving the stack of papers in front of the publisher.

"If you mean I covered the trial, yes, of course."

"Look at these damn headlines. They're crucifying me before we've even had a chance to respond to the opening statement! The media isn't even giving us a chance. Come on, Tom, you know it's bullshit."

"What am I supposed to do? I've covered cases like this before. Today, you could get all the supportive headlines, assuming, of course, you've got a case. It's a daily roller coaster. With a man like Paris Diamond, you'll get some of the headlines you're after."

"Some drunk puts all this crap down in a diary, and you think a jury will believe that more than what's on public record from the state mining inspector at the coroner's inquest?"

"Well then, you have nothing to worry about. What I won't do is be the PR flack for Bradford Mining Enterprises. I'm a reporter. I'm not going to have this conversation with you again, Lawrence."

"You'll see," Bradford mumbled as the publisher turned to enter the courtroom.

Inside, already seated, Robert Ren turned to Delena, motioning her to lean down for a whispered conversation. "I think the old man is losing it. He gave one of the weakest openings I've ever heard in my life. Stay calm like we've rehearsed. Feel free to cry when the prosecutor makes any references to the deceased."

"This isn't some kind of show, Robert," Delena looked offended.

"I'm sorry, Delena, but it is. Be prepared for all kinds of theatrics from Diamond. He's known for building cases in that fashion."

"Is the prosecuting attorney prepared to call his first witness?" The conversation was interrupted by the judge's voice.

"Yes, Your Honor," Robert stood and addressed the judge. "I'd like to call Lawrence Bradford to the stand."

The middle-aged Bradford looked more like a polished Wall Street analyst than a Montana coal mine owner. He sailed determinedly toward the witness stand and was sworn in. He sat and stared directly at Robert.

"Mr. Bradford, what is your occupation?" Robert asked.

"You know what it is, for hell sakes. I'm the guy getting sued."

The courtroom spectators burst into laughter.

"For the record please," Robert said calmly.

"I'm Lawrence Bradford," He turned a side glance to the jury. "Owner of the Bear Creek Mine."

"Would you describe Brent Harrison's title while working at the Bear Creek Mine?"

"Harrison was a shift foreman at the time of his death."

"What were his responsibilities as they related to the health and safety of the men on his shift?"

Bradford rolled his eyes up like the series of questions were a bore. "A mine foreman has a twelve-point checklist he's responsible for every day. He examines the roofs and timbers each day to see if they're safe. He checks out the careful handling and where we keep the explosives; he makes sure there are enough escape tunnel routes; he checks out air quality each day, as it relates to white, black, and fire damp."

"Will you explain to the jury white, black, and fire damp?"

"Sure, they're gases that are always a part of mining. Carbon monoxide, carbonic oxide and methane. Carbon monoxide is the worst one in coal mining."

"Thank you. After the foreman gets the information every day, what does he do with it?"

"He records it in the safety book and signs it. The state mining inspector reviews the book regularly to make sure the mine is operating within established safety standards."

Robert raised one eyebrow in a questioning slant. "What happened to the records after the explosion and cave-in?"

"They were all destroyed, of course."

"I have no more questions; you may step down."

"Does the defense wish to cross examine this witness?" the judge asked.

"Not at this time, Your Honor," Paris Diamond said, looking up from his notes for the first time since his client took the stand.

With a nod from the judge, Robert continued. "I call Delena Harrison to the stand."

As the tall, attractive woman arose from the plaintiff table, a loud murmur erupted from the courtroom spectator benches. Robert waited for her to be sworn in and watched as she sat down in the witness stand.

"Mrs. Harrison, what role do you have in this case?"

"My husband was the foreman on duty when the accident happened."

"Did you understand his role as foreman at the mine?"

"Objection, Your Honor," Diamond said. "Mrs. Harrison isn't qualified to address the full scope of the multiple roles a coal mining foreman plays."

"I'll rephrase the question. Did your husband ever discuss his work with you at home?"

"Every day I was married to him."

"Did he ever show you anything relating to his daily safety reports?"

"Objection, Your Honor," Diamond said softly. "Mrs. Harrison is not trained to provide expert witness relating to safety or any other jobs performed by Mr. Harrison."

Robert turned to the jury, then swiveled on one heel around to the judge. "Your Honor, there is a direct relevance to critical evidence in this trial if I am allowed to proceed."

"Mr. Ren, keep your questions relevant to the appropriate role of the witness," the judge said. "You may continue."

"Did Mr. Harrison ever show you anything relating to his daily reports of safety in the mine?"

Delena pulled the black diary from her purse, holding it up for the jury to see. "I'm not the one to ask about what's in this daily diary my husband kept, but here it is."

"Your Honor, I'd like to enter into evidence this diary Bear Creek Mine Foreman Harrison carried on his person each day to take down notations relating to his twelve-point checklist official log he filled out before the end of each shift."

The judge nodded to proceed.

Robert turned back to Delena. "Did your husband make reference to any concerns he had relating to safety near the date of February twenty-seventh, 1943 when the disaster occurred?"

"Yes, he said conditions were extremely dangerous."

"Again, I object, Your Honor," Paris Diamond said in a near whisper as he lurched up from his seat. "I make a motion that Mrs. Harrison's last comment be stricken from the record."

"Too late, the jury heard it anyway, you stupid bastard," Lawrence Bradford whispered to his legal counsel.

"Strike it from the record," the judge said. "Mr. Ren, I don't want to cover this same ground again or I'll find you in contempt of court. Do you understand?"

"Completely, Your Honor. I have no more questions for the witness."

"Do you wish to cross-examine, Mr. Diamond?"

"Not at this time, Your Honor."

Robert cleared his throat and looked at Alice, then back at the judge. "I call Robert Dunn to the stand."

A walrus-looking man with a drooping mustache and shuttering gait, like a rowboat on a stormy sea, was sworn in.

"Mr. Dunn, what is your occupation?"

"I'm an administrator for the Federal Bureau of Land Management here in Billings. I was formerly Montana's state mining inspector, before Howard Wellington, who died recently."

"Would you take a few moments to review and read to the court page thirty-two through thirty-four in Mr. Harrison's diary, identified as 'Exhibit A'?"

"Yes, I would," he groaned as the diary was handed to him.

Robert didn't say a word. Ten endlessly quiet minutes passed. Diamond continued to slowly turn pages on his notepad, seldom glancing up with any sign of interest in the proceedings. Lawrence Bradford sat amazed over the disoriented and lax manner his big city-priced legal counsel was displaying to a gawking jury.

"I've read it closely enough to respond," Dunn spoke, finally.

"Do you feel comfortable, in light of your former role as state mining inspector, in interpreting all of the notations?"

"Oh, absolutely. His penmanship leaves a lot to be desired, but I was able to make it out. Do you want me to read it?"

"Just what you interpret to be relevant."

"He writes here on page thirty-two what he again repeats on the following two days dated February eighteenth and nineteenth. He states, 'Dangerous carbon monoxide levels. Inadequate ventilation.' Then he records readings that bear out his concern."

Robert Ren turned to Paris Diamond, trying to conceal his satisfaction. Mr. Dunn's testimony had a perceptible effect on the jury. They were casting disapproving glares at the defendant. Robert was curious to see how his opponent would get out of this one. "Your witness."

Diamond glanced up. "What? Oh, no questions."

The judge looked at him in surprise. "Mr. Diamond, you don't wish to cross-examine the witness?"

Paris Diamond rose to his feet. "No, Your Honor. Mr. Dunn seems like a totally honest man." He sat down again.

Robert couldn't believe his good fortune, Diamond not even putting up a fight. Maybe his magic had vanished. Robert was already starting to picture his victory.

Judge Snider turned to the prosecuting attorney.

"You may call your next witness."

"Murderers! Murderers!" a deep graveled voice screamed from the back of the spectator benches.

A pounding gavel nipped the wave of amazement and vocal disgust washing over the room like a tidal wave. The judge used his gavel like a pointing finger. "If I have to, I'll remove all spectators and the press from the room. Outrageous. Not in my court. The gentleman in the back out of the courtroom, if I hear one more word from you mister, you'll be talking behind bars."

Bradford yanked Diamond by the shoulder to force his attention to how their case was deteriorating on only the second day of trial. "Now you listen to me, you little bastard," he whispered. "I'm not about to pay you five hundred thousand dollars to sit there and study your notes. It's getting away from us and you act like you don't even give a shit. You keep this up and I'll make sure your career dies in this courtroom. Am I communicating?"

Paris Diamond's eyes focused intensely on Bradford's. He said nothing, but the undeterred fury that he seared into Bradford's brain couldn't have responded with more velocity.

"I mean it," Bradford added, losing resolve.

Lawrence Bradford would have been appalled if he could read Diamond's thoughts. If only he knew how fast Diamond could permanently close his filthy mouth and empty head. After he wins this case, Diamond smiled, he'd see who got what they deserved.

"I call Sean Campbell to the stand," Robert said.

The burly Scot rose and stretched his thick arms to the ceiling before sashaying down to the front of the courtroom.

After he settled in the witness seat, Robert began his questioning. "Mr. Campbell, what do you do for an occupation?"

"I'm a coal miner at the Bear Creek Mine."

"How did you know Brent Harrison?"

"The lad was my friend. 'Twas about three years ago we became friends. We worked on the same shift many times."

"When did you last speak to Mr. Harrison?"

"Oh, about two days before he died. I didn't pay much bother to what he kept tellin' me until the accident."

"What was that?"

"About how dangerous the gas levels was gettin'. The man called the mine a time bomb that could go off at any minute."

"Did he show you the diary marked as 'Exhibit A', detailing his concerns?"

"He didn't, but there was no need. Most of us knew there was no stoppin' the diggin' for anything."

"Did you personally ever overhear the state mining inspector agreeing with Mr. Harrison or any other foreman that the mine was unsafe?"

"Not much attention paid to the subject. Overtime pay was great. Most of the lads would talk of money. There was a time I heard Brent arguing with the inspector outside the mine over somethin' about safety. Brent wanted the mine shut down and the man said Mr. Bradford would never go fur it."

The judge cleared his throat, giving Paris Diamond a signal that thunderous objections were in order for leading the witness, but the attorney continued to look busy, doodling as though nothing significant was being said.

"Mr. Campbell, how would you characterize Mr. Harrison?"

"If you mean what kinda man was he, 'twas hard to find a lad better to his family or harder workin'."

"No further questions, Your Honor."

"Mr. Diamond, would you care to cross-examine the witness," the judge queried, anticipating the answer.

"No, Your Honor."

Sean Campbell's character reference was followed by another high-spirited mine employee who had more interest in justice than in his future with the Bear Creek Mines.

Robert Ren decided to press his advantage. "Then Mr. Pappas, you would agree that Brent Harrison's diary accurately represents what was recorded on the official mine log, the log that was so conveniently destroyed in the fire?"

Diamond was on his feet. "Objection! Leading the witness. Unsubstantiated slurring of the defendant." The outburst was the first dramatic animation the jury had seen from him since his under-whelming entrance into the courtroom.

"Sustained." The judge exhaled deeply in relief, then ordered the last question and witness comments to be stricken. "I don't want to remind you again, Mr. Ren, that reckless leading questions and comments like that last one don't belong in my courtroom."

"Yes, Your Honor." Robert turned to Delena and winked with a smile.

Despite persistent urging by Robert to have Tony Pozereli take the stand, the union president declined the exposure, cautioning his legal counsel to keep him and the union as far away from the jurors' and press's ears as possible. Robert wanted him to express concern the union had to unanswered questions at the coroner's inquest.

"Does the plaintiff have any further witnesses relating to liability?" the judge asked Robert.

"No, Your Honor."

"You may now move to the area of damages. The jury will note in your case instructions that the plaintiff has to establish legitimate grounds for an award of money, based first on the actual wages lost over the balance of the life-times—based on a typical employment period—referred to as hard or general costs. The plaintiff must justify an amount for a gray area referred to as compensation for pain and suffering. Proceed, Mr. Ren."

With the presentation of information on each large easel card set up close to the jury, Robert continually nodded his head. By the time he got to the challenging area of a substantial award for pain and suffering most of the jurors were unconsciously nodding with him.

Lawrence Bradford went back and forth from shock to anger. His legal counsel didn't even attempt to pose any objections that might break the powerfully persuasive trance Ren was free to weave on everyone in the room.

After Robert was done, Judge Snider rapped his gavel on the bench and shook his head in disgust. "This court is adjourned until nine o'clock tomorrow morning."

There was a rumble as everyone in the courtroom rose. The judge stood up and walked through the side door to his chambers. The jurors filed out of the room.

From the back of the courtroom the noise began to build, like approaching thunder, until there was pandemonium. Reports on progress of the trial were not only in the news that evening, they were the news. Publicity continued to be showered all over Robert Ren and Delena Harrison. The story was being covered from all sides sympathetic to the plaintiffs' wrongful death position. Delena wanted desperately to flee from the radio and newspaper reporters hovering just outside the courtroom hoping for exclusive interviews, but her pride wouldn't let her. She knew she was the voice for every man who had died and they had to be heard.

"Does it look like an open-and-shut case?" a reporter asked shoving a microphone in Delena's face.

"I'm confident justice will prevail," she responded, sounding almost too confident in what did look like an easy victory.

A *New York Times* reporter turned to the wide-eyed woman's attorney. "Mr. Ren, have you ever studied Mr. Diamond's courtroom style? He's not to be underestimated."

Like Judge Snider, Robert was ignorant of Paris Diamond's courtroom magic.

Over the years, Diamond had cultivated jury and courtroom spectator manipulation into an art form. Lawrence Bradford's crude language and primitive mind wouldn't begin to understand his mastery of courtroom drama. For those many business giants who felt they could keep up with him, he would lay out every scene of the play to avoid concerns during their enactment. The angrier and more indicting Bradford got, the more Paris Diamond decided to leave him groveling and cussing for pure spectacle enjoyment.

Chapter 40

At six that evening Delena's house overflowed with congratulatory partying by many of those who promised to be the abundant beneficiaries of her crusade. Many of Clara's former schoolmates from Bear Creek Middle School joined their mothers for the surprise party. Mrs. Mastro's potato gnocchi, Mrs. McFadden's Scottish potato and lamb ragout, and Mrs. Korbut's Slavic cucumber cream soup all contributed to a feast that most said wouldn't soon be forgotten.

"A toast to the most courageous woman in Montana," a heavyset Italian widow announced as she lifted her glass of port for all to pay homage.

Through tears of amazement, Delena interrupted the ceremony. "You have your heroes confused. Alice Beck was the fire behind everything good that's happened in my life since Brent died."

Mrs. McFadden raised her arm to hush the crowd. "That crazy river woman? Delena, you're too modest. We know you're the one who lost your home and stood up to Bradford. I, for one, will never forget it."

"No, it was Alice who gave each of you back your money from her own savings. She's the one who convinced Tony Pozereli the union should provide us the legal support required to be where we are right now."

"That Robert Ren is fantastic," said Mrs. Korbut.

"Please ladies." Delena's tribute to her one loyal friend was interrupted by a knock at the door. Instinctively she rushed to open it. Alice and Robert stood hand-in-hand with a bottle of champagne. Delena pushed it away as she threw her arms around her guest of honor.

When Alice saw the house so full of people she tried to escape Delena's grip. She had avoided social gatherings most of her life and her soaring joy was tempered by her nagging insecurities. Robert shoved the two interlocked women into the living area of the tiny house, positioning them in the center of the crowd.

Delena continued holding her elusive companion by the arm as she motioned for everyone to quiet down. "This is the woman I was just talking about – Lieutenant Colonel Alice Beck. She may be a little rough around the edges, but she's one of the sweetest people Clara and I have ever known. If we have any chance of winning, it will be because of her courage under fire. America may not be as safe as it was when she was in the Philippines, but the Harrisons have been." She turned a lovely smile to Alice. "Thanks for all you've done, Alice."

Alice dug her nails into her palms and bit her lip. "I haven't done a thing." She turned in a full circle to eye some of the same women who had coldly rejected her help at the mine. "You haven't won a thing yet. Delena's living hand to mouth in this little bitty house and she can't find enough sewing work to keep her and Clara away from the wolves for a month. You want to say thank you, have her make you and your family some clothes. This woman is the best damn design and sewing whiz this town has ever seen."

The festive ambiance fell to a dead silence. Many of the women dropped their heads, having been reminded of their own hardships.

"Just like my Alice to keep 'em laughing," Robert said. "We have something else to raise a toast to. Alice has asked, I mean, I have asked Miss Beck to be my bride, and she has agreed to share every day and eternity with me."

"I can't believe it, I can't. Oh, Alice!" Delena screamed in delight as she pulled her to her generous breast once again. Knowing it would be painful for Alice to express her emotions to a throng of strangers, Robert pulled her into the security of his arms as he told the women the wedding was going to be on the grounds of his father's beautiful home sometime in the fall. Everybody was invited to witness what would be one of the most elegant ceremonies ever held in Red Lodge.

"A toast to Colonel Alice Beck!" Delena proclaimed. Glasses rose immediately. The widows of Bear Creek Mine would never again refer to Alice as the crazy river woman. Alice broke Robert away from a long line of well-wishers to get some time alone.

~

Since Alice's knock at the door, Robert's abdominal pains had vanished for the first time in days. As the two reached the turnoff to her cabin, the excitement calmed enough for him to finally broach the inevitable. "Have you treated a patient with pancreatic cancer, Alice?"

"Please, Robert, not today. Let me celebrate the moment."

"Have you?"

"There have been patients my nurses have served with abdominal cancer. There are so many kinds of cancer. I can tell you, it's not a new disease. It's been plaguing the human race since ancient times. I didn't want to see or believe your symptoms, but recently I've been rereading about the disease in an old issue of a medical journal I had in my bookcase.

"Did you know cancer was detected a year ago in the bones and skull of Egyptian and Peruvian mummies embalmed as far back as 3000 BC? Greeks and Romans wrote about it not long after the death of Christ. I forget what year in the mid-1800s a German pathologist—Muller, I believe—first recorded the use of a microscope to distinguish between normal and malignant tissues. He was the guy... I'm boring you."

"No, please, since the doctor told me I have cancer I've done all I could to avoid reading or dwelling on it. It might be less scary if I knew more. Now that I have a reason to live, I want to know everything about it."

"There are a lot of new procedures and treatments, Robert." She pulled his hand down from the steering wheel and firmly held it in hers. "Why didn't you tell me?'

"I didn't want your pity. I put you through enough pain. Sounds crazy."

The ache in Alice's chest and throat was almost suffocating. She waited in silence before proceeding with a review of her fresh research on what the Romans called Carcinoma, meaning crab. "Physicians of the ancient empire likened the disease to a crab because of its claw-like extensions that keep growing and reaching out, mutating everything in their path.

"In today's medicine, cancer is considered by many physicians to be not a single disease, but maybe two hundred different diseases, each with a related cause and each calling for its own treatment. How many cigarettes a day did you smoke before you were diagnosed with cancer?"

"This is pancreatic, not lung cancer. I've read all the talk lately that there might be some remote association between smoking and cancer, but they haven't proved it. Besides, that's not what's killing me."

"How many?" Alice persisted.

"A pack and a half, sometimes two packs a day when I was under pressure at the bank. Since I lost my appetite I've cut way back. Probably don't smoke more than twelve a day."

"Epidemiologists think the likelihood of developing cancer increases with age and really accelerates if you smoke or drink too much. A lot of cancers are slowly advancing diseases that go through a number of steps, from less malignant to more malignant and invasive diseases. If you discover it early enough your chances are much better."

"Alice, we're talking about pancreatic cancer. The doctor was a little lacking in bedside manner, but at least he laid it out for me. It's about the most highly malignant cancer there is. I'll admit it, the doc said cancer of the pancreas has been tied to smokers quite a bit."

"You've had your last cigarette, buddy," Alice said. She lurched for the pack in his shirt pocket and threw them out the window.

"Wait a minute, it's a little late for that. By the time the doc checked me out, he said there wasn't a damn thing they could do. It's gone too far. He said my liver is a lot bigger than it should be and jaundice is just one of the treats ahead." Robert dropped his head and rubbed his brow. "It scares the hell out of me, Alice."

"We're not giving up that easy. We'll learn more about pancreatic cancer than most physicians that specialize in it. I want you to get an examination at a real hospital."

"It was a real one in Pennsylvania. I've got the full diagnosis at my father's house. I'll show it to you. If you see anything that we could do, I'm for it. You think I want to end it all now when my life has just begun?"

"There are answers. There have to be. We're going to start with nutrition. No more faking it. I'm going to put together a strict and healthy diet, and damnit, Robert you're going to eat it."

"Hold on here, Colonel. I think you're going to like this," He laughed, breaking the tension. He then pulled the car over to tenderly kiss his bride-to-be.

Chapter 41

Diamond was comfortable, even amused. The trial was proceeding nicely. Everybody was convinced the outcome was history. The only thing left was for the widows to count their money. This was his favorite part.

Judge Snider reopened the trial for the defendant's response to liability and damages charges.

Diamond glanced behind him to be sure his surprise witness was in attendance. He was, along with the rest of the cast.

"Mr. Diamond, are you ready to call your first witness?"

The frail attorney misfit in a gray single-breasted pinstripe suit rose, giving a barely audible response that he was ready for the play to begin.

"I call to the stand Denny T. Palmer."

A thin, older man, with impish and soft rounded facial features, pushed up a long strand of his thin, bone-straight white hair as he moved to the witness stand at a brisk pace to be sworn in.

"What is your occupation, sir?" Diamond asked.

"I am an American History professor at the University of Montana in Helena."

"You wrote a comprehensive essay recently on the dangers of mineral and coal mining in America, did you not?" Diamond asked in a wispy voice while staring into the faces of the jurors with both hands on the gallery rail.

"I didn't hear all of that. What was it?"

Diamond turned to the witness. "You wrote a comprehensive article detailing the deaths of every coal miner in Montana since the late 1800s, did you not?"

"Oh, yes. I spent three years researching mineral and coal mining in the state. Yes."

"I submit to the court the essay Professor Palmer wrote, along with approving comments on the document's thorough accuracy by leading national authorities on mining and current health and safety standards. I have retained a copy for myself to indulge the jury in historical facts that have a direct bearing on the question of wrongful death."

"Objection," Robert said. "Historical references detailing the dangers of mining have no bearing on whether the defendants violated current standards."

"Oh, but they do, Mr. Ren. There is a direct correlation. If I may proceed?"

"Objection overruled," the judge ordered. "Proceed."

"Is the work of a coal miner dangerous, Professor—even if all current safety regulations are being met—from a historical point of view, of course?"

"My answer would have to be yes. The current standards aren't doing enough to protect lives. From the very beginning, the work of a miner, both coal and hard rock, has been extremely hazardous.

"In 1889, the founding fathers of the territory had the foresight to create the State Mine Inspector office. G.C. Swan, the first Montana mine inspector, stated that there was great opposition to the passage of the bill. Miners pushed it, and in 1892, the legislature made it law. But there were still deaths."

"Objection. This lesson in history isn't relevant to the case," Robert said.

Judge Snider shot a scorching glance at Robert. "Overruled. Continue Professor Palmer."

"In 1891 or 1892 Deputy Inspector Jacob Oliver stated that the Silver Fork mines in Red Lodge had air that was good, except for a few places. The following year, the mine met established safety standards, but the ventilation was again noted as a problem.

"In 1893, eight men died in that mine after one of the miners fired a blast that cut off the air from a cave-in, the explosion ignited gas that blew the men up. Same gas as reported to have exploded at the Bear Creek Mines.

"In 1894 Charles Shoemaker, the state mining inspector, pleaded for more laws to be enacted for the protection of human life."

Diamond stepped up close to his witness, then looked into the eyes of the jury. "Professor Palmer, would it be fair to say that Montana's state mining inspectors have been the greatest crusaders in mining history in the state for forcing stronger and stronger safety codes to help save lives in a business where danger can't be eliminated regardless of the standards?"

"Objection, leading the witness," said Robert.

"Sustained. Be careful, Mr. Diamond."

Paris Diamond paused to ensure riveted attention before he proceeded.

"I will rephrase the question," he said, his voice soft as satin. "Would you give examples of the role state mining inspectors played as it relates to the protection of coal miners?"

The professor nodded and followed Diamond's lead, looking at the jury when responding. "Montana's state mining inspector, Richard Welch was instrumental in creating the first compensation act for workers in Montana. He pushed through a general law requiring all employers employing more than a certain number of people, say twenty-five, to pay certain sums during idleness caused by accidents received while at work, and for death caused by accidents at work."

"And was it from the law that went into effect in 1915 that the poor widows and other survivors from the Bear Creek Mine disaster were each paid one thousand dollars by the defendant's company profits?"

"Yes."

"All because of the hard battle fought and won by the state mining inspector?"

Robert was on his feet. "Objection, leading the witness."

"Sustained."

"Many recommendations the coal mining inspectors made were later passed into law," the witness volunteered.

"Thank you. No more questions."

"Would you care to cross examine, Mr. Ren?" the judge asked.

"No, Your Honor."

"With no cross-examination, you may call your next witness, Mr. Diamond."

"I call Second District Court Judge Wally Kessel to the stand."

A potbellied man in a red and white plaid western shirt with a sweat-stained straw cowboy hat in hand walked up to the stand with a horse-rider's waddle.

"Judge Kessel, did you oversee the coroner's inquest held April third, 1943 following the Bear Creek Mine disaster which took place February twenty-seventh, 1943?"

"Yup."

"Yes or no, please," the judge interjected.

"Yes."

"Your Honor, I enter into exhibit the minutes from the inquest, complete with testimony relating to the cause of the mine disaster and observations and recommendations made by the now-deceased Howard

Wellington, who was acting as the Montana state mining inspector at the time of the accident."

Diamond turned back to Kessel.

"Judge Kessel, have you had an opportunity to closely review these minutes recently?"

"Yes, I have. You provided me with a copy last week."

"Would you tell or read to the court what the state mining inspector said in the inquest?"

"Don't need to read it. He said all the safety codes were being followed, but even in light of that, there should be stronger national safety standards to help prevent further tragedies."

"I have no further questions of this witness." Diamond had the cocky attitude of a man in complete control.

Robert Ren clutched the desk edge. A stabbing pain ran up his back. He used the desk as a crutch to rise. "I'd like to cross-examine the witness, Your Honor."

"Proceed."

"Judge Kessel," Robert relaxed his furrowed brow as the pain left as fast as it came. "Wasn't it the decision of the inquest to seek to amend the law to allow state mining inspectors to close a mine if they determined it unsafe? Something they have no power to do today?"

"It was."

Robert had recovered enough to chance walking to the jury box rail and stare into jurors' eyes for his next question. His back was to the witness, but he acknowledged the professor with sidelong glances. "If all the safety standards were being met at the Bear Creek Mine, why did the state mining inspector and you feel so strongly about this new empowerment?"

"The issue wasn't what was done wrong by Lawrence Bradford." Judge Kessel shrugged his shoulders while looking at the jury foreman. "If you can't trust the state mining inspector, who can you trust?"

Delena leaned over to whisper to Robert after he dismissed the witness and sat back down. "Howard Wellington lived high on the hog. He was on the take. Alice and I could tell."

Robert nodded. "I know. Don't worry about it. We have enough going for us already and trying to prove a dead man was a crook could hurt our case. We're doing fine."

Their words were interrupted by Diamond's announcement. "I call Tony Pozereli to the stand."

Lawrence Bradford grabbed the back of Diamond's jacket, pulling him back and rising to meet him at the same time. "What in the hell are you doing now?" Bradford hissed. That guy will crucify us. Don't do this. Why didn't you tell me, you sneaky bastard?"

The sound level in the courtroom rocketed from a steady murmur to a loud noise. No one was more shocked than Pozereli. He was familiar with Paris Diamond's reputation, the snake that tried to twist anything around to sound wrong. It was sure to be a no-win situation. Pozereli was sworn in, still wearing a look of stunned surprise.

"What is your occupation, Mr. Pozereli?" Diamond asked in a slow, quiet, high-pitched voice.

Pozereli cleared his throat, then spoke in a jittery voice. "I'm the president of the United Mine Workers of America."

"Why did the union take the unprecedented action of not accepting Montana's state mining inspector's word at the inquest?" Diamond asked the most dangerous question he could.

There was no right answer for Pozereli to give. He cleared his throat again, nervously tugging at his collar. "After a careful review of the inquest minutes, and hearing what I felt was incomplete information on all aspects of the cause of the disaster, I volunteered to look into the matter further."

"Are you saying the union isn't officially supporting a guilty decision, but rather helping facilitate a more complete investigation to get answers to unanswered questions?"

"Objection," Robert said. "Counsel is leading the witness."

Judge Snider glanced at the jury and other faces in the courtroom. It was no longer a sure-fire case.

"Sustained."

"What is the union's position regarding the outcome of this trial?"

Pozereli's discomfort was evident. "We, we have no position. We just want to make sure every precaution is being taken to protect our miners."

Diamond did his damage. The union members and the mining companies would be after Pozereli with that response. "I have no further questions, Your Honor."

"I'd like to cross-examine the witness, Your Honor," Robert nearly yelled.

"Proceed."

"It's been inferred that the union inappropriately took action to investigate the deaths beyond the decision of the coroner's inquest, as well as the word of Montana's state mining inspector." Robert expected an objection, but got none, so he proceeded. "Why did the union take the chance of raising ire from all sides of the lawsuit by continuing to investigate?"

Pozereli had to pick a side, and there was only one choice. "I met with Mr. Bradford's legal counsel in my Washington, D.C. office and he couldn't answer enough questions." Pozereli hesitated. "He seemed to be hiding something."

The courtroom erupted.

"Quiet, quiet or I'll go to closed sessions," the judge yelled with a pounding gavel.

Diamond slowly stood up. "Objection. Unfounded supposition by the witness."

"Sustained. Mr. Pozereli, please just answer the questions."

"What kind of questions?" Robert asked, then turned to the jury and spoke before Pozereli could respond. "Nobody has brought up that Mrs. Harrison's house was burned down as soon as she decided to sue the Bradford Mining Company. Mr. Wellington's death was, well, it happened at such a fortuitous time."

Diamond pounced to his feet, his shrill voice on the edge of rage. "Objection! Unfounded innuendoes of blame on a death the police report stated was clearly an automobile accident."

"Sustained. Please remove the last comment from the record. Mr. Ren, one more mistake like that and I'll hold you in contempt of court. I ask the jury to dismiss Mr. Ren's last statement."

Robert smiled at his witness. "No more questions, Your Honor."

Diamond's next surprise was calling Sean Campbell to the stand.

"Did you and Mr. Harrison ever share an alcoholic beverage together?" "'Course we did. The lad was no teetotaler. No drunk neither, if that's what ya up to."

"Did you ever have a drink or two or three before you went to work together? Remember Mr. Campbell, you're under oath," Diamond said in a whisper. He once again had his back to the witness and faced the jury, diving into curious eyes.

"'Twas a rare occasion we tipped a few before work."

"I submit to the court Exhibit 'C'. The rules and regulations for employees of the Bear Creek Mining Company. I read the following: 'Employees are expected to be sober and orderly at all times. No drinking of any kind before or during the shift will be tolerated to insure the safety of all mine employees.' How many times did you and the foreman of the Bear Creek Mines have drinks before you went to work?"

"Can't tell ya. I've known the man for years. The lad was no drunk and never went to work drunk, I'll promise ya that on ma mother's grave."

"More than ten times?"

"'Can't remember."

"Just yes or no," Diamond insisted.

"Over many years, yes."

"I have no further questions, Your Honor."

Diamond was a bit nervous before he called up his star witness. A devilish grin appeared, then vanished at the thought of his own resourcefulness.

Chapter 42

Richard Yakel had successfully dodged Robert Ren's attempts to locate the former Bear Creek Mine foreman for the trial. Life was good. His puffy, Mack Truck face smiled between swigs of whiskey, compliments of his benefactor, Lawrence Bradford.

Life in Rock Springs, Wyoming had its up sides. The motel and his monthly allowance from Bradford made possible luxuries he'd never enjoyed before, including regular clean bedding and indoor plumbing. He realized he settled for too little considering his testimony could have cost those assholes millions, but he still thought it was a damn good deal. He smiled, noticing more daylight than amber color in his bottle.

The only competitor who could louse up his plans to up the ante was William Flockhart, the other foreman at the time of the mine disaster. The dumb Scot ran back to Edinburgh with his wife and two children shortly after the catastrophe, completely unaware of the pot of gold he could have been paid to keep out of sight and mind.

Paris Diamond had no trouble finding the Eagles Nest Motel, home to down-and-outers, one-night stands and a regular destination for the desolate little town's two prostitutes. Having grown up among thieves, drunks, and perverts, the attorney was as comfortable moving around the underbelly of society as he was in his own wealthy suburban neighborhood.

Diamond knocked on Yakel's door with confidence.

"Who the hell is that?" Yakel slurred in an explosive, gravely voice.

"I have some more money for you, Mr. Yakel. Open the door."

Still coherent enough to pick up the words "more money," he lifted himself to the door like a hungry dog lured by roast beef leftovers on the kitchen table. "How could you be here? I was only just thinking of asking for more money. I haven't even talked to anybody yet. Hey, who the hell are ya?"

"The name is Paris Diamond. If you'll let me in, I can explain how you can earn another one thousand dollars before you vanish back into oblivion."

~

Diamond had spent hours with the creature, trying to make him credibly presentable to the jury. He instinctively took a quick look over his shoulder before he called his witness. His dark blue beard line had come back since he got him out of bed, and watched him shave less than two hours ago. He savored the anticipated response to his closing act.

"I call Richard Yakel to the stand."

Robert tensed as he heard the name. Where the hell had Diamond found the guy? Robert had two detectives working full-time and they hadn't turned up a single clue. Bradford must have hidden him.

Yakel mechanically repeated the oath, surveying the room until his eyes locked on Lawrence Bradford.

Diamond kept his eye on him to guide everything Yakel said. "Mr. Yakel, what was your occupation February 27, 1943?"

Yakel's eyes turned back to Diamond. "I was a foreman for Bear Creek Mines."

"Did you know your fellow foreman, Brent Harrison, well?"

"Of course," he shrugged, a sullen expression on his face. "All the foremen knew each other."

"Was there anytime Mr. Harrison smelled of alcohol or drank on the job?"

Robert slammed a pencil down on the table. Delena reeled back as her attorney sprang out of his chair. "Objection, Your Honor. Jury instructions made it crystal clear that with no family, medical, or employment record of Mr. Harrison having a drinking problem, there are to be no references that would suggest his judgment on the job was impaired in any way. This is the second time…"

"Your Honor," Paris Diamond said in a syrupy voice, "we only just found this witness. His testimony is critical to understanding exactly what was going on at the time of the accident."

"Objection overruled. You may answer the question, Mr. Yakel."

"Happened pretty regular. He even offered me a drink from a flask he kept hid in the mine. Homemade whiskey. Considering one outta three houses in Bear Creek had a still at the time, lots of miners got it down to a tee. I told him to throw it away or he'd get fired. Don't think he listened though, cause a couple days before the accident I saw him taking another nip from it, at shift change."

"In your opinion, was his judgment ever impaired from drinking?"

"Objection, leading the witness," said Robert.

"Sustained."

Paris Diamond approached the jury, staring into their faces before uttering another word. "Mr. Yakel, like Mr. Harrison, you had to fill out the twelve-point safety checklist every day, reviewing it at the end of each month with the state mining inspector. Is that correct?"

"Yes, sir."

"Please tell the jury what you wrote down in the log book that was destroyed in the explosion a month, a week, a day before the disaster."

"Nothing, nothing was outta the ordinary. The men were workin' at lightnin' speed, but everything was done by the book."

"Did you or State Mining Inspector Howard Wellington ever talk about concerns regarding unsafe conditions?"

"We talked a lot about how hard the men were drivin' themselves, by their own choice, to make more overtime money and get coal to Uncle Sam to help win the war. No talk about safety problems, 'cause there weren't any. It's that simple."

Robert felt weak, dizzy from too little food and too many eyes on his vulnerable condition. "Objection," he said softly, without rising. "Your Honor. The witness is in no position to make final determination on the safety of the mine."

Diamond's eyes were alive, dancing from the witness to the jury to the judge. "Your Honor," he said in a highly excitable tone, "In the absence of the state mining inspector, whose opinion would be more appropriate than the man who shared the same miner health and safety oversight responsibilities as the plaintiff's husband, whose diary is the singular foundation for their case?"

Judge Snider sighed. "Objection overruled."

Diamond focused on his witness. "Thank you, Mr. Yakel. No more questions, Your Honor."

"Lying two-faced traitor," a miner yelled from the back of the spectator benches.

Before further comments could ignite the overflowing crowd, Judge Snider slammed down his gavel. He gave his final warning to quiet down or the trial would go to a closed courtroom.

"I'd like to cross-examine the witness, Your Honor."

The judge nodded and Robert stepped forward.

"Mr. Yakel, it's nice to finally meet you. With no forwarding address and not a soul you worked with aware of what happened to you since the accident, I must say I'm surprised to see you here today. What have you been doing for a living for the last eight months since that dark day?"

"I retired. I had enough of that dirty business."

"How old are you, Mr. Yakel?"

"Just about fifty-two." Yakel glanced over at the jury with a crooked rotted-teeth smile. "My ol' lungs just can't take that coal dust no more."

"Where do you live? As a normal procedure I should remind you that you're under oath. If you fail to answer any of Mr. Diamond's or my questions with accuracy to the best of your ability, criminal charges could be brought against you."

A monstrous glare came and went. "'Course I understand that. I live in Rock Springs, Wyoming. Don't have no family or many friends so I guess I coulda been hard to find. I never imagined it would have mattered to anybody until Mr. Diamond over there called and asked me to just tell it like it was. That's what I've been doin'." He looked over at the jury. "Big city attorney like him wouldn't know squat about the dangers of mining."

Judge Snider cleared his throat. "Mr. Yakel, try to confine your answers to yes and no." He looked at the jury, silently hoping they weren't buying all the witness had to sell. Solemn expressionless faces gave no clues of how the defendant's case was going.

"Did Mr. Diamond offer you any money?" Robert said slowly so the jury had time to scrutinize Yakel's face when he answered.

"Objection!" Diamond nearly screamed. "Outrageous character defamation of the witness, as well as me."

"Objection overruled. Please think about your answer Mr. Yakel. You're under oath."

Yakel's lip twitched and his eyes darkened. "Don't need to. 'Course not. I had a lot of friends that died in that mine. I'm just giving the facts as I'm asked."

Robert silently stared at Yakel, allowing the jury more time to size up the creature. "No more questions, Your Honor."

"This court is adjourned until tomorrow at nine o'clock."

Unlike previous case adjournments, the crowd left the courtroom in near silence. The press no longer swarmed for interviews from either party as reporters were trying to carefully weigh their words in light of inflammatory indictments and innuendoes in previous stories.

Publisher Tom Lloyd didn't buy it. Brent Harrison's highly documented word against one man of extremely questionable ethics. Knowing it could be the last day of the trial, with the plaintiff's and defense's closing remarks likely revealing nothing new, the publisher concluded the widows were about to lose.

As he fled from Billings to his Bear Creek Corona typewriter, Tom Lloyd was thankful his paper was coming out the next day. He knew he'd have to make a last minute change to the front page, even if it took him all night.

Without the jury being sequestered, he could get the paper into their hands. Somehow. Even if he only got it to one juror, he rationalized, they'd share it with the others before they came to a decision. He knew the faces, and would bring a boy from Red Lodge to find at least one of them in front of the courthouse before the trial began. It wouldn't hurt for the other national reporters to see what they didn't have the courage to report.

~

On the drive back home, Alice was the only one to express what they were all thinking. "That dirty Bradford must have paid that liar a fortune for him to stick his grimy neck out that far."

With the trial always taking care of tomorrow, Delena hadn't been forced to wrestle with the thought of long-term poverty until she watched the jury swallowing poisonous lies, bit by bit.

Alice sensed Delena's premature feelings of defeat. "Trials are won and lost on the persuasive skills in closing remarks," she swung an arm over the back of her car seat to look at Delena. "You've got to keep in mind, Robert had everybody eating out of his hand until today." She glanced at Robert. "You're one hell of an attorney, Robert. By the way, how're you feeling?"

Robert lifted a hand and used his fingertips to wipe sweat away from his forehead. "Got a little fever."

Delena was deep in thought. "They'll think my husband was a no-good drunk who couldn't be trusted."

They silently rode, whisking past the one-hundred-foot pines bordering Beartooth Highway.

Chapter 43

Lawrence Bradford paced back and forth in his study like a wild animal circling its prey. Everything he had killed for was on the line and in the hands of an arrogant eastern-trained attorney who acted passive about the outcome of the trial. Even now, Diamond was sipping his expensive scotch and peacefully closing his eyes in one of Bradford's leather chairs.

"First, you feed the jury everything it needs to get sympathy for the poor widows, never posing an objection." Diamond lazily opened his eyes. "Even the judge was trying to get you to take a stand. I've never been involved in any kind of court case," Bradford rose from behind his chair. "But I'll tell you, Diamond, if you've won so many times before, it couldn't have been with people like you'll find out here. They've got a heart, and nearly sixty widows going against some rich mine owner stacks the odds in their favor from the get-go."

The frail attorney sat upright in his chair with a blank expression, listening to every word his client was spewing. After a long pause, he slowly stood and walked to the fireplace mantel, examining the disparate array of photographs with Lawrence Bradford standing next to President Roosevelt, some celebrity he couldn't recognize, and a host of other famous people. Those standing near his client had one thing in common, an uncomfortable look of obligation.

Before Diamond could respond, Mrs. Bradford made a grand entrance in a gold sequined, skin-tight dress with a diving neckline cut just above the nipples of her generous breasts. Most men stopped whatever they were saying mid-sentence when she entered. She immediately commanded a room. To Paris Diamond, the bleached blond just looked like another whore on the take.

"Darling, there is a call from Tom Lloyd I think you'd better take. I told him—"

"You better have told him nothing." Bradford's nostrils flared. "That man isn't my friend anymore. He's made that obvious. What the hell did you say?"

"I just said you'll be right with him," she said in a bad little girl voice, not lifting her eyes from her feet. "Oh, and I thanked him for that story he ran a while back about you meeting with the President."

"Don't ever say a word unless we talk about it first. I never..." Bradford stopped his usual reprimand, waking to the fact that Paris Diamond was astutely watching the exchange with a hint of pleasure on his face.

"Please leave us alone, dear. I'll pick up the phone here, if you could hang it up in the kitchen." He waited for her departure then reached for the phone. "I want to get back to your strategy in a minute, Diamond. First, I want you here when I talk to that turncoat publisher. The son-of-a-bitch is the one responsible for all the national press buzzing around the place, with his one-sided stories he's been sending out all over the country. The slippery bastard is probably snooping around for another angle. The worse it gets the better it is for his career. I know exactly what he's up to." Bradford grabbed the telephone when it sounded. "Hello, Tom. This is Lawrence. What can I do for ya?"

"I just wanted to alert you that I'm running a story in tomorrow's paper that includes an editorial I wrote, taking an open position in support of the widows' case."

"You what? You son-of-a-bitch. Who do think you are?"

"I want to read you a couple of sections and get your response before I go to press."

Paris Diamond didn't need to be on the other end of the line to comprehend the treacherous waters his client was entering. He signaled for Bradford to put his hand firmly over the mouthpiece.

"Just a minute, Tom," Bradford's hand covered the phone and he turned to Diamond. "What is it?"

"Change your tone right now," Diamond whispered. "If he's calling, it's because he hasn't yet gone to press and he's making sure there aren't any suppositions on his part allowing you to sue him for defamation of character. Calm down and talk like you were doing a radio interview. Remember, you have nothing to be ashamed of, and look forward to the right decision tomorrow."

Bradford's eyes maniacally raced around the room as he began transforming his demeanor.

"Sorry, Tom, there was a knock at the door. Just some delivery. What were you saying?"

"I've referenced that your attorney, or former attorney, Jed Patterson, attended a meeting arranged by Delena Harrison four months ago. He interrupted Mrs. Harrison to point out that it was only the Bradford Mine owner's generosity that was making the one thousand dollar settlement possible. He intentionally misled the women relating to their legal entitlement. He also told Delena Harrison she wouldn't get a cent since she was stirring up trouble.

Without pausing for comment, Lloyd continued, "Mr. Patterson also went to Washington, D.C. on the same train as Mrs. Harrison. He accosted one of her traveling companions, Robert Ren, after Mrs. Harrison turned down an offer the attorney made in your behalf. The offer was for a free house for three years and a handsome annual allowance if she terminated pursuing the suit. Lawrence, are you there?"

Bradford smiled slightly. "Patterson was fired for a lot of reasons, mostly relating to incompetence, but I'll tell you right now, Tom, he had no authority to hit somebody or make a settlement offer. That's why I fired the son-of-a-bitch."

"Lawrence, you've got one disgruntled former attorney. He told all this to me today and said that if he'd been asked he would have said it under oath."

"Come on, Tom. He's just pissed off over getting canned."

"I talked to Robert Ren, Lawrence. He said, if necessary, he could track down the witness who was close enough to him and Patterson on the train to see the fist hit Ren's stomach and watch him double over. I'm going to go with it."

"Why are you doing this, Tom? What did I do to you?"

"I'm a reporter, Lawrence. I told you before that my job is to tell it like it is. You have a cunning attorney, but I think this time he's in over his head. There are a lot of facts that haven't come out in the trial that surprise me. I won't even get into what I personally believe happened to Howard Wellington." There was an excruciating silence. "But it's obvious. Mrs. Harrison's attorney didn't or wasn't able to uncover enough dirt to get to the bottom of what was really going on."

"If you print—"

"Harrison was no drunk and we both know it," Lloyd said.

"If you print anything like what you just said, you'll never report again. These lies are character defamation and I've got the money to nail your ass to the wall for trying, unjustly and without evidence, to ruin my company and my reputation. Watch your step, Lloyd."

"Just wanted to let you know and get your response. See you in court."

"That man is trying to destroy me!" Bradford slammed down the receiver.

Diamond watched his puppet dangle from the strings of his own self-destructive ignorance.

Chapter 44

The young man moved his weight from one foot to the other as he grew more and more confused by the publisher's obscure descriptions of the jurors given him earlier that morning. The best answer, he concluded, was to leave the side entrance where he had been stationed and hand a copy of the paper to everybody that entered the courtroom.

In anticipation of a quick same-day jury decision, the suit drew the largest crowd it had since the trial started. A long line formed outside the courtroom an hour before the proceedings were to begin.

The boy's hundred copies of the *Carbon Courier* were all handed out before nine o'clock. Not one of the recipients was a juror. All entered the main building by the side entrance as the publisher had anticipated.

Bradford and Diamond were among the first recipients of the indicting newspaper.

"My God, Diamond, look at that headline. 'Miner Widows Unite For What's Right.' If a juror gets their hands on this shit with that kid out there handing out piles of free papers, we can declare a mistrial, can't we?"

"That, Mr. Bradford, is the first thing you have ever said that I agree with. But it won't be necessary." Diamond saw it getting better and better. Everybody was charging for victory and he planned to steal it right out from under their noses. It couldn't get better than this.

Opposite Paris Diamond and Bradford were Robert and his client, holding the same paper up to their faces and huddled in conversation.

All stood as Judge Snider entered the room. The judge pounded his gavel and the murmur quieted.

"Have any of you, any of you seen this morning's *Carbon Courier*?"

In unison every head jerked back and forth like a gallery observing a heated tennis match.

"I have held the jury in my chambers for a moment so I could address a gravely serious matter. Fortunately, none of the jury has seen this paper." He held up the *Carbon Courier*. "May I remind the spectators and press in this room that, in this country, the jury decides guilt or innocence? The media taking a position, regardless of which one, is irresponsible, and it won't be tolerated in my court. Mr. Lloyd, I will have to ask you to leave this courtroom, and let this be a lesson to you."

Tom Lloyd's face was flush. He painfully rose from his seat and began excusing himself, stepping across a crowded row of feet and purses. Low heckling from other journalists accelerated his efforts to escape. It was the most embarrassing moment of his professional life.

"I would like to also caution those in the courtroom that you, too, can be ejected from this room if I hear one outburst similar to the other day." The judge scanned the spectators until he found what he'd been warned about before entering the courtroom. Every Bear Creek Mine widow was wearing a large red felt heart pinned to her dress over her heart. Each heart had the name of the woman's husband and his birth and death date beneath it. Many wore several hearts for the sons they also lost in the mine disaster. They all sat in three rows with their families, creating a crimson memorial the press photographers were eating up.

The judge motioned to have the bailiff show the jury to their seats. They filed in and sat down, unaware of why they'd been detained. The judge scanned the courtroom. When there was absolute silence, he turned to the jurors. "Ladies and gentlemen, I urge you to follow your case instructions carefully. The decision you make should be singularly based on the facts presented in this courtroom. The plaintiff's attorney, Mr. Ren, will offer his closing remarks today. As long as there is no gross negligence relating to your case instructions, it will be his job to attempt to convince you with the facts and his own conclusions that his position is correct. You will last hear from Mr. Diamond, who will have an opportunity to respond to the plaintiff's conclusions and give you his final words of appeal.

"I strongly urge you to judge beyond what each persuasive attorney says here today, weighing the testimony from each witness and all that has been said throughout the trial. With those cautions, I'm sure you'll do the American system of justice proud. Mr. Ren, you may now give your closing remarks."

Robert Ren took a deep breath and approached the jury box. "Thank you, Your Honor." He picked up the black diary, held it up in his hand and turned to the spectator benches. "Ladies and gentlemen, in his final summation, Mr. Diamond is going to tell you that coal mining is inherently dangerous. He will be correct. He's going to tell you that the actual record of how safe the mine was February 27th, 1943 was destroyed in the explosion and cave-in. He will be correct.

"He'll tell you the documented testimony from the state mining inspector at the coroner's inquest and the testimony by another foreman at the time of the disaster are in direct conflict with the concerns recorded in this diary. The picture that has been so meticulously and falsely painted for you by the prosecution could make you think this is a simple open and shut case. But ask yourself this before you jump to any conclusions: What motivation did Brent Harrison, a sober, responsible work and family man, what motivation did the foreman have to continually record specific readings of the gas gauges that by professional interpretation proved the mine was a ticking bomb?

"With Howard Wellington dead and no back-up documentation by the state mining inspector, what it really gets down to is Brent Harrison's word against Richard Yakel's." Robert took a long intentional pause, then returned to his desk and pulled out a piece of paper. Adrenaline alone was driving him past the now-knifing stomach and back pain.

"I have here a telegram from William Flockhart, from Scotland. He was the other foreman besides Mr. Yakel and Mr. Harrison whose testimony is central to the outcome of this suit." The paper shook in his hands. "It reads..."

"Objection, Your Honor," Diamond said. "It's out of order to submit new testimony in closing remarks. I've neither had the opportunity to review or respond to whatever the plaintiff's attorney is about to read. I find this conduct absurdly unprofessional and undermining to the accepted procedures under which the legal profession operates. I strongly object to this being read."

"Objection sustained." The judge shook a pointed finger at Robert. "Counselor, you know better than that. If you don't, you had better refer to any first-quarter college law book. This court does not have time or the inclination to give you instructions in the law. Mr. Diamond is quite right. Before coming into this courtroom today, you should have reacquainted yourself with the basic rules of evidence. That mistake will cost you the ability to even introduce it. Proceed with your closing remarks with no further reference to the telegram or any other new evidence at this stage of the trial."

Robert Ren stood there with a jaw-dropping look of shock. "Your Honor, it isn't without precedence that late-arriving evidence central to a better understanding of the facts is submitted at the time of closing remarks, with a provision that the defense be given an opportunity to review it and address the jury."

"That's enough! You may file an exception."

"Your Honor, I respectfully submit that my client is being done an injustice." Robert had a hangdog expression. "I will, however, honor the wishes of this court and not refer to the telegram again."

"Mr. Ren, I understand what you're doing." Judge Snider narrowed his eyes. "If you go any further with these antics, I'll hold you in contempt of court."

"Yes, Your Honor," Ren politely responded. He gave Paris Diamond a flashing dour look. He then turned to the jury with pleading eyes and replaced the telegram into his pocket.

Diamond raised his hand as though asking permission to be excused. "Your Honor, while I recognize this late-arriving evidence is being submitted for the jury's consideration at a totally inappropriate moment in judicial process, I, too am curious as to what it says, and concede protocol allowing it to be read into the record."

"Mr. Diamond, that decision isn't yours, it's mine," the judge said. "There will be no further reference." He turned to the court stenographer. "Eliminate any reference to said telegram. Now may we proceed?"

"I understand and will honor your instructions," Robert said again in solemn tones.

"We want to hear it," more than one person in the gallery yelled.

The gavel came down. "I remind all those in attendance your desires and comments have no place here. One more outburst and I'll clear the room."

One of the heart-covered widows stood up, naïve of her action. "Shame on you, Judge. That telegram could clear up everything."

Judge Snider motioned to the officers at the back of the room. "Clear the courtroom right now before another word is said. If anyone resists I'll send you right to jail for contempt of court, and don't think for a minute I won't." Silence fell over the assembly as a reporter for the *New York Times* spoke up. "Judge, you don't mean the press, too, do you?"

"Especially the press. I only have one job here, to see that justice is done, not contribute to a dramatic public exhibition that's good for headlines."

Robert Ren glanced down at the message from the Scot.

"Mr. Ren, Missus and me don't want to be dragged into a mess with the law. Don't contact me again. W. Flockhart"

The jurors began whispering among themselves while the courtroom cleared. Alice and Tony Pozereli gravitated together, pushing through the throngs of people to the crowded corridor.

"What do you think, Alice?" Tony queried.

"I think we're privileged to have such a brilliant attorney representing our mutual interests. He showed me the telegram last night. Knowing how strict Judge Snider had been so far, he played his cards so that he wouldn't be able to read a word before his opponent's objections shut him down."

"What did it say?"

"Enough."

Pozereli smiled. "It seems your Mr. Ren is always full of surprises. Looks like the thing isn't over yet," he said with twinkling eyes and a nod of satisfaction.

"Did you see the faces of the jurors when they didn't get to hear it?" Alice asked. The union president nodded his head again. "Better than any words of support that he could have written. Brilliant."

Robert Ren's calculated experiment had worked its magic on the room, including those sitting in judgment.

"Your Honor, I rest my case." Robert didn't feel better. He felt great.

"Mr. Diamond."

Bradford pulled his attorney back to his seat once again as he began to rise. "This better be good," he threatened. Diamond dismissed the comment. He'd grown to detest Bradford more than any client he'd ever represented, from soul-less drug dealers to men who'd murdered women and children along with their main target.

Paris Diamond rose again and headed straight for the jury box. As he approached, he never took his eyes off the jury foreman. "My compliments to Mr. Ren. He was right in many of his observations, including the one that all the evidence provided in this case does make your decision an easy and quick one. Yes, I will certainly refer you back to Montana's finest mining historian who recounted the gruesome history of mining deaths in your state, deaths that legally placed no blame on the mine owners. Just coal-black facts that mining is a deadly business.

"Tony Pozereli, national president of the mine union, has been on a crusade for the last four years to strengthen the current codes governing the health and safety of miners as well as better provide for survivors of mining accidents like the one at Bear Creek. My client is in full agreement with the fact that their mine and every coal mine in the country isn't safe enough." Diamond stopped his soliloquy in almost mid-sentence, preparing to lower his voice to his signature whisper.

"Where Mr. Ren went wrong was in positioning your decision of guilt or innocence over the word of Frank Yakel. There's another deceased man, Brent Harrison, who may have taken an entirely different approach to his concerns than blaming his employer. This is a company that's been working around-the-clock in accordance with the President of the United States, and I quote 'to put the energy behind good, battling the ultimate evil.' The plaintiff's attorney has tried to confuse you as to who is good here and who is evil.

"It is evident by every action my client has taken that he, too, is horrified by the tragic death of husbands, grandfathers, fathers, and sons. He has and will actively support whatever efforts the union makes to improve and make conditions safer for his miners who bravely flirt with death every time they enter the mine. Lawrence Bradford feels the state mining inspector should have the authority to close a mine if the official determines conditions are unsafe.

"There's been a lot of talk about speaking for the dead. Who speaks for Howard Wellington, whom the plaintiff's attorney has failed to discredit in his clear testimony at the coroner's inquest, underscoring the fact that no safety codes were being broken? It isn't just the other foreman who testified, under oath, that what was recorded in the deceased's diary was not the case. You must each reject the written testimony of the state mining inspector if you find Lawrence Bradford guilty." He paused for effect.

"Yes, your decision is an easy one. The final word should be that of the man whose position has always represented the protection and welfare of the miners, the word of Howard Wellington, Montana State Mining Inspector."

There was a long silence as Diamond hung his head and sat down.

The judge gave the jury final instructions, and they filed out. They deliberated for eight hours.

Robert Ren and his client lingered, then slowly left the room to take a break, as did Bradford. Only Paris Diamond stayed in his seat, unwilling to tear himself away.

When the jury filed out of the room, Alice had been observing through a crack in the door and signaled Robert to join her in getting a word-for-word accounting of what they'd missed from Delena. When Delena finally stood up to walk out she was afraid to move, only dimly aware of the dispersing crowd. It was over. She'd done her best. While she knew nothing of law, it appeared her attorney had swayed the minds and hearts of every juror. She'd watched their faces closely as the debate over the mysterious telegram went back and forth. They hungered for a reason to find the defendants guilty. She could feel it. The hearts on the widows' clothing had been her one substantive contri-bution to the case. She'd stayed up all night cutting out and lettering the information Alice and Clara had gathered door-to-door. She closed her eyes and tried to pray, but the fear was too strong. What if, for some strange reason, the jury came back with a verdict of not guilty?

As Delena approached Alice, her exhausted expression said it all. She held her friend tightly, finally letting out the tears she'd been holding back since the trial began. Maybe they were for Brent. Maybe for Clara. Definitely for her.

At last, the jury filed back into the room, their faces grim and foreboding. Delena's heart began to beat faster. She felt like throwing up.

Normally Paris Diamond could read the verdict in the foreman's eyes, or in somebody else whose body language was trying to communicate the outcome of the decision to the victor. It was inevitable. He'd have to accept it this time. Something didn't feel right. Not one of the jurors would give eye contact to anyone in the room. All eyes were cast down or directed to the foreman.

At that moment, Diamond realized he must have been insane to go up against widows and children. Diamond looked down momentarily into his own private thoughts. His ego had gotten in the way of his judgment this time.

Delena stole a look at Lawrence Bradford. He sat immobile as a park statue. She could feel no hatred coming from him now, only a deep fear. For some strange reason she wanted to say something to comfort him.

Judge Snider was speaking. "Has the jury reached a verdict?"

"It has, Your Honor."

The judge nodded and his clerk walked over to the foreman of the jury, took a slip of paper from him and handed it to the judge. Delena felt as though her heart was going to explode. The pounding grew so hard it actually hurt. She couldn't breathe. She thought of stopping time right at that moment so she wouldn't ever have to know the outcome.

Judge Snider studied the slip of paper in his hands, then slowly looked around the courtroom, paying particular attention to the widows once again sitting side by side in a sea of crimson hearts. His eyes finally rested on Delena Harrison and Robert Ren.

"The defendant will please rise."

Lawrence Bradford got to his feet, his movements slow and tired.

"Will the jury foreman please read the verdict?"

"Yes, Your Honor. We find the defendant, Lawrence Bradford, not guilty."

Chapter 45

There was a momentary hush, and then the judge's further words were drowned out in a roar of horror from the spectators. Delena sat there, stunned, unable to believe what she was hearing. She turned toward Robert, speechless. He stared at her, lost in the same surrealistic moment. And then tears welled in his eyes and streamed down his cheeks.

"I'm so sorry."

Alice had already recovered from the outrageous verdict and was singularly focused on getting Delena away from the other widows and the press. Though small in stature, she easily cleared a path through the throng of sympathizers.

"We're getting out of here. You and Clara will be staying at my extra cabin for a few days. Robert, grab her purse. I need to get both of you out of here."

Delena heard distant voices but couldn't discern what was being said. She stood

motionless until Alice gently tugged her by the arm in the direction
of the exit used by the jurors. Once on the other side of the door, they
ran face-to-face into one of the jurors. A man of medium height and
indiscernible features. A rancher. A member of the jury.

Alice couldn't help herself. "Get the hell out of our way, asshole. I
hope you're happy, because the decision you made today is going to
kill a lot more miners."

The man was stunned by her aggressive rudeness, momentarily
leaving him speechless. "We had to go with the evidence. I hadn't seen
the paper," the rancher said. His shoulders drooped and the *Carbon
Courier* released from his hand and fell to the floor. "It was…"

Robert patted the juror on the shoulder. "I'm sure you did the best
you could. We're a little emotional right now."

"A little emotional!" Alice raged. "Mister, did you see the families
in that room? The women and children who have no idea how they're
going to find a way to survive? Howard Wellington was murdered for
what he knew. How could you?" Alice couldn't go on.

Paris Diamond's bitter lambasting client, Lawrence Bradford, was
all smiles, giving him and every well-wisher within earshot his assurances that he knew the truth would prevail. "I couldn't have done it
without the thorough research and determination of the greatest
attorney in America today, Paris Diamond," Bradford proclaimed to
two reporters madly jotting down every syllable. Flash bulbs popped,
and one by one Lawrence welcomed any exposure he could, pulling
Diamond into the picture with his arm around him whenever possible.

Tony Pozereli couldn't get out of the building fast enough. A
reporter trapped him at the courthouse front door.

"Mr. Pozereli, as a result of the decision today, do you see the potential of a massive strike?"

"Of course not. What happened here today was our system at work.
Every question I had leading to the union's decision to represent the
mine disaster survivors has been answered."

"So the union is satisfied with the outcome of the trial?"

Pozereli hesitated, knowing his answer could trigger a massive response from either side.

"I've made my point. That's all I have to say at this time. Thank you."

The press had come to see a spectacle and they weren't disappointed. Near frantic widows left the courtroom, wailing, many braced up on both sides by relatives and friends. Publisher Tom Lloyd acted as a buffer to the unrelenting throng of reporters and photographers who placed no value on allowing the losers their privacy.

A jury of twelve found Lawrence Bradford innocent, but every spectator and newsman in the room—before they were ejected—had come to a steadfast position on his guilt. Speculation of what the telegram actually said couldn't be quieted.

Right after seeing Delena and Alice to his car, Robert bolted to a telegraph office. To his relief, it was empty. The message he never imagined sending read,

> "Mr. Flockhart, Got your telegram. Understand why you didn't want to be summoned. Tried to use what you did send in the trial, but it wasn't allowed. Tragic news for the widows. Bradford won.
>
> R. Ren"

The *New York Times* reached Mr. Flockhart in Edinburgh the next day. He gave them an exclusive interview. The headline with Flockhart's response read, "State Mining Inspector In Mine Owner's Pocket." Flockhart, like many of the miners who hadn't spoken up at the coroner's inquest for fear of losing their jobs, knew Bradford had given the inspector free land for his cabin because he was always bragging about it at the station house during break. He, too, had pleaded with Wellington to urge Bradford to close the mine because of inadequate escape routes and too little oxygen.

~

Pozereli rushed back to Washington, D.C. to be greeted by sign-carrying protesters, making a news-creating public protest over the union's position supporting the outcome of the trial. While Tony Pozereli had intentionally maneuvered around the issue, a *New York Times* reporter took the liberty of filling in the blanks. Being satisfied with the process was interpreted to mean the union supported the verdict of not guilty.

Coal and mineral miners from coast to coast went on strike within forty-eight hours of the verdict. There was no greater reaction to learning of the other foreman's confession than in the towns of Washoe, Bear Creek, and Red Lodge. Miners not only went on strike, many of them quit with thunderous exits that would live on as campfire stories. Fists were flying and mine property was smashed. Coal cars were intentionally de-railed and equipment sabotaged to force operations to close.

The evening after the trial, Lawrence Bradford was burned in effigy across the street from his home. Rocks were hurled through his windows before the Red Lodge police arrived.

"It'll all settle down in a few weeks. Everything will get back just the way it was," Bradford told his panicking wife at one of the few moments he had ever worried about her fears and concerns. Abandonment by the other city fathers and the local press forced him to consider his wife a last-resort companion.

~

President Roosevelt declared a national emergency, summoning Tony Pozereli and large mine owners to his office to resolve conflicts immediately for the sake of national security.

Pozereli sat outside the Oval Office. Dropping his usual distin-guished and distant demeanor, he nervously licked and bit at his mustache, a nasty little habit he'd picked up during the trial. Next to him sat Steven Cochran, one of the youngest and largest mineral mine owners in the country. The man's chiseled features and lean muscular body were enhanced by a dark farmer's tan on his face and arms.

The two watched the President's entourage dart around the room in a hopeless attempt to bring order to the serendipitous schedule that wartime circumstances created for the President.

"Why in the hell did you get us all into this mess, Mr. Pozereli?" the mine owner whispered.

Tony Pozereli had given the question a lot of thought, and had made peace with himself regardless of the outcome.

"The union's job is to protect its members. Yes, we do it through salary and health benefit negotiations with mine owners such as you. It's also our duty to do everything we can to get those men and boys home safely to their families every night. That isn't done through just giving lip service to get stronger safety codes; being as courageous as the men who are risking their lives, does it? I took a risk that caused a volcanic eruption, regardless of the outcome of the trial.

"I've thought a lot about this, and I'd do it again. Those men had no reason to die."

The rancher watched the man's eyes as he spoke every word. "I believe you would."

"The President will see you now, gentlemen. Right this way."

Tony Pozereli experienced that youthful sensation of butterflies, the kind he got as a young man about to meet a potential employer.

"I don't give a damn! I don't trust him and you shouldn't either," the President was shouting into the phone as the men entered the office. He shot a glance at the new arrivals and lowered his voice, "Winston, sorry. I've got to go. Big mining strike I need to untangle. Yes, good luck at the conference. Talk to you Monday. Goodbye."

He looked long at the two men before hanging up. "Gentlemen. No need to get up." The President patted the steel on the metal wheel of his chair. "Now, how in the world are we going to get those miners back on the job? I've asked just you two here today to help me strategize on the answer. And we will get one before you leave. Let's start with you, Mr. Pozereli. To the point now."

Pozereli cleared his throat and tried to appear confident. "The United Mine Workers of America have been trying to get coal and mineral mine owners like Mr. Cochran here to place a royalty on every ton mined, allowing the capital to create the kind of health and death coverage our members need and deserve. I've personally attempted to make an appointment with you or your designate in the Department of Interior to help get this done. Now we're at a point where it's got to happen."

The President's gaze was intent as he spoke, "And the Union openly supporting a multi-million dollar lawsuit pointing a gun directly at mine owners' heads was going to help in the détente needed to get the job done?" he asked, his voice thick with sarcasm.

"I think Mr. Pozereli is right about this, Mr. President. If it weren't a lawsuit, it would have been something else. The situation's been a hot one for about two years. Working around the clock for Uncle Sam has men's tempers flaring," Cochran said.

"You agree with that, Mr. Pozereli?"

"I do, sir."

"Good, good," the President said. "Have to commend you, Mr. Cochran, on being so rational, a trait I trust distinguishes you from your peers in the mining business. One question. Can both sides work this out together in less than two weeks?"

Cochran responded. "No, Mr. President. The mine owners have been resistant, fearing losing competitive price positioning in the international marketplace. They'd need government guarantees that you wouldn't go shopping elsewhere once this all blows over. You may even have to subsidize the industry."

"Mr. Cochran, we're fighting for our lives. This is no time to be talking subsidies when Americans are being rationed on everything from automotive rubber and gasoline to the most basic food products. Good God, man, even cigarettes and liquor are rationed. We're all making sacrifices, and so must our industries. What do you two think of the idea of me pulling out the Smith-Connelley Act, allowing me to negotiate with the union and get people back to work?"

"You can do that?" Cochran asked.

"If it affects our country's national security, I can. Gentlemen, we need that coal. Not one of us can afford to lose a day. Coal is the lifeblood that keeps our war machine running."

Pozereli's face grew chalky. "Before you meet with the union, I request, Mr. President, you run your settlement ideas past a roundtable of mine owners I'll organize."

"Done." The President steered his wheelchair around to his two guests, aggressively shaking their hands and commending them on cutting to the chase and helping him decide how to resolve the national strike.

Before the two men parted, Pozereli stopped Cochran outside the White House walls.

"You didn't have to support me with the President. I'm all too aware of the feelings about the union, and me specifically, as it relates to the strike. Thank you, Mr. Cochran."

"Funny how the President, in a ten-minute meeting, is trying to convince us that we helped hatch his plan to jump in the middle of everything. I've heard threats of this for months, but you know, I think it might be the only way out. I'll see you, Mr. Pozereli." The young man's bowed legs made Pozereli smile as he basked in the aura of bare-fisted honesty.

Chapter 46

As weeks passed, Delena regressed to a point even lower than that immediately following her husband's death. Her indomitable spirit and willingness to face life's obstacles as a challenge had been replaced, nearly overnight, by dark, morose behavior. Uncontrollable anger interspersed with long periods of silent isolation in her bedroom even had Clara concerned.

Panic. It's how every day started and ended for Delena. Even being able to provide for a modest survival had become overwhelming. Before her husband died, she'd always been insulated from any real difficulties and hardships. Once she'd broken herself away from Alice's support, she had no idea what to do.

While there was an abundance of coal as winter approached, Delena ran out of food staples and was left with twenty dollars of her mining disaster settlement money. She lifted her head up from a glassy gaze to Clara as if to speak, but dropped it down again. Clara noticed that her mother's thick mane of rich dark chocolate hair was dull, dirty, and tangled, causing the greatest fear she'd experienced since her normal childhood had vanished.

"Twenty dollars is a lot of money, Mom. It'll buy us milk, butter and lots of other things."

Delena threw her head up to respond, her long, wild hair shooting up as if it was a fireworks explosion. "What do you know about how far twenty lousy dollars will go? We need every penny of it to pay the rent, child. We've run out of food. I can't even feed you tonight."

That was the first of many nights Clara spent tossing restlessly in the night, napping, waking, unable to settle because of gnawing hunger. Piece by piece the furniture was sold to keep the two alive. The new icebox Alice bought for them as a housewarming gift was sold to the local pawnshop and replaced with an old one less than forty days after the trial.

Clara went to school without breakfast and only a slice of bread for lunch. Her mother warned her each day to tell no one at school about the severity of their hardships. But Clara's disintegrating appearance was enough to tell the tale.

Stretching every morsel of food out to last another day for Clara, Delena looked even worse than her daughter. While she never adjusted to gripping hunger pains, her greatest challenges were the fainting spells she faced on her daily walks from one business to the next pleading for any kind of work.

Unfortunately, the Harrison's desperate circumstances weren't unique in Red Lodge. Mines remained closed while the government desperately tried to calm violently protesting striking miners at Bear Creek and every other mine in the country. Even Bradford's threats to close the mine forever and leave Red Lodge, Bear Creek, and Washoe ghost towns couldn't stop the depth of anger of the desperate miners.

One widow committed suicide, leaving behind six children. The Red Lodge sheriff discovered the body lying in a pool of blood shortly after a neighbor reported hearing a gunshot and uninterrupted screaming of an infant. Five of the Jones children were at school when their mother put the shotgun in her mouth and pulled the trigger, but the woman's two-year-old had been napping in the other room before being awakened by the explosion.

There was open crying in the streets of Red Lodge for the tragic loss, but Delena didn't shed a tear, wondering if the woman had taken the only realistic course of action to end what felt like an eternity of hopelessness.

The only way Delena could make enough money to keep herself and her daughter alive was going door to door and offering to sew buttonholes for the growing number of homemade clothes replacing financially out-of-reach store-bought wardrobes.

The national strike was finally settled after nearly a month of negotiations. A week later the United Mine Workers of America sent a group of government and union officials, led by Tony Pozereli, to the Bear Creek Mine for a thorough inspection before allowing operations to resume. Prohibitively expensive requirements for over one hundred new safety exit tunnels and a long list of other related safety stipulations kept Bear Creek closed, clamping a death grip on the company towns.

Alice's attempts to mail money to Delena were unsuccessful. Delena repeatedly returned the checks with a note each time politely thanking Alice for all she had done, and assuring her that everything was fine. Alice had watched her dear friend's plunge into poverty with a continuing sense of responsibility and failure. Only Robert's comforting embrace and daily discussions and plans for the wedding distracted her from her worries. She'd alerted the community's priest, urging him to assist the family with the aid of her anonymous contributions to a relief fund for the destitute.

As the priest came to the Harrison's door, he felt again for the one hundred dollars Alice Beck had given him as a first installment to the fund. The door opened and an apparition stood before him. A willowy woman draped in a soiled, woolen garment, with dark, matted hair that hung in rat's tails over the waif-like face. She had pencil-thin legs encased in old nylons with holes at both knees. The young priest looked closely at the woman who was near his age, then stared down at the ground in horror of her deterioration. Behind her stood a porcelain-faced child who looked through him as though he were a ghost.

"Father!" Her voice was bell-like. "This is an unexpected pleasure! Come in. Do sit down." Delena ignored poor Clara, who stood dumbly, staring at the high church robes the Episcopalian was wearing.

Nervously the priest began to speak of the Church's traditional role of helping out God's children when they are in need.

"I'm sorry, Father, for being so rude. Let me get us some tea and maybe..." Delena stopped in mid-sentence realizing she had no food to offer. She got up and retreated into the kitchen, returning moments later. "I'm afraid we just ran out of tea. Clara put that on our grocery list, will you? I'm sorry."

Clara didn't respond, knowing they hadn't bought enough food to constitute a list for longer than she could remember.

"No problem," the priest assured her. "I'm here with some good news. The Church has a relief fund perfect for people like you and your daughter," he began, reaching into his pocket.

"That's good," Delena offered with a rigid smile. "There are so many people in need. I'm afraid I can't donate anything at this time, Father. Times are tough for a lot of us right now."

"You don't understand." The priest put a comforting hand on her shoulder. "I'm here to give you money."

"No, thank you," Delena said suddenly. "You've been most kind. My family doesn't need or take charity."

"How much?" Clara blurted out.

"Clara! Please leave the room. This is grownup talk, dear. Not for you to concern yourself about."

The priest watched sadly as the child turned and erratically walked like a lifeless toy to the bedroom, slowly closing the door behind her.

Turning back to Delena, he said, "Since she brought it up, I have a sum here of one hundred dollars to get things started. You'll be able to obtain a similar amount monthly as long as needed."

Delena wouldn't let her instincts go to snatch the money from his extended hand. "Use it for a needy family." Her down-turned eyes hid her shame.

"That's what I'm trying to do," the priest whispered.

Chapter 47

Unemployment was rampant in Red Lodge, even after Bear Creek Mine reopened with less than half the miners it formerly employed. A stubborn refusal to acquiesce to government and union demands resulted in less than half of the vast catacombs of rich coal deposits being mined until safety demands were met.

"I'll show every one of you bastards who runs this town!" Lawrence Bradford yelled across his Red Lodge Cafe breakfast table to Tom Lloyd and any one else within earshot. "My mine built this town and it just might destroy it."

"You might at that, Lawrence," Lloyd shot back at him, fed up with his arrogance. "I assume you don't mind me quoting your endearing remarks, because I think we finally have ourselves that front-page story you wanted."

Before the publisher could lift his *New York Times* back up to read, Bradford ripped it out of his hands, hoisted him up to his feet by his suit coat lapels and threw him up against the wall. Lloyd's head hit the round wood frame edge of the landscape picture with a loud thud. Bradford pulled the unconscious man back to his seat, extending his arms and dropping his head on the table. Lloyd's coffee cup shattered into pieces as it was swept from the table and crashed to the floor.

As the mine owner's blind rage began to ebb, he looked around the room at gaping mouths and coffee cups frozen in air by shocked onlookers.

"All right, then. Anybody else with a smart-ass remark? I didn't think so." Bradford slowly walked away from a sea of accusing eyes, then stopped at the entrance. "Let's see what happens to you after I leave town."

~

The first tight grip on Alice's heart finally released when the priest recounted Delena's eventual, grateful acceptance of the money. Robert realized that without a resolution to the Harrison's financial struggles, any hope for joy in the brief time that he had left with Alice would be severely limited. Based on the near-constant abdominal pain and weakness enveloping him, he was beginning to wonder if the wedding was too far away. While Alice had encouraged him to move in with her, he'd resisted, not wanting her to endure the daily burden of his advancing disease. He'd been trimming down the time they spent together to less than three hours a day before noon, his easiest time of the day.

When the idea hit him, he suddenly felt a zooming excitement he could hardly contain. He made a quick review of his remaining savings and investments, assuring himself of the viability of the idea before springing it on Alice. It would work. It had to.

The ritual of a trout and wild rice breakfast together at the cabin went as usual. He would time the announcement of his well-researched plan while the two went on their one-mile walk along Rock Creek.

"Alice, do you think Delena is a talented seamstress?" he broached the subject.

"Of course. Given the right circumstances, I think Delena would have been a kick-ass fashion designer. Why do you ask?"

"I found a shop on Main Street that just went out of business, Betty's Western Clothing."

"Betty's out of business? That place has been around for years! This town's in serious trouble, Robert. I don't see a way out of it either."

"I see a way out for two people, Delena and Clara. Now Alice, hear me out on this before you jump in like a Marine, okay?" He didn't wait for an acknowledgment. "I made an offer for the building."

"What? There's no business in this town."

"The name of the new establishment will be 'Delena's'. She'll not only offer her designs to the people who drive along Main Street on their way to the Beartooth Mountain Highway, she'll also be an outlet for the arts and crafts made by any willing and talented widow from the mine disaster." He paused to gauge Alice's response. Since it seemed positive, he continued. "There's more. Here's the big idea. The town is desperately low right now. Life has to go on. We've got to put this mining disaster behind us."

"Come on, Ren, what's your point?" Alice was catching his enthusiasm.

"A Festival of Nations."

"What in the world are you talking about?"

"You and I are going to meet with Tom Lloyd to have him recommend to the City Council that there be an annual event, paying tribute to the nationalities that have settled in Red Lodge since the turn of the century. Alice, this town is totally unique, with the potential for a tourist attraction that could bring in hundreds of people from other towns. Maybe even other states."

Alice smiled for the first time in a long time, watching the pleasure Robert was having in hatching some bigger-than-life scheme.

"English, Irish, German, Finnish, Scottish, Slavic, Swedish. Alice, the list of nationalities settling in Red Lodge is as long as all of Europe. Oh! You're going to love this."

"Will you get to the damn point?" she said, laughing.

"As you know, all these foreigners drifted into their own nationality groups, with Little Italy, Finn Town, and Scottish Caledonia, for example. Nothing will bring back hope more powerfully than a celebration of their roots. The Finn Opera House has been vacant since the mine disaster, but before that, the plays and music were spectacular. And what about the Finn band that used to tour the state? And the Finnish symphony orchestra? The Italian band." Robert's heart was pounding at a runner's speed as his imagination and his mind could hardly keep pace with each other. "The Italian women's chorus performed all over the state. The Yugoslavs have that picnic spot a few miles from town, The Happy Brothers Picnic Grounds, where they used to have that annual event of old country festivities. Even the Slavs had a thirty-member tamburitza orchestra.

"Let's get started early in creating one huge annual tourist-based celebration, a Festival of Nations. This town should never again rely on coal for its lifeblood, but tourism. It'll start small, but with the proceeds, the city fathers could build a large civic center to serve as center stage for all the activities."

Alice leaped from a crouched position by the stream's edge to her feet. "And it could be expanded to sell arts and crafts from the various lands represented in the town. Oh, Robert, this really is a great idea."

"Why limit it to arts, crafts, and concerts? We could have a festival of the nations parade, with every nationality represented by authentic-looking native attire. There's hardly a Scot here that doesn't have outfits for their annual march from Bear Creek to Red Lodge."

"And for the many who don't have costumes, 'Delena's' will make them. Robert, you are brilliant!" Alice jumped into his arms, giving him a wet warm kiss that would have led to making love on the spot had he not broken away in laughter.

"Behave yourself, Colonel; we're talking business here. Red Lodge can be reborn as a tourist town. We've got it all. An incredible history, the Beartooth Mountains, fishing, a rip-roaring rodeo, and the most beautiful women on earth." He swept her up into his arms and held her tightly to his chest. Hungry lips pressed hard as their lively tongues entwined. The stream reflection of the warm morning sun danced on their tenderly melded bodies.

~

Robert's arms were flailing in theatrical motions. Tom Lloyd sat without interruption, listening to the proposed birth of a Festival of Nations and what it could mean to his dying community. "We'll get flags from every nation represented in Red Lodge and line the streets with them to set off the grand parade." "The Kiwanis Club could obtain flags from anywhere in the world," the publisher surprisingly interjected.

"Then you think it's a good idea?"

"I think it's the best idea in this town since coal was discovered. I don't think we ought to bill it as a moneymaking venture, though. It could be the backbone of turning this into a tourist town, and people are broke with the war and all. It will be a local tribute that, if I can get the Council on board, will be designed for the benefit of the community. It should be educational, with the creation of a museum exhibit from around the world that builds every year. Robert, you've really got something here that could save this town from an early grave." The editor was on his feet enthusiastically shaking Ren's hand.

The Red Lodge City Council greeted the idea with the same enthusiasm as the publisher, each embellishing it until it was rooted in a rough action plan less than a week from when Robert first unveiled the concept to Alice.

The approved plan swept through the town overnight, with only a handful of people unaware. Delena Harrison was one of those people. With the buttonhole business now coming to her, and the life-saving monthly allowance from the priest, she never left the house except to purchase household necessities.

~

Alice and Robert pounded on the recluse's front door. "Delena Harrison, I know you're in there. Open this door right now. That's an order!" Alice commanded.

"Alice, that's not the way to get her to answer," Robert took over. "Delena, this is Robert. I need your help. Please come to the door."

The relentless pleas dragged her from her bed to the door. Her raw-boned appearance made Alice suck in her breath.

"Delena, what in the hell are you doing with yourself?" Alice said, not bothering for an invitation to enter the house. "You've been such a shut-in. You make me look like a socialite. I'm not going to stand for this another minute, whether you want my help or not."

Delena said nothing. She mechanically motioned for her company to sit on the remaining couch and she seated herself opposite them on a kitchen chair she dragged over.

Alice was too excited to sit. She paced, with hands locked behind her back like an inspecting general. "Now, Delena Harrison, we have a business proposition for you. Are you up to listening to this?"

Delena slowly agreed. Voices in her head told her to prepare for another attempted handout.

"I assume you haven't sold your sewing machine," Alice asked.

Delena shook her head.

"Robert has put money down on a business space for you on Main Street so you can create beautiful dresses, jackets, blouses, you name it. You can sell them to our growing drive-by traffic and locals over at High Bug, for example. Of course, you'd also want to strut your stuff for clothiers in Billings for a high percentage of the profit."

No response.

"Now hang in there with me for a minute. You're not the only widow suffering since the mine disaster. You can be their savior, because... Delena, are you listening? Because this is the best part; your store will display and sell whatever reasonable arts and crafts they can conjure up, with all the profit going to them."

Delena looked up from her worn shoes. "I let them all down."

"Of course you didn't, but I'll tell you this: Nobody will play a greater role than you in not only giving the unemployed a means of a living, but also at giving them new hope."

Alice and Robert proceeded to explain his Festival of Nations idea and the enormous array of costumes Delena's would be commissioned to create for the city and individuals. They told of the enthusiasm of each city council member, and described their unanimous vote to endorse the project. With each idea, Delena cautiously allowed a glimmer of hope to rush through her. By the time Robert finished painting a picture of all the rallying potential of the Festival, Delena was alert and smiling.

As foreign and uncomfortable as it made Alice feel, she walked over to the couch, gently pulled Delena up from her seated position and awkwardly hugged her. Delena shook uncontrollably, then let loose of the crippling darkness that had been feasting on her and her child.

"It's over, Delena," Alice whispered in her ear. "We'll have our beautiful girl back in no time. You've got to look your best, you know, to greet the public at your new store."

"The money I get from the church isn't enough to buy fabric for clothes."

"A small investment from us already is factored in," Robert said. "We're also going to provide materials initially to those widows with a talent to showcase arts and crafts. We'll keep an accounting, and I bet in no time at all you'll be able to pay us back." He paused for a moment. He'd likely be dead before the shop had a chance to return a dime. As though she read his mind, Alice reached for his hand, giving it a tight squeeze before turning her attention back to Delena.

"All right. Mind if I take a look in your closet?" Now that they had a plan, Alice was ready to get to work. Without waiting for an answer, she marched directly into the bedroom. The clothes she'd bought Delena were gone. In their place were drab past-their-day clothes that desperately needed washing.

Alice shook her head in amazement. "Nothing. Nothing. Delena, the first thing we're going to do is go to Billings tomorrow morning and get you some presentable clothes. Shame on you for letting things go this far. I can't imagine what Clara has to wear to school. Poor kid. Well, enough of that. I want you to make a list of every clothing and furniture and food item this house needs to get it on its feet again. And I want that list by morning." She poked her head around the bedroom doorway to get eye contact with Delena. The nodding head was all she needed before continuing her complete inspection of the house for her own list, in case something was left off.

Robert sat on the couch, chuckling over his spitfire's way of taking charge in a crisis.

Hours later when Clara returned from school her mother sat her on the bed. She literally screamed with joy when her mother told her every detail of the surprise visit. The two sang songs together while rushing through the shack, making a dream list of everything imaginable. First, a paint job, including interior eggshell white and a pale yellow siding and white door and window-casing exterior paint. Drawings of forest green window flower boxes and a wildflower garden kept them up most of the night, like teenagers at a slumber party.

Shortly after sunrise Delena was up, washed and dressed in her only marginally presentable dress. They'd already decided that Clara would miss school for the day so she could accompany the shopping party in Billings and pick her own school wardrobe.

"I promise right now that I'll keep an accounting of every cent you invest in us, Alice, and I'll pay you back with interest," Delena declared the second Alice walked in the door.

"I've got to tell you, woman, you gave me a real scare. You of all people giving up hope and letting go of one of your most valued possessions."

"What's that?"

"Washed and combed hair along with carefully applied makeup."

~

Robert's celebration over his idea to save the town and his happiness with Alice was abruptly interrupted by the passing of his father, who died as he lived, alone.

He felt a strange relief when he found his father in the middle of the day, dead in his bedroom with a Vaughn Monroe record still playing. It was a bittersweet event that did little to replace Robert's awareness of his own impending death.

Robert, Alice, and the Harrisons were the only onlookers as his casket was lowered next to his wife at the Red Lodge Cemetery. The same young priest who'd come to Delena's house to offer aid performed the service for a man he never met. The fill-in-the-blanks service was as meaningless as the man's life.

~

Red Bovine, a fiery, carrot-topped rancher and Red Lodge attorney tapped Robert's shoulder as he and Alice left the doctor's office later that day. "I need to see you about your father's will," he whispered. Robert turned to the man with sun-worn skin who smelled like sage-brush after a summer rain.

Robert nodded and reached for Alice's hand. "I'll go with you," she said, and tightened her fingers around his.

Red had to dip his head to avoid hitting the awning on the boardwalk outside his two-room, ranch-style law office. His father's saddle was slung over a half-rail in front of his paper-piled desk. Aged amateur paintings of horses, Indians, and Montana mountain scenes covered the walls. Robert noticed the tiny signature of R. Bovine on the bottom right corners.

"Never mind those," Red said in a raspy drawl. "My wife says I'm less ornery when I'm painting. Got a house full of 'em." He made a wheezy chuckle.

"The will?" Alice asked, anxious to get Robert into a bed for rest.

Bovine raised his eyebrows, but didn't respond. Instead, he turned his attention to Robert. "Yes. Robert, your father had me come out to your house about a week before he died. Place looks great, by the way. He went on and on about all the work you did. What a thoughtful and loving son you are."

Robert swallowed hard. "He did?"

"Sure did. Insisted I change the will so you got everything he had. The house, his savings, stock, real estate holdings, the works. Quite a tidy sum. Robert, can you believe it adds up to just over half a million dollars?"

Alice stared at the man frozen in the seat next to her.

"He said 'loving son'?" Robert struggled to pry the words out of his throat.

Red's clear azure blue eyes looked into the man's tear-pooled eyes. "He wandered back like a lost steer that found a campfire, didn't he?"

Robert took a long, deep breath and nodded.

~

The next day Robert slipped away from Alice long enough to create his own will with the help of Red Bovine. He awarded half of the estate, including the house, to Alice Beck and/or Alice Ren, depending on her marital status at his time of death. His daughter, Karen, was to receive the sizable balance upon his death. He left out where he was to be buried, knowing the awkward moment would arise with Alice before his death. Anticipating her refusal to accept the house and money, he elected to have her discover her good fortune after he was gone.

Chapter 48

August 6, 1945 was like any other hot summer day in Red Lodge with one exception: President Harry S. Truman gave the green light for the U.S. Air Force to drop the atom bomb on Hiroshima, Japan. Three days later, a second atom bomb was dropped on Nagasaki, Japan. Just five days after that the world was alerted of an unconditional surrender by Japan.

Even Alice's regular corresponding contacts in the war zone had given her no idea what was up Uncle Sam's sleeve to end the war. Having spent most of her adult life in and around war victims, she felt no relief in reading bold front-page headlines detailing the extent of annihilation resulting from splitting the atom. First-hand experience watching vicious enemies become allies nearly overnight had blurred the lines on the merits of global warfare. While she'd never seen pictures of the German concentration camp victims, she was enough of an insider to know the rumored atrocities were true.

Two acquaintances had died in Japan's bombing of Pearl Harbor, but Alice felt no retribution. She imagined the horror of the scorched landscape and charred bones of women and children whose only crime was being born in a blindly aggressive country.

To her surprise, Robert expressed the same unsettling sadness when the two walked hand in hand through the swarming crowds in celebration on Red Lodge's Main Street. They stopped frequently for Robert to rest. The cancer had nearly incapacitated his ability to walk without her assistance. Regular visits to the Saint Maurice Hospital for increased morphine injections to ease the pain reminded them weekly of what the future held.

"Robert," she ventured, "would you mind stepping the wedding up?"

He stopped and gazed at her. "It's less than a month away. All the invitations are printed, ready to send out." Robert draped an arm over Alice's shoulder and started the walk again. "I'll make it, you know."

She looked up at his ashen face. "I'm not exactly the type to parade down an aisle blowing kisses at people and checking later to see if they got enough punch," she said without smiling.

"Oh, Alice Beck, be a good sport. We invited every widow that day at Delena's house, and believe me, this is one feed and spectacle nobody in this town is going to want to miss." He stopped to watch her eyes. "Even Tom Lloyd grabbed me on the street and shook my hand like my best friend when he heard the news." Robert tenderly rubbed Alice's back. "Since the trial, you're about as close to a local hero as this town has got."

She shook her head. "That's ridiculous."

"Haven't you noticed how everybody waves at you every time we step foot into town?"

"I've never cared about being popular. Robert, I want to have the ceremony at the cabin with only Delena, Clara and Autumn as best dog. There's a little grassy place in front of the cabin by Rock Creek."

"To hell with a few invitations," he said. "Besides, we can still have a reception next month. The cabin, it is."

"Next week, if I can get the minister," Alice added.

"Alice, I have a requirement, too. I'm not about to get married without my daughter present. A week doesn't even give her time to make arrangements. Let me call her and see how flexible she can be."

"Fair enough." Alice snuggled under his arm again.

"I know this kind of thing is taboo before a wedding," she said without looking up, "but I don't want to spend another night away from you. Leave that big empty house and move in with me. Today."

"That idea requires no negotiation, Colonel."

~

As Karen's plane made its descent into Billings, she retrieved a compact makeup mirror from her purse to make a last minute inspection before seeing her father again. The well-read telegram he'd sent fell out onto her airplane food tray. Even though she'd already memorized every word, her eyes scanned it again.

"Dear Karen, wedding has had to be moved up to September 1, but only if you can come. Can't wait to see you. Let me know soonest. I'll pay all your expenses.

Love, Dad"

It always gave her a funny feeling when he signed notes or letters "Love, Dad." She'd never admit it to him, but she couldn't feel emotionally whole until she knew that he really meant it. Childhood hugs and kisses somehow weren't enough.

~

"How do I look, Alice? No bullshit," Robert said nervously adjusting his tie.

"If you're scared, what do you think I am? You look fine. When are you going to tell her?"

"After the wedding."

"Robert, the last time your girl saw you, you looked a lot different."

"That bad, heh?"

"Not to me, but you've lost nearly forty pounds, your coloring is yellow and you barely made it out of bed to the airport without the morphine."

"I can't be all doped up when she sees me!"

"She's your daughter."

~

Karen stepped off the plane in a powder blue suit. The slim figure and fluffy sun-blond hair belied the darkness that consumed her when she realized that the frail old man coming toward her was her father.

With tears in his eyes, he embraced her with all of his limited strength. There was no concealing his condition. Karen couldn't avoid feeling his bony frame when they embraced. She pulled back and stared for a moment into pained eyes.

"Now my life's complete with the two women I love." His words of the heart flowed more freely than ever before. The thought that he was dying seared Karen's mind as she looked over his shoulder at "the other woman."

"How rude of me," Robert laughed nervously. "Karen, this is Alice. Alice, Karen."

"Plenty of time to get to know each other later," Alice said with a terse smile. "Let's get back to the car and on our way."

Assuming Alice's brusque behavior was related to her father's frail appearance, Karen tucked a hand beneath his arm and looked to his companion to lead the way. Once seated in the back seat of Robert's large convertible, Karen anxiously waited for her father to begin talking.

"I've changed, obviously, since I saw you last, Karen. I didn't want to tell you at the time, but, I've got pancreatic cancer."

Karen gasped and lurched, planting both arms on the top of the front seat. "My God, Dad. How serious is it?"

"At this point, every day I get is a blessing." Karen watched her father reach over for Alice's hand. She eased back to her seat, her sinking feeling growing worse by the second.

As his one-way conversation wafted from the front seat to trivial points of interest during the drive through downtown Red Lodge, she couldn't stop replaying what he said. "Every day left is a blessing."

"Can we go to your childhood house first? I've heard you talk about how grand it is for years. I really want to see it," Karen asked, not sure he'd be up to leaving the house again once they arrived.

"You won't be disappointed," Alice said, joining Karen in a lighter topic. "Thanks to your father's hard work, it's one of the nicest homes in town."

"Will you do me a favor, Honey?" Robert said, glancing quickly in the rearview mirror. "Would it be okay if we don't talk about cancer again? I want our time together to be wonderful. Besides, I'm just about to get married. Cause for a celebration, not a wake."

Nodding her agreement, Karen didn't trust herself to speak. Gazing out the window as they cruised the quaint streets, she wondered how much he'd changed. Before, he would never talk about real feelings. His deteriorating health may have changed that.

~

Alice was as lost as Karen seemed when the two of them were finally alone on the front porch of the cabin. The excitement of meeting his daughter again had taken a toll on Robert. Karen had watched in horror when only the morphine needle stopped his writhing pain and they'd left him resting uneasily in bed.

"So, how long have you and my dad been in love?" Karen asked, her head intentionally turned away.

"Since I was nineteen."

"What?" Karen's head jerked around in surprise.

"Since I cared for him when he was wounded and sent to a small hospital in Savenay, France," Alice explained simply. An hour later Alice had shared nearly every detail of how they fell in love.

"Robert's return to Red Lodge was as big a shock to me as it was to you. I believe there was never a day that your father was unfaithful to your mother in their twenty-three years of marriage. He's not that kind of man."

Karen doubted that. He was the kind who was worse. "He never loved my mother," Karen said, whispering each word slowly. "I knew it from when I was little. She didn't have him any more than you did. That's why she left him."

Too restless to stay still, Alice got up and motioned for Karen to join her at the river's edge. "Your father probably never told you about Rock Creek, did he?"

"He hardly ever spoke of Red Lodge or his father. The only thing he talked about was his mother. I wish I could have met her."

After a moment's hesitation, Alice decided to include Karen in every dimension of her father's life. She told of his father's abuse and Robert's escape from his domineering control by running every day along Rock Creek. She even confessed that she lived by the stream to be close to him, knowing it was the only thing that brought him peace in those turbulent years.

Alice's compassion for her father was openly evident; the woman was one with her father's pain. While still protective of her unyielding loyalty to her mother, Karen couldn't help but admire the insight and passion the stranger felt for her father.

"When he wakes up, I'll be gone for a few hours, making arrangements for the wedding. If I were you, Karen, I'd tell him everything you've felt since you were a child. Don't pull any punches. Sometimes, he doesn't want to talk about the things that really matter, but it would be good to get it all off your chest." Alice stepped a little closer. "He's really proud of you, you know."

Karen stared at the woman whose ghost had ripped apart her life. "He doesn't get away with much with you, does he?"

"Kiddo, nobody gets away with much around me, especially your father."

Chapter 49

When Robert awoke, his daughter was directly over him, staring, in hopes of arousing him from slumber.

"Are you awake?"

"I am now, Honey. What time is it?"

"You've been sleeping for a few hours. It's nearly six p.m. I've got a few questions I need to have you answer. You might get mad, but..."

"No," he struggled to sit up, "go ahead. I expected I'd have a lot to answer when you arrived."

"It doesn't have to do with what's happening now." She paused to wait out the strain from holding back tears in the base of her throat. "It has to do with when I was growing up. It never felt like you loved me any more than you did Mom. You always wanted a son. I could tell because you and I would go to ball games, shoot basketball, all the things you would have done with a son. I was just like Mom to you. I mean..."

Robert exhaled a tremulous sigh. "I know what you mean. I'm not going to try to explain myself away. I was a lousy father. I buried myself in my work to escape what was missing between your mother and me. I'm sorry, Karen. All we can do is start right now." He sighed again, thankful the morphine hadn't overtaken his mind yet. "I will tell you that I never wanted a son. I guess that's just how a guy who never had a sister or decent parents tries to do kid's stuff. Does that make sense?"

Karen nodded hesitantly.

"Karen, I've loved you with all of my heart since the day you were born." Robert knew his mind was fading into a blissful stupor. "Like it or not, we have to discuss funeral arrangements and my will, Karen. I probably won't live much longer."

Karen looked down, studying the intricate embroidery of the quilt. Denial was the safest place.

"Your grandfather left me his estate, together we'll be leaving you over four hundred thousand dollars."

The number was unfathomable and meaningless. Karen continued her examination of the kaleidoscope of greens, red, yellow, tan, all creating windmill patterns in each square. A brown road led to the pastoral rolling hills crested by the looming wood structures, with four wedge arms forming a perfect circle.

"Karen, please listen to what I'm saying. I thought people leaned over to a dying man's lips and tried to hear every last profoundly meaningful word, you know, like in the movies." He laughed, then winced. The pain was returning. "Instead, I'm surrounded by a couple of bull-headed women I'll probably find rolling in the dirt pulling each other's hair out. I'll be a referee as my last dying act!" He chuckled.

"Who made this beautiful quilt?" Karen asked in a distant voice.

"Alice had it made in France in 1919 by one of the village women who spent her life doing nothing but creating these incredibly detailed covers. Beautiful, isn't it?"

"Was that after you left and stopped writing to her?"

Robert paused. "You two have sure covered a lot of ground for a short visit. These windmills represent the circle of love between us that wasn't broken then, or now. Some things are best left to the private corners of people's lives. We all have them, Karen. I'm sure you have a few that you'll never share with me. Sometimes I wonder if any of us ever really know each other. The subliminal mind is nearly always running contrary to the conscious one."

"And your subliminal mind was never with the woman and child who loved and needed you, was it, Dad?"

"Not always. Karen, I can't talk about my death with Alice, she couldn't handle it." Sharp pain gouged his stomach like a jagged-edged knife.

Karen looked away. "And I can?"

"You're family. My child and my blood. I know I wasn't there for you a lot of times, but I never stopped loving you or used harsh words."

Karen numbly considered his words. It was the first time in her life she could study the thought processes displayed across his face. "What can I do, Dad?"

They'd talked more from their hearts at that time than any time before. Karen prayed to God that He wouldn't take her father now. She promised she'd go to church and dedicate her life to Him if He'd only show her a sign that her prayers were being heard, but she knew it was ridiculous.

"Alice won't have anybody but that dog after I'm gone. I don't want her retreating back to an isolated life here at the cabin. That's why I'm going to give her your grandparent's house rather than sell it. You'll get the value back in an equal split of my money and your grandfather's. I don't expect you to have any feelings for Alice. Maybe you'll even resent her at first. She's got a lot of rough edges. Most people think she's rude, but that little soldier out in the stream up to her hips in icy cold water and fish has the most tender heart of any woman I've ever known."

Karen put a hand on her father's arm, then opened his fist and inter-locked her fingers with his.

"Karen, will you do this for me? Just stick around a month or so after the funeral to help settle Alice into her new surroundings."

"Okay, Dad, but I'm not making any promises about how it's going to go. We just might end up rolling around in the dirt. I'm not exactly the shy type myself."

He smiled at the thought, and then continued, "I want to be buried near my parents at the Red Lodge Cemetery. Buy a plot next to me for Alice. I'll give you the money so it's all done before the wedding in four days." He clutched his stomach. "I've got to rest now, dear. "Would you go get Alice for me? I could use some more morphine."

Fortunately, Alice was on her way inside the cabin when Karen reached the porch. The need for morphine was getting to be constant, allowing precious little unaltered mind time for the two of them to plan anything relating to the wedding.

Chapter 50

Robert died at three in the morning.

At first, Alice thought he was in a stupor from the amount of morphine she had given him near midnight, but his body grew cold with the dawn. Golden streaks of light pierced through the cabin window forcing Alice to release her desperate hold on his lifeless body. Her first action would be one of the most painful: telling his daughter, who was staying in the cabin next door.

Alice trudged to the cabin and let herself in. Karen was still asleep, and Alice envied her the few remaining moments of believing that Robert was still with them.

"Karen, wake up." Alice gave her cool exposed arm a jiggle.

Karen sat up immediately, muttering from a disturbed sleep. "What is it? What happened? Is Dad all right?"

"He's gone."

"What? What are you saying? No. He isn't dead. He isn't dead. God, no. God, no. Don't let this happen. Please God." At first, she fought off Alice's attempts to hold her, but wouldn't stop. Couldn't stop. The two rocked in each other's arms in silence with only the sound of Rock Creek, forever unchanged despite the generations of human tragedies played out by its banks.

Even when Alice returned to her cabin, Karen's wails of soul-deep pain echoed in the morning air. Unable to face the cabin they'd planned to share, Alice sank down on her cabin's front porch and hugged her knees to her chest. Her soul felt as dry as her eyes.

~

Word of Robert Ren's death traveled as fast as expected from the funeral home to the community. While the mine disaster widows and the rest of the community had received word that the wedding was canceled at the Ren family home, everybody was aware of Robert and Alice's generosity in making Delena's possible for the sale of widow arts and crafts. The anticipated wedding had been the joyous talk of the town for days. The news of Robert's death once again dragged the community into the depths of despair.

The widows quickly organized a meeting at the site of the partially built civic center. The first annual Festival of Nations was still months away. Virtually hundreds of people from all over Montana and neighboring states had asked for further information about the festival from articles Tom Lloyd had written and published characterizing and promoting the seven-day event.

~

"I'm standing on the site of a magnificent new building that would have never existed, if not for the imagination of one man, Robert Ren," one of the festival organizers observed to the settling congregation of widows. "Robert Ren and Alice Beck, along with Delena, of course," she announced, glancing at the Harrisons sitting in the front row, "they've been the best friends we have. I propose each of us prepare our finest dinner and set up a schedule to take it out to Alice and Robert's poor daughter every day for the next month. It wouldn't hurt for each of us to tell Alice how we feel for her and invite her and Robert's daughter to our homes at a future time. That's all I have to say."

~

Alice, with Autumn close behind, returned from one of her mountain escape meadows near dusk. There was a note from Delena taped to the front door asking her and Karen to come to her house immediately. Inside the cabin, Karen sat looking into a fireplace glow, as if the answers to her questions about their loss were hidden among the burning embers.

"He had instructions," Karen said in a monotone voice without acknowledging Alice. "You get the house and I agreed to stay for a month to make sure everything is all right."

Alice expelled a deep breath and put a hand to her forehead. "The house. You mean your grandparent's house?" She kicked a kitchen chair over, causing Karen to flinch and turn towards her. "I have as much use for that as a deaf man has for a radio. House is yours. I don't want a damn thing. Not a damn thing."

Karen turned as the door slammed. She gradually rotated her head back to the flames, mindlessly nodding in agreement to the rambling of the strange woman who had invaded her meditation.

~

Karen acted as the intermediary that evening for the first well-wishing widow to arrive with a basket of fruit and a hot dinner.

"Now you tell Miss Beck that she's always welcome at our house. And make sure you tell her how bad we all feel. We'll all be at the funeral. We've arranged a get-together after the service at the town hall.

There were so many people who wanted to be there, it was the only place big enough to fit everybody in."

Karen said nothing, but acknowledged each statement, giving the necessary body language to assure her understanding.

Knowing that Alice would never attend a large gathering of mourners, Delena elected to surprise her following the service. She alerted her to the throng of widows who would be at the graveside service, after which Alice drove straight to the mortician and priest to make an unannounced change of the time of the service.

Alice, Karen, the Harrisons, and Autumn stood alone as a cold wind brushed across the graveyard during the priest's highly emotional soliloquy guaranteeing a better life on the other side. Before the casket was lowered, Alice placed the quilt covered with windmills over the top of the cherry wood box. Karen put her hand to her mouth and squeezed back tears. After the service, Karen nervously put her arm around Alice, guiding her back to her father's convertible.

Delena lingered behind until they got to the car. "Alice, if you don't mind, I'll drive you back."

"Where's your car?" Alice started to ask.

"I need to be with you right now." Delena didn't wait for an answer. Clara and Autumn piled into the back seat next to Karen. Delena drove from the mountain ridge graveyard down to Red Lodge's Main Street, then turned right instead of continuing straight to go to Alice's cabins.

"Delena, where are you going?" Alice asked. "Take us back to the cabin." She turned to Karen in the back seat. "That is, if you want to join me there for a while."

"I don't want to be alone. Can I stay in the guest cabin for a couple of days?" Karen asked.

"Of course!" Alice felt a twinge of surprise. "Long as you like."

Delena tried to act natural. "I just have to run into town for a minute. Then I'll take you right out there."

As the convertible pulled into the town hall parking lot Tom Lloyd followed his prearranged instructions and rushed to the car.

"Alice, there's a nice plaque recognizing Robert's role in coming up with the idea of the Festival of Nations. You and Karen have got to see it." There wasn't a sound coming from the other side of the door when they approached the entrance. Delena positioned herself behind Alice to avert a quick getaway.

The room exploded in cheers at the sound of the door opening. Over a hundred people raised glasses in a toast. Festival Chairman Tom Lloyd went to the microphone, flanked by Red Lodge's mayor.

"Ladies, please come on in. I know a funeral is a time to mourn and reflect on the life and loss of a loved one. All of us are here today to do just that, but also to honor the living. Delena Harrison, would you come to the podium please?"

Alice nervously shifted her weight from one leg to the other while scanning the room for a quick getaway route.

"I appreciate nearly the whole town coming to this tribute to Robert Ren and Alice Beck. Before speaking of the living, I want to say a few words about our loss. From the day Robert Ren walked back into Red Lodge, things started to change. He beautified his father's home, made it possible for Alice and me to go to Washington, D.C. to get the union's support to try and set right the wrong done by the Bradford Mines. He valiantly acted as the widows' attorney for no fee. And last but not least, he gave birth to the idea behind the Festival of Nations, an event that promises to bring us all back together and begin building a future for our community."

The mayor was on his feet. "This commemorative plaque acknowledges him as the founder of the Festival." With a flourish, the mayor unveiled the architectural rendering of the soon-to-be completed cultural center. "We've named this wonderful facility the Ren Civic Center. And now, a toast to Robert Ren."

Alice was handed a full glass of champagne. Delena intercepted one from the tray Tom Lloyd had been carrying. Alice held up the glass of champagne.

"To Robert Ren," she proclaimed through mounting tears. In Alice's peripheral vision she saw Karen standing alone and realized that most of the people there didn't even recognize that it was her father being praised. She grabbed the full glass from the tray and handed it to the young woman. As their red, teary eyes met, Karen looked down, confused by how her feelings had evolved in a matter of days.

A long line of caring handshakes and well wishers followed. Alice even allowed her private space to be violated by strangers. All for Robert Ren.

Chapter 51

Delena had been overwhelmed with business since she hung a shingle and the Festival of Nations became a confirmed reality. The raw material and money Robert and Alice provided to interested widows was rapidly being transformed into quilts, rag dolls, miniature playhouse furniture, and a vast array of wooden toys, play houses, rocking cradles, tables, and chairs.

No one was more delighted by Delena's near-overnight success than Tom Lloyd. He'd personally written numerous front-page stories in the *Carbon Courier*, highlighting them with pictures of the most attractive woman in Red Lodge. At least he thought so since the first day she and Alice Beck had walked into the bachelor's office.

Thoughts of her had become a near obsession, contributing to his irrational writing and distribution of his one-sided story the last day of the trial. As far as he was concerned, though, being thrown out of the courtroom was a small price to pay for defending Delena Harrison. During her period of extreme hardship he didn't know what to do as he painfully watched her slide into poverty.

Once he and Delena were on the committee for the Festival of Nations, he could no longer contain his feelings. Today he would approach her at her shop, expressing just how he felt. A bold action, necessitated by the fact that he'd accepted an offer to be the *Associated Press*'s Montana, Wyoming, Utah, and Nevada western bureau chief. The requirement that the position base out of Billings was considered a small concession, considering the impressive national reputation he'd garnered for his highly sensitive and interpretive coverage of the Bear Creek Mine widows' trial.

After pacing up and down Red Lodge's Main Street to rehearse the perfect words, Tom Lloyd finally entered Delena's shop. Her deep brown hair had a hint of illuminating auburn revealed by the afternoon sun as she put her last artistic touches to the perfect positioning of an eclectic array of objects.

"Excuse me, Delena," he cleared his throat awkwardly.

"Yes?" Her hair flew up and back in a dramatic motion that swooped away what little confidence he had mustered.

"Would you consider, ah, would you have…? I would appreciate it if…"

"If I would have dinner with you? Yes, I'd love to, Mr. Lloyd," she chirped, smiling up at him.

"How did you know?"

"Call it a woman's intuition. Of course, since the first time we met in your office you've been staring at me. Kind of gave me the idea you were interested."

"You ought to be an investigative reporter."

"You, Tom Lloyd, ought to follow your heart a little more. I've known you were trying to find a way to ask me out for quite a while. I'll make it easy on you." She reached out and shook his hand. "I am, and have been, greatly indebted to the way you stuck your neck out for me and the other widows. I think any woman would have to be crazy to turn down such an invitation," she proclaimed with both hands on her hips and a fresh relaxed smile that made him blush.

"I have a feeling I won't have much to say. You seem to speak handsomely for us both."

"Good, it looks like we are off to a great start."

~

When Delena told Alice about Tom Lloyd and his new job in Billings later that day, Alice usurped her friend's move and initiated a far-stretching hug. "That's just great. Tom Lloyd is one of the best men I've ever met. He'll make a perfect husband."

"Hey, wait a minute! I'm talking about a first date and you have me married already."

"Somebody's got to have a happy ending. You're my choice."

~

Alice found Karen in the attic of her grandmother's house, systematically filtering through memorabilia from her father's youth: a baseball mitt, his first shoes, and first year baby clothes. Treasures she would keep for life. Maybe she'd dress her own son, if she ever had a family, in the shoes worn by her own dad. She was thankful and changed from the last brutally honest and tender conversation she had with her father.

"I never wanted a son. Of course, I always loved you." Those words kept repeating like healing medicine in her mind.

Alice looked up to the dark hole and partially extended pull-down ladder, anticipating it could only be Karen.

"Karen, you up there?"

"Yes. I'm not doing much," she yelled.

Alice pulled down and climbed the ladder.

"Only looking at a steamer trunk full of things from my father's childhood," Karen said.

"Okay if I join you?"

"Not much here."

After the two carefully unfolded and refolded a large stack of baby clothes, then inspected a collection of agate marbles and torn and yellowed public school paperwork, they sat in the center of the attic, cross-kneed, bartering over each item.

"Alice, I know this will sound strange, but I've never felt better. It isn't just the money, even though I admit I never dreamed I'd be rich. I don't know, I just feel good about Dad and everything. I'm giving half of my money to my mom. I called her this morning and she about fainted."

"Don't be giving it all away. You'll need a good amount of the inheritance to buy the *Carbon Courier*. This county needs a good publisher with the current one running off."

"I'm a cub reporter. I wouldn't know the first thing about owning and putting out a paper." Karen's words and thoughts were as far apart as the two polar ice caps. She hoped for further encouragement.

"A reporter from the *Boston Globe* should be able to handle gripping news like social functions, births, and deaths. Besides, the town civic center is named after your father. You'll have clout. To look the part, I'll be giving you back this fancy home. I'd have no use for it. You could have garden parties regularly for all the High Bugs and mucky mucks."

"If I owned the paper, it would be a lot more than a neighborhood social calendar. I'd deal with the real issues facing this county and state."

"Exactly," Alice smiled. "You'd be one hell of a publisher. Want me to talk to Lloyd to get the price down to a reasonable number, or will you?"

"How in the world did my father keep the pants on in your relationship?" Karen laughed and she threw her arms up with a yelp of joy, then virtually floated back into a pile of clothes.

"I assume you mean I wore the pants in the relationship. Well, girl, as a matter of fact the only thing I'm comfortable in is pants, army issue."

Epilogue

He hated weakness of any kind. His wife and her lover would suffer the penalty of death for such bitter betrayals.

Arlis Camilo was almost as rich as he was powerful. He owned one of the largest fleets of cargo ships in the world. Originally headquartered in his native land of Singapore, he'd moved to Los Angeles after months of seductive persuasion by his latest wife who was almost half his age.

He was tall and lean with an English nose and had a well-bred aura befitting his privileged background. His third wife was one of the most beautiful redheads he'd ever seen. While she shared none of his passions outside the bedroom, her social graces allowed her the title of Mrs. Camilo, at least until the blush of youth had faded.

"I should have known she would take up with such a low life," Camilo spat at the man sitting in the shadow of his luxuriously appointed office building overlooking the Pacific Ocean. "You'd never believe the man is my partner; we're exact opposites. He came from uneducated stock, slithering his way into the shipping world and my life. Well, he just dug himself into an early grave."

Vincent "Vinnie" Rosalini sat up, creating a line of light across half of his face. His sharply defined eagle's beak nose and smoked glass eyes gave him the appearance of a soulless predator. When he chose to, he could be extremely persuasive with his tongue or his fists. He spoke three languages, could fly his own plane, had two large homes and an impressive collection of art. Not bad for a man who'd murdered for a living since he was nineteen-years-old.

"It'll need to look like an accident, of course," Camilo continued. "I tapped my partner's line about a month ago for another purpose, when purely by accident I discovered the animal was cavorting with my lovely wife. They're off to the Mojave River Forks Reservoir this weekend to camp out and savor the sparkling night sky in a cozy sleeping bag. Charming picture, isn't it? Such a shame that you're going to interrupt their bliss."

~

The night air was as cold as a tomb. Vinnie pointed his black four-door Buick across the county line into the silent world of the desert. The road twisted left and right, dipping in and out of tight ravines, climbing by slight degrees to the couple's fire-burning campsite that overlooked the reservoir.

"Perfect," Vinnie said, parking the car off the road and venturing out into the night. "A remote location few will attempt to navigate in a car. Only dip-shits like me," he said out loud to himself, breaking the eerie silence of the desert.

The desert sand ripped into Vinnie's eyes. He unzipped the left-hand pocket of his jacket and produced a half-pint of whiskey. After taking a deep, long drink he pulled a dark, smoke gray object from his other pocket, cocked it, and held it up waist high while using the other hand to shield his eyes from the unrelenting sand storm.

It only took a few moments to make his way to the place the couple had camped. They'd evidently had no concern about being found. He stood for a moment, a shadowy figure towering over the entwined couple. When he spoke, the harshness of his voice shattered the night.

"Party's over, kids. Get out of that bag. Now."

~

Arlis Camilo's wife had never been accused of exceptional brightness. She had a tendency to live in the moment. True to form, she was caught up in her lover's embrace and never heard the assassin's approach. Even when he spoke, things seemed to happen too fast for her mind to grasp. There was a flash of light and a small explosion, then her lover grabbed his chest and tried to lunge at the black-haired hawk of a man, now fully recognizable in the glow of the firelight. Eyes wide in horror, she watched as her lover doubled forward, head close to his knees, and sank to the ground. The sound went off again, the bullet entering his back this time. A slow, deliberate death. Grasping and clutching at his chest, he rolled slowly over to one side.

Acting purely on instinct, she'd backed away from the nightmare, finding comfort hiding behind her lover's car.

"Mrs. Camilo, where are you?" the sinister voice provoked a shiver of terror.

The woman couldn't say a word. Her body and legs reacted for her. She stumbled backward, turned, ran. Ran madly into the swirling curtain of sand and near total darkness of the cloud-covered moon. She heard the gun go off but felt nothing. She ran straight, unseeing, into the front of Vinnie's car and the force knocked her to the desert floor.

Dazed, she shook her head, fighting for consciousness. As she rose she could barely make out the letters BLT 535 on a California license plate. Bacon, Lettuce, and Tomato foolishly rushed into her mind as she leaned on the car bumper to get her footing.

Wishing she'd paid more attention on the trip in, she plunged through brush, Joshua tree branches, and over the edge of a sand dune ravine. She felt herself rolling, tumbling, then a stunning blow as she crashed into sand and went sliding all the way down to the bottom of a great dune.

She tried to move. A sickening jab of pain coursed through her shoulder. She lay still on her back staring up at the sky. As the clouds rolled across the moon's surface, partially revealing a sky speckled with bright white stars, she looked up. There was Vinnie silhouetted against the sky like a giant apparition. He paced back and forth, hunting for a way down. The woman, the desert, and the night waited in perfect unmoving silence for the monster's next move.

~

Morning came and she was still alive, stirring and whimpering on the heating desert sand. After some time, moaning softly, she got up on her knees. One of her large blue eyes was swollen shut. Her right arm hung limply from a dislocated shoulder. When she tried to lift it, a wave of sharp pain surged through her body. Nausea rose from her bowels.

She waited. When the pain and sickness subsided she hugged the injured limb to her large-breasted chest with her good arm and slowly got up to her feet. She never looked back or upward.

At noon she found water. Beneath the shade of boulders, jammed in the middle of the streambed was a basin of sand with a pool in the center. The heart-shaped prints of deer led in and out. Mrs. Camilo waded through the mud, cleared the slime from the surface of the water and managed to drink. Most of the afternoon she lay there. When the sun had moved beyond the dune above her, she carefully crawled out of the sucking sand and went on.

All through the day clouds gathered, the wind whistled, and by evening she could hear the far-away mutter of thunder. That night, whenever she awoke for a few moments she saw flashes of lightning reflected in the sky. No rain fell where she was. Her hunger made her sick with misery, worse than the pain in her arm and shoulder to which she was now accustomed, or the fiery discomfort of her sun-scorched back.

She wasn't going to walk anymore. She was tired, and decided to lay down in the streambed and go to sleep.

She might not have heard the coming of the flash flood. It began as only a distant rumble. Gradually the ground started to vibrate, until the water's volume created a dull and heavy roar. The flood rumbled down upon the woman and everything else in its path. Dust sailed into the air as it crashed into mud banks. Chunks of dried-out earth slid or toppled into the torrent. On the crest of the flood as it came, above the churning debris of bushes, vines, weeds and logs, floated the delicate figure of a woman giving herself freely to the water's wild movements.

Gasping for air, she crawled onto a tree trunk and rode it down the Mojave River.

Now what began for the woman was an unreckoned, uncountable series of days and nights. Her life became dreamlike. The nightmare, with its unacceptable disasters seemed long ago, happening to someone else. She entered a world of dreams and soft colors.

Fourteen days after Vinnie had murdered her lover, recreational boaters along a recessed inlet of the river discovered Mrs. Camilo. The stagnant water smelled of rotting algae as they carefully pulled what resembled a shriveled human figure from the tree trunk.

The body was covered with a mass of second- and third-degree burns. The woman appeared to be quite dead. Then they detected a trace of life, or thought they did. They carried the body to their motor-boat and jetted full-speed back to the boat ramp and the awaiting ambulance they had alerted through ship-to-shore communication.

She was still alive. They put her in an oxygen tent and pumped quarts of saline into her veins. She lived long enough to choke out her story, with a detailed description of the campsite, the murderer, and the Bacon, Lettuce and Tomato license plate number.

~

Paris Diamond looked across the gray metal table at his client. The conspicuous, two-way mirror made him almost laugh at the covert attempts of the arresting officer and the state prosecutor to listen in on a hoped-for confession.

Diamond had been Camilo's attorney for over twelve years, representing more than one family lieutenant caught in far more incriminating circumstances than Vinnie. Diamond had agreed to return to criminal law when he heard the lieutenant's name. There was a debt to pay a man who had insulted him personally and professionally.

"I urge you to be cautious in whatever you might say, Vinnie. There could be some misinterpretation that could lead the prosecuting attorney to believe you had some role in the death of Mr. Camilo's wife and her husband's partner," Diamond said as his eyes led his client to the large sheet of glass behind him. "I'll get us some privacy."

Moments later the accused and his legal counsel were in a one-person jail cell sitting on the bed side by side.

"A confirmation of a man fitting your description by a National Park Ranger at dawn. Your license plate number and an incredibly detailed description of what you, the killer, looked like. Hey, they've got you this time. We need to make a deal," Diamond whispered in his signature quiet voice.

Diamond knew he was a dead man if Camilo found out he tipped off the police to get this scumbag. He rationalized that it was all part of the game as he admired the cool exterior his client kept, regardless of personal danger.

"You need to give 'em something. Like the resolution to past hits you've made that have never been discovered or solved." Diamond almost smiled in anticipation.

"Are you out of your mind?" Vinnie snarled. "They don't have enough evidence to pin the Camilo murder on me. Not if you're any kind of attorney."

He would come around.

~

Lawrence Bradford was having another bad day. In fact, since the trial and mining operations were producing less than half of what they had at his former peak production, he hadn't been a happy man. It was irrelevant to him that he was now socially blackballed from every meeting or event of any consequence. What did matter was the personal role Tony Pozereli had taken in helping the state determine the appropriate qualifications for the new state mine inspector. It was time to sell and move on.

The ring of the doorbell surprised him. He hadn't had a visitor for over two weeks. Rather than wait for his manservant to answer it, curiosity compelled him to head for the door himself. Two steel-faced suits created a wall in his entryway.

"Mr. Lawrence Bradford?"

"Yes."

"You're under arrest for your role in the murder of one Howard Wellington and a Miss Lillian Hutton."

~

About the Author

Lon LaFlamme is a former AP wire service and daily newspaper reporter. He was CEO of one of the largest marketing communications companies in the western U.S., receiving numerous national advertising and public relations awards. LaFlamme has served as marketing professor at the nation's largest private university. He divides his time between Seattle, Washington and Salt Lake City, Utah.